REIKSGUARD

As Helborg raised his arm he knew all his brothers' eyes were upon him, expectant.

'Reiksguard!' he called. 'To battle!'

As one, the Reiksguard knights spurred their mounts to a trot, heading straight at the Skaeling warriors. The line was packed so tightly that the flanks of each horse near touched its neighbour's. Helborg had drilled them to precision, and despite the broken ground each brother adjusted his pace instinctively to keep the line unbroken. The rumble of the hooves striking dirt rolled down the slope, and each and every warrior, whether Nordlander or Skaeling, knew what was coming. The Empire soldiers who had fallen back across the Reiksguard's path needed no further prompting and scurried out of the way. The Skaelings followed suit, their lust for death and battle insufficient to face down the tons of man, beast and metal bearing towards them.

Also by the same author

RELENTLESS
by Richard Williams

More Warhammer from the Black Library

· **GOTREK & FELIX** ·
GOTREK & FELIX: THE FIRST OMNIBUS
by William King
(Contains books 1-3: *Trollslayer, Skavenslayer & Daemonslayer*)

GOTREK & FELIX: THE SECOND OMNIBUS
by William King
(Contains books 1-3: *Dragonslayer, Beastslayer &
Vampireslayer*)

Book 7 – GIANTSLAYER
by William King

Book 8 – ORCSLAYER
by Nathan Long

Book 9 – MANSLAYER
by Nathan Long

Book 10 – ELFSLAYER
by Nathan Long

EMPIRE IN CHAOS
by Anthony Reynolds

GRUDGEBEARER
by Gav Thorpe

OATHBREAKER
by Nick Kyme

HONOURKEEPER
by Nick Kyme

TALES OF THE OLD WORLD
Edited by Marc Gascoigne & Christian Dunn

A WARHAMMER NOVEL

REIKSGUARD

RICHARD WILLIAMS

For Graham,
One day it shall be the name for heroes, and not merely the
name of heroes.
With thanks to Jules, McCabe, Marc Harrison,
and in remembrance of the Thirtieth.

A BLACK LIBRARY PUBLICATION

First published in Great Britain in 2009 by
BL Publishing,
Games Workshop Ltd.,
Willow Road, Nottingham,
NG7 2WS, UK

10 9 8 7 6 5 4 3 2 1

Cover illustration by Clint Langley.

Map by Nuala Kinrade.

A CIP record for this book is available from the British Library.

ISBN 13: 978 1 84416 727 2
ISBN 10: 1 84416 727 5

Distributed in the US by Simon & Schuster
1230 Avenue of the Americas, New York, NY 10020.

See the Black Library on the Internet at
www.blacklibrary.com

Find out more about Games Workshop
and the world of Warhammer at
www.games-workshop.com

Printed and bound in the US.

THIS IS A DARK age, a bloody age, an age of daemons
and of sorcery. It is an age of battle and death, and of the
world's ending. Amidst all of the fire, flame and fury
it is a time, too, of mighty heroes, of bold deeds
and great courage.

AT THE HEART of the Old World sprawls the Empire, the
largest and most powerful of the human realms. Known
for its engineers, sorcerers, traders and soldiers, it is
a land of great mountains, mighty rivers, dark forests
and vast cities. And from his throne in Altdorf reigns
the Emperor Karl Franz, sacred descendant of the
founder of these lands, Sigmar, and wielder
of his magical warhammer.

BUT THESE ARE far from civilised times. Across the
length and breadth of the Old World, from the knightly
palaces of Bretonnia to ice-bound Kislev in the far north,
come rumblings of war. In the towering Worlds Edge
Mountains, the orc tribes are gathering for another assault.
Bandits and renegades harry the wild southern lands of
the Border Princes. There are rumours of rat-things, the
skaven, emerging from the sewers and swamps across the
land. And from the northern wildernesses there is the
ever-present threat of Chaos, of daemons and beastmen
corrupted by the foul powers of the Dark Gods.
As the time of battle draws ever nearer,
the Empire needs heroes
like never before.

PART ONE

'Our history teaches us that the heart of the Empire once beat in the chest of a single man. His name was Sigmar. On the day of his coronation, the creation of our Empire, he planted that heart in Reikland. Since that day, that heart has been uprooted and carried to each corner of our nation. On its long journey it has gained great victories and suffered terrible scars; it has been split into pieces and been reformed; it has learned fortitude, defiance, justice and nobility.

'Now it has returned to Reikland. Sigmar grant that it may be sustained here and its stay be so pleasing that this honour never depart.'

– Emperor Wilhelm III,
Elector Count of Reikland, Prince of Altdorf,
Founder of the Reiksguard, 2429 IC

PROLOGUE

HELBORG

The Nordland coast, near Hargendorf
2502 IC
Twenty years ago

KURT HELBORG GUIDED his horse carefully through the frozen mud up the side of the ridge where the Imperial army had set its positions. As he climbed, he risked a glance beside him, down the snow-covered slope. The land was grey, muffled under the blanket of the morning fog, which was only now, grudgingly, beginning its retreat. Helborg could see the bleak coastline starting to emerge, and the shape of the Norscan tribe's encampment that lay out near the beaches. He could not make out individual figures at this distance, but he could sense the tribe beginning to stir.

He crested the ridge. Spread out before him, the Empire's army was also making its preparations. The tents of the Nordlanders were clustered in their regiments. The state troops, their blue and yellow uniforms faded and ragged, had congregated around the cooking fires. Long lines of men had formed before the armourers, each wanting a new edge for their swords and halberds, and they traded old stories to pass the time. Their gravelly voices were loud and boisterous, even this early in the day. The militia companies were quieter; fewer of them were yet out of their tents, but those few who were awake were conscientiously sighting their bows and testing their arrows. Even for these woodsmen, levied soldiers though they were, a battle against sea-raiders was no unusual event.

'You had best bring up the rest of your brothers, preceptor, if you plan to fight the day,' a sonorous voice chided. Theoderic Gausser, the Elector Count of Nordland, had emerged impatiently from his tent half-dressed to admonish the Reiksguard knight. His page and attendants hurried out after him, garments and pieces of armour piled in their arms. Nordland ignored them, directing his belligerent stare straight at Helborg.

'Good morrow, my lord,' Helborg replied as he brought his steed to a halt. There was a moment's pause as Nordland waited pointedly. Courtly ceremony demanded that a knight dismount rather than remain at a higher level than an elector count; however here on the battlefield, when the army was at such risk, Helborg was in no mood to pander to Nordland's misplaced sense of propriety. The elector count scowled.

'Good morrow, indeed. Now answer me, preceptor, will the Reiksguard stand or will they flee?'

Helborg bridled at Nordland's insinuation, but held his temper in check. He had come here for a reason.

'The Reiksguard will stand, my lord, as your shield-bearer, but not as your pallbearer.'

'What?'

'My brothers and I have ridden out already this morning to test the ground. It will not hold your attack.'

'Again with this? You had your say last night. We have heard all these words before–'

'And they have been borne out, my lord.' Helborg cut the elector count off. 'There the enemy stands exactly where I said they would. Proceed as I advised, fall back to Hargendorf. The enemy must follow for there is no other escape, their ships are sunk, there is no route west but through Laurelorn…'

'I need no aid from those of Laurelorn,' Nordland spat.

'When that sun rises…'

Nordland jammed his fist into a gauntlet and held it up at Helborg.

'Hear me well, Preceptor Helborg. You may well be ordained to become the captain of your order, you may be a favourite of your Emperor; he may even make you Reiksmarshal one day. But until that day, you do not tell me how to command an army of Nordland on Nordland soil.'

His point made, the elector count turned his back to the knight and motioned one of his attendants to fix his neck-guard.

'He is your Emperor as well, my lord,' Helborg replied firmly, and then waited for Nordland to explode at him.

Nordland's shoulders rose and his attendants backed away, but he did not turn around. Instead, he exhaled and then clipped the neck-guard in place himself.

'Karl Franz is a pup,' Nordland said, quietly but clearly. 'Elected no more than one month, he brings his cannon and his mages to save us all from these raiders. He picks his battle, burns their ships and turns the sea to blood. And then no sooner does the tide go out, than he takes his toys and his mages back to Altdorf to garner his laurels and enjoy his triumph. And while he has gone home, I am still here, to finish what he started. He is my Emperor, yes, but how long he will last we shall see. The men of Nordland have been fighting this war long before the Reikland princes took the throne, and we will be fighting here still, long after it slips through their fingers.'

Nordland finished speaking. The air around him was still. He took up his helmet from the paralysed hands of his page. Helborg had not moved, but he felt as though his body must be shaking with rage. Carefully, he unclenched his jaw.

'You will never speak of the Emperor in that manner again.'

Nordland gave a bark of laughter and then half-turned to look Helborg in the eye.

'Or what?'

Helborg held his gaze as easily as he held a sword in his hand.

'I do not say what will happen; I only say that you will never speak of the Emperor in that way again.'

Nordland pulled the helmet over his head and stomped away.

'Just be ready, Reiklander, if you are called.'

A troop of horsemen galloped into the camp, young noblemen to Helborg's eye, and Nordland hailed the lead rider and beckoned him over. The rider pulled his horse up and fair leaped out of the saddle, the frost on the ground cracking as he landed.

'My boy!' Nordland exclaimed. 'You made it in time.'

Helborg knew that there was nothing to be gained by pursuing Nordland further, and he turned his steed away.

THE SUN WAS rising and the battle had begun. The soldiers of Nordland stood ready in their disciplined regiments of halberdiers and spearmen; the woodsmen with their bows stood in groups of skirmishers down the frosted slope. The Norscan tribesmen, Skaelings he had heard they called themselves, had sorted themselves into a rough line and formed a shield wall. They had used the long beams from their wrecked dragon ship to build a crude war altar to whatever petty sea-god it was that they worshipped. Obviously, it was there that they intended to make a final stand. Some of them wore armour, a few were as completely encased in plate as a knight, many wore barely anything at all. The cold was nothing to them.

The cold was something to him, though, Helborg reflected, as he sat in the saddle in the front line of the Reiksguard knights. The interior of his helm was near frozen enough that his cheek might stick to it. Still, better too cold than too hot. He had boiled under a hot midday sun in his armour too often to resent the frost. The cold would allow him to fight all the harder.

Nordland had positioned the Reiksguard out on his right flank in the midst of a scrub of dead trees. The elector count had said that this position might conceal them, so they could ambush the foe. However, Helborg knew that such a strategy relied upon the enemy advancing close enough to be surprised. All the Skaelings need do was sit and wait for the Empire regiments to come to them, and the Reiksguard knights would be left too far from the battle to do any good. When the Emperor had returned to Altdorf, he had left Helborg and his Reiksguard knights behind deliberately to ensure that his great victory would not be reversed. How could Helborg carry out these instructions if he was not allowed into the fight?

The woodsmen began to pepper the Skaeling shield wall with arrows, and the Empire drummers took up a marching beat. Helborg looked to his side to check the front line of his knights. The young knight beside him, Griesmeyer, sensed his concern.

'Perhaps, Brother Helborg, this show is meant to entice them towards us.'

'No, Brother Griesmeyer,' Helborg sighed, 'the elector count means to win the battle without us.'

'Then, with such a commander, we are sure to fight this day indeed,' Griesmeyer responded lightly.

Helborg could not find it within himself to chuckle. Instead, he turned to the younger knight.

'I did not say so before, but I am glad you could persuade Brother Reinhardt to rejoin us.' Helborg nodded over at another knight, Heinrich von Reinhardt, who was sitting intently at the far end of the squadron.

'I am glad also,' Griesmeyer replied carefully, 'but the credit is not mine to claim.'

'You have not spoken to him of late?'

'Not since the campaign began, preceptor.'

'The two of you were very close as novices.'

'And after, preceptor.'

'Indeed. And after. A pity.' Helborg turned away. 'Perhaps you will change that after today.'

Griesmeyer paused. 'Yes, preceptor.' But Helborg had already returned to watching the battle.

The uneven slope had frozen hard during the night and the sun had yet to rise high enough to begin to melt it. Despite the steady beat of their drums, the Empire regiments advanced slowly, the officers working hard to keep the ranks in order. Even the normally sure-footed woodsmen slipped and slid on the ice-covered ground.

At the bottom, the Skaelings stood quiet behind their shield wall. They did not shout or chant as Helborg had seen before. Norscans were normally impetuous; their shield wall was an imposing defence indeed to an army without cannon or gunners, but once they had worked themselves into a frenzy, it was easy to goad them to attack and to break their line. These Skaelings, however, even with their backs to the sea, stood calm as the Empire's drums carried the regiments towards them.

The sun finally rose clear above the ridge; Helborg imagined that many of the Nordland soldiery were grateful for its warmth on the backs of their necks. They did not know, as Helborg did, that that warmth would doom their attack.

The regiments advanced and the woodsmen fell back, unable to scratch the Skaelings behind their solid shields. As they ran to the sides, a flurry of movement went through the Skaeling line. Lightly armed young-bloods, stripped to the waist to display their woad, burst through the shield wall and ran a dozen paces forwards. They skidded to a halt and hurled their weapons into the face of the tightly packed Empire regiments. Barbed javelins, razor-sharp axes and knives all whistled through the air. The spearmen regiments instinctively raised their shields, knocking the missiles aside. The halberdiers had no such protection and the brightly uniformed men in the front ranks fell, feebly groping at the blackened shafts of the weapons buried in their bodies.

Shamans, cowled in furs and feathers, flung bloated heads at the Nordland soldiers. The heads burst apart as they hit shield or weapon, enveloping the ill-fated soldiers they struck, leaving them clawing at their throats and eyes.

The cries of the wounded and the dying rang out. The woodsmen lifted their bows and sighted the young-bloods who had abandoned their shield wall. Without that protection, the woodsmen's arrows easily found their marks. The reckless youths died where they stood, even as they reached back to throw again. Most of the survivors scampered back from the killing ground, but some, incensed by the proximity of their enemy, ran instead for the regiments, shrieking oaths to their dark gods.

The Nordlanders were unimpressed and held firm, catching the youngbloods' first wild blows and then chopping them down without breaking step. And all the while the Imperial drums marched them on.

Their advance down the hill had been painfully slow; it had taken the better part of an hour. But their discipline had held their formation together over the broken ground. The slope dipped sharply two dozen paces in front of the shield wall and then flattened out before rising slightly to the Skaelings' line. So for a moment, as they closed on the foe, the front lines of the regiments disappeared from sight as though they were swallowed by the earth. It was at that instant that the Skaelings gave a mighty roar, all together, and hauled their profane standards high.

Helborg felt a tiny jab of alarm and he could see that the elector count far to his left shifted uneasily. But then the blue and yellow banners fluttered back into view; the regiments were on the flat. Over the last few yards, the halberdiers raised their blades high and the spearmen lowered their points. The Empire regiments struck the enemy line in a single hammer blow, and the battle proper commenced.

All down the line, weapons swung, clanging against shields and slicing into flesh. The regimental banners dipped and rose as their bearers struggled forwards, urging their men on. The spearmen bashed their shields against the wall and then stabbed low, impaling the legs of the Skaeling warriors and bringing them crashing to the ground, opening a gap in the wall. The halberdiers, meanwhile, were more direct and hacked down with their heavy blades, splintering apart wooden Norscan shields. The Skaelings struck back; their strongest warriors, in their heavy armour, bullied their way through the soldiers who opposed them. Spear stabs skittered off their greaves and the halberd blades merely dented their metal shields instead of smashing them to pieces. These champions fought past the soldiers' polearms and cleaved Nordlander men apart with each blow from their massive swords.

For all their efforts, though, they were too few. Gradually, inevitably, the Empire regiments were winning. The shield wall was weakening, disintegrating, as the lightly armoured Skaelings fell and their victorious champions pushed forwards. The Skaelings were holding their line and the shield wall had not yet moved, but the famous Norscan ill-discipline was finally showing.

Helborg saw the elector count begin to relax, the satisfaction clear on his face. Nordland spurred his mount forwards, his bodyguard staying close behind, so he could be there for the victory.

Helborg would not be held back any longer, and took the elector count's advance as tacit permission for himself. He led his knights from their pointless concealment and formed them up in two lines, ready to fight. For Helborg could see, as Gausser had not yet realised, that Nordland's battle plan was about to unravel.

A halberdier, hefting his weapon around for another blow, suddenly had the frozen mud beneath his right foot slip away and he tumbled backwards, the head of his halberd lodging itself in the shoulder of his comrade behind. A grizzled spearman brought his opponent, a tattooed brute with teeth like a boar, wailing to the ground. The spearman lunged forwards to finish the boar-man off and felt his front foot bury itself in the sludge and refuse to move. He threw his arms forwards to break his fall and looked up just in time to see the head of an axe sweep down towards his undefended face.

All down the line, the Empire soldiery had begun to stumble. The ground beneath them, which had appeared frozen solid by the night's chill, had melted under the pounding of the battle, the warmth of the capricious sun and the hot, spilt blood. Weighed down by their breastplates, shields and weapons, the soldiers' heavy tread was shattering the surface ice and trapping their legs in the shifting, treacherous bog beneath. The officers still shouted their orders, but the soldiers were no longer listening as each began to look to his own safety. The advance had stalled. With every step now, each soldier edged back towards the steeper slope behind him. The blue and yellow banners themselves began to droop as their bearers fought to keep their own footing.

In a matter of minutes, Nordland's army had gone from a half-dozen solid, well-ordered regiments to a mass of struggling individuals, fighting for their lives. The Skaelings, who had arranged their shield wall on firmer ground, hooted at the Nordlanders' plight. Once more, the shield wall opened and the youngbloods ran out, spinning their axes and knives at the flailing soldiers.

The horrified woodsmen, close at hand, raised their bows again. The youngbloods, dancing their way across the bodies and rocks stuck within the half-melted ice, had sprung upon the backs of the retreating Nordlanders, and there were no easy targets. The woodsmen fired. A few hit home, catching the crowing youngbloods in their throats and faces, but most flew wide, the woodsmen unwilling to risk hitting their ill-fated comrades. Even while hundreds of soldiers were still clawing their way out of the bog, the nimble youths had crossed and scrambled up the bank, joyfully cutting and slicing as they went. In the face of this, the woodsmen too stepped back.

The army was on the verge of collapse. The Nordlanders were a hardy and resilient stock, and were certainly no cowards, but in the great confusion none of them knew where to look for their orders. The veterans sought for the regimental banners, desperate for direction, but the flags had been left behind in the ice-bog, their bearers prize targets for the Skaelings' blades. No soldier who had gone to retrieve them had survived.

One banner, however, still flew. A wildly moustachioed officer, bleeding heavily from a barbed javelin in his side, had dragged himself to the foot of the bank. With the hollering Skaelings on his heels, he tried to pull himself up the steep slope. His leg gave out and he slipped back down. A young spearman above him saw his distress and turned back to aid him; with the last of his strength the officer pushed the banner up high towards the reaching arms of the spearman. He took hold and the officer sighed in relief; relief that turned to despair as a whirling axe took the top of the spearman's head off like a knife through an egg. The banner wavered. The officer, a Norscan knife between his shoulders, groaned his last and the banner sank down with him.

Though his attack had turned to disaster, the elector count was not slow to react. His army needed their leader and he would not disappoint them. He seized his personal standard and galloped forwards, urging his mount as fast as it could go down the slippery slope. He held his banner high and bellowed as he went, 'Nordland! Nordland! To me! Rally!'

His men responded and hurried towards him. The day had been lost. Nordland's advantage in numbers, which had been slight even before, had been stripped from him in the mud-pits before the shield wall. However, if the Skaelings relented, held back in their position, then Nordland could at least reorder his regiments and retreat in good order back to Hargendorf. The Skaelings, however, had no intention of allowing their foe the time they needed. Their brutal young-bloods were already running up behind the Nordlanders, slicing at exposed backs, but veering away where bands of soldiers had stopped and were making a stand. Of more concern, Helborg could see that the heavily armoured warriors were now crossing the bog and forming up on the bank. They had stripped the long ship beams from their war-altar and had laid those across the unsafe ground. Hundreds of them had already made the near side and were starting to stalk up the hill, dispatching the enemy wounded as they passed. If this juggernaut reached the Empire's line before it had reformed, Helborg doubted the shaken Nordlanders would rally a second time.

As Helborg raised his arm he knew all his brothers' eyes were upon him, waiting to be released.

'Reiksguard!' he called. 'To battle!'

As one, the Reiksguard knights spurred their mounts to a trot, heading straight at the Skaeling warriors. The line was packed so tightly that the flanks of each horse pressed against its neighbour's. Helborg had drilled them to precision, and despite the broken ground each brother adjusted his pace instinctively to keep the line unbroken. The rumble of the hooves striking dirt rolled down the slope, and each and every warrior, whether Nordlander or Skaeling, knew what was coming. The Empire soldiers who had fallen back across the Reiksguard's path needed no further prompting and scurried out of the way. The Skaelings followed suit, their lust for death and battle insufficient to face down the tonnes of man, beast and metal bearing towards them.

For a split-second, Helborg saw the warriors at the bottom of the slope hesitate, some turning to retreat behind the relative safety of the bog and their shield wall. But then one of their chieftains stepped forwards, arms encased in long bladed gauntlets shaped as the claws of a crab. He shouted for his men to hold their ground. They brought up their shields, readying another wall.

Helborg gave the order and the Reiksguard knights broke into a canter. The rumble of the hooves grew into a storm, and everyone on the battlefield who was not engaged in mortal combat turned to watch the Reiksguard's charge.

The Reiksguard's first line was aimed straight at the centre of the new shield wall. Helborg nudged his steed with his heels to turn him a degree to the left, confident that the correction would be fed up and down the line. He was not ashamed to admit that the first time he had been a part of a charge of the Reiksguard knights he had felt fear, but now he could only feel the eagerness, the excitement, the power flowing through his brothers and into him. This new Emperor Karl Franz said his dearest wish was an Empire at an honourable peace, and as the Emperor wishes so does the Reiksguard; but in Sigmar's name Kurt Helborg could not deny that he loved war.

Scant yards away, Helborg yelled his final command; the Reiksguard dropped their lance points and shot forwards into a gallop. This was the moment where they showed their enemy the fate that awaited them. The Skaelings were braced for the impact; they knew it would hurt, but their line would hold and then, once they had stopped the horses, they could bring down the knights from their saddles and slaughter them. They knew this in their minds; but as they saw the lance points lower, their spirits quailed and, on animal instinct, they leant back, off-balance.

The Reiksguard struck. The force of his lance's impact hammered Helborg back in the saddle. He twisted, held the lance for a split-second to ensure it penetrated and then released. The years of drill made his actions automatic. As his hand released the lance's grip, it went straight to his sword's hilt and pulled it from its scabbard. He drew back and high to avoid the brother beside him, then arced around and cut down like the sail of a windmill: First to his right, then to his left, catching any foe that came close. Helborg did not need to think; his body did what it had been trained to do. But Helborg's thoughts raced; while his body fought, his mind seized every sound, every sight it could to determine if their charge had been a success. How many brothers had fallen? Had the shield wall broken? Were the Reiksguard winning? Should they run? He could not tell and so his body fought on.

His steed butted forwards, burying the spikes on its champron into a howling face. Helborg stabbed down at another who was aiming a cut at his horse's unarmoured legs. Helborg felt a blow to his hip on the other side, but ignored it and stabbed down again. His armour would hold, but he would not survive if his mount was crippled. Though the Skaeling line was a hair's breadth from collapse, they had held and were pushing back. The knights had been pushed apart so that the enemy could get in between and swarm them down. Blows from maces and axes pounded on the knights' armour, chains and ropes sought to tangle the warhorses' legs. Having withstood the initial shock, barely, the enemy's numbers were beginning to tell.

And then the Reiksguard's second wave hit. Helborg was near jolted from his saddle again as his brothers slammed in, filling the spaces that had formed between the first wave and knocking the Skaelings down the hill. Within an instant, the wall broke and their warriors scrabbled down the bank still littered with Nordlander dead. Helborg called his knights to a halt. As much as he wished it, he knew he could not pursue the Skaelings into the bog. Already the main body of the Skaeling tribe were making crossings on either flank, and his knights, stood still, could not hold the centre. The day had been lost, but the Empire's honour had not been surrendered.

There was still much to do, and the Reiksguard spurred away from the top of the bank before they could be trapped there. Helborg ordered his squadrons to the left and to the right, to break up the skirmishes being fought there and allow the Nordlanders to disengage. Helborg looked up the hill. The elector count was still there, readying to lead the next assault himself. Helborg cursed.

'You cannot attack again!' he said as he rode up to the elector count. 'You must hold them at Hargendorf.'

'You've done well, Reiklander,' Nordland said, not even turning around. 'I don't deny it. You've given us our chance and now we can turn the tide.'

Helborg hastily dismounted and strode over to the man. Nordland's bodyguards closed ranks and kept the bloodied Reiksguard knight a yard back from their lord.

'If you are killed here today,' Helborg insisted, 'then it will throw the defence of the north into disarray. I cannot allow you to attack!'

'Who commands Nordland's army? Some Reiklander or–'

'Just look!' Helborg, in frustration, pointed down at the dark mass of Skaelings crawling up the slope, whooping and chanting in victory.

Nordland looked, and then gasped.

'My boy…' he whispered.

Helborg followed his gaze.

A dozen richly dressed horsemen were charging down the slope on the left at the advancing Skaeling flank. They were the young nobles that Helborg had seen early that morning, and Nordland's reaction left him without a doubt that it was the elector count's son at their head. They whooped as the first few Skaelings they encountered dived out of their way, and rode further in, searching for kills. The Skaeling flank halted when the nobles struck, almost as though bemused by the foolish valiance of such an unsupported attack. And then the Skaelings swarmed. For a moment, Helborg saw the nobles realise their predicament, rein in their mounts and try to turn back, and then the dark horde swallowed them up.

As his son's mount fell, Nordland cried again and made for his horse. Helborg held him back and this time the elector count's bodyguards did not stop him. Helborg looked for his Reiksguard brothers, but they were dispersed, struggling all across the field to keep the Skaelings back. Then one of the bodyguards shouted. Helborg looked: a single Reiksguard knight had broken away from his squadron and had plunged into the horde, carving his way through Norscan warriors surrounding the site where Nordland's son had fallen. It was one man against a hundred; it was suicide.

Then suddenly Helborg saw Griesmeyer break away and gallop towards the lone knight. As Griesmeyer charged, he called the knight's name.

'Reinhardt!'

CHAPTER ONE

DELMAR

The Reinhardt estate, Western Reikland
Spring 2522 IC

'Reinhardt! To your right!'

Heeding the warning, Delmar von Reinhardt flattened himself in the saddle. The beastman's clumsy swing sailed over Delmar's head. The young nobleman slashed back, cutting open the beastman's head. Black blood gushed from behind its horns as it staggered and then fell into the undergrowth.

Delmar did not look back. He did not dare. Riding fast this deep into the woods, he had far greater chance of being unseated by a low-hanging branch or crashing into a bloodhedge than being struck by an enemy's weapon. He had to keep riding, keep the exhausted beastkin from escaping further into the woods. None of them could be allowed to escape.

The forest burned with the red light of the setting sun, and Delmar caught glimpses of his men amongst the trees as they chased down the survivors of the beastkin tribe. Each band blew their horns to mark their positions, but they had no breath spare to shout oaths or curses at their enemy. Delmar too was tired; his horse, Heinrich, was drenched in sweat, but Delmar urged him on all the harder. Every last one of these killers had to be brought down. If not, then other villages would pay the same price as Edenburg.

Another beastman burst from a thicket and blundered into Delmar's path. There was no chance to avoid it and Heinrich crashed forwards, knocking the creature to the ground. Delmar felt Heinrich drop away beneath him, pitching him forwards, almost out of the saddle. Delmar's heart leapt into his throat. He threw himself hard to the other side and Heinrich managed to catch his footing and stumble back up.

Delmar reined Heinrich in and instantly slid down from the saddle. His legs felt like water, but they still obeyed his commands. Sword ready, he trod carefully back over the vines and rotten logs to where the beastman had fallen. It had not moved.

This one was smaller than the rest, almost human in its looks. It was pale and thin, with sunken eyes and wispy hair. Its chest was a mass of spear-cuts. It was still alive, but only barely. Its breathing was shallow, rasping, and the blood oozed from its wounds. Death seemed close, but Delmar knew these mutant creatures were tough. With the luck of its unholy gods it might just heal, escape, and then return the stronger to slaughter again.

Delmar did not hesitate. A single blow severed the beast's head from its body. The dead eyes bulged for a moment and then were still. Delmar turned away to see the alderman of Edenburg and his hunting band riding up behind him, bloodied boar-spears in their hands.

'My thanks for your warning, alderman.' Delmar's voice remained steady, despite his fatigue. That was good.

'I would only wish I could have kept up with you better,' the alderman replied. 'You ride these woods faster than I could a level field.'

'Heinrich is a good steed,' Delmar replied, stroking his horse's neck to calm him.

The horns blew again around them. Delmar silently gritted his teeth and hauled himself back into the saddle.

'My lord,' the alderman protested, 'you have been riding a night and a day. The foe is beaten. You have done enough.'

Delmar turned back to the alderman. His blue eyes were bright with exhaustion, but the determination in his face was the only reply he needed to give. The alderman recognised the look; it was that same one his father had.

Delmar tapped Heinrich's flanks with his heels and, once more, the two of them chased after the horns.

THE ALDERMAN DID not see Delmar again until the next morning. At some time in the night, Delmar had returned to the remains of Edenburg and collapsed next to the village's boundary wall. The alderman would not have seen him hidden there, but Heinrich still remained over him, standing sentinel.

Delmar had not even lain himself out properly. He had slept sitting, his back against the wall, his blood-blackened sword still in his hand. The alderman thought it prudent to wake him from outside its reach. Delmar struggled back to consciousness; he instinctively tried to rise and clattered back down. The alderman handed him a gourd of water then sat down beside him.

'I've sent word back to your mother and your grand-father that you are safe.'

Delmar, still drowsy, nodded his thanks as he took the gourd.

'Sigmar be praised,' the alderman said. 'To Edenburg,' he toasted.

Delmar took a swig from the gourd, then splashed the rest over his face, slicking his brown hair back from his eyes. He blinked the water away and then stared at the burned-out houses.

'Praise Sigmar indeed,' Delmar replied wearily. The villagers of Edenburg were already awake, sifting through the remains of their homes. As hard as the battle had been the day before, they would have to work harder today if they wished to sleep beneath a roof by nightfall.

'I learnt long ago,' the alderman said 'that a village is not in its structures, but in its people. And those we have saved. *You* have saved, my lord.'

Before them, the bell of Edenburg's small temple of Sigmar began to ring. It tolled for the dead.

The beastman tribe had come down from the mountains in the depths of the last winter; it had been another blow to a province already reeling from the failed harvest the summer before and teetering on the brink of famine. The state troops had been called away for the war in the north, and so there were no soldiers to oppose them. The beastkin journeyed east, attacking all in their path, slaughtering the adults, carrying off children and stealing precious livestock supplies. If villagers stood they were killed, if they ran they were chased down, if they hid the tribe burned them out of their refuges. The beastmen killed for food and they killed for sport. But then they had reached Edenburg.

'We were fortunate,' Delmar replied. 'It could have been far worse.'

The beastmen had struck the night before. The villagers of Edenburg barricaded themselves within the temple of Sigmar and rang its bell to signal their distress. While some of the beastmen tried to batter their way in, the rest ran wild through the streets. They had little use for gold, but snatched food or flesh of any kind. Their favoured target was always a village's inn, for the stores it held and for the drink these degenerates craved.

They broke open the cellar of the inn of Edenburg expecting to find a few casks of mead and ale. But they were to be surprised. The cellar held whole vats of wine, racks of spirits, enough not just for a village, but for a city. The word of this discovery quickly spread amongst them and the streets emptied as more of the beastmen hurried to take their share of this treasure.

'Fortune, my lord,' the alderman gently admonished Delmar, 'had a great deal of help on this occasion.'

In the temple, the villagers had heard the battering against their barricades slow, and then stop altogether.

Fearing a trap, they stayed still until the sun rose and they could make sure that the beastmen had gone.

But the beastmen had not gone. Beyond all restraint, they had drunk what they had found in a single night. The first villagers who emerged found Edenburg littered with these monsters prostrate in the streets. And in the distance, from all directions, came the militias, every able man from every neighbouring town. With them was Delmar von Reinhardt. Delmar, who had ordered every last bottle to be taken from the cellars of the Reinhardt estate and planted in Edenburg, and who had now ridden all night from village to village to bring the militias to arms.

The beastmen had awoken then and tried to stagger back to the cooling shade of their forests, their once-fearsome tribe reduced to a mewling rabble. They had been caught against the cliffs of the Grotenfel, and there they had been destroyed.

'I do not know what it cost you, my lord. But I take Verena's oath that we shall repay you.'

Had the alderman not sounded so serious, Delmar might have laughed. Those wines and spirits had been everything from his family's cellars. The collection had taken them generations to build up and, beside the estate itself, it had been quite the most valuable thing that his father had left him. It had been his reserve, his last gasp, to sustain the family should their finances grow dire. This one village alderman could not repay it.

'Save your coppers, alderman. Whatever value others placed upon it, this was its true value for me. Our villagers are safe again, for a few years at least. And what has greater value than that?'

'We shall find a way, my lord,' the alderman replied stiffly, for lord or not, no man doubted that he might make good his bond.

Suddenly, the villagers began to stir from the ashes of their homes. For a moment, Delmar thought the foe might have returned, but the villagers were excited, not fearful. He rose to follow them.

Another horseman had entered the village, but this was no town official nor messenger. It was a warrior. A knight. A knight who was robed in red and white and who wore the symbol of the skull encircled by a laurel wreath.

'Sir knight!' the alderman hailed him. 'If you come for battle then I fear you are a day too late!'

The alderman glanced at Delmar, only to see the nobleman's face wide with amazement.

'Griesmeyer!' Delmar shouted with delight.

It HAD BEEN eight years since Delmar had last seen his father's old brother-in-arms. Griesmeyer appeared older now than Delmar remembered, of course. His dark red hair, kept close-cropped in the young man's fashion, was shot through with grey. The lines on his face were etched deeper. But the greatest difference was not in the knight, but in himself. He had grown from a child to a man and now was almost half a head taller than the knight who used to tower over him. It felt wrong: he should not be able to look down upon such a great man as Lord Griesmeyer.

The timing of the knight's return could be no coincidence. His grandfather, in one of his few lucid moments, had written to the order recommending

Delmar to their service not two months before, and now surely Griesmeyer had brought their reply. Delmar burned with the urge to ask, but it was not his place to demand answers from a Reiksguard knight.

Griesmeyer had visited the Reinhardt estates often, though given his service to the Emperor, his arrival could never be predicted. But eight years ago his visits had ceased entirely. When he had asked his mother why, she did not reply. She could not stand even to hear Griesmeyer's name mentioned, and Delmar had acquiesced in her wishes. But he had been barely more than a child then; now he was a man. As the two of them rode into the estate's courtyard, Delmar vowed to himself that whatever his purpose, Griesmeyer would not leave so abruptly this time.

'Lance and hammer, Delmar, you are so changed, and yet your estate is exactly as it was,' Griesmeyer called over the clatter of the horse hooves on the cobblestones.

'We change nothing here. Not in the last eight years, not in the last twenty.' Delmar jumped off his horse, his fatigue forgotten.

'Come,' Delmar continued, calling for the family's manservant to attend. 'Take your ease with us. Let me take your saddle and come inside.'

Griesmeyer looked as though he was about to accept, but then glanced up over Delmar's head. 'No, my boy, I have arranged lodgings in Schroderhof. I will spend the night there and return tomorrow.'

'In Schroderhof?' Delmar was taken aback. 'We have more than enough room for old friends of my father's. You will stay here.'

Griesmeyer glanced above again and this time Delmar half-turned to see what had caught his eye. His mother stood at the nursery window, staring down at them.

Griesmeyer's tone turned serious. 'Your father, Morr allow him rest, would have advised you better than to gainsay your elders.'

The knight reached into his saddlebag, pulled out a sealed parchment and handed it to Delmar. 'Here. My mission today was solely to deliver you this. You will need the day to rest from your exertions and then say your goodbyes. And so I leave you 'til tomorrow.'

Delmar looked at the parchment; he could scarce breathe with excitement. The seal was that of the Reiksmarshal, the Captain of the Reiksguard, Kurt Helborg himself. The letter had to be what Delmar hoped; it could be nothing else.

'And there was one other matter…' Griesmeyer reached again into his saddlebag and pulled out a sword, its sheath marked with the Reiksguard colours.

'Your sword?' Delmar asked.

'Not my sword,' Griesmeyer replied, turning his horse away. 'Your father's. And now yours. Keep its edge keen, young Delmar von Reinhardt, for the Reiksguard will need it, and you, before long.'

DESPITE GRIESMEYER'S ASSURANCES, Delmar was not content that the knight felt unwelcome at the estate. Nevertheless Delmar was ultimately grateful for Griesmeyer's tactful retreat. When the household learned that the Grand Order of the Reiksguard had received his grandfather's recommendation and were willing to consider him, there was an outpouring of emotion from family, friends and servants alike that would have mortified Delmar if Griesmeyer had been there to witness it.

Much had to be done, though in truth less than Delmar expected. His mother had been readying for the day that her only son should follow his father's path for years. The estate's steward was an experienced, sensible man and well trusted in the locality. He advised Delmar to call an immediate conclave of the aldermen of the neighbouring villages. They gathered quickly and applauded Delmar's success. Many of their sons had gone away to war already. Now the threat of the beastkin was gone, they were proud that their lord would be there with them. The aldermen readily reaffirmed their oaths of loyalty to the Reinhardt family, as Delmar reaffirmed his family's oaths to them.

When Griesmeyer returned early the next morning, he found Delmar already waiting, packed, horse saddled and his duty done.

'I was surprised yesterday, my lord,' Delmar said, as they walked their horses to the Altdorf road. 'I had expected... that is, I had hoped that a messenger would come. I could never have dreamed that a knight would deliver the message personally.'

Griesmeyer rode slowly, bareheaded, enjoying the sun. Delmar watched as the knight drank in the soft countryside that they passed, the blossom on the trees, the bright spring flowers in the field.

'Lord Griesmeyer?'

The knight turned back to him. 'Apologies, Delmar. It has been a long, harsh winter. I am glad to be reminded that there are still places in the Empire of peace and beauty.'

Delmar briefly thought of the blood that had been spilt not two days before, but said nothing. What had been a great battle to him was little more than a skirmish when compared against the clash of armies in the north.

'The order would not normally send a knight on such a mission, no,' Griesmeyer continued. 'I requested it specifically. I have been looking for an excuse to travel back here for years now, but my duties have prevented it. When I learned of this though, a chance to welcome the next generation of Reinhardts into the Reiksguard, how could I pass it up?'

Delmar felt his chest swell with pride, but it did not deflect him from his purpose. 'Has it been your duties then, that have kept you from returning to us?'

'Aye,' Griesmeyer replied. 'I swear I must have travelled to every province, eaten in every town and slept in every field following our Emperor. People will say that he will slow down as he grows old, and I say to them that I believe the sun will slow in the sky before our Emperor Karl Franz!'

'I do not doubt it,' Delmar agreed.

'I was glad to see your grandfather looking so well also, I had heard he had been taken very ill last winter.'

'He is recovered now. His body at least.'

'And what of his other condition, has there been any improvement?' Griesmeyer asked.

Delmar's mind flicked back to his grandfather last evening. He had been happy then, but it had been the happiness of an infant. He had no understanding of what was happening around him; he merely watched in wonder at the celebrations. Delmar had tried to speak to him, tried to say goodbye, had hoped that his departure might raise a spark of the great man who had once lived inside that body, but he was disappointed. Delmar had nodded and smiled, and his grandfather had nodded and smiled back again. He wondered now if he would even notice that his grandson had left.

'I am afraid not, my lord. We had some hope that his mind might recover in those first few years, but now we have reconciled ourselves that he will never truly return to us.'

'A great regret,' Griesmeyer said. 'I never had the honour to fight beside him, but whenever we speak of those days, he is always spoken of in the highest regard. Just as his son is, and his grandson will be, I am sure.'

Delmar wished to ask then of his father. It had been eight years since he had last heard Griesmeyer's tales of their time together in the order. But after eight years of wanting, Delmar found himself hesitant to ask.

Instead, they rode for two days, talking of everything but. Griesmeyer asked of all the events of Delmar's life that he had missed and, in return, the knight recounted tales of eight years of the Empire's wars. It was not until they were in sight of Altdorf itself that Delmar dared ask about his father's last campaign. Griesmeyer held silent for a few moments. For the first time, Griesmeyer's contented mask slipped, and Delmar saw the look of sorrow that he wore behind.

The old knight's tone was sombre. He described it all in great detail: the argument between the elector count and Helborg, Nordland's failed assault, the Reiksguard's charge and dispersal across the slope, and then the young nobles' foolish attack. Delmar's father, Brother Reinhardt, had been the closest. Without hesitation, he had plunged into the Skaeling horde and pulled the youth from the ground. Griesmeyer had seen Reinhardt's horse run clear, Nordland's son unconscious across its saddle. He and his brother knights had cut their way through the Skaelings, trying to reach where Reinhardt still fought, but their efforts had not been enough. Reinhardt disappeared under a mass of the savage warriors and it was all the knights could do to turn about and escape themselves.

Delmar had only the faintest memories of his father. All Delmar could remember was of playing with a toy that his father had given him, and of a knight tending to his mother when she was bedridden. He would not even know his father's face if his mother had not kept a portrait. Even so, Delmar felt proud to be associated with his father's heroism, the only sadness he felt was that he had had no chance to know him.

THE ROAD TO Altdorf ran to the western bank of the Reik, and from there it followed the river until it reached the great Imperial city. The river was crammed with boats, traders journeying back and forth to Marienburg, but also ferries and transports, anything that could float, stacked with people heading upriver from Altdorf. Delmar stared at them from the bank; these were not travellers by choice, they were farmers, trappers, village folk. They were refugees.

'Surely,' he said to Griesmeyer, 'the war cannot have reached so far south that the Reik is threatened?'

'I do not know,' Griesmeyer replied, echoing Delmar's concern. 'Perhaps there has been news in the last few days. The foe's great armies are on our northern border, it is true, but the Empire is riddled through with their allies and followers. The beastkin in the forests, the greenskins in the mountains, the marauder bands who may ride where they will, now our armies are distracted. It is a time that any man of sense looks for a thick wall to stand behind.'

They left the slow-moving boats behind and approached Altdorf itself. The closer they rode, the more noxious the river became. For the Altdorfers, the Reik was not only their trading lifeline, it was also their sewer, and the refuse they dumped washed up along the banks. Griesmeyer cut away from the river then, and headed for the main road leading to the western gate. An hour's travel along a track through the woods, and finally there it was.

Delmar had been to the capital before, but only as a child. He had wondered if, like Griesmeyer, the city might appear lessened now he was a man.

It did not.

The city of Altdorf rose high above the forest, as though a god had lifted the towns from an entire province and stacked them all one atop the other. A grand wall had been built about it for its defence, but the buildings inside had long since risen above the wall's height. Every scrap of land, no matter how unpromising, had been built upon, and when the land within the walls was exhausted, Altdorf had begun to build upon itself.

They approached through the western gate, solidly fortified and flanked by two stone statues of watchful griffons bearing hammers. The gate was jammed with wagons, once again some traders and some refugees who were clamouring to get into the city, but one look at Griesmeyer's insignia and uniform were enough for the guards there to wave them in. Once inside, Delmar was plunged into a greater darkness than he had experienced in the forests. The sky disappeared amongst the towering buildings. The crowds, the noise, the stench of the place were overpowering; so many people all pressed close together. The villagers around the Reinhardt estate had weathered the famine, but others had not. When the crops failed last summer, men took their families from the starving countryside into the cities to find what work they could. Altdorf, the glorious capital of the great Empire, had become a meat barrel crammed with the desperate and the dying.

Delmar constantly soothed Heinrich as they pushed their way through the hawkers, the labourers, the vendors and the beggars. He kept as close as he could to Griesmeyer, steering his own horse calmly ahead. They were not far from the Reiksguard chapter house when a trumpet sounded ahead of them. The mass of people parted and crammed against the buildings. A squadron of Reiksguard cavalry had appeared, thundering through the streets. Delmar moved aside, but Greismeyer hailed them and their leader brought them to a a halt.

'Brother Griesmeyer,' the lead knight commanded. 'You have returned in time. The invasion has begun and the Emperor needs our swords.'

'Aye, Marshal, we will come at once.'

Marshal? Delmar nearly exclaimed. This was the Reiksmarshal! This was Kurt Helborg himself before him. Delmar stared at the knight on his fearsome grey steed. The man was powerfully built, far more so than the slighter Griesmeyer. His eyes were stern, unyielding, but the most distinctive feature of his face was his mighty moustache. It was thick as a plume and stretched nearly twice the width of his face, curled with precision to either side. Truly it was a monster that doubtless scared any opponent as much as any weapon in his hand.

'Who is this?' Helborg demanded, his deep voice stern.

'This is Delmar von Reinhardt, he will be joining our novices.'

Delmar thought he saw Helborg give a flicker of recognition when Griesmeyer said the Reinhardt name. But if it had been there, it had quickly vanished in the Marshal's scowl.

'This is a matter for the inner circle, Brother Griesmeyer. Send the novice on his way.'

'At once, my lord,' Griesmeyer replied. Helborg spurred his horse and the party was away.

'You know the chapter house?' Griesmeyer asked. Delmar nodded. 'Good. Give them your name. You are expected.'

With that, Griesmeyer rode after them and the crowds swarmed back into the middle of the gloomy street and Delmar made his way onwards.

The chapter house of the Grand Order of the Reiksguard was not hard to find. It was a separate citadel within Altdorf, encircled by its own wall and defences so that a hundred trained warriors might hold it even if the rest of the city should fall. Unlike the rest of the city, the houses around its wall had been kept low, only a couple of storeys, and none higher than the wall itself. Stringent city ordinances stipulated these restrictions, and where these ordinances were ignored the Reiksguard's own ordnance enforced them.

Delmar had found the large black gates of the chapter house imposingly barred and locked. He was challenged from above. Delmar looked up and saw a guard on duty, standing beside the ornate frieze of the coronation of Emperor Wilhelm III that arched over the gates.

'I am here with a letter. I am to join the order.'

'Are you? We'll see,' the guard replied, a snicker in his voice. 'Keep going around. You want the white gate, the next one.'

Delmar thanked him despite his rudeness, and continued on. The next gate was smaller, decorated only with a small sculpture of Shallya, but no less closed. The guard there challenged him. Delmar shouted up over the raucous bellowing of the street vendors.

'I am Delmar von Reinhardt. I am one of the novices.'

'Wait there, Lord Reinhardt,' the guard shouted back, 'someone is already coming.'

Delmar nodded and urged Heinrich to the side to move him from the middle of the street.

'You there! On the horse! Do not move!'

Delmar looked back up, but the shout had not come from the walls. He turned and there, in a knot of the crowd, he saw a pistolier, weapon drawn and pointed straight at him.

'Do not move!' the pistolier shouted again, and fired.

The bullet whipped straight over Heinrich's head and Delmar tipped back on instinct. Heinrich, spooked and sensing his rider's distress, reared back. As Heinrich went up, Delmar felt his balance begin to go and threw his weight forwards to stay in the saddle. The Altdorfers nearby backed away from the horse's flailing hooves. Heinrich landed, and before he could rear again Delmar dragged its reins to the side, forcing the horse to turn, preventing him from balancing evenly on its hind legs and rearing again. Delmar gripped the reins and jumped from the saddle, searching for his attacker.

The pistolier was still there, but he was not reloading his gun, nor even making his escape. He and the women around him were laughing!

Enraged, Delmar pulled Heinrich forwards and shoved his way through the gaggle. The women, street jades interested only in passing distraction, fell back leaving the indolent pistolier alone. Automatically, Delmar sized up his opponent. This was no petty Altdorf cut-throat: his clothes were black, but richly made, cut to show red cloth beneath. He was bareheaded, for he had given his hat as a mark of favour to the prettiest of the jades, who in turn planned to barter it for liquor as soon as she could. His thin face, more accustomed to a cockily ingratiating smile, was frowning with irritation.

'Hey!' the pistolier shouted as Delmar seized him by the neck.

'Who are you?' Delmar demanded. 'What in Sigmar's name were you doing?'

'What was I doing?' The pistolier twisted in Delmar's grip. 'What were you doing wandering into my shot?'

'Your shot?'

The pistolier pointed past Delmar's head. Delmar glanced around and saw the weathervane upon the chancery behind him still spinning from being struck by the pistolier's bullet.

'Trust me,' the pistolier spat back, 'if I had been aiming for you, you would be dead already. The only harm I cause is that which I intend…'

The pistolier wrenched himself from Delmar's grip, spun about, snatched his hat from the jade who had been sneaking away and tossed back his cloak, revealing the sword at his hip.

'…and I do not intend any to you. If you had been a better horseman you would have been perfectly safe.'

Delmar released Heinrich's reins and moved his hand to his own sword's grip. 'I will have your name, sir.'

The pistolier's hand inched closer to his rapier.

'I am Siebrecht von Matz. And if you are such a fool as to think you can beat me with a blade,' Siebrecht held up his left hand, little finger outstretched, displaying the ring bearing his family's coat of arms, 'then you can kiss my signet.'

Siebrecht gave a sharp, self-satisfied smile, but Delmar had already taken hold of his sword's hilt. Just as quickly Siebrecht gripped his own. Before they could draw, they were interrupted by a crash as the gates beside them slammed open and a second squadron of knights galloped past. The crowd ran from the horses and drove the two fighters apart. Delmar was pushed back, but then forced his way through the cram of bodies after his opponent. He caught sight of Siebrecht, but then another knight blocked his path. What remained of him, at least, for one of his eyes was covered by a patch, one of his legs was a wooden peg and his right hand had no fingers.

'Delmar von Reinhardt? Siebrecht von Matz?'

Moving their hands cautiously from their swords, Delmar and Siebrecht answered in unison, 'Aye.'

'Come inside, novices. I am Brother Verrakker. Welcome to the Reiksguard.'

CHAPTER TWO

SIEBRECHT

INSIDE, THE REIKSGUARD citadel was no less formidable. Unlike out in the city, where the houses and shops had grown tall haphazardly as each occupant had tried to outdo his neighbour, the home of the Reiksguard Order was commanding by design. Each building locked firmly into the next and each corner the novices turned revealed another imposing sight. Monuments and memorials were crammed in every courtyard, and statues of the heroes of the Empire stood at guard beside every entrance. The walls were decorated with the heraldry of the multitude of noble families who had served and, once their service was done, had poured money into their old order. Greater even than these were the Grand Hall of the order and the Chapel of the Warrior Sigmar, and, greater still, at the citadel's heart soared the tower of the chapter house of the Order of the Reiksguard itself, emblazoned on each side with the skull, the wreath and the cross of the order, watching over its warriors and the city beyond.

Siebrecht von Matz tried hard not to be impressed, and failed.

Less impressive, though, were Siebrecht's fellow novices. The interfering horseman, Delmar, had pointedly ignored Siebrecht after they had entered the citadel and Siebrecht had returned the favour. Reiklanders, Siebrecht muttered. He swore that their pride was more precious to them than their own lives. Siebrecht was sure of his aim; he was the best damn shot of any he knew in Nuln, and there had been no danger. No, if only that Reiklander Delmar had not overreacted, all would have been well.

The crippled knight who had come to meet them, Brother Verrakker, had forgone comment at seeing them about to draw on one another. Instead, he had merely bid them follow him inside and led them to a side-court where the rest of the novices were assembled.

No sooner had the three of them arrived than half the novices gathered around and greeted Delmar boisterously. They shook his hand and slapped his back and loudly congratulated each other for their privilege of joining the hallowed ranks of the order.

'Reiklanders,' Siebrecht muttered again, shaking his head. He could recognise them with ease; they all had the same close-cropped hair and simple but well-cut clothes in the military style that was the current Altdorf fashion. So slavishly did they follow the fashion that Siebrecht did not know how they could tell each other apart.

He had known that a greater proportion of his fellow novices would hail from the Imperial city and its surroundings. Reikland prided itself on having more of its sons in the service of the Emperor than any other province. There was no service more convenient for the offspring of the Altdorf aristocracy than a knightly order established within their very walls, and there was no order more prestigious for the status-obsessed nobles than the personal guard of the Emperor. So Siebrecht should not have been surprised that, once the novices were all together, fully half of them were Reiklanders and had ostentatiously gathered in a tight-knit group to the exclusion of the rest.

Siebrecht instead regarded the remaining novices, those left standing at the fringes of the Reiklander huddle. The 'Provincials', as the Reiklanders were already referring to them. None of them were speaking; instead, they eyed each other warily. All of them were armed, and most kept their hands near their weapons. They had all come from quite a distance.

One of them, who carried a small mallet as well as a sword, was an Ostermarker; Siebrecht could tell by the severe expression on his face as much as by the darker hue of his skin. The next was an Averlander, his clothes ribboned with the province's colours of yellow and black. Most recognisable of all was a Nordlander who stood half a head taller than even the burly Middenlander beside him. He carried not one, but three heavy blades at his belt and had a round shield strapped to his back.

So these, then, were to be his companions. Siebrecht sighed. Savages and inbreds from every backwater the

Empire possessed. It had been too much to hope that he might see another from Nuln, anyone he might know already. As he searched around, though, one of the other Provincials stood out, for he was regarding the Reiklanders with exactly the same contempt that Siebrecht himself felt. A good enough place to start.

Siebrecht watched him for a moment as the novice shifted his intense stare from the Reiklanders to the others. Siebrecht caught his eye and the two warriors held each other's gaze for a moment. One of them would have to make the first move, and in such situations Siebrecht prided himself that the first move would always be his.

He crossed the distance between them. Unlike the rest, this novice's attire was more restrained, and did not scream his origins as the other novices' had, but as Siebrecht stuck out his hand he noticed the golden glint of a small talisman around the other man's neck shaped like a comet.

'Siebrecht von Matz,' Siebrecht introduced himself. 'You are from Talabheim?' he said, with confidence.

The Talabheim novice glanced down at the proffered hand and then looked back up at Siebrecht. If he had been put off by Siebrecht's hearty salutation, he did not show it.

'That's right,' the novice replied, gripping Siebrecht's hand with equal force, 'Gunther von Krieglitz.'

Krieglitz's eyes quickly flicked down Siebrecht's attire. 'How was your journey from Nuln?'

Siebrecht flashed a smile. This Krieglitz was quick.

'Not long enough to this destination,' he replied, then leaned in closer. 'After we are done here, I need to find a tavern and get a drink. You coming?'

Siebrecht waited, expressing an air of innate confidence he did not feel, while Krieglitz considered for a moment. These first encounters, the first alliances you formed within a new group, they marked you for the rest of your time. It dictated the friends you would make, the opportunities you would have, the kind of life that might be yours.

'All right,' Krieglitz replied, 'but let us get the Nordlander along as well.'

Krieglitz took Siebrecht's shoulder and guided him towards the big northerner.

'No one's going to stop us with him beside us,' Krieglitz concluded.

Siebrecht smiled again. He liked the man already.

KRIEGLITZ IN FACT invited the rest of the Provincials as well.

'It's the Reiksguard way, you know. Everything in big regiments,' he told Siebrecht.

And the others, not wishing to be left with the Reiklanders, all agreed. Brother Verrakker returned to show them where their belongings might be stored, apologising as he hobbled along that the knight commander had not also been available to greet them. Commander Sternberg, he explained, had just departed to join the order on the road to the north, as had Marshal Helborg himself.

At that, one of the Reiklanders spoke up.

'If the order are heading to the war, then surely so should we. We have seen battle before.'

'Oh, you may go as soon as you wish, Novice Falkenhayn,' Verrakker replied. 'But if you wish to go as one of the Reiksguard then you will have to wait until you have proven yourself worthy of the order first.'

Siebrecht warmed to Verrakker. He was a crippled warrior whose only role now was to play nursemaid to arrogant novices, but he still had some steel to him.

Falkenhayn stayed silent in a bad humour. Siebrecht took a moment to inspect the Reiklander. "Falkenhayn", Siebrecht knew it to be the name of a powerful family, and this novice obviously enjoyed that power. He had even trimmed his sideburns sharply across his cheek to resemble the markings of a bird of prey. Siebrecht noticed that the other Reiklanders were already looking to him as their leader. All except Delmar, who did not appear at home even amongst his own kind.

Once the novices' belongings were stored, Verrakker showed them to their sleeping quarters and then left them to their own devices. As soon as he had gone, the Reiklanders left as a group to explore the citadel further. Siebrecht nodded to Krieglitz, and the Provincials went back to the white gate and brazenly strode out into the city.

THE NORDLANDER INTRODUCED himself as Theodericsson Gausser, and Siebrecht and Krieglitz realised that they had been joined by the grandson of the current elector count. Unlike Krieglitz, who was the eldest son of a younger branch of the noble family of Talabheim, and Siebrecht himself, whose own family had little influence in Nuln's affairs, Gausser's grandfather was one of the most powerful men in the

Empire. Gausser himself was reluctant to speak of his connection or much of anything else for that matter.

'Your grandfather is a great man,' Siebrecht ventured. If by great, Siebrecht considered, one meant a rapacious land-grabber for whom dominion over half the Empire would be insufficient.

Gausser merely grunted.

Siebrecht eyed their surroundings carefully again. Altdorf was not short of publicans or taverns, but Siebrecht had instinctively guided the novices away from the finer establishments and towards the poorer quarter. The tavern he had decided upon was no den, but it was rough enough to have some life to it. It reminded him of the drinking spots that his band of bored noble sons had frequented back in Nuln. In any case, Siebrecht reasoned, the swords the novices wore on their belts kept them safe from the casual violence of the tavern's other patrons. It was better than out on the street where they had been assailed by legions of beggars: men and women, aged and young, whose desperation overruled their fear.

Once they were seated, however, Siebrecht found easy banter between the novices in short supply. The Averlander, Alptraum, watched everything but had little to say of his own; and the Middenlander, Straber, and the Ostermarker, Bohdan, had gone to the bar with some complaint about the liquor. Weisshuber at least offered to buy the drinks, even if he did stare at everything as though he was a newborn.

'Are you sure we should have left?' the wide-eyed Stirlander, Weisshuber, piped up. 'No one said we could leave.'

'No one said we had to stay either,' Siebrecht blithely replied.

'If you're so concerned, Weisshuber,' Krieglitz said, 'then head back now.'

'Let's not be too hasty, Gunther,' Siebrecht intervened. 'As long as our new friend wishes to enjoy the city, and has coin and a generous spirit, then he should stay. We will not be missed before the evening service.'

'It is a wondrous city,' Weisshuber continued, 'I have never seen the capital before today. It is so alive.'

Siebrecht and Krieglitz shared a glance.

'Alive like a rat's nest.' Siebrecht made a dismissive noise. 'It is nothing to Nuln. You wish to see beauty then see Nuln, my friend. Do not forget, Nuln was the capital of the Empire for more than a century, before Altdorf.'

'And Talabheim before that,' Krieglitz said. Siebrecht raised a sceptical eyebrow at his fellow novice. 'In its own way,' Krieglitz admitted.

'Talabheim is a great city,' Siebrecht graciously conceded.

'It is strong,' Gausser stated. 'That is good.'

'Thick walls,' Alptraum murmured, staring off through the window at the spires of Altdorf, 'but full of paper and lawyers.'

Krieglitz scowled. 'At least we *have* law. Is there any law in Averland these days?'

'We have lawyers,' Alptraum said. 'Saw a lawyer once.'

'Only the one?'

'It would have been more... but the rest of them escaped.'

The Averlander's strange comment hung over the table for a moment.

'Taal's teeth.' Krieglitz said in disbelief. 'I would never have expected to meet someone like you here.' Siebrecht chortled, spilling some of his wine. Krieglitz continued, 'Nor one like you either, Novice Matz.' This time the touch of concern was clear in his voice.

'I tell you, my friend,' Siebrecht said, wiping the spilt wine from his face with his sleeve, 'I did not expect to meet me here either.'

'I DID NOT expect to see you here, old friend,' Falkenhayn said to Delmar. 'How many years has it been?'

'A fair few,' Delmar replied. 'I could not come to the city…'

'…and I would never be seen in the country,' Falkenhayn laughed, and led the way on. He seemed quite familiar with the chapter house, and Delmar remembered that Falkenhayn's father had been a knight of the Reiksguard as well.

Falkenhayn had shown them the Grand Hall first, which, as its name implied, was very grand indeed. Tables long enough to seat a hundred at a time stretched down its length. Stone arches criss-crossed its ceiling. Shafts of light shone through lined windows and warmed the rich, dark, oak-panelled walls. It was also currently very empty. Aside from the novices, there were scarce half a dozen knights taking their afternoon meal.

'Wait, my brothers, 'til we see it full with the whole order,' Falkenhayn said to the others. 'It is a sight to be seen.'

Most of the knights who were present were accompanied by one of the order sergeants to aid them. Delmar was surprised to see them here, aiding the crippled, but apparently their duties extended far beyond merely protecting the chapter house's walls. The knights themselves had a great need of aid, for they had such a diverse range of injuries as to be more likely patients in Shallya's wards.

They were clustered near the far end of the hall, close to the top table where places were always reserved for the Reiksmarshal and the order's senior officers. Behind the top table was displayed a tapestry depicting Sigmar granting the land of the Empire to the tribal chieftains who would become the first Imperial counts. And above that were displayed the personal coats of arms of each of the grand masters of the order who had served to date. Delmar saw Kurt Helborg's own heraldry in the eighth position along.

At the opposite end, where the novices had filed in, there was another display of shields. These were far smaller, though, for there were dozens, hundreds of them. It was a wall of remembrance, Delmar realised, and there, a foot or so above his head, hung the shield of his father.

'Come on, brother, let's move on,' Falkenhayn told Delmar in a hushed voice, and he started to lead him outside.

'Come on, Proktor,' Falkenhayn said, louder, to the other Reiklander who had stayed behind, staring at the wall.

Outside, Delmar released his breath. He was no stripling youth any more, he had fought, killed, commanded others in battle. His father had gone from his life long ago, and Delmar had thought he had reconciled himself to that loss. Still it felt strange to be walking these corridors that his father had walked, seeing the traces of his existence that still lingered here.

The courtyard beyond the Grand Hall opened up into a wide expanse of empty ground. After seeing so many buildings crammed atop each other, Delmar was surprised to see open space left untouched.

'It is the practice field,' Falkenhayn answered. 'Where the novices train, the knights as well, when they are here.' Falkenhayn's tone was tinged with disappointment that the order was on the march without them.

The other Reiklander novices stretched their legs around the field. The day's events and the anticipation of the formal induction tomorrow had got their blood up, and they began to spar with each other.

Watching with Falkenhayn from the side, Delmar saw how companionable the other novices were with each other.

'It seems you are all old friends already,' he said.

'We are,' Falkenhayn replied. 'We have all been serving in the pistolkorps together this past year.'

'Of course,' Delmar said quietly.

'Proktor there, you remember Proktor,' Falkenhayn continued, indicating the slightest of the novices. 'He and I enlisted together.'

Delmar nodded. Proktor's family and Falkenhayn's were related and, throughout their youth together, he had ever been Falkenhayn's shadow.

'Harver and Breigh were already there,' Falkenhayn said, pointing out the two novices wrestling with each other. 'And Hardenburg came a few months after. You don't have any sisters, do you, Reinhardt? I should keep them away from Hardenburg if you do.'

Delmar looked at the pleasant-faced young man as he adjudicated over the other novices' bout.

'No, no sisters or brothers.'

'Ah, Reinhardt,' Falkenhayn said, 'do not doubt that you have brothers now.' Falkenhayn looked out to the other novices, 'Doesn't he, Falcons!'

The Reiklanders looked up from their sport.

'Falcons!' they cried back.

'What's that?' Delmar asked.

'Just a name the pistolkorps called us. The others are quite fond of it.'

'Falcons?' Delmar said. 'After you?'

Falkenhayn shrugged.

'It is a shame you were not with us then. We could have used your strength. But come on, let us make up for lost time.' Falkenhayn took him over to join the others. 'And let us only hope that the war continues long enough for us to show the Empire's foes how the sons of Reikland fight!'

SIEBRECHT AND THE other Provincials made their way, slowly but steadily, back to the chapter house. Siebrecht and Krieglitz walked side by side, Bohdan and Straber supported each other, Alptraum walked on his own and Gausser carried the unconscious Weisshuber over his shoulders.

The wine had insulated Siebrecht nicely against the cool night and the human squalor in the streets around him. He was far happier now he was on the other side of the cup. He found himself singing an old nursery song, written as a learning rhyme to teach common children the provinces of the Empire. As Siebrecht recited the first line, Krieglitz and Gausser, strangers from across the Empire who had never met before that day, joined in and sang together.

A voice from a window above gave the novices a short, sharp critique of their abilities as minstrels. Siebrecht responded by launching into the second verse with all the greater gusto. Krieglitz very firmly clamped his hand over Siebrecht's mouth.

'Be quiet, you idiot. You'll get us into even more trouble.'

Siebrecht flailed but could not slip from the Talabheimer's grip.

'Talabec! Talabec!' One of the beggar women rose from the gutter and stumbled towards Krieglitz. 'You are from Talabecland?'

'What of it?' Krieglitz said, pushing Siebrecht away and moving his hand to his sword. The beggar woman saw the movement and cowered away.

'Nothing, noble lord! I did not mean any harm. Be generous and spare your fellow countryman.'

Krieglitz let his sword drop back. 'You would have been better to stay at home.'

'Our homes were burned, noble lord. The beastkin in the forests.'

Krieglitz grudgingly flicked her a coin, which she caught and hid instantly beneath her clothes. 'That is my last one. Do not send your friends after me looking for more.'

'More trouble,' Krieglitz muttered under his breath as he led the Provincials on.

'You concern yourself too much,' Siebrecht said, far more sober than he had been a few moments before. 'We will be fine.'

'I doubt that indeed.'

'I would wager it.'

'What?'

'Come, I shall prove it,' Siebrecht retorted. 'A gold crown that we have not been missed.'

'You are ridiculous, Siebrecht.'

'Think of it as simple prudence, Gunther. Would you pay a crown to guarantee there was no trouble?'

'Perhaps,' Krieglitz admitted.

'Then if we are not, you have your money's worth. And if we are, you have another crown to console you for your loss. It is prudent, I would say. Are you Talabheimers not known for your prudence?'

Krieglitz shook his head but said, 'Very well.'

'Done and done. Come on, Gausser, let us get the young Stirlander to his bed.'

'I cannot believe it, Siebrecht,' Krieglitz said. 'You have got me gambling on my very career.'

Siebrecht laughed at his friend. 'And it is only the first day. Imagine what there will be tomorrow!'

'ARE YOU AWAKE, Novice Matz?' Brother Verrakker said gently.

Siebrecht groggily cracked an eyelid. It was still dark. He closed it again.

'Good,' Verrakker said. 'Take him.'

* * *

SIEBRECHT WAS VERY much awake as the sergeants hurled him into the deep pool of black water beneath the chapter house. He gasped at the shock of the icy water and quickly surfaced, then instinctively ducked again as the struggling forms of the other Provincials were thrown in after him. All of them rose, spluttering protests.

The only one of them still dry was Gausser, who was wrestling on the side with three sergeants trying to restrain him. One of them lost their grip, and Gausser picked him up and launched him bodily into the pool. The sergeants who had been handling the other novices glanced at each other, then threw themselves onto the struggling Nordlander.

'Enough!' Verrakker said, and the sergeants carefully loosened their grip. 'Novices, you will clean this pool. You will empty the water, scrub its walls, wash them clean, then refill it.'

Siebrecht's foot strained to reach the bottom while keeping his head on the surface; he found he could stand, so long as he stayed on tip-toe. He tried to shout back at Verrakker, but his breath still had not returned.

'Novice Gausser,' Verrakker continued, and the Nordlander shrugged himself free. 'You may leave with us, or you may stand with your brothers. It is your choice.'

Gausser stood for a moment beside the pool, then, staring at Verrakker with bloody-minded defiance, he slowly lowered himself into the water.

'As I thought,' Verrakker concluded. 'We shall return when you are done. And here, something to help...'

Verrakker dragged a bucket through the water and then held it up. Water poured out through its perforated base.

'You can't leave us. We could catch our deaths in here!' Siebrecht finally managed to gasp.

'We have excellent healers, Novice Matz,' Verrakker replied as he and the sergeants filed out. The sergeant Gausser had soaked left with a pointed backwards glance.

'And if they should fail...' Verrakker continued. 'Well, you shall not be the first.'

THE COLD REMAINED in their bones the rest of the day, and Siebrecht spent most of their induction around the chapter house either shivering or yawning. He had expected the other Provincials to attach a certain degree of blame to him regarding their unfortunate experience. Weisshuber took it with equanimity, though; Alptraum acted as though nothing had happened; Gausser accepted it with his usual impenetrable stoicism; and Bohdan and Straber thought it had been a great joke.

Only Krieglitz appeared to hold a grudge. Siebrecht decided to shake him from it. That evening, once the novices were sent back to their quarters, he wandered over to him and flicked him a gold coin.

Krieglitz caught it sullenly. 'You really do not care, do you?'

'That I do not.' And Siebrecht did not. The Reiksguard had been no choice of his. Throughout his childhood, his father, the old baron, had done nothing but blame the Reikland emperors for all the woes in the world. He clutched his bitterness still, his one solace, as he blindly brought the Matz family to its knees. He allowed candles to be lit only rarely, as he said he could not afford them. He detested any sounds of laughter or mirth, and so Siebrecht and his brothers and sisters crept around like mice. The baron had turned the family home into the family grave.

Of all them, only the baron's younger brother, Siebrecht's uncle, had escaped the poison of the household completely. And once he left, the baron never allowed him back. The uncle had gone into the merchant trade, and would return once every few years, laden with gifts. Even then, Siebrecht's mother had to take him and his siblings into Nuln to meet him as the baron refused to have his brother set foot upon his land.

As he grew older, Siebrecht had also kept away as best he could, gaming, drinking; he and his friends had even joined the pistolkorps when the war came and they took what excitement they could from the tedious patrols and brief alarms. Siebrecht had hoped that they might stay together and join the city regiments. He would have cut a fine figure indeed in their black uniform, and the Countess of Nuln was renowned for her fondness for having young officers entertain her at her grand dances.

Instead his family had sent him here, far from his friends and his ambitions, to protect the life of the very man they had raised him to detest. So, no, he did not care.

'Understand me, Siebrecht,' Krieglitz said, with deliberate import. 'This may not be important to you, but it is to me. To my family. So I will be your comrade, I will be your friend, but I will not let you be my undoing. Agreed?'

'Agreed,' Siebrecht said, and they shook hands on it. 'I will not be your undoing, Gunther, I would wager a crown upon it.'

'Of course, you would.' Krieglitz shook his head.

VERRAKKER CALLED THE novices to the practice field and had them stand in a loose semi-circle at the corner. They each wore their plain cloth tunics and had been given a sword, a wooden waster.

They were met there by several of the order's sergeants and two of the Reiksguard's fightmasters. The first fightmaster stood formally at ease, his feet a shoulder-width apart, his hands behind his back. Or, to be more precise, hand, singular, for the fightmaster's left arm ended no more than an inch below his elbow. Nevertheless, the knight held the arm at the perfect angle, as though his hands still grasped each other. The second knight stood a step directly behind him. Unlike the first, his face was downcast, his eyes were bandaged and his head was completely bald, not a hair upon it, not on his scalp, nor above his eyes, nor on his chin. He had his hand on the shoulder of the fightmaster before him.

Verrakker introduced his brother-knights: 'This is Brother Talhoffer and Brother Ott,' Verrakker said, indicating the lead knight and then the second. 'While you are novices, you will not address them as such. Until you can prove yourselves worthy and become full brothers, you will address them as Fightmaster Talhoffer and Fightmaster Ott, or simply as master.'

Verrakker bowed to the fightmasters deferentially and hobbled away. As the other novices turned their attention to the fightmasters, Siebrecht, thoughtfully, watched Verrakker go.

'We are well met, noble sons,' Fightmaster Talhoffer declared. 'I see in you the burning need to serve your Empire and I can tell you now that the Empire has great need of that service. You will have heard already that before you may become a brother of this grand order you must prove yourself in three disciplines: strength of body, strength of mind and strength of spirit. Of these three, strength of body is the most important, for without a strong body you will never protect the Emperor from those who seek to do him harm. Strength of body is what you will learn from me.'

There was a shifting amongst the novices. Some of the Provincials and the Reiklanders were not impressed. They were not children who needed to be taught basic drills.

'You have all served before,' Talhoffer continued. 'You have all fought. You all show promise, else you would never have been allowed here. Promise, though, is not enough. We do not entrust the life of our Emperor to those who merely have promise, we entrust it only to those who have proven their ability. Not simply to fight, but to fight as a knight of the Reiksguard must. We will train you to fight and we will test you. You may think you are a great warrior already, but if you cannot or will not learn what we have to teach, then there is no place for you here.'

Talhoffer drew out the pause, waiting for one of the more prideful novices to speak and knowing that none of them would. The novices stayed silent.

'We will teach you how to fight as a Reiksguarder in every circumstance, on horse, on foot, in the crush of a regiment, in a single combat, against one opponent and against many. For we must be prepared to serve in whatever manner the Emperor demands.'

Talhoffer beckoned to one of the sergeants attending him, who passed him a halberd.

'You must become adept in all the arms of the Empire as well.' Talhoffer easily hefted the heavy weapon in a single grip. 'Skill with lance and sword are not sufficient, you must be ready to use whatever weapon is to hand.

'While you will spar with each other to learn and to practise, the purpose of your training is to fight the enemies of the Empire. Not each other. Some of you, I warrant, have drawn your sword in anger against a comrade because of injury to your honour. That ends here. Duels of any kind between members of the order are strictly prohibited. For we are a brotherhood, and from this point on you must be brothers to each other.'

Siebrecht stole a glance in the direction of Delmar, but he and the rest of the Reiklanders merely looked on.

'Now, I shall call each one of you up in turn to judge what you have learnt already, or rather, how much work I will have to undo the bad habits that poor teaching has already instilled within you.'

He told the novices to sit and then called Harver forwards. Siebrecht had expected that Talhoffer himself would spar, but instead one of the sergeants squared off against him. It was a surprise: the sergeants were all common-born, and while noblemen learned to use a sword from childhood, few commoners had the money or the time.

In a few blows it was over, and Harver was flat on his back.

Siebrecht dropped his pretence of uninterest and watched the bouts closely. He had been quietly confident, for in Nuln duelling was a constant pastime for his band of libertines. He had had to defend himself not only in single combats but also in the sudden and deadly street fights that erupted between different bands over the important things in life: wagers, women and honour. But these sergeants had been taught well.

Novice after novice stepped up and, no matter what their past experience, each was defeated. Siebrecht allowed himself a small smile when Delmar had his sword knocked from his hand.

'Novice Matz, your turn to spar,' Talhoffer ordered. 'Let us see whether you Nulners are as eager with the sword as you are with your pistol.'

There was a stir amongst the Reiklanders: news of the clash between Delmar and Siebrecht on their first day had spread quickly amongst them.

As Siebrecht rose, he whispered to Krieglitz, 'A crown of mine says I mark him.'

Siebrecht stood up and walked over with his typical swagger. He took his position and settled into his guard, ready for the sergeant to attack.

'Novices!' Talhoffer interrupted before the fight could begin. 'You did not tell me that the Reiksguard had accepted a Tilean!'

It took Siebrecht a moment to realise that the fight-master was talking about him.

'I do not follow your meaning, master, I am no Tilean.'

'If you are no Tilean, Novice Matz, then why do you stand like one?'

Confused, Siebrecht looked down at his feet.

'Take up a proper Imperial guard, novice, we shall have none of the Tilean "arts" here. They are fit only for women.'

The other novices, realising the fightmaster's joke, laughed hugely, the Reiklanders especially. Embarrassed, Siebrecht shifted to a fair approximation of the 'plough' guard that the sergeant had adopted, holding his sword at waist height, pointed at his opponent. Siebrecht cursed under his breath. All the duelling instructors of Nuln taught the Tilean style, there was no fault in it, and now he had allowed himself to be forced into a style in which he was less comfortable.

Before Siebrecht could reconsider, the sergeant took the initiative and advanced, raising his sword into a roof guard, hilt by the shoulder, blade pointing straight up as he went. Anticipating the downwards slash, Siebrecht gathered his blade in and, when the blow came, was ready to lift his own blade in reply. The sergeant's weapon crashed down upon his own with full force; Siebrecht felt his elbow give way and grabbed his hilt with his free hand to prevent his guard collapsing. On the sidelines he heard the fightmaster *tut* disapprovingly. Siebrecht had intended to beat the sergeant's sword away and twist his blade to respond with a cut of his own, but it was all he could do to keep his opponent from his neck. The sergeant drew back, preparing another strike, and Siebrecht took the opportunity to step quickly backwards, giving him a few precious seconds to recover.

The sergeant advanced again, but this time it was Siebrecht who attacked with a lightning thrust, not to his opponent's chest but to his thigh. This was what true swordplay was about, Siebrecht knew, not words, nor tricks, but simply being faster than any opposition, and in that he excelled. The sergeant corrected his strike, sweeping his blade down early to deflect Siebrecht's thrust away. Siebrecht was ready for it and, just before the swords made contact, he flicked his wrist and brought the point over the sergeant's hilt and up against his chest. It was a move designed for lighter, slimmer weapons than this ungainly practice sword, and his wrist muscles protested at such treatment. But the sergeant was surprised and had to throw his body back to evade the sword's tip. Siebrecht thrust forwards again to realise his advantage, but the sergeant found his feet and managed to stumble backwards, before finally knocking Siebrecht's sword away with a desperate swipe.

There was another moment's pause as both sides reassessed the other. Siebrecht could tell that his fellow novices had been impressed; none of them had managed to so much as trouble the sergeant, let alone drive him back. But he also knew that the sergeant had been too confident; he would not be caught out so readily next time. The sergeant, though, appeared to have learned nothing from the last engagement and once more advanced with a high guard, exactly as he had done the first time. It was obviously a trap, evidently the sergeant hoped for Siebrecht to draw his sword in again ready to block and allow him a chance to close the distance, perhaps even reverse his guard into a downwards thrust. Siebrecht did the opposite and threw himself forwards, thrusting straight at the sergeant's chest this time, trusting to his sheer speed to succeed without any tricks.

As Siebrecht moved, the sergeant leaped forwards, keeping his sword high but twisting to evade the novice's point. Siebrecht's blade slipped past the sergeant's side and so he hurriedly stepped back to pull away. Too late. The sergeant's free arm slammed down, pinning Siebrecht's blade between his arm and his chest. Desperate, Siebrecht tried to twist the weapon to cut its way clear, but the sergeant had already snaked his arm around Siebrecht's sword hand and locked the elbow. Dropping his own sword, the sergeant gripped Siebrecht's shoulder and dropped his weight, dragging the novice down with him. They both hit the ground, but the sergeant landed on top and still with his grip. In mere moments, Siebrecht was face down with the sergeant's knee in the small of his back.

At an order from Talhoffer, the sergeant released the lock on his arm and the pressure of the sergeant's knee lifted. Feeling humiliated, Siebrecht clambered to his feet.

'You still have your sword in your hand at least, Novice Matz, though you would find it of little use where you were.'

Aware of the mocking stares of the other novices who were enjoying his defeat, Siebrecht did not say what he wished and instead muttered something under his breath.

'What was that, Novice Matz?'

Ah, curse them, Siebrecht thought, he had a legitimate grievance.

'I thought this was sword sparring, master, not wrestling.' If he had known that he would have to defend himself against wrestling moves as well, he would not have been taken off guard.

Talhoffer considered the novice from Nuln. 'Did I ever say that this was sword sparring, Novice Matz?'

No, he hadn't, Siebrecht recalled. They had all simply assumed.

'No, master,' he admitted.

'Was it simply because you were given a sword that you thought a sword was the only weapon with which you could fight?'

Siebrecht did not speak, but gave a half-nod.

'Though it is true that you will learn sword from me, and wrestling from Master Ott, we draw no distinction between them in combat. We fight with the whole of our body, Novice Matz. Every resource at our disposal.'

CHAPTER THREE

FALKENHAYN

'I AM MASTER Lehrer,' the grey knight announced from his throne behind the solid oak desk in the depths of the order's library. 'You will have heard already that before you may become a brother of this grand order you must prove yourself in three disciplines: strength of body, strength of mind and strength of spirit. Of these three, strength of mind is the most important, for without a strong mind and the ability to reason, even the strongest body is easily outwitted or dumbfounded. This is what you will learn from me.'

'In this place,' the master continued, 'you shall learn the full meaning of knightly duty, to the Emperor, to his people and to yourself. You shall also learn judgement; for if you are to be a knight, rather than merely a soldier, you shall have to be a judge, of your own actions and the actions of others'. For there is no better judge than an honourable knight, who has truth in his words, duty in his heart and a sword in his hand.'

Beneath his shaggy beard, the old master's mouth slowly twisted into a smile. Delmar listened closely. He thought of Griesmeyer; aye, there would be a knight Delmar would trust as a judge.

'As well as that, we shall also examine the Empire's greatest victories and its greatest defeats, for our ability to reason and learn from our mistakes is what sets us apart from beasts. We shall study the Empire's most successful generals and its most terrible foes. We shall begin today with Emperor Wilhelm III.'

Behind Delmar, at the back of the novices, someone scoffed.

'Novice Matz,' Master Lehrer called, 'you wish to speak?'

Delmar turned around, as did every other novice, and stared at Siebrecht.

'No, master,' Siebrecht replied. 'A cough only.'

Delmar once again found himself growing angry at the Nulner's disrespect towards the order's masters.

But Master Lehrer, who took a degree of malicious enjoyment in hooking impertinent novices, was not to be disabused.

'Well, Novice Matz, you are called upon now. So we will sit silently until you share your thoughts with us.'

Delmar watched as Siebrecht paused for a moment, testing the master's pledge, but Lehrer's amused expression was impenetrable.

'My only thought, master,' Siebrecht began, 'was that there might be emperors worthy of study before more recent times.'

'You mean, before the Reikland emperors?' Lehrer replied, dryly. 'Go on then, novice, who would you suggest?'

Delmar could see Siebrecht's cockiness return to him. 'I, for one, master, have learnt much from the great Emperor Magnus the Pious,' he said, then adding, 'of Nuln.'

Master Lehrer sat satisfied. 'I take your meaning, novice. I prefer to start with Emperor Wilhelm because that is where our order's own records begin. But Emperor Magnus's reign was two centuries ago, long before our order was founded, and there are precious few contemporary accounts of his great victories.'

'Master,' Falkenhayn spoke up, giving Delmar a wink, 'I feel I must say that is greatly unfortunate. For if we are only to study the last hundred years I scarce think we will find any general of Nuln of note.'

Siebrecht scoffed again. 'Small surprise when the Reikland princes allow scant few from other provinces to command the Empire's armies.'

. Falkenhayn bridled at that. 'The surprise is that any provincial might be given command, when it is Reikland that must provide half the men of the Emperor's armies and all the officers.'

'Ridiculous,' Siebrecht shot back.

'Is it? Reikland is but one province in ten, and yet we Reiklanders here are half the novices. Truly we are called the Reiksguard for a reason!' That brought a small cheer of support from the other Reikland novices, but Delmar stayed silent. He saw the look of disquiet on the faces of the Provincial novices, and pulled at Falkenhayn to try and sit him down.

'Oh, I do not dispute it,' Siebrecht countered. 'I only say that it is ridiculous that Reikland officers prefer and advance their own kind ahead of any other.'

If Siebrecht expected Falkenhayn to deny it he was mistaken.

'And why should they not?' Falkenhayn declared. The room went silent. 'Why should they not when it is Reikland blood being spilt on every border of the Empire? When it is Reikland lives that are lost defending each and every province?' Falkenhayn looked over the other novices.

'We are a nation under siege,' he continued, 'attacked not only by force of arms, but also by the worship of dark gods and the snares of foreign culture. There are wolves to the north, warmongering princes to the south, barbarians to the east...'

'I hope,' Krieglitz interrupted, standing, 'that you refer to those beyond the borders of the Empire.'

'Of course, brother,' Falkenhayn responded stiffly, 'those beyond the borders of the *true* Empire. And those within our borders who have thrown over our ways in favour of these others. With such danger riddled throughout our realm, can you blame a Reikland general looking first to those of his own province, men that he knows hold the interests of the Empire higher than any other...?'

The quiet library burst into uproar as the Provincial novices shot to their feet in outrage, followed just as quickly by the Reiklanders.

Master Lehrer thumped a bronze skull ornament against his desk until he could make himself heard.

He shouted at them all to be seated once more, and, finally, continued to speak.

'Excellent!' he chortled, as the room simmered. 'I sense we may have potential for some lively debates here. Let us then begin, not with Wilhelm, nor with Magnus, but rather with that great victory which defined the Empire at its birth, the First Battle of Black Fire Pass, and in particular Sigmar's unification of the twelve peoples of the Empire. I trust my point will be lost on none of you.'

'I AM BROTHER Verrakker,' Verrakker said. 'You have heard many times now that before you may become a brother of this grand order you must prove yourself in three disciplines: strength of body, strength of mind and strength of spirit. Of these three, strength of spirit is the most important, for without a strong spirit one can stray from the true path. And one's strength and one's mind can be turned to betray all you once defended. Strength of spirit is not to be learned, and I shall not be your teacher. Only your judge.'

'THIS IS THE Empire.' Talhoffer declared.

One of his sergeants stood, ready, in the middle of four of the Reiklander novices. They each carried a waster in their hand wrapped in cloth. The cloth was damp from red dye so that a blow would mark the fighter struck.

'The Empire is surrounded by its foes. All of whom, whether they admit it or not, desire to see us brought to our knees.'

The novices eyed the sergeant warily and closed in on him. So far he had done nothing but casually shift his position to keep track of his opponents. He held his sword loosely by his side. From across the circle, Delmar saw Falkenhayn gesture at him to attack. Delmar stepped forwards, swiftly lifted his blade high and cut down.

'Encircled as we are, we cannot allow our enemies the chance to strike together.'

As Delmar swung, the sergeant moved, slipping inside the arc of the blade and using the flat of his sword to guide the cut away to the side.

'And therefore we must allow ourselves to stay fixed to our guard, to hold on the defence.'

The sergeant shot forwards, maintaining the contact with Delmar's blade even as the novice instinctively drew back, keeping it off the line between them.

'Every defence must contain an attack. And every attack must contain a defence.'

The sergeant slammed his weapon down Delmar's sword arm onto his shoulder, then without pause drew it down his chest to his belly. Delmar looked down and saw the lurid red slash it had left across his body. The sergeant did not pause, but gripped Delmar with his free hand and pivoted around behind him, pushing the novice forwards. Falkenhayn's charging swing, intended to strike the sergeant down from behind, instead smacked into Delmar. Still twisting, using Delmar's body as a shield, the sergeant spun about and struck a heavy blow into Falkenhayn's side.

'Reinhardt, Falkenhayn, stand out.' Talhoffer ordered. The frustrated novices reluctantly stood aside and the sergeant squared off against the remaining pair. No one doubted the outcome.

'Attack and defence are the same. That is our overriding tenet. We fight as the Empire fights. Man and nation, there is no distinction. If an enemy should strike at us, we must first try to evade the blow. If we cannot, then we must control it so that it does not hit us with its full force. And that deflection of force must itself form a riposte to strike back. Only with such a principle can our Empire stand against the myriad foes that surround us.'

'THAT WAS PREPOSTEROUS,' Falkenhayn complained afterwards as he and his fellows suffered in the washing room, scrubbing the red dye from their shifts. 'In any battle, we would be wearing armour. That cut would never have got through our armour and so I should not have been stood down. It was no fair test of our martial skills.'

'It is a fairer test of your laundry skills then,' Gausser spoke up from the other pool. Falkenhayn ignored the jibe, for he never dared face the Nordlander directly.

'We will get better, brother,' Delmar said calmly.

Falkenhayn recommenced, 'If we are to wear armour to fight, then we should practise in armour. That is obvious.'

'THANK YOU, BROTHER. We got your wish,' Hardenburg remarked bitterly, struggling to lever himself to his feet. The novices stood in the arming room, all encased in heavy grey plate.

'It's as heavy as a Stirlander matron! Pardon my word, Weisshuber,' Hardenburg laughed.

'This isn't proper armour.' Falkenhayn was still complaining. 'These are just segments of strapped iron plate; they do not even fit together properly.'

'It is so they can be adjusted,' Delmar answered, even though Falkenhayn had not asked a question.

'It would need to be,' Siebrecht said to Krieglitz at the other end of the room, 'to fit over Falkenhayn's head.'

'He has enough spare room down there though.' Krieglitz knocked his armoured fist against his armoured crotch. The clang of metal against metal drew the Reiklanders' attention.

Hardenburg thought to join in the Provincials' banter. 'This is the one piece I'm glad for,' he said. He and the Provincials laughed together, until Falkenhayn put his hand on Hardenburg's shoulder. 'Leave them be, Tomas,' he ordered. Hardenburg looked back, but the moment's unity was gone and the old division between the novices was back.

As WELL AS the long sword, Talhoffer demonstrated the other weapons of the Empire's armies: spears and halberds, which allowed a knight to keep a greater distance from particularly dangerous foes and, when fighting on foot, to ward away enemy horsemen; greatswords, heavy two-handed blades feared by many of the Empire's foes; maces and warhammers, which could break limbs and skulls in a single blow; even the dagger, though with such an array of weaponry at their disposal the novices could barely imagine when they should need such a short blade.

Though he had been introduced alongside Master Talhoffer, Ott had not involved himself in any of Talhoffer's sword teaching. The fightmaster was something of a mystery to the novices. He barely made any sound and certainly never went to speak. And Siebrecht had seen that he wore around his neck the symbol of peaceful Shallya, the healer, similar to that beside the white gate. It was a strange god for a warrior to venerate. In training he merely stood behind Talhoffer, eyes closed, listening. Delmar had occasionally seen him make subtle gestures to the other fightmaster, the same gestures that Delmar had once seen a village girl without hearing make in order to communicate with her parents, but Talhoffer had never made them back. He replied instead with speech.

Once the novices had been equipped with their armour, however, Ott's sessions on close-quarter fighting began in earnest. While Talhoffer never fought with the novices directly, leaving his well-trained sergeants to provide the demonstration of what he dictated, the same was not true of Fightmaster Ott. Instead, Ott practiced the reverse, he spoke only through his sergeants and fought himself, demonstrating his staggering repertoire of grapples, locks, limb-breaks, throws and strangles upon the novices personally. They fought in practice bouts, often with small blunted stakes to represent daggers. Against a fully armoured knight who was standing and mobile, a dagger presented little threat; however if that same knight could be brought to the ground or held in position then that small blade became deadly, as it could be forced between openings and joins in the armour. The novices had all wrestled as youngsters, in horseplay with their fellow youths, and now they began to see the deadly art from which their childish games had derived.

Delmar had been one of the first to face Master Ott in a practice bout. While Delmar did not expect to win, he thought that he would provide a fair showing, just as Siebrecht on the first day of duelling. Though Ott had experience, he was not very tall. Delmar had the advantage in both height and reach, and his skill at riding had given him a sure sense of balance. When Delmar had squared off against Ott, the master had barely even opened his eyes; the eyelids were raised only a crack and the eyes themselves hidden in the shadow. Delmar got his first hold on Ott easily, and just as easily Ott slipped out of it, taking Delmar's arm with him. The master twisted as he went and, for all Delmar's steady feet, he found himself forced to the ground; it was either that or have his arm ripped off at the shoulder. The master's dagger pricked him at the back of his neck and the bout was over.

Once Ott had 'assessed' the skill of each of the novices, and left them choking on the earth, his tuition began. He took the novices through the move and then paired them off to practise, ending each session with a proper practice bout.

Against the other novices, Delmar fared far better, winning most of his bouts. The novice who excelled was, of course, Gausser. Not only was he far larger and stronger than the others, but Nordland was infamous for settling disputes through trials of combat.

Despite his domination, his training did not go without incident. It was near the end of one of the sessions.

Most of the novices, exhausted, preferred to rest in wrestling clinches rather than continue to try to trip or throw their opponents. In the midst of that amiable lethargy, however, a violent argument erupted.

'Can you not hear, Nordlander? Can anything penetrate that head of yours if it is not drummed upon it?'

'You did not say it, Falkenhayn. I would have heard it if you had said it.'

Ott had tapped Falkenhayn to wrestle Gausser. But before the bout was done, Falkenhayn had cried out loudly and accused Gausser of ignoring his attempts to concede the bout.

'I said it again and again and you ignored it! I swear he's broken my arm.' Falkenhayn gingerly presented the injured limb to the sergeant beside him.

Delmar and the other novices crowded around. Proktor gently took hold of Falkenhayn's arm, but Falkenhayn suddenly jerked it away with another cry of pain.

Gausser now turned to the sergeant as well; he was getting uncomfortable having to defend himself.

'If he had not been squirming so much, I would not have needed to hold on so tight.'

'You admit it then!' Falkenhayn exclaimed. 'You were holding tighter than you should to hurt me.'

'I did not mean to hurt you,' Gausser answered, but without conviction. His dislike of the Reikland novices and Falkenhayn in particular was well known.

'But you did not stop when I said relent.'

'That, I did not hear you say,' Gausser stated, his accent thickening as he grew more flustered. He was not accustomed to such duels of words.

'How convenient that you can ignore the rules when it pleases you.'

That charge, effectively calling the Nordlander a cheat, pushed Gausser over the edge.

'No, no, no,' Gausser bellowed, taking a menacing step forwards. Siebrecht and Krieglitz rushed to either side to prevent him going further, just as Delmar and Proktor pulled Falkenhayn behind them to protect him. 'No to your clever lying words. I fight fair. You did not say relent. You carry on fighting and now you complain. It is you Reiklanders who ignore rules when it pleases! You take back what you say or we fight again! Here! To prove who is right.' Gausser stomped back a few paces to free himself of his friends' grip and started to tear off the practice plate.

'You are just proving all I said. Did you not hear through your skull?' Falkenhayn called back, safe behind the other Reikland novices. 'You broke my arm! A fair fight that would be.'

'Then choose your champion,' Gausser snarled, throwing his breastplate off his shoulders. 'If you can find an honourable man who will stand in place of a worthless lying slug like you.'

'That barbarian,' Falkenhayn muttered to his fellow Reiklanders. 'He has insulted my honour. I have no choice but to fight him now.'

'No, Franz, no,' Proktor urged, 'your arm. You'll not stand a chance. Let me fight for you.'

'You are a good brother and a good cousin, Laurentz, but even with an arm broken I stand a better chance against him than you do.'

'I will do it,' Delmar said.

Falkenhayn's face lit up. 'My thanks, and my honour, are with you, Delmar.'

'Here is my champion!' Falkenhayn shouted to Gausser.

'No duels!' Weisshuber cried from the middle. 'Don't you remember, no duels.'

'This is no duel,' Siebrecht jibed back. 'This is training!'

'Novices! Stand apart!' The sergeant yelled. Obediently, they did so, edging back, but eyes still fixed on the other side.

Master Ott stepped in between them. He turned his head from one side to the other, as though inspecting the two groups of novices with his closed eyes. The sergeant stood by his side to interpret his gestures.

'Master Ott says,' the sergeant stated, 'that it is not the privilege of novices to change his rota. But if two novices wish to train, then let them train. But let them train well, in accordance with what they have been taught. Alone, without aid from any other, with plate and daggers, and with these sergeants in place to ensure the rules are followed.'

Delmar did not know how it had come to this. This did not feel like the right thing to do, and yet he was defending his comrade's honour; how could there be wrong in that? Falkenhayn had looked at him so imploringly, what could he do besides offer his aid? And yet he knew that he could not win. He had done well in practice, but Gausser was half a foot taller than he and built like a great cannon. He had trounced all the other novices, and Delmar had been no exception. Gausser would expect the first few moments to be tentative, each testing the other. If Delmar struck fast he might catch him off-guard. If he managed to knock Gausser to the ground in the first few seconds, that might be his only chance.

The sergeant gave them the signal to begin and Delmar charged, and so did Gausser. As soon as he saw the Nordlander run at him as well, Delmar tried to check his stride, side step and trip him. Gausser merely kicked the tripping leg out of the way and crashed into Delmar. Delmar managed to pivot rather than fall and spun to the other side of the circle, grasping the moment to recover. The two went at each other again, this time more warily. Delmar ran through the techniques that Ott had taught them. He dived in to try to lock Gausser's arm, but the novice held it in close and then smacked Delmar across the chest, knocking him back over the Nordlander's hip. Delmar felt his balance go and rolled himself away. Gausser came in for him, grabbing around his torso. Delmar kept low, seized Gausser's knee and then drove into his gut with all his strength. Surprised, Gausser took a half-step back to regain his footing and Delmar pushed all the harder. It was not enough, Gausser's leg was like a tree trunk and refused to shift. Delmar was suddenly crushed to the ground as Gausser intentionally collapsed forwards onto Delmar's back. They both went down on their fronts, but Gausser was on top, and after a brief scramble Delmar felt the wooden dagger push through a gap in his armour. The sergeant called the point and Gausser allowed Delmar back to his feet.

They began again. From the initial clinch, Delmar desperately tried to wrap his arm around Gausser's neck, but the Nordlander simply allowed him to get his hold and then heaved Delmar off the ground and knocked his legs out from under him. Again Delmar went down to the groans of the Reiklander novices. Another point against him.

Delmar could see that Gausser was growing confident, and he had good reason. Though Gausser did not have the technique of Master Ott, his experience, his weight and reach, were more than enough. Delmar would have to surprise him. Gausser came at him again and Delmar grabbed his arm and spun into him, ready to roll the Nordlander over his shoulder. Gausser was ready for it, had planted his feet and was about to use his strength to pull his arm back and wrap it around Delmar's throat. Delmar, however, kept spinning, under Gausser's arm and out the other side. With a twist of his hands, Delmar locked Gausser's arm and the strength went from it. Delmar went to his belt and drew his dagger, ready to hold it to the back of Gausser's neck and win the point, when the Nordlander twisted himself around, stepping into Delmar's body and punching him hard in the stomach. The metal plate protected Delmar from the worst of the blow, but the lock was broken, and Gausser lifted him high and then dropped him on the ground once more.

'Stay down this time, Reiklander,' Gausser said as he was awarded the point again. With three points against him, the result seemed conclusive. 'I win!' Gausser announced. 'The gods have found for me, Falkenhayn, they agree you are a slug too.'

Gausser turned back to be congratulated by his fellows, but they stared past him.

'My champion still stands,' Falkenhayn crowed back. Gausser turned about and there, indeed, Delmar had got back to his feet and was readying to fight.

Gausser shook his head in bewilderment. 'What are you doing, Reiklander? Have you not had enough?'

Delmar did not trust himself to be able to speak, to open his mouth and be able to form words. His legs felt like water. His head was ringing and stuffed full of fog. His balance was shaky. But he stood ready to fight and the Reiklanders gave a great cheer.

Gausser knocked him down again, with ease. Gausser held him down and whispered to him, 'I have no anger against you, Reinhardt. Relent. Your honour is not at stake here.'

'But,' Delmar gasped back, 'the honour of my brother is. And I will not relent,' was all he could say.

The sergeant called the point and Gausser backed away from him warily. He sensed that the tone of the fight had changed. The Provincials were no longer cheering his success. Instead, it was the Reiklanders who cheered, each and every time Delmar rose back to his feet. The more points he scored and the more Delmar clambered back up, the more Gausser grew frustrated. The more Gausser grew frustrated, the more the Reiklanders cheered.

'Why do you still call points? They mean nothing any longer,' Gausser berated the sergeant and threw his dagger away.

'Novice Gausser!' the sergeant warned over the hooting crowd.

'No! No! If this is how he wishes it then this is how it will be.'

Delmar could no longer speak, he could barely think. All his energy went to staying on his feet. His vision had narrowed and he could only see straight ahead. He saw Gausser come at him again and half-heartedly threw an arm out to grapple. The Nordlander easily blocked it, took his legs out from under him and brought him down to the ground again. Delmar felt himself being flipped over onto his back and then Gausser's elbow pressing down onto his throat in a strangle.

'Relent, Reinhardt. Relent!' Gausser demanded, both fearsome and fearful at the same time. Delmar struggled to breathe.

'That is enough, Novice Gausser,' the sergeant interrupted. Gausser, conscious that all eyes were upon him, broke his hold at once.

'You see,' he muttered as he got back to his feet, 'these Reiklanders, they are stubborn until the end.'

The sergeant watched Master Ott's gestures. 'Yes,' he said on the fightmaster's behalf. 'You fought well, Novice Gausser. It is a lesson to you all, that when an enemy will not relent then your only safety lies in its destruction. But we are only training today, so I will not require you to demonstrate to the fullest extent.'

Gausser nodded and then retreated back to the Provincial novices, as the Reiklanders tended to Delmar. Neither side said anything to the other, but there were many looks exchanged, and none of them of brotherhood.

From that day on Falkenhayn refused point-blank to spar with Gausser any more, and Gausser replied by refusing to spar with either Falkenhayn, Proktor or

Delmar. The Reiklanders swore as a group that none of them would train with Gausser any further, and the Provincials returned the favour by refusing to train with the Reiklanders.

OTT ORDERED DELMAR to spend a day in the order sanatorium to recover from Gausser's rough handling. Delmar spent the morning deep in thought, reflecting on the division between the novices. Falkenhayn had treated him well; he and the other Reiklanders had accepted him like a brother. It was as much as he had hoped. Nevertheless, in keeping his Falcons together, Falkenhayn had driven a wedge between the novices. A wedge, Delmar realised, that he himself had initiated. Siebrecht continued to show nothing but contempt for the Reiksguard and his instruction, but he should not have let that one novice's attitude poison his to the rest of the Provincials.

As he turned these grim thoughts over in his mind, he was happily surprised to be visited by Griesmeyer. The knight had returned from the main army with correspondence from the Reiksmarshal. He still had the dust of the road on him.

'My apologies that I was not able to see you all the way here that first day,' Griesmeyer said, taking a seat on the bed beside Delmar's.

'All was well, my lord, I was able to find my way.' Delmar winced a little at speaking, as his throat was still sore. 'How goes the war? The foe has invaded?'

'Yes, Kislev has fallen. Their armies are in the Empire, into Ostland. There are attacks from the east as well, into Ostermark. And everywhere throughout the forests there are reports of beastkin or marauder war-bands on the march.'

'To where?'

'Hochland, without doubt. From there, perhaps Tal-abheim, perhaps Middenheim, though they would be fools to besiege either of those. Perhaps they even intend to strike here.'

'Will you be able to stop them?'

'The Emperor is pulling in our allies. We are gathering a mighty host. We will stop them.' Griesmeyer seemed confident. 'But let us not talk of it for a few moments. Instead, tell me how you have found your time with the order.'

'It has been… an honour.'

Griesmeyer looked at Delmar with a sceptical eye. 'A restrained answer for one I'd have thought would be so full of excitement.'

'I am sorry, my lord.'

'I am not interested in your apologies, I will have an answer from you,' Griesmeyer insisted.

Delmar hesitated, but could think of no other avenue than the truth. 'It is all… not quite as I expected.'

'What all is this? Come, novice, clarity of thought is what we strive for here. What did you expect?'

'Just… more! When I think of how I pictured the Reiksguard barracks before I came here…'

'Yes? How did you picture it?'

'Fuller. Full of people: knights training, hurrying back and forth to the Imperial Palace to be at the Emperor's side. Stories of old campaigns, talk of new ones, the Reiksmarshal in the chapter house convening meetings of the order where matters of the Empire's defence would be discussed and decided. To be full of life, instead of quiet like the grave. There's just us, the sergeants who keep to themselves, and the tutors...'

Delmar was embarrassed by his outburst.

'And none of those are the image you had of a Reiksguard knight, correct?'

'I apologise, my lord. I do not mean to disrespect them. I know, I have been told, that they were all formidable warriors before...'

'Before they were crippled, yes. Oh, I did not think you meant them any disrespect. I know you well enough for that.' Griesmeyer got to his feet and strode over to the sanatorium's window looking out onto the practice field. 'I understand you better than you realise. When I have visited here when the banners are away the place resembles a Shallyan infirmary more than a knightly order. But we must find a role for them all.'

Griesmeyer turned back to him. '*You* must understand, Delmar, that these men have dedicated their lives to the order, many of them have nowhere else to go. Their lands have been lost, or are managed by others, relatives who they barely know perhaps, and who would have little use for a warrior who cannot fight. As they have given for the order, so must the order provide for them. Your tutors are the lucky ones in that respect; they can remain active in the martial way, others can only contribute by different means.'

'I understand, of course, my lord,' Delmar replied, his shame deepening. Griesmeyer saw the novice's contrition and changed the topic.

'What do you think of them? Your tutors?'

'Master Lehrer is a good teacher. I like him, though I sometimes find it difficult to understand how some of the matters he speaks of relate to a knight's duty. Master Talhoffer can be… hard on us at times, but there is great value in what he teaches. Master Ott…'

'Yes?'

'I do not know. It is hard to know what to make of him.'

'Hmmm… If you know Master Lehrer well, I should talk to him about Ott. You may find you understand him better. And what of Master Verrakker?'

'Master? He said he was merely a brother.'

'Did he?' Griesmeyer pondered. 'Well, who should know better than he. How have you found him?'

'I believe he has a thankless task.'

'That is true indeed. I spoke to Brother Verrakker earlier this morning. Is the peace and quiet all that is concerning you? He mentioned that there were some disputes between the novices. Are you involved in those?'

Delmar did not speak at once. Griesmeyer had been very kind to him, but if Delmar confided in him would he then take formal action? That would only deepen the divide between the two groups.

'If I am,' Delmar replied, 'then those disputes would be mine alone to resolve.'

'Ah!' Griesmeyer replied, laughing. 'The old Reinhardt pride, I remember it well from your father. Do not think, though, that the masters are blind. It was the same in my day. Even more so, for I was a novice before Karl Franz was elected. The old Emperor was failing, showing his age, and all my fellow novices could talk of was the succession.'

'I was with novices from every single province,' Griesmeyer continued, 'each of whom thought that their ruler was the only conceivable candidate. Sigmar alone knows what would have happened to the Reiksguard if another Emperor had decided to move his capital to a different city, to Middenheim or Talabheim. Can you imagine the White Wolves, the Panthers and ourselves all barracked together? You would not be able to move in the streets for knights on their warhorses.'

Delmar smiled at the image.

'As it resulted, the throne stayed in Reikland and went to Karl Franz, and he has made a good job of it, though he has faced hard enough times. The arguments though, that even we novices had at the time...'

Griesmeyer cut off the thought with a curt gesture.

'I remember when, in learning our history, I first heard of the civil wars in the Time of the Three Emperors. I remember that I could not believe that there were so many people then who honestly considered it best to tear our nation to pieces. However, as the years have passed, and I have travelled, and met hundreds of my fellow subjects... I become more and more surprised to meet those who wish to hold it together.'

Griesmeyer shook away the memory. 'I will leave your disputes to yourself, Delmar, but I will say this. Do not forget that you do not have to follow the same path as others do. It is you who are responsible for your conduct, no one else.

'And know this, Delmar, it is politicians who conquer through division. And you know what little the Reiksguard thinks of politics. No, it is leaders who unite and rule.'

Delmar thought on it. 'Is the same true of the Emperor?'

Griesmeyer gave his half-smile of amusement. 'It is not the Reiksguard's place to judge their Emperor. The elector counts are more than willing to take up that duty.'

'You have seen him?'

'The Emperor? Often. I could not call myself one of his guard if I had not.'

'What is he like?'

Griesmeyer was about to reply, but then paused. 'You will find out soon enough once he returns.'

'If he returns,' Delmar whispered. 'Not all return from the north.'

Griesmeyer's tone softened. 'I will not deceive you, Delmar. There have been times in our history when our realm has been in greater peril, but never in my lifetime. But I am only one man, and our nation has ever had its spirit tested by those who hate us. They spill our blood and we spill theirs. For centuries, for tens of centuries now. Do I like it? No. Would I give my life to banish them for ever? Without a moment's doubt. But do I fear their coming? Never. Never again.'

'I am due back to the north,' Griesmeyer said, rising from his seat upon the bed, 'and it is true, I may not return. But the Empire cannot be killed as can a single man. It will live still.'

'We should go with you,' Delmar suddenly declared. 'When you leave, we novices should ride with you. We can do no good here. Let us come and fight for the Emperor.'

Griesmeyer looked archly. 'You think your dozen swords would make the difference?'

'Perhaps,' Delmar ventured.

'Well, I do not. And neither does the Marshal. You will stay here until you are ready, though you may believe me that your tutors are pushing you as fast as you are able.'

Griesmeyer looked down upon his friend's only son. 'Do not concern yourself, Delmar, that all may be done before you may serve. There is a war being fought far greater than this single campaign, and it holds the entire Empire within its grip. Take my word, we shall not be free of it for many years.'

DELMAR, ONCE RECOVERED, returned to the novices. The two groups were keeping their distance on the practice field: the Reiklanders were training at the pell whilst the Provincials rehearsed the close-order drills under a sergeant's supervision. Falkenhayn was attacking the wooden pell with a fury, and Harver and Breigh had looks of thunder upon their faces; Hardenburg just lay on the grass, covering his face.

'What has happened?' Delmar asked.

'There is word from the north,' Proktor supplied.

'What is it? Has Ostland fallen?'

'Ostland!' Falkenhayn shouted from the pell, in a voice loud enough for the Provincials to hear it. 'Ostland proved to be little more than a bump in the foe's path. It's Middenheim.'

'Middenheim?' Delmar was shocked. 'Middenheim has fallen?' It was impossible; the fortress-city of the White Wolf could never have been taken so quickly.

Proktor shook his head. 'It is besieged, and by such a great horde that… the army's hope for victory is slim.'

Delmar immediately thought of Griesmeyer, already riding hard back to the north. He looked over at the Provincials but could not see the novice from Middenland.

'Where is Straber?'

Proktor looked to Falkenhayn, but the other novice turned back to the pell.

'What is it?' Delmar asked.

'A messenger came for him,' Proktor said quietly. 'His estates have been burned. His father's body was found. The women were missing. It is thought they are dead as well. At least… it is hoped. Death would be a mercy to being captured by those monsters. He has ridden for home.'

'As they all will.' Falkenhayn, sweating, came across from the pell. 'It is as I always said, Reinhardt. They cannot be relied upon. It will be us Reiklanders who will carry the Empire.'

'Brother,' Delmar replied, 'Straber's home is in peril. His father is dead. That means he is the lord of those lands. Of course he must go back and defend them.'

'And when Middenheim falls and Nordland is threatened, will Gausser then go? Then Bohdan back to Ostermark, Krieglitz to Talabheim?' Falkenhayn flicked his sword as if knocking those novices away. 'Perhaps, Delmar, each man should only defend that patch of ground on which he stands? Is that how we should defend our Empire?'

'Calm yourself, brother,' Delmar said.

'No, brother, I shall not calm myself,' Falkenhayn shouted. 'You answer me, is that how we should defend our Empire?'

Delmar looked to the others, but there was no sign of support from Harver or Breigh; Hardenburg still lay there, his face covered; Proktor was the picture of misery.

'No,' Delmar conceded, 'it is not.'

'Thank you, brother,' Falkenhayn spat, and took his sword back to the pell.

IT WAS TO be a full day before Falkenhayn had calmed down sufficiently to make his peace with Delmar. It was frustrating; they all felt it. To be closed up in the chapter house whilst the Reiksguard was fighting the Empire's enemies was intolerable, but there was nothing that could be done except leave the order as Straber had, and none of the Reiklanders wished to do that. As the news of the siege of Middenheim raced around the city, it drove the masses of starving refugees to even greater desperation. If Middenheim could fall, where would be safe within the Empire? The Altdorf officials began to stockpile food in case a similar fate befell the capital. Traders, priests and storekeepers followed their example. What food had been available to the refugees in the streets was cut off. The officials proclaimed that everyone in the city had to tighten their belts. But for some their belts could be tightened no further, and their desperation drove them to greater acts of violence.

As the tension built in the streets, so too did it grow amongst the novices. To gain peace, Delmar decided to follow Griesmeyer's advice and inquire about Master

Ott of Master Lehrer. Lehrer directed him to a section in the Reiksguard's annals. The passage was still relatively fresh, having been written only a few years previously.

There had been a battle, but Delmar could not tell where as, unlike the others, there was no location specified. It must have been at night, however, for there were repeated references to the dark in which the enemy had concealed themselves and in which the battle was subsequently fought. There was no specific mention of the name of the foe in this instance, merely the ambushes and traps they sprung upon the Reiksguard as they advanced. There was mention of Brother Ott, however.

During one of their attacks, a foul missile had exploded over him. He had been covered with an evil smoke which had burnt his skin and filled his lungs with its poison. It was one Brother Talhoffer who had covered himself with his cloak and dared plunge into the cloud of gas. He had emerged, dragging the unconscious Ott with one hand and still carrying his sword with the other. Talhoffer had just called for aid when one of the frenzied creatures charged at him. Both of them had struck at the same time, the knight running the creature through with his sword, the creature chopping through the knight's other arm, by which he held his brother, with a jagged glaive. At the loss of his arm, Talhoffer had apparently kicked the creature's corpse away, dropped his sword, seized Ott with his remaining hand and continued to pull him to safety until other brothers arrived.

'It is a noble tale,' Master Lehrer commented from behind his desk after Delmar had finished reading.

'Our healers went to work on them both as soon as the army emerged from the pit. Talhoffer was recovered within a few days, though of course his arm was left behind. Brother Ott, however, languished for weeks. It was not until he had been brought back here, swaddled in bandages like a newborn babe, and was treated by the High Priestess of Shallya herself that he finally awoke. That daemon-smoke had taken his voice, and burned his eyes so that to see daylight gave him great pain; while it took time for his body to mend, so far as it could, it took longer to heal his spirit, for him to find some useful purpose again.'

'He has found that, master,' Delmar replied earnestly.

'Treat such knowledge with discretion, though, I ask you, novice. The moment of such an injury marks the end of a knight's ability to serve in battle. For proud men such as Talhoffer and Ott, it is a type of death. I believe that you should know it, though, to help you to understand. They are men of experience, and it is beholden on you novices to learn all you can from them. They are all honourable knights, each with his own story.'

'Do you have a story yourself, master?' Delmar asked. 'Is it among these shelves?'

'Aye, a short one,' Lehrer replied with mock weariness, 'but that one you will have to find yourself. I will not aid you there.'

THE UNREST WITHIN the chapter house was not limited to the novices. Talhoffer grew more and more critical of the novices' progress as the days of the siege progressed. He dismissed Weisshuber from their ranks with an almost casual disregard. The novices discovered his possessions gone from their quarters; it was that abrupt. It came as a regret, but no surprise; the genial Stirlander simply did not have the proficiency for the violence inherent in the knightly occupation.

Yet still Talhoffer reserved his most scathing words for his favourite target, Siebrecht von Matz.

'If you stand there with your sword stuck out, Novice Matz, waiting for it to be beaten aside, then your opponent will oblige you.'

'Guards should be moments of transition, Novice Matz, not poses for your heroic memorial. Keep moving.'

'If you insist on cutting from your wrist instead of your elbow, Novice Matz, then your arm will fall off. I guarantee it.'

'Ah, so that's what happened to you,' Siebrecht, sore and harangued, muttered bitterly. He had had enough of this.

'HE'S FAST,' VERRAKKER commented, 'and skilled. You have to give Novice Matz that.'

'So he has some skill, brother,' Talhoffer said through clenched teeth, trying not to move. 'What of it?'

The two knights stood with Brother Ott upon the top of the tower of the chapter house. It was as good a place for privacy as any. All Altdorf was lain out below them; the Imperial Palace, the Great Temple, and buildings, so many buildings crammed with people.

Talhoffer had commissioned a portrait of himself and had judged this the perfect backdrop. He might have reconsidered if he had known what a hash the artist was to make in bringing his canvas and easel up the small spiral staircase.

'Please hold your pose, my lord.' The artist, already irate and behind time, tried to keep the chiding tone from his voice.

'I had hoped that you were driving Matz all the harder because you recognised his potential and wished to prevent him being complacent. Yet you dismiss that skill so easily, brother,' Verrakker said. 'Is he not one of the ablest fighters of all the novices you have tested?'

Talhoffer took his time in consideration. 'On foot, perhaps. On a horse he has little to distinguish himself from the rest.'

'Then why have you made him your whipping boy?'

Talhoffer turned to his fellow knight. The artist let out a small grunt of irritation, and Talhoffer rounded back on him.

'Oh, paint your backdrop, man, and give us a few moments' peace.'

The artist duly bent back down to his work, and Talhoffer and Verrakker crossed to the other side of the roof.

'Is there a reason you take a particular interest in this novice's wellbeing, brother?'

'That is the very question I am trying to ask you.'

Talhoffer ignored Verrakker's words and continued on his original line. 'You and he are both from Nuln, are you not? Some old loyalty there perhaps?'

'You tell me, brother. Is his home the reason you dislike him so?'

'Ah!' Talhoffer scoffed. 'Petty provincial prejudices are beneath one who has schooled counts and kings, brother.'

'So I would have thought.'

Irritated at Verrakker's insinuation, Talhoffer dropped his usual superior air.

'I have no cause against his skill or the city of his birth, brother. It is his attitude to which I take offence.'

'And what of that?'

'That he does not wish to be here. Even Ott can see that. The other novices, as unskilled, raw or insufferable as they may be, they all have the spirit that comes from understanding what a privilege they have been given. For Matz, the sooner he plucks up the courage to leave, the better. For all of us.'

'It is not your place to judge his spirit, brother. It is mine, of which you are well aware.'

'Oh, yes, you and Brother Purity.'

'Where did you hear that name?' Verrakker snapped, his tone so sharp that it cut Talhoffer to the quick.

Talhoffer, in surprise, stumbled over his words, then began again.

'You are not the only one to know some of the order's secrets, brother,' he said.

'That is a matter for the inner circle. And until and unless you are elevated to those ranks you shall not speak that name again. On your oath, Talhoffer.'

Talhoffer backed down and Verrakker was glad of it. He did not like having to push his authority with the fightmaster. Ever since he had been admitted to the order's inner circle and Talhoffer had not, it had been a sticking point between them. Evidently, the matter still rankled with the fightmaster.

'You and your secrets,' Talhoffer started again. 'Even your little pretence to the novices that you are some doddering invalid.'

Verrakker saw that the fightmaster was trying to salvage a little of his own dignity and adopted a more conciliatory tone.

'You learn much of a man by how he treats his lessers.'

Talhoffer gave a short bark of a laugh. 'Just like the sword, Verrakker, those who live by secrets will die by them.'

'I have enough people telling me my destiny, brother,' Verrakker said, indicating an end to their conversation. 'We should concentrate on the novices and the task in hand.'

'Very well, then,' Talhoffer declared, once more gathering up his haughtiness around him. 'I will judge Novice Matz solely on his skill, and leave the question of his spirit to you and... your judgement. Let it be on your heads,' the fightmaster chuckled at his own joke, 'as to whether this weak-willed stripling should ever be allowed to call himself a Reiksguard knight.'

'Thank you, brother,' Verrakker replied, but Talhoffer was not finished.

'So, as I have answered your question, brother, will you do me the privilege of answering mine? Why do you take a particular interest in this novice?'

'I take a particular interest in all my charges, and I do believe that we shall need the sword of every single one of them in the weeks ahead.'

'You have heard something more from the siege?'

Verrakker nodded. 'Our army is converging upon the siege lines. There is a battle, a great battle that is about to occur. Our scouts have a count of the size of the enemy. And I do not believe we will win.'

The two knights both turned and stared out over the battlements, over the city, over the maddened crowds, over the river and the forests. Though it was far too distant for them to see, they both looked to that great bastion of the north: Middenheim, where the fate of the Empire was being decided.

CHAPTER FOUR

HERR VON MATZ

THE TEN REMAINING novices marched, fully armed and armoured, in close order. At a command from Talhoffer, they halted, drew their swords and instantly began the drills that he had taught them, stabs from high, from low, and downwards swings.

Talhoffer looked the novices over with a critical eye. Only Krieglitz was performing up to the fightmaster's standards; Gausser had power behind his blows but they were too slow; Bohdan and Alptraum were slow to learn them, Bohdan especially, as he was older than the rest and more set in his habits. Siebrecht, though, was quick, of sword and wit, but he was lazy and only did the least he could to escape the fightmaster's censure.

The Reiklanders' progress, meanwhile, was far more acceptable. Talhoffer could tell that they had fought together before. They attacked in unison, covered each other and responded to Falkenhayn's orders in an instant. Harver and Breigh in particular, Talhoffer noted, fought beside each other as though they had done so their entire lives. None of the Reiklanders had the strength or innate skill of a couple of the Provincials; Proktor was too slight and Delmar's swordsmanship far too untutored, but they fought far better as a squadron and that was how they would have to fight in the Reiksguard.

If he had had enough time Talhoffer knew he could have brought the Provincials up to that standard. This could have been one of the finest novice squadrons he had taught, but Verrakker was adamant that there was not the time. Push them on, push them on, he had told Lehrer and the fightmasters, they will rise to it. They will be ready.

Well, Talhoffer would show Verrakker how ready they were not. He had given the sergeants a small mission of their own, and they were now strapping something to the pell. One of them raised his hand to show that they were finished, and Talhoffer called the novices over.

'Though we are part of the greatest realm of man, mankind exists in other nations all around us,' Talhoffer announced, 'Bretonnia and Estalia to the west, Tilea and the border lands to the south, Kislev and the tribes of the Norse to the north,' Talhoffer's eyes glossed quickly past Gausser, for the Nordlanders' heritage was more intertwined with the Norse than they would ever admit, 'and the horse brigands of the east. It is our nature to march under different banners and test our strength against each other. Just as we have our knightly orders, so too do they have their champions. Here!'

The pell was dressed in a full suit of armour, so that it could almost be a man stood there. It was not Reiksguard armour though. It was crudely forged and painted black.

'The men of the north: some wear little more than furs and skins and can be fought like normal men, but others are encased within plate as thick as a Bretonnian's, even as thick as a dwarf's.' Talhoffer walked slowly around the armoured pell.

'Hammers and maces at the head. You don't need to cut the skin if you can bash their brains loose instead,' he said as he indicated the helmet. 'If you only have a sword, however, and most likely you will... Novice Reinhardt, Novice Gausser, step forwards.'

The two novices did so, and a sergeant gave them each a sharpened metal long sword. Talhoffer stepped away.

'Novice Reinhardt,' the fightmaster ordered, 'one of your strongest cuts, if you please.'

Delmar took up a roof guard with the weapon and then, after a breath, stepped forwards and drove the sword down with all his weight against the armour's shoulder pauldron. The blade struck the plate with a crashing ring and the impact nearly jarred the weapon from Delmar's hands. With the novices crowding around, Delmar stepped up to look at the damage and was disappointed to see that there was only a slight dent.

'Back. All of you,' Talhoffer chided. 'Novice Gausser, can you do better?'

Gausser stepped up and targeted the pauldron on the other side. Delmar could see the Nordlander's massive shoulder muscles knot, then release as he swung the sword down like a mallet. The ring was even louder this time, and Gausser stepped forwards with a satisfied look on his face to examine the plate. His face fell, however, when he saw that the dent he had created was only slightly deeper. It had certainly not penetrated the armour.

'Do not be disappointed, novices. It takes a blade of magical keenness for a man to slice apart full plate. No, if you only have a sword with which to strike at these armoured warriors then here is what you may do. First, the murder stroke.' A sergeant wearing armoured gauntlets stepped up, grasped Gausser's long sword in both hands by the end of the blade and then brought the hilt down on the armour's helmet. He stepped away, leaving a sizeable dent in the helmet's crown, enough to have killed the wearer.

'Come in and look now,' Talhoffer said to the novices. 'You see the cross-guard acts as a rudimentary hammer. It can also be used to hook your opponent's weapon away if you wish to wrestle him to the ground. Second, the thrust with the half-sword. Better when the foe is on the ground, but as circumstances demand. Novice Reinhardt, a thrust, but through the gap in the armour. Use your free hand to grip the blade half-way down its length and use that to hit your target. It is accuracy, not speed that matters here.'

Delmar looked for a gap and twisted the blade so that it was pointed at the join in the armpit. Up close now, he could hear a slight buzzing noise from within. With a glance at the fightmaster to ensure he should continue, Delmar slid the blade firmly through the join and into the space for the body. There was a second's resistance inside, but then the blade slipped easily through.

'Well done, Novice Reinhardt.' Talhoffer smiled a cold smile.

Suddenly, Delmar coughed and gagged. A foul stench erupted from the armour, and the other novices who had come in close to watch stumbled backwards, spluttering.

'That is the last lesson about fighting these casements,' the fightmaster warned. 'When you do break it open, you can never know what you will find inside!'

Talhoffer ripped open the helmet's visor to reveal an inhuman face, rotted through, its maw hanging open in seeming surprise. From its mouth emerged a stream of flies, disturbed from their feeding by the blow to the head. The novices scrambled back a distance.

The sergeants laughed hugely. It had not been easy to manhandle the dead pig in there at first light this morning. But it had been worth it to see their charges' faces.

Talhoffer did not laugh however. If Verrakker thought that they were ready for the test of spirit then he was sorely mistaken.

'Novices!' Talhoffer called them back to order, but his instruction was fated not to continue.

'Brother Talhoffer! Brother Ott!' a knight called from the steps of the chapter house. Talhoffer, Ott and Verrakker went over and gathered in a tight huddle, exchanged a few words, then hurried into the chapter house together.

'Do you sense it, brothers?' Krieglitz asked the others.

'No,' Siebrecht replied, 'but I see it.'

'The tension,' Alptraum spoke up, 'the concern they have. They don't count us at services; they don't care if we whisper at meals. None of them raises his voice any more. It is as if they must stay quiet so as to hear whatever may come.'

'All the better for us,' Siebrecht joked, but even he could not convince himself that he enjoyed the oppressive atmosphere. It reminded him too greatly of home, where his father was always waiting for the next disaster to befall them.

The wind picked up. Alptraum stopped and turned into it.

'It's from the north,' the Averlander stated, his eyes closed.

'There's blood on it.' Gausser's great nostrils flared, as though he were a whale dredging the sea.

Siebrecht looked at Krieglitz in bemusement at their friends' strange behaviour, but Krieglitz too was staring with them in the same direction.

Out in the city, a bell started to strike. It was one of the bells of the Great Temple and it sounded a doleful, sorrowful note. Then a second bell rang; this one with a lighter tone. Then a third chimed, and a fourth, and a fifth. And now they were ringing all across the city.

'Victory! Victory! The siege is lifted! The foe are on the run!' the cry went up from the chapter house. Victory. Victory. The word resounded in the novices' heads so loudly that they no longer heard the bells. Victory! Gausser gave a giant whoop of delight. Krieglitz clasped Siebrecht's hand and shook it with delight.

'Victory!' Delmar shouted to the Reiklanders, and even Falkenhayn could not help but smile with relief.

Delmar saw Talhoffer step out of the chapter house.

'Master!' he called out. 'The war is over!'

Talhoffer strode quickly over. 'We are done for the day,' he ordered the novices. 'Be back tomorrow at first light. We will need to make up for the time we have lost.'

'Master, is the war over?' Delmar asked.

'We have a victory, Novice Reinhardt, that is all. Tomorrow, first light, all of you.'

But the city did not share the fightmaster's dour assessment. They had endured a hungry winter and a spring of fear. The news of the great victory around Middenheim was their first glimpse of hope and they would make the most of it.

As the novices' training intensified, all they could hear for days beyond the walls of the chapter house was the city celebrating with everything it could. The beggars in the streets and the refugees from the other provinces, who had been despised as parasites dragging Altdorf down, were treated once more as fellow subjects. The Altdorfers' hatred would turn back upon them, the refugees knew, so the most hopeful of them departed the city to journey back to their homes, though none of them knew what they would find left.

In such a time of general wellbeing, Siebrecht could not resist slipping out into the city to enjoy the jubilation. He had thought he had covered his tracks well, but he had no regrets when the sergeants came for him again.

Siebrecht, prepared for the worst, was escorted to the guardhouse by the white gate. There, however, he realised that, for once, it was not him that was in trouble.

'Ah, there you are, Siebrecht,' a familiar voice greeted him. 'Be a good boy now and explain to these suspicious gentlemen that I am no spy or pilferer.'

There sat a man whom Siebrecht instantly recognised. The forehead was higher, the hair greyed, the skin sagged slightly over the distinctive cheekbones, but the family resemblance, alas, was clear.

'You can stand testament for this man?' The sergeant asked.

'He's my uncle,' Siebrecht said.

'You sound surprised.' his uncle retored. 'Did you not receive my letter? I could scarcely pass through this great city without paying a visit to my dearest nephew.'

'We discovered him concealed within a goods cart,' a sergeant said, his posture stating clearly his desire to drag their captive out feet first.

'I was not concealed and I resent your implication,' Herr von Matz said, taking umbrage. 'I was inspecting the guildmarks upon the seals. My good brother, the Baron von Matz, has entrusted his eldest son into your order's care and I will report back of the dubious origin and the even more dubious quality of the food you serve here. I am certain that he will apply most readily to your commander as regards your treatment of his son and your rough handling of me.'

'Uncle!' Siebrecht admonished him. 'Sergeant, my uncle's name I can stand surety for, to his nature I cannot. Do you wish to hold him further?'

'I do not wish to hold him, nor see him again.'

'Wishes, sergeant…' his uncle began, but Siebrecht shot his uncle a sharp look and he subsided.

'Come on, uncle.'

'If I may be permitted to speak, I would like to ask for my hat back.' He stared pointedly at the sergeant, who disdainfully retrieved the ridiculously plumed hat and handed it back.

'Novice Matz,' the sergeant said as he showed them out. 'Herr Matz.'

'Herr von Matz,' the uncle corrected tartly, and the sergeant closed the door on his face.

Out on the crowded street, Siebrecht saw his uncle drop his pretence of petty indignation and straighten into the role of a respectable man of means. Herr von Matz led his nephew a short way through the busy streets back to his lodgings, ignoring all of Siebrecht's attempts to question him along the way. Finally Siebrecht gave up, and followed in silence as his uncle entered an unremarkable house, nodded his greetings to the housekeeper and sat down in a private room where some food had already been laid out.

Herr von Matz produced a small wooden case, delicately inlaid with sculpted bone. He took out his knife and carving fork and sat down to eat. Seeing his chance, Siebrecht took control of the conversation.

'So, my uncle, is your purpose here solely to embarrass me before my order?'

'Embarrass you?' Herr von Matz paused mid-slice. 'I am quite certain I took considerable pains to ensure that I only embarrassed myself.'

'What?'

'You, meanwhile, played the role of the mortified and reasonable relative superbly. I can assure you that the next time those sergeants see you they will not be thinking how exceedingly arrogant you are, rather they will reflect on how great an improvement you are on the previous generation.'

Siebrecht could not believe his uncle's gall. 'Are you claiming that you provoked the entire thing in order that I would appear less annoying to some common sergeants?'

Herr von Matz waggled his fork at his nephew. 'Don't be dismissive of your lessers, my boy. An Emperor may give you titles, but he'll never clean your boots. Those sergeants there, I'm sure they have the run of the chapter house, am I right? Keys to every lock, an ear to every door? Very useful.'

Siebrecht lavished scorn in his reply. 'So you crept into a cart and hid so that I may have the opportunity to befriend them.'

'No, of course not. That was a mere fortuitous opportunity.'

'Then what were you doing?'

'Trying to see the seals, the guildmarks, as I said.'

'You truly care about the freshness of the food?'

'Why should I? I'm not going to eat it, am I? If I wanted to trade in food then I would buy it at home, or Averland, and I would send it north. Far too dangerous though, the cost of escort would be prohibitive. And so few people in the north have the money to pay these days.'

'Then what were you interested in?'

'The ore, of course. The ore, the charcoal, the cloth. Anything that can travel. You see the seal, you know the supplier.'

'You wish to supply the Reiksguard? Is that it then?'

'Perhaps. Perhaps there are some suppliers who are taking too great a profit, or have one too many middlemen that might be circumvented. The value of good ore is high now because of the war; charcoal is short because of the danger in the forests; so much cloth is needed for all the uniforms for the Emperor's armies; but when the war is done will the values stay high? Or will the wars never end?'

'Did you not hear the bells, uncle? The war has just ended.'

Herr von Matz gave a tiny short laugh, which fully encapsulated his opinion on his nephew's naïveté.

'There cannot be a new campaign,' Siebrecht said. 'Not already.'

Herr von Matz sized up his nephew carefully.

'You will find, young Siebrecht, that the beginnings and ends of wars are marked by historians. Not by those who are still fighting them long after some man of letters has declared that a victory was won. Here's a piece of information for you. See how you fare in realising its value. Have you ever heard of a dwarfen hold named Karak Angazhar?'

'No. Should I have done?'

'Not a youth in your position, whose only interest is in the next bottle, no.'

Siebrecht bit back a sharp remark. 'What about it then?'

'It has been besieged, for several months now, by the goblin tribes of the Black Mountains.'

'Dwarfs and goblins fighting. My word, uncle, what astonishing news you bring me,' Siebrecht replied, barely trying to conceal the sarcasm in his voice. 'I am truly staggered.'

Herr von Matz gave his nephew a sharp clip around the ear.

'Oh, I did forget how clever you are. Very well then, I will leave it at this. Karak Angazhar is not one of the great dwarfen strongholds, it is no equal of Karaz-a-Karak or Barak Varr, and yet before this month is out the soldiers of the Empire will march from Altdorf to go and rescue it. And, most likely, the Reiksguard will be at their head.'

'What? Why would we? The old alliance is strong of late, but we are stretched to the limit. And if it is a choice between dwarfs and our own realm, then I know which we should defend.'

'That, I will leave you to discover. And when the Reiksguard marches, you had better ensure that you are still with them. And still in a condition to give a good account of yourself.' He pointedly picked up Siebrecht's glass and placed it on the far side of the table, out of his reach. 'It would not do to have the order think ill of you.'

Siebrecht snorted. 'I would not care if they did.'

'Decide upon your opinions, Siebrecht,' his uncle taunted him. 'First, you are ashamed that I have embarrassed you before your brothers, and now you say you do not care what they think.

'Let me be sure that you rightly understand the truth of your circumstances.' Herr von Matz fixed Siebrecht with his glare. 'The Reiksguard was not so willing to consider your application, simply because of your name. Your name, our name, has little to recommend it any more. No, the Reiksguard's consideration was bought; yes, with that same coin that you so quickly squander.'

'You bribed the Reiksguard to accept me?' Siebrecht could not believe it.

Herr von Matz sighed heavily. Under his brother's indolent upbringing Siebrecht had obviously experienced much of the world, but had never thought to understand it.

'No,' he said patiently. 'I would not even try. Men of honour are simply too expensive for the worth they can provide. And as soon as they accept, they lose their one source of value. Their honour! You do not bribe men of honour. You bribe the amenable men whom the men of honour trust. You needed recommendations and there are nobles highly placed in Wissenland, all around the Empire, who are willing, nay eager, to be influenced. Some of them near ripped my hand clean off, so keen were they to grasp their gratuity.'

'For what purpose then?' Siebrecht pushed himself away from the table and stormed around the room. 'For what purpose was I sent here, away from my family, away from my friends, away from my life? To be run ragged by Reikland martinets? To have insults hurled at me by Reikland boors? To die, protecting a Reikland prince?'

Herr von Matz met his nephew's fiery outburst coolly. He continued eating without even looking up. Siebrecht felt stymied, and yet he was unwilling to give up his temper. Instead, he stomped over to the shutters and slammed them back hard. The sounds of the city burst in, and Siebrecht leaned into the street and sucked in the air.

'When you're finished,' Herr von Matz remarked between mouthfuls, 'do close those shutters and sit down.'

Siebrecht stubbornly held his post at the window for a minute more, but then did as his uncle told him.

'What do you think of Novice Gausser?' Herr von Matz asked as he sat.

'Gausser?' Siebrecht was taken off guard by the change in topic. 'Well… he's as strong as an ox and about as bright.'

'Do you think he's good to his friends?'

'I suppose.'

'He could be Emperor one day, you know.'

Siebrecht laughed at that. 'Is that another certain prediction of yours? I'll take your wager on that one for sure.'

'Why not?' Herr von Matz replied calmly. 'He is the grandson of an elector count, if he inherits that then all he need be is elected. Alptraum?'

'A loon!'

'His family hold the Averland guilds and merchants in their pocket. Falkenhayn?'

'A Mootland cesspit!'

'He will inherit whole streets here in Altdorf, indeed the one this very house is in.'

'Ranald's balls, uncle, do you know all the other novices? Have you had your spies on me ever since I arrived?'

'Spies? Who would need a spy for that? You and your fancies, Siebrecht. You think I wouldn't ask who you were training with? It's not a secret. If a family have their son in the Reiksguard they proclaim it from their rooftops.'

'Excellent, then! Now you've shown me that they are rich and I am humble, I feel a whole new joy at my internment with them.'

'The point is, Siebrecht, that they are rich and you are *with* them. These men whom you have so quickly dismissed, each one of them is of ten times the consequence of any of your drinking partners in Nuln. You are here so that, in years to come, when you have long quit the Reiksguard, you may enter the court of any province in the Empire and be welcomed there by its ruler as an old and dearest friend. Money has less relevance than you assume, those sergeants' treatment of me today is ample proof of that. Look at Reinhardt, you know Reinhardt?'

'Oh, I've met Novice Reinhardt.'

Herr von Matz ignored the rancour in Siebrecht's tone.

'The Reinhardts have little money beyond their estate. But his great-grandfather was one of the first Reiksguard knights. His grandfather served. His father died in battle. Do you think he had to buy the recommendations from petty nobles for the order to consider his application? No money can buy the influence his name has in the order and, through them, with half the rulers in this land. The privilege will flow to him like honey. All I want for you is to be able to taste it. This is an opportunity that you will have at no other time in your life.'

'An opportunity for you, you mean,' Siebrecht struck back, 'to say that your family has a son in the most prestigious guard of the Emperor.'

'It will get you coin if you want it. Titles, if you want those. Do not doubt that women come with both if that is your only desire. Forgive me then for a design which meets both our ambitions.'

'We have coin. We have titles. You make us sound so desperate, uncle.'

'You think there is coin in the barony?' Herr von Matz said as he poured himself another glass. 'For generations now its wealth has been ebbing away. Your father inherited the barony and then sat on it, like an addled hen that sits on a stone and waits for it to hatch. He feels his way of life slipping away but he does not know how to stop it. He's become quite solicitous to me these last few months, did you know? Why do you think that is? Brotherly love? Not a chance. It is my coin that he hosts, not his brother. No, Siebrecht, it is well you know now: there are no riches in the barony. And that means that you must either be a great Baron von Matz, or you will be the last.'

Siebrecht sat, silenced by his uncle's frank admissions.

'It is only for a few years,' Herr von Matz continued, his tone more conciliatory. 'Serve well. Make your name. Resist the urge to plunge your breast onto the enemy's sword. Then come back to your life, though I predict that you will not look on it the same as you did. You will help your father in managing the estate, and you will have the privilege to do what it will take to restore the family's fortunes.'

'For just a few years.'

'Three at most. Enough to establish yourself, to get yourself known for more than drinking, impertinence and wild gunmanship. There is no purpose in exposing you to needless risk.' Herr von Matz gave an honest smile. 'You and I, Siebrecht, we're the ones on whom the family name depends.'

Siebrecht said nothing. His head stayed downcast, his sight fixed on the grain of the wood in the table, not wishing to meet his uncle's gaze. He knew his uncle was right; he'd known for years. Something he knew but could never admit.

Herr von Matz was satisfied with the impression he had made upon his nephew. He sat back in his chair and wiped his mouth.

'Emperor Wilhelm,' he began, 'as much as any good man of Nuln should detest him, I cannot but admit that his creation of the Reiksguard was a masterstroke. Other emperors had founded knightly orders before, but none of them ever saw their true potential. Other orders...' Herr von Matz waved his hand dismissively. 'The Order of the Black Bear want the strongest, the Knights of Sigmar's Blood want the learned, even our own great Emperor Magnus, when he founded the Knights Griffon, asked only for the most devout.

'It was only Emperor Wilhelm who ever asked for the eldest. The heirs. More than any of the others, Wilhelm looked to the future; for after ten or twenty years, once their fathers were dead, the heirs were the nobles themselves. And each of them had been taught and drilled to have absolute loyalty to their Emperor. To leave the rule of the Empire to him. To shun politics altogether!

Everyone knows that the Reiksguard have vowed to never interfere in the political world. Loyalty, first, last and always, isn't that right? And an end to civil wars as well, because it is so much harder to shed the blood of one you have called brother.'

Herr von Matz paused a moment to catch his breath, the ancient wiles of a long-dead emperor exciting him far more than any scheme of his own.

'Yes, Siebrecht. Emperor Wilhelm was a very clever man.' His meal finished, he wiped his cutlery clean and replaced them in their box. 'And it behoves clever men like Wilhelm and *you* and I not only to know the world, but also to understand *how* it works. There are the spoken reasons, and then there are the unspoken reasons. And it is the unspoken reasons that are by far the most valuable.'

Herr von Matz stood, ending the interview. Siebrecht was most relieved to be away. His uncle, however, insisted on walking him back to the barracks. Once there, Siebrecht thought he would leave. However, he blithely strolled up to the same guardhouse from which, an hour before, he had been so roughly ejected. The sergeant was less than pleased to see him return, but Herr von Matz laid on such a spectacular display, alternating between profuse apologies for his earlier conduct and the highest praise for the close attention that the guards had taken in ensuring the safety of his nephew, that even the stoniest of them could not help but mellow a little.

When he finally took his leave, he asked both Siebrecht and the sergeant to walk him back out onto the street, where he engaged the sergeant in a few minutes more of animated, good-natured conversation, so that to any passer-by the two of them might have appeared as the warmest of acquaintances. Herr von Matz then bid them a friendly farewell and crossed over the square to his next interview: a timber supplier who, impressed by Herr von Matz's ostentatious connections within the prestigious Reiksguard, found himself agreeing to a far greater discount than he had originally intended.

'THESE, NOVICES, ARE the files.'

Master Talhoffer had brought the novices in their awkward plate armour down to the far end of the practice field. Set up there were lines of thick wooden fence posts, each one six feet high, arranged in neat rows a pace or so apart. The novices had assumed the posts had been set up for building or cultivation. They were wrong.

'You have been taught how to march in formation. Some of you even manage not to fall over your own feet while you do so. You have been taught the drills to use so that you do not strike your brothers beside you. But rehearsing drills is very different to facing another man in the crush of combat.

'We could simply pack you together and let you go swing at each other, as I see you do each day with your wasters, but then we would flood the sanatorium with unconscious novices, brained by their fellows in the battle line. Therefore we have this. The files. Each one is a corridor, roughly the width of what you might have to fight in battle proper. We will begin here, and when you have all eventually mastered the art of not smacking your blade in a wooden post, you will finally have the chance to embed it in your fellow's skull.

'Split into two groups, one man at the end of each corridor. When I say begin, you will all enter your corridor; the first one out the other side is the victor. Understand?'

The novices split, once again into Reiklanders and Provincials. However this time it meant that instead of sparring between themselves as they usually did, they would face each other.

'Reinhardt,' Falkenhayn whispered to Delmar, 'come, let us stay together and fight side by side.' Falkenhayn indicated the file to his right and Delmar took up the position there. He looked down the column and realised that Falkenhayn had matched him against Gausser again. He checked the files beside him: Falkenhayn himself was facing Siebrecht, who, even aside from his cavalier behaviour that first day, had failed to impress Delmar. This training was wasted on him, he truly did not care to be here and rarely bothered to stir himself to action even when sparring. He would happily fall if it was less effort than fighting. No doubt Falkenhayn would have an easy time against him. Beyond him, Proktor faced Krieglitz. There, Delmar considered, was a proper fighter. He did his province proud, though as Falkenhayn said, a man should be judged not only by prowess but by the company he chooses, and Delmar considered that Krieglitz's friendship with Siebrecht had firmly held the Talabheimer back.

Talhoffer called on them to be ready, and Delmar concentrated once more on his own column and the hefty Nordlander at the end of it. Talhoffer ordered them to begin and the novices entered the files. Delmar saw Falkenhayn sprint forwards on his left, charging Siebrecht down. He had decided to approach Gausser more cautiously. He had charged the last time they fought and little good it had done him. Gausser was slower than he, but the plate weighed Delmar down far more than the Nordlander. The two warriors walked steadily towards each other until they met in the middle. Already Delmar heard the crunch of armoured bodies hitting each other from either side and the yells of success of those who had already emerged. He ignored them and kept his focus.

He and Gausser exchanged a few stabs, each testing the other's guard. However Delmar quickly realised that in confined quarters such light blows against an armoured opponent were insignificant. What counted was strength and weight, and in both Gausser would best him. Gausser obviously came to the same conclusion, for he reversed his wooden sword and swung the hilt in a murder stroke at Delmar's head.

Instinctively, Delmar gave ground; he would ordinarily have gone to the left or right, but in the files there was nowhere to go but back. He brought his own sword up with both hands and blocked the murder stroke. Gausser had no fear of Delmar's retaliation and no thought of relenting, so he swung again to batter his way past Delmar's guard or force him back out of the file. Delmar let the Nordlander crash against his sword once more, but on the third stroke he stepped back even further and allowed the murder stroke to knock his weapon out of his hand completely. Gausser had expected to meet solid resistance, and so for a second was left off-balance, overextended. Delmar grabbed the hilt of Gausser's sword and pulled his opponent hard, forwards and down. Gausser refused to release his own blade and so as Delmar pulled, Gausser came with it.

They stumbled back together a few steps and Delmar almost had Gausser trip, but the Nordlander twisted his body and killed his forwards momentum by slamming into a post with his shoulder. Delmar was ready for it. As Gausser reared up to steady himself, Delmar dropped low, wrapping his arms around Gausser's knees and gripped them tight in a bear hug. Gausser was solid, but in the mud even he was not strong enough to keep his stance. Delmar heaved his legs together and shoved hard against them as low as he could. Unable to bend down and grab the Reiklander without falling over himself, Gausser held tightly to the fence post, but with one final surge Delmar finally took the legs out from under him. Gausser toppled to the ground with all the majesty of an oak felled in the forest. Delmar ran for the exit and did not look back until he was out. Only then did he turn around. Gausser was still picking himself up. Delmar went to Falkenhayn beside him to congratulate him as well, but his friend had a face of thunder.

'It was a trick, Reinhardt, he won with a stupid Nulner trick,' Falkenhayn railed. Falkenhayn had charged, as Delmar had seen, and Siebrecht, ever insolent, had stepped out of his way rather than bother with the exercise. Falkenhayn had run for it; he would be out of the files before any other. But as he passed, Siebrecht had kicked out, and Falkenhayn had lost his footing and slammed the side of his head into a post.

It had been a trick, Delmar decided, but it had been a fair one, only accomplished because of Falkenhayn's own mistaken assumption. Proktor too had, predictably, lost against Krieglitz and the two victorious Provincial novices stood at the other end of the files commiserating Gausser on his comeuppance.

Delmar raised his hand in salute.

'What are you doing, Reinhardt?' Falkenhayn bristled. 'Put that hand down.'

Delmar let his friend pull his arm down. The Provincials had seen it, but did not return it.

THAT DAY WAS only their first at the files. They continued to train there each day, sometimes sparring with sergeants armed with long spears or pikes, sometimes packed three, five or even ten novices to each file. The novices learned how, even stuck in the rear ranks, they might aid the fighter at the front to win his combat, while those at the front learned how to maintain the pressure on the enemy, knock down their opponents and then step over them to allow those behind to finish them off. All of them learned the danger of falling in the middle of a melee, and Delmar was not the only one of them to suffer the indignity of being kicked around on the floor for several minutes before he could finally crawl clear.

In armoured combat, Gausser continued to dominate, though Delmar gave a good enough account of himself to regularly best the other novices. Where the sergeants sparred with them intentionally without armour, however, Delmar noted that it was Siebrecht, with his new determination, who began to demonstrate the greatest ability. His technique still included some remnants of his Tilean instruction, but now that he was used to the heavier weight of the Reiksguard's swords his skill became apparent. His sheer speed, in particular, led him to fare far better than the rest in exercises where a single fighter was left to face multiple opponents. Though Talhoffer did not go so far as to praise Siebrecht for his improvement, the fightmaster relented in his previous criticism.

When they weren't performing close-order drills on foot, the novices were doing so on horseback. In this, Alptraum had great proficiency. Averland was renowned for its horses and riders, and indeed most of the Reiksguard's own mounts bore Averland markings.

Delmar, though, surpassed even him. At last, Delmar prayed thankfully, after being bested in every other way, he had at least one discipline in which he could be proud. A discipline in which he could be the one to help others.

Horsemanship was inherent within the noble classes. They had all learned to ride as children, but to ride so close as to be stirrup to stirrup with your brother beside you, whilst carrying a heavy lance and shield and controlling your mount with your knees, required a higher level of experience entirely. These urban nobles who visited their horses twice a week in their stables and took them for a jaunt outside the city walls simply had not developed the same familiarity that Delmar had on a country estate where he rode Heinrich out every day between village and town and was responsible for every aspect of his horse's care.

Delmar had not been allowed to use Heinrich in the Reiksguard's training; Talhoffer had told him that a knight of the order had to be able to control any mount owned by the order, which were all specially trained to carry the weight of a man in full armour. As hard as battles were on men, they were far worse for horses and a knight might find himself changing mounts as many as half a dozen times; his control could not rely on a personal connection with his steed. Therefore a novice was given a different horse for each exercise, and he was personally liable if his mount bit or kicked at another as they walked or practised their charges. A kick, if it struck the other animal badly, had the potential to cripple the leg and render a hugely expensive warhorse useless, and so all of Delmar's friends were eager to learn the danger signs of an agitated steed and the correct preventative measures.

The danger was not only to the horses. In a close formation charge, Harver's horse misstepped. In trying to right his steed's course, Harver barrelled into Breigh beside him. Both horses fell, Harver was knocked from his saddle and was left bruised, Breigh was caught in his mount, his horse fell hard upon its side and Breigh's leg was snapped.

Breigh spent a night in agony while the order's healers worked upon him; Falkenhayn and the distraught Harver stayed with him. Breigh went home the next day, forgiving Harver with every breath, and vowing to Falkenhayn that he would return as soon as he was able to walk once more.

ONCE AGAIN, THE sergeant stood at the ready in the middle of four novices. Delmar caught the eyes of

Hardenburg, then Bohdan, then Siebrecht. They yelled and charged as one. The sergeant pulled no punches; Delmar only just caught sight of the sergeant's sword as it pierced his guard and smacked him soundly on the side of the head before moving on.

'Reinhardt out. Hardenburg out.' Talhoffer paused. 'Sergeant, you may stand down.'

The sergeant hauled himself back to his feet, his shift covered in bloody marks landed by the remaining two novices. He scowled at Delmar and stalked away.

'Killed again, Novice Reinhardt,' Talhoffer said to him afterwards.

'Yes, master.' At least this time it had been to his head and it would not take so long to wash the dye from his shift.

'Your skill with the sword is not great.'

'I will improve, master.'

'Still, I should not like to be you in battle.'

'No, master,' Delmar replied, unable to prevent the tinge of failure from colouring his voice.

He would never be a great swordsman, Talhoffer could tell. But he had nevertheless led the charge against a superior opponent, knowing what it would cost him but trusting that his brothers together would be victorious. And he had been right.

'No, Novice Reinhardt,' Talhoffer considered. 'I would not wish to be you in battle. But I would stand beside you.'

CHAPTER FIVE

KARL FRANZ

THE NOVICES' ROUTINE was broken one day when, after
the service at the Great Temple, Verrakker did not take
them back to the barracks, but rather into the grounds
of the palace. The gardens themselves were not huge, as
befitted a residence that had been largely carved out of
the existing city, but they were beautiful. The summer
had not yet reached its height and everything there was
in bloom. The flowering plants were clustered around
statues of heroes of the Empire, both ancient and mod-
ern, and had been carefully chosen to represent some
aspect of each hero's character or achievements.
Beyond the cultivated gardens, the grounds settled into
a verdant lawn bordered by the cooling shade of the
trees and hedgerows, which softened the sounds of the
city.

Despite the beauty on offer, there were few around to
enjoy it. With the Emperor on campaign with the army

in the north, the palace was quiet. Without the Emperor, or the frenzy of supplicants who typically surrounded him, the staff had little to do but keep the apartments in order. Those noblemen who were officers to the Imperial court had mostly left with the Emperor, and those who stayed preferred to perform their official duties from their own residences, where they were more comfortable and could manage their personal business matters away from prying eyes. Those administrators who were left in the palace kept themselves busy enough, maintaining the flow of correspondence between the court on campaign and the court left in residence, and had little reason to trespass out of their own domains.

The one part of the palace grounds that was still frequented was the Imperial Zoo, and it was there that Verrakker was leading the novices. Delmar had seen it before, years ago; everyone who came to the capital made sure to visit and gaze in wonder at the bizarre creatures of the Emperor's menagerie. The zoo predated the return of the Imperial capital to Altdorf and it had displayed hundreds of different animals from across the Old World and beyond, though not all survived long once they were resident. But it was not the exotic animals that were the true draw of the zoo, it was rather the monsters. They were warped and terrifying, and Delmar, along with men, women and children alike, had queued patiently for the chance to be scared witless by such things as the Spawn of Hochland.

Verrakker walked them past the line of Altdorfers waiting outside the spawn's tented cage, and all the other public enclosures that radiated out from the central pavilion. He took them back into the working areas of the zoo, where the grisly tasks of feeding and cleaning the animals were kept hidden from the sight of the public behind tall hedges .

'Here we are,' Verrakker announced.

The novices had been led to a set of stables, not greatly different from the Reiksguard's own at the citadel. The horses were all fine specimens, all warhorses and mostly of Averland stock, Alptraum proudly noted, but there was nothing particularly special about them.

At the rear of them, Delmar noticed one horse that was special: a pure white charger, though Delmar could see little more than its head over the herd. Then it reared and spread a pair of giant swan-like wings.

'These are the Emperor's mounts,' Delmar whispered.

'That's right, Novice Reinhardt,' Verrakker replied.

Delmar stared, his mouth open, at the pegasus as it whinnied and bucked while its handlers tried to calm it.

'Come on, this way,' Verrakker said. 'There is more to see.'

Here, behind the stables, there were a series of other enclosures, each one containing a majestic beast: griffons, pegasi and more. In one massive, darkened enclosure they could see nothing in the shadows, yet Delmar felt a cold, ancient gaze bearing down upon him.

Delmar asked why the bars on the enclosures were only ten feet high. 'These beasts can fly,' he said, 'those bars will not keep them in. Why is there no roof?'

'The bars are not meant to keep them in,' Verrakker replied, 'these creatures are here by their own will. The bars are there to keep inquisitive fools out.'

At that moment, the Emperor's mounts all lifted their heads as one and gave an ear-splitting cry. The novices jumped away from the enclosures; even Verrakker took a step back. Then their cry was answered from above. Delmar looked up and saw a griffon in the sky, wheeling and swooping above the zoo. And on its back was a rider, whose distinctive profile was known across the land.

'The Emperor!' someone shouted, as handlers and retainers raced to the stableyard where the griffon was coming in to land. The novices ran with them.

Delmar arrived first, in time to see the fierce griffon Deathclaw slow his flight with backwards beats of his mighty wings and settle on the ground with incongruous grace. The handlers took the griffon's reins and helped the rider out of the saddle. There he was, Delmar realised, no more than a dozen feet before him. Emperor Karl Franz, Prince of Altdorf, Grand Prince of Reikland, Count of the West March. Delmar stared at him and, for the merest instant, the Emperor looked back. Delmar was struck by the tiredness in his eyes. Then the Emperor was distracted by one of his attendants, and turned back to give Deathclaw an affectionate rub behind its ears and on its beak. Delmar found himself surprised to see this legendary figure make such an ordinary gesture. He noticed then that the griffon was sweating and shaking with exertion. There must be some emergency for the Emperor to come back alone, unexpected, with the army still so far distant.

Then a band of Reiksguard knights, who were on guard at the palace, came running up and formed a crude protective circle around the Emperor. Verrakker grabbed Delmar's shoulders and ushered him and the other novices out of the way.

THE NOVICES WERE left in a state of high excitement and yet they were told little of what had transpired to hasten the Emperor's return. Their regular training was curtailed, as the order required every able knight to stand guard duty at the palace until the Reiksguard squadrons returned. Talhoffer, Verrakker and even Ott took up their old ceremonial guard armour and joined the regular garrison. The novices were left to spar with each other and run drills under the supervision of their sergeants; of their tutors only Master Lehrer remained, and they had never seen him out of his library, or even out from behind his desk.

Three days after the Emperor's arrival, the squadrons of the Grand Order of the Reiksguard processed into the capital with Kurt Helborg at their head. They were the first of the regiments from the victory at Middenheim to return to the city, and the novices joined the hundreds of citizens of Altdorf who sweltered in the summer heat to line the route and cheer them home. The knights, their silver armour dazzling in the sun, marched their warhorses in close order through the streets up to the chapter house, as stoic in the face of popular acclaim as they had been in the face of the enemy. Delmar and the other novices, swept up in the jubilation, yelled their praise. The great Wilhelm Gate of the chapter house opened and received them home again.

It was Siebrecht who first spotted the second group of arrivals. They appeared at the chapter house in covered wagons through the white gate to the side of the barracks. That caravan carried the injured knights who had survived, but had not been fit to ride back in with the main procession. It also carried the precious armour of the knights who had not been so fortunate and had been buried on the battlefields of Middenland.

DELMAR FOLLOWED THE knightly procession into the grounds of the barracks and around the side of the chapter house through to the stables. When he arrived the yard was full of sweating horses, irritable in the heat of the midday sun. Stablehands hurried back and forth as fast as their dignity allowed, helping the knights out of the saddle and leading their steeds to the next empty stall.

Delmar skirted his way around the edges until he saw Griesmeyer, his red hair matted and darkened with sweat. He was still mounted, waiting patiently for a stablehand to attend him.

'Lord Griesmeyer!' Delmar cried as he squeezed his way past two warhorses.

Griesmeyer turned in his direction, and in that instant before recognition dawned, Delmar saw the tightness around his eyes and the furrows in his brow. Then his face broke out into a smile and the ghosts were gone.

'Delmar!' he said. 'I thought it would not be long until I saw you.'

Delmar respectfully took hold of the knight's reins and stroked the horse's neck. 'My lord, how went the battle?'

'Sigmar's breath, novice! I shall tell you all, but give me a moment.'

GRIESMEYER WAS EVEN better than his word. He went with Delmar to the novices' quarters and there sat and answered all their questions of the siege. The knight conjured up images of the ravening hordes of savage northern warriors; the horrific mutants and monsters that they held captive to unleash upon their enemies, the daemonic war engines made of metal which pulsed with life, and the dark champions that strode through the ranks, gripping ancient weapons inscribed with arcane markings that burned with power.

But then he spoke of the Empire's army, where the most famous regiments stood in a single battle line: the Carroburg Greatswords, the cannon of Nuln, the Scarlet Guard of Stirland, the Death's Head of Ostermark, huntsmen from Ostland, the Hochland rifles, and halberdiers, spearmen, swordsmen and archers from across the provinces.

The novices felt a surge of pride at that, and even more so when Griesmeyer described the Reiksguard's final charge which broke the last of the foe's resistance. None were more proud though than Delmar, for the other novices knew that the knight had visited them because of him. And he was proud also, he realised, to see his fellow novices united.

Afterwards, Griesmeyer asked Delmar to walk him back across the yard.

'Do you think they enjoyed my stories?' he asked.

'Aye, my lord,' Delmar replied, 'I think that their only regret was that they could not be there to see it themselves before it was all done.'

'Good, for the war is not done at all.'

'Pardon, my lord?' Delmar could not quite believe what the knight had said.

'This war could not be won in a single battle. Some of their warbands have scattered, but many have stayed together under one of their generals and retreated into the mountains or the forests. It is a snakebite, the fang has gone but the poison is left behind. I am sure we will march north again soon, unless the Emperor has another purpose for us, and then your friends will have their chance. Presuming you have been found worthy of joining, of course?'

'The masters have said that the testing is concluded. But they have not yet told us their decision. Have you heard that I–'

'I have not spoken to them,' Griesmeyer cut him off, 'but I am sure you have trained hard and that your dedication will be rewarded. When is your vigil to be held?' he asked.

'The night after next,' Delmar replied.

'For certain you will know before then,' the knight replied unhelpfully. 'I am glad they waited until the order could return.'

'Is that why they have delayed?' Delmar queried. 'For our testing is finished. We do not know what we should be doing.'

At that Griesmeyer stopped in his tracks. He peered into Delmar's eyes for several long seconds, as though he was searching for something there.

'Keep your guard high, novice,' Griesmeyer finally said. 'It is not finished until you take the oaths.'

'I will, my lord,' Delmar muttered, then Griesmeyer dismissed him and went on alone.

DELMAR SAT QUIETLY in his small cell, trying to pray. The novices had all been moved from their dormitory for that night and each was placed in a separate cell within the chapter house. It was supposed to allow them some privacy and rest before their vigil the next night. The vigil was to be the last test they would face as novices. Should they pass, then they would be called to take their oaths to become a full brother-knight of the Reiksguard. Throughout their vigil they would pray and be prayed over.

Rumours abounded amongst the novices that the prayers the priests used were ones of exorcism and that in times past novices had had daemons discovered within them, had been driven mad, attacked their fellows or even burst spontaneously into flames. Griesmeyer had scoffed at such tall tales, though he could recall an instance where the intensity of the ceremony had been such that one novice, who had been put under great pressure by his family, burst out laughing and had to be removed and calmed down.

The purpose of the event in truth, Griesmeyer had said, was to give each novice a final chance to reconsider whether they could honestly swear the binding oaths of loyalty that would then be asked of them. The oaths of a brother-knight to the Reiksguard and to the order's rule superseded any others that a warrior might take, whether to family, province, friends or gods, short of those he took to the Emperor himself. As strange as it seemed to Delmar, Griesmeyer said that there had been occasions where it was only at the vigil itself that a novice had realised that he could not swear sole loyalty to the order and so had had to withdraw. The brother-knights who successfully completed the vigil together would, from then after, forever be witnesses to the fact that each of them had taken their oaths to the Reiksguard with the full knowledge of what that entailed.

Delmar did not believe that this would present any difficulty for him. He knew the oaths, he had learned them by heart from his grandfather ten years before he would set foot in the chapter house as a novice. He would not baulk now at swearing them in earnest. Nevertheless, he could not settle at prayer. They had each been given an icon bearing the cross, skull and laurel wreath, the insignia of a full brother-knight, to aid them. He had felt a surge of pride as they placed the icon around his neck, but he found it of no help in prayer. It was quiet outside his cell, dark also; he could think of no reason why he should not be at peace and yet he was not. Disappointed at himself, he gave up on his prayer and instead decided that rest was what he needed. He lay down on the cot and closed his eyes. He felt his breath deepen and sleep quickly took him.

Delmar woke. There was a sharp smell in his sinuses and he sleepily rubbed the bridge of his nose with his fingertips. It was still quiet. He turned onto his side to get back to sleep. No, it wasn't quiet, it was completely silent. There were no croaks or calls from the night animals in the chapter house's grounds. No murmurs from the ever-wakeful city around its walls. Delmar opened his eyes. There was a flickering light from under his door. A lantern. Something, someone, was outside.

The door-bolt began to slide back.

Delmar shot up as though ice-water was in his veins. He dived from his bed; he did not have his sword, but his hand reached for a weapon, for any weapon. The intruder heard the noise and slammed the bolt back. The door flew open. A man stood there, silhouetted by the lantern light.

'Delmar?' the man asked. His voice deep, thick, but not harsh.

Delmar squinted at him and took a grip on one of the bed legs, readying to throw the entire piece of furniture at the assailant if need be.

'Who is that?'

The man held the lantern in front of him and its light fell upon a face that Delmar had only seen in portrait but yet knew better than his own.

'Delmar, my son.'

'Father?'

'FATHER?'

'Yes, son?'

'Father.' Delmar rose to his feet and took the hand held out to him. The hand gripped him back. It was flesh. It was real.

'Father,' Delmar said again and grasped the man's shoulder. It was solid.

'Yes, son?' Delmar looked into the blue eyes, greyer slightly with age.

Delmar clutched him close, expecting the body to evaporate like smoke. It did not. Delmar hugged his father tightly to him, unable to contain his joy.

'It's all right, son. It's all right,' Delmar heard him whisper in his ear.

Then, and only then, did the questions tumble out. 'What are you doing here? Where have you been? They said you were dead, Father. They told Mother you were dead.'

'They were lies, Delmar. Everything they told you was a lie. But come, quickly, I cannot be found here.'

DELMAR FOLLOWED HIM out of the cell and down through the corridors. His father wore a long travelling cloak, but beneath it his clothes were matted dark red.

'Is that blood? Are you injured?' Delmar asked.

'It is not mine,' his father replied, and Delmar saw the slumped bodies of sergeants hidden in the shadows. Delmar looked away, and his father led him out of the buildings and towards the stables.

'What has happened to you?' Delmar asked, hurrying to keep up.

'Many things, Delmar. Many things,' his father said, moving quickly between the horses' stalls. 'I have seen marvels. Experienced wonder. I have touched the edge of existence and my eyes have been opened.'

'Here,' his father said, stopping at the stall of Delmar's horse. 'Put a saddle on Heinrich and let us be gone.'

Delmar hesitated.

'What is the matter?' his father asked.

'Is this for the night? Is it for good? I… I cannot just leave.'

His father looked at him for a moment, then saddled the horse himself. 'I am leaving, Delmar. Stay if you wish, but if you do, you shall not see me again.'

'Wait! That is not fair!' Delmar exclaimed. 'Of course I wish to come with you. But I have taken oaths...'

'Then all you have done is lie to liars. Do not concern yourself with your oaths, for they do not if it does not suit their interest.'

Delmar reached into his saddlebag.

'Let me then at least leave a note for Lord Griesmeyer. I shall not mention anything, but merely say that I left of my own accord.'

His father pulled himself into the saddle.

'Leave your note then,' he said. 'But your Lord Griesmeyer will never read it.'

Delmar looked up at his father and saw again the blood on his clothes, on his hand.

'Do not judge me, Delmar,' his father said. 'He took your father from you. He took my life from me. It was quicker than he deserved.'

Delmar took a step back, then steadied himself against his horse.

'If it is any comfort,' his father continued, 'he died with honour. Such honour as he had left.'

'Give me your hand, Delmar,' his father reached out. 'Give me your hand. We must go. We must go now.'

Delmar looked up at his father. His hero. His measure of nobility. He looked at the bloodied hand held out towards him. Sigmar help him, he took it.

THE WHITE GATE was unbarred and open for them. Delmar could see no sign of the sergeants that should be at posts there. Instead, as they rode through, Delmar saw the shadows shift in the corner of his eye. He turned but the movement was gone. His father paid it no heed and guided Heinrich through the quiet streets towards the tenements of the poor quarter. The houses' windows were all battened and shut, those refugees who'd stayed lay crammed in the gutters and did not look up as the lone horse walked by. A pox had begun to spread amongst the poorest of Altdorf and the word was out that the refugees were to blame.

As they rode, his father pressed Delmar for details of his life, the estates, his grandfather and mother. Delmar related all he could remember, and then asked him of how he had returned to them. His father grew quiet; he spoke softly of his time as a captive of the Skaelings, how he had been sold as a slave to another tribe further north, of his failed attempts to escape and, finally, how he had rendered such service to his master that he had been freed.

'When was this?' Delmar asked. His father appeared fit and strong, he was not fresh from a slavedriver's whip.

'Over five years past now.'

'Five years?' Delmar gasped. 'You stayed away so long.'

'I was freed, Delmar, but I was not free. I had obligations to meet and debts to repay. If I had fallen in the midst of them, well, I did not want you to have your father returned to you only to have him snatched away again.'

'But now you are done? You are free?'

'No. But I had to come back now. I had to because of you, Delmar. You have disappointed me.'

Delmar felt a hole open in his chest as he heard his father's words. 'Disappointed? How?'

'When I heard you had joined the order, when I heard that you had left your mother and your grand-father behind to pursue your own selfish ambition.'

'What?' Delmar gasped. 'It was nothing of the kind. They *wanted* me to come.'

'They wanted to be left alone? Vulnerable? Eking by on what little fortune the family has left until some passing marauder takes even that from them?'

Delmar could not believe it. For all his life he had hoped for his father to return, had dreamed it, but never had he conceived that he would return for this.

'I do not understand, I thought it was my duty. I thought it was *your* duty, your path that I was to fol-low.'

'You will learn, Delmar, that you will make mistakes that you cannot correct. Only pray that your child does not make the same ones.' His father carried on riding calmly. 'I know now that my prayers were in vain.'

'Here.' His father pulled Heinrich up into a small walled courtyard amongst the tenements. 'We shall spend the rest of the night here.'

He dismounted, tied the horse up and locked the gates behind them.

'And what will we do tomorrow?' Delmar asked, fol-lowing his father into the house.

'Tomorrow,' his father said, walking down the steps into the cellar, 'we take you back home. Where you belong.'

'Home?' Delmar said. 'I can't just go home. I've sworn to the order, they need me.'

'Need you? Need you more than your family?' his father replied. He looked at Delmar. 'Oh, I understand now. You thought the order was waiting, expectant, for you to arrive at their door. That they would laud you and praise you, because you were special? That they would give you some magic sword and dispatch you to Middenheim, where you would stand against the Chaotic horde beside Helborg and Karl Franz and that they would look to you to save the city? You live in a fantasy, Delmar. No, if you stayed you would serve and you would die and be little more than a footnote. Just as I was. You do not choose your fate in the Reiksguard, it is chosen for you.'

Delmar looked down, confused. Yes, he had dreams, what young man did not? But there were dreams, and there was duty. He looked back up at his father.

'If service is all the order can offer me, then it is all I require. And the only sword they gave me, Father,' Delmar reached back and drew his blade, 'is yours.'

'The only sword that is mine, Delmar, is the one I carry within me.' His father held up his bloodied hand and, with a stroke of shadow, his hand and forearm flattened and discoloured, transforming into a bloodied blade. He drew a spiral in the air with its point and, wherever it touched, it leeched the colour from the world.

'You see, Delmar, the Reiksguard is nothing. Your oaths to them are nothing. Give them up and come home with me.'

'No,' Delmar said. His father's sword-arm drew a circle at Delmar's feet and the ground burst into a grey flame.

'Do not disappoint me again,' his father ordered. He gestured again and Delmar's sword melted through his hands.

'No!' Delmar bellowed, and that sharp smell once more burst in his sinuses.

THE GREY GLOW dimmed around the illusionist and a sergeant opened the cover from around the lantern. Verrakker checked on Delmar, but the novice had already fallen back into a natural sleep.

'We are finished here,' Verrakker announced. 'Go and prepare the next.' He nodded at the sergeant, who ushered the illusionist out of the cell.

One other figure remained. A woman. A crone, doubled over. She hobbled over to the bed where Delmar lay.

'If,' the crone began, 'my last maternal feeling had not already been burnt from me, I might almost feel sorry for the boy.'

Verrakker did not reply. He did not enjoy this testing, but he knew better than anyone how necessary it was. He had overheard the novices and their talk; they had thought the test of the spirit would be one of simple courage. To face a monster, perhaps. They had had little idea of what the enemies of the Empire were capable of. The dark mages and daemons that whispered in a man's mind to plague them with their most personal terrors, or tempt them with corrupting dreams of glory. Too many strong men had been lost, not to fear, but to pride. The belief that they were greater than their oaths, that their ambition trumped the order's own. Too many had fallen and turned their swords against their homes. Truly, man's most determined foes came from his own ranks.

The crone continued her inspection. 'The father, though,' she tutted, 'so predictable. All these boys, driven by their fathers, one way or another. Never a thought for their mothers. No.'

'We are finished,' Verrakker interrupted. 'Let us move on.'

'Oh, I am in no hurry,' the crone continued. 'You let me out of my hole so little, you cannot blame me for savouring the moment.' She played her splintered nails across Delmar's sleeping face.

'Do not touch him!' Verrakker ordered and grabbed her hand away. The crone whipped about, her free hand going for his neck, and Verrakker grabbed it and held both puny wrists in a single grip.

The crone, hands pinned together, smiled up at him. Her blind eyes flickered from side to side.

'I do not need to use my talent to know this boy's fate. Testing, acceptance, service, a little glory, death, a modest memorial, then oblivion. Same as his father. Yours, however...'

The crone stretched out her smallest finger and placed it against Verrakker's wrist, below his glove. 'Your destiny is far more interesting, Master Verrakker.'

'Do not think that you may read my weakness as easily as this boy's. I am one of the inner circle and I have faced far worse than you.' Verrakker replied, his voice level, his composure like steel. 'As to my destiny, I reconciled myself to that long ago.'

The crone tried to spit at him, but nothing but dry air reached Verrakker's face. He tightened his grip around her wrists in warning.

'Break them then, if you wish,' the crone declared. 'I can do nothing to stop you. But I know you will not. For the first fate we learn to read is our own.'

Verrakker paused for a moment, then pushed the crone away. She rubbed her wrists.

'It amuses me greatly,' the crone said, as she ran her hands over her shaven scalp and retied the last vestiges of hair into a braid.

'What has?'

'That you bring me out to use the very gift for which you keep me in my cage.'

'Your "gift" was not our concern, though there are witch hunters and templars enough to burn you for that alone. I would have cared not if you had spent your life where you were, reading commoners' fates. But to try to read the fate of an emperor? To know his terrors and temptations? That I care about a great deal.'

'An emperor who died only a few years after? Do you not wonder, Verrakker, if the Reiksguard had let me read him whether he might have been saved? Do you not wonder why I did it, knowing I was destined to fail? Do not answer, I can tell you do.'

'Hence you serve your purpose, and it is that alone that has kept you alive for all these years.'

The crone chuckled. 'When you threaten the life of one who knew their fate before she could even speak, Verrakker, you sound like a fool.'

'On,' Verrakker ordered, his tone brooking no further postponement, 'you have delayed long enough. On to the next.'

'Yes, on,' the crone concurred. 'Let us see what you have next for old "Brother Purity".'

TWO OF THE novices did not return from the trial of the spirit.

The novices were excused services and gathered in the Great Hall for the morning meal. Siebrecht was the first there. He was still shaky, but already the details of the vivid dream he had had during the night were fading. As he saw the haunted look upon the faces of the first novices who joined him, though, he knew that some machination of Verrakker's had been at work.

Siebrecht watched as Delmar, Falkenhayn, Proktor, Hardenburg, Gausser, Bohdan and finally Alptraum, entered the Great Hall and took their seats. No one could explain what had happened to them, but Siebrecht could guess. Proktor said that he had seen Harver's possessions being taken away, and there was no doubt in any of the novices' minds that whatever test they had faced, he had failed.

Siebrecht could surmise why. The accident with Breigh had affected him greatly. Carrying such guilt, a man's spirit could easily be broken. Unlike Breigh, however, Harver would never be allowed back. Harver, though, was not Siebrecht's first concern. The face that he most expected to see, most wanted to see, did not appear.

'My lord, my lord Verrakker,' Siebrecht interrupted the knight when he appeared in the Great Hall.

'Matz, what are you doing? Novices should not be speaking at meals.'

'Where is Gunther?' Siebrecht's determined expression convinced Verrakker not to try to quiet him there, within the hall that was quickly filling with hungry knights. Verrakker bustled Siebrecht outside.

'Show some courtesy,' he berated the novice as he went. 'If you cannot hold your questions for the proper time, at least have a respectful tongue in your mouth.' But Siebrecht did not care for Verrakker's censure, only the answers he might give.

'Where is Gunther?' he asked again.

'You mean Novice Krieglitz?'

'Yes, yes,' Siebrecht demanded. 'He did not return last night. He cannot have failed; I know him too well, my lord. If I have passed then he must too, for he has twice the courage that I do.'

'I cannot talk of it,' Verrakker said, but Siebrecht heard the note of hesitation in his voice.

'Please,' he asked and, in desperation, he added, 'brother?'

Verrakker relented. 'He received news last night that has meant that he has had to delay.'

'What news?'

'I cannot and I do not wish to say. And you will get no more from me.'

'But he is still here? He has not gone?'

'Yes, he is in a room in the upper corridors, but he is not to be seen or spoken with. Do you understand me, Siebrecht?'

'PERHAPS NEXT TIME, Novice Matz, you will recognise an order when I give it to you.'

Brother Verrakker was seriously displeased. He had been called to the guardhouse and there found the wretched novice in the corner of his cell and under the sergeants' watchful guard.

Even crammed into a corner, Siebrecht maintained his composure. 'In my defence, my lord, I did not see or speak with Novice Krieglitz.'

'Only because the sergeant saw you climb atop the antechapel and try to scale the side of the chapter house.'

'I would have succeeded as well,' Siebrecht muttered.

'Quiet!' Verrakker snapped and slammed his good hand down on the cell door. Siebrecht near jumped from his skin.

'It beggars belief, novice.' Verrakker did not shout or bawl; his voice was quiet, but no less chilling for that. 'That for all your attempts at dedication, you still carry this air about you. That your opinions, that you yourself, are somehow greater than this order. That you are more right than your superiors, and that therefore you may obey or refuse their instructions as you think fit. This order is not a pastime; it is not some indolent band of aristocrats playing at soldiers. It is a sacred duty and no one is greater than it, not you, not I, not the Reiksmarshal himself.'

'I am sorry, my lord. I truly am…' Siebrecht mumbled.

'I doubt it,' the knight interrupted. 'And it would not be enough, in any case. I realise now that you cannot help yourself saluting with one hand and biting your thumb with the other.'

Siebrecht struggled for something to say, but he could think of nothing.

Verrakker spoke again, his tone more level this time. 'Tell me this instead: why did you do it?'

Siebrecht's mind went blank for a moment, then every possible reason he could have had tumbled into his thoughts. His perverse amusement in defying the order; how if there was a secret he desperately wanted to know more about it; how he wanted Krieglitz back to help him endure the insufferable Reiklanders.

'Well, novice?'

Siebrecht scrabbled down through his own thoughts, and therein found his true reason.

'Because he is my brother,' Siebrecht said, unfolding himself and standing to his feet. 'And because a Reiksguard knight should not allow his brother to feel he has been abandoned. Not even at the last.'

Verrakker tested Siebrecht's gaze for a long moment, before finally speaking.

'Well put. Master Lehrer would be proud of you.'

'It is no rhetoric, my lord.'

'No. I realise.'

The silence stretched between them, Verrakker's knuckles twitching as he drummed his missing fingers.

'You have a day, Novice Matz, to reconsider your position within this order. Tomorrow night there is the novices' vigil and then their oaths. Until then, I do not want you in the citadel. Your uncle has agreed to take you into his custody for the duration. If you decide not to return after that time, then I will understand.'

Siebrecht nodded. Verrakker paused, deciding something for himself, and then continued. 'You caused a great deal of commotion, you realise? I would warrant that there are none within the chapter house, even those in a room along the upper corridors, who would not know of your actions or why you undertook them.'

Siebrecht understood the meaning in the knight's words. 'I thank you, my lord.'

'Thank me? You have nothing for which to thank me.'

'For a knight's judgement.'

For a moment Verrakker looked genuinely touched, then he scoffed at such flattery and left Siebrecht alone.

'IF YOU HAD wanted information,' Herr von Matz scolded his nephew when he collected him, 'then I do not know why you did not simply ask me. Yes, the young Novice Krieglitz, a sad case, indeed.'

'What is?' Siebrecht asked. 'What is happening to him?'

'Not to him, rather to his father, the Baron von Krieglitz. He has been accused of consorting with dark powers.'

'What?' Siebrecht could not believe his ears.

'A rather melodramatic turn of phrase, I know, but not a charge to be taken lightly in any case.'

'Can it be true, uncle? I cannot believe that it can be true.'

'Who can say? Talabecland is rife with intrigue at present. Since their little internal coup all the noble families are manoeuvring themselves into position, each trying to undermine and outflank the other. And a scandalous legal charge has ever been a favoured weapon in the political armoury of the Talabheim families. Krieglitz's father is of little consequence himself, but his family's connections run straight up to the countess.'

'So this is just politicking. Talabheim will sort itself out and Gunther will be fine.'

'That would be true in any ordinary accusation, but this one has been endorsed by the Order of Sigmar. It is their investigation now.'

'The witch hunters?' Siebrecht gasped.

'Indeed,' Herr von Matz replied. 'Have you ever seen the witch hunters at work when they have discovered their prey? I have. A common family that I knew slightly. It was not the punishment that chilled me so, it was the hunters' dedication to it, their thoroughness. The woman was exposed as being tainted, mortally corrupted; she and her family were hounded from their home. They caught the husband there, and he refused to denounce her, so they burnt him. The witch hunters and their templars pursued the rest into the hills, but still that was not enough and they chased and chased, until finally their quarry was spent and they lay down on the cold hillside to die. I saw them bring the bodies back, the clothes cut open to reveal the marks of corruption. I remember thinking how small those marks were, and yet how significantly they were treated.

'She had asked me to stand as a witness of her character at the trial. I refused for I did not want their attention drawn to me. And I am glad I did so. That is why from that day forwards I have been careful to display my worship of Sigmar, Ulric, Taal and Rhya, Morr, Myrmidia, Manann, even though I hate the sea, Shallya and Verena. So that no matter what kind of templar may break down my door and drag me out, they will find me a model devotee of whatever god they worship.

'Fear evil men, Siebrecht, for they will take all you have and destroy all you are. But fear the good man with a righteous cause more, for they will do the same and convince you that they were right to do so.'

THE DREAM OF his father had unsettled Delmar and he had returned to Master Lehrer's library. After reading about Talhoffer and Ott, he had gone back often to learn more from the annals of the Reiksguard. He had discovered what had happened to Lehrer who, in his first campaign after taking his oaths, had lost both his legs to a scythed chariot on a campaign in the Southlands.

Delmar's favourite accounts, though, had been the ones that included his father. Searching back, Delmar had found his name mentioned in several records before Karl Franz. He had even found the listing of the knights of his father's vigil and saw his name there beside Griesmeyer's. Delmar had read of his father's first battles, but then there had been no mention of him at all for a year. Delmar thought back and realised that that was because it was the year that Delmar himself had been born. Heinrich von Reinhardt had returned to his estate to be with his wife.

A year on, there was his name again: a brief notation amongst those assigned to guard the Supreme Patriarch on some expedition to Ostermark. Then his name vanished once more. He had been injured on that expedition and had taken a long time to heal. Then there were swathes of notes from the period of Karl Franz's election. The Reiksguard prided itself on staying above political matters, but as the Emperor's guard they could not afford to remain ignorant of them, especially at such an uncertain time.

Afterwards, when Karl Franz led his first campaign against the Norse who plagued the coast of the Sea of Claws, there was Heinrich von Reinhardt. Delmar had read all he could about his father, yet there was one book which he had not yet had the courage to open.

'Ah…' Lehrer replied. 'I did wonder when you would finally ask to see it.'

Lehrer reached down below his desk and pulled out the volume. 'I have marked the passages that you will wish to read.'

It was a brief account, for the Reiksguard had not considered the battle against the survivors of the Skaeling tribe of any great significance. The war had already been won, after all; the fact that the fighting still continued was neither here nor there to the annalist. Furthermore only a few squadrons of Reiksguard knights were involved, and had only been left behind to placate Count Theoderic Gausser as the remaining regiments of the army returned home. The account merely reported the bare facts: the Count of Nordland's disastrous attack, Helborg's charge, then noted that the knights dispersed to cover the army's retreat. And then, Delmar could not believe it, it was literally a footnote: the death of Heinrich von Reinhardt was a footnote below the account of the battle.

Delmar read the line a dozen times, willing more to appear. 'Is this all?' he asked Lehrer.

'Not what you expected, is it.'

'This cannot be all there is.'

'You tell me, Novice Reinhardt. You are the one who has supposedly been paying attention when I have spoken of the internal functions of our order.'

'What else…? Wait,' Delmar realised, 'he's on the wall of remembrance. And before a knight is added, you said there is a hearing to ensure that a knight did not pass through want of bravery.'

'That is correct. And there would have been a hearing in this instance, because of the circumstances.'

'What circumstances?'

'Brother Heinrich von Reinhardt died because he disobeyed the orders of his preceptor,' Lehrer explained. 'He broke ranks from his squadron and rode into the heart of the enemy. He did it for the noblest reasons to be sure, but to be a knight of the Reiksguard is to renounce one's own will and subject oneself to the will of another. It would have had to be deliberated. Alas…'

But Delmar was already moving through the shelves into the depths of the library. He returned a few minutes later, bearing an open document holster.

'It's empty.'

'Alas,' Lehrer continued, 'our records of those deliberations were taken from us. I was here by that time. I recall the master librarian then was quite put out by it.'

'Who took them?'

'The orders came from the inner circle. But the knight who took them was—'

'Griesmeyer.' The name jumped unbidden to Delmar's lips.

'Yes.'

Lehrer took the holster from the novice's hands and closed it. 'You should not consider it too unusual. Brother

Griesmeyer was the only one who was with your father at the end. The deliberations were almost entirely his testimony. And they were great friends.'

'So I have been told.'

'I was relieved, in a way, when I heard that they were together when your father passed. I do hope that they had had a chance to put their differences behind them before the end.'

Delmar was still thinking of how he might retrieve those records when Lehrer's words sunk in.

'Put what behind them? I did not know of any argument between them. What were their differences?'

'Oh,' Lehrer remarked, placing his forefinger on his temple as if it would aid his recollection. 'Well, this was all a long time ago. I do not think I ever knew. They certainly were great friends as novices, and then after... But it was...' Lehrer rocked back thoughtfully in his chair.

'Yes, I remember, it was when your father came back from the Patriarch's expedition in Ostermark. That was the time I met you, in fact. Your grandfather brought you and your mother here. We thought that your father might heal quickly once he was back, but it was not so. Rather than keep you and your mother in lodgings in Altdorf, he decided to return to his estate for his convalescence. At that time, I am sure that he and Brother Griesmeyer were still as close as they ever were.

'When your father returned, it was after the election and so it must have been no more than a year later, but the two of them were much changed. They had previously been inseparable, but by then they were never seen in public together. There were stories of some terrible arguments between the two of them in private. I would never have spoken to them about it, but it was well known at the time. Still, when the new Emperor gave the call to march to the north, they both went. Perhaps being on campaign together again may have made the difference. I certainly hope it did.'

'Yes,' Delmar muttered.

'What of you, novice? Do you not have any memories of that time?'

'A few,' Delmar thought back. 'My mother, crying in the ursery. Over my father, I think. But then sometimes when I remember it I see him there as well, or a shape at least, of a man. A knight, most definitely a knight. So perhaps it was before he passed, but then it should not be that she was so distraught. I do not know.'

'Or perhaps they are several memories blended together,' Lehrer mused. 'Memory is an uncertain record when set against ink and parchment. I have discovered many people who will swear in all honesty that they remember as red what was blue, and as white what was black. Do not let it trouble you. Keep to your reins, Novice Reinhardt.'

THE VIGIL BEGAN at dusk and was held in the Reiksguard's chapel, sited beside the chapter house's main chamber. The eight novices who still remained had processed in, wearing simple white shifts. They were each first interviewed by two knights, brothers that none of them had seen before, and questioned as to their beliefs, their faith, their families and whether there was any hidden infirmity or physical corruption that would prevent their serving the order. Once this was satisfactorily completed, they were reminded of the oaths that they were to swear, and of the rules and regulations of the order, and then they were left to pray.

There was little to see within the chapel. The interior was lit only by a few evenly spaced candles, and without the sun outside, the glorious scenes set in the stained-glass windows were dark and could not be seen.

Siebrecht knelt. His thoughts chased round and round his head. He told himself that though he did not know enough, there was no way he had at present of finding the answers, and so he should concentrate on being at peace. He settled his thoughts for a time, and then a minute would pass and he would notice Krieglitz's absence once more and the thoughts would chase around again.

Delmar knelt, and tried not to think. He tried not to think of how his father and Griesmeyer had knelt together in this exact same spot twenty-five years before at their own vigil. He tried not to think of his ancient memory of his mother in mourning, and yet another knight being there. He tried not to think of the chill in his mother's voice when she spoke of Griesmeyer or the look in her eyes when she saw her son with him. He tried not to think of the dream of his father and the doubts that it had placed in his mind. Above all, he tried not to think of that battle in which his father had paid his final service, and how the only witness to his last few minutes alive was Griesmeyer. Delmar tried not to think. He tried to pray, but to no avail. Either the gods did not hear him, or they had sent him these thoughts themselves.

The novices remained there until dawn when the light from the rising sun shone through the glass windows and the image of Sigmar Triumphant blossomed before them. They were led from the chapel into the chapter house where every brother of the order without duty had gathered. The novices recognised some of the knights, their tutors: Talhoffer, Ott, Verrakker, even Lehrer was there in his engineered chair, a cloak covering the stumps of his legs. In the centre sat the grand master, Reiksmarshal Kurt Helborg himself, the officers of the order by his side, and by them Delmar saw Griesmeyer, a smile of pride on his lips. Before the assembled order, the novices swore the solemn oaths of fraternity and, one by one, their names were called for the order's assent.

'Brothers of the Grand Order of the Reiksguard, here stand before us those who would join our ranks. Each one, the eldest son of a most noble family, and able to bear arms. They have proven themselves of sufficient strength in body, mind and spirit. They have sworn to uphold our duties and they have pledged themselves to our cause without doubt, without condition, without restraint. Will you call them brother?'

The eight of them, four Reiklanders, four Provincials, stood as a single squadron. Each man stepped forth when his name was called and, as the order confirmed him, the Reiksguard insignia was placed over his shoulders.

Delmar listened as the knight acclaimed each novice in turn: Alptraum of Averland, Bohdan of Ostermark, Falkenhayn, Gausser of Nordland, Hardenburg, and Siebrecht von Matz. When they reached Proktor, the knights' shout was so loud that it fair rattled the glass in the windows. Then came his turn.

'Delmar von Reinhardt?' the officer called.

'Aye!' The knights bellowed and cheered their new brothers.

And with that they became Reiksguard.

CHAPTER SIX

KRIEGLITZ

WHILE THE EMPEROR had been away, his palace had been in hibernation; once he was back it awoke with a surge of vitality. The Imperial officers returned and re-established themselves and their staffs in their appointed chambers. Servants bustled from room to room, preparing each so that no matter where the Emperor chose to walk he would find his path furnished and well fragranced against the smell of the city outside. Noblemen flocked back so that they might garner the Emperor's favour, and the Reiksguard tripled the palace guard to ensure that each of these different groups did not trespass where they should not.

'As part of the palace guard,' Verrakker briefed the new young knights, 'you must be ever vigilant, ready at a second's notice to halt an assassin or an enemy assault. What you will find, however, is that you spend most of your day telling some persistent perfumed fop of a courtier to step back and allow the Emperor his privacy.

'It is the Emperor's will when he wishes to make himself available and when he does not. It is their duty to obey, and not to substitute their own wishes for his. No matter who they are. They will all be noblemen and lords, unused to being denied. Some may even try to pull rank over you; if they try they shall not be successful.'

Delmar, Siebrecht and the other young knights laughed.

'And finally, I would remind you all: though it is rarely glorious, being a guard at the palace is one of the most solemn duties within the Reiksguard. A lapse on your part could be the means by which our Emperor is murdered, a civil war erupts and the Empire collapses in flames. So consider that. And then consider that any negligence, any dereliction, any reckless act committed whilst on this duty is considered treason. And guards have, and will continue to be, executed for that crime.'

THE PROBLEM OF protecting the Emperor was made all the more difficult by the Imperial Palace itself. Though the Reikland princes had only been elected to the Imperial throne a hundred years previously, the palace had been built long before. Some even said that part of its structure dated back to the first time Altdorf had been the capital of the Empire, centuries ago. The place itself had been built and rebuilt, extended and redesigned as it had been put to different uses over the years. This rate of expansion only increased when the emperors took occupancy and adapted it to be the principal seat of government. Separate buildings were sited nearby for these purposes and, as the palace grew still further, these buildings were connected and subsumed into the whole. A past Imperial architect had described the result as, 'a residence where the differing architectural styles were not so much at odds as in outright conflict,' and had begged the emperor of his day for the funds to build a fresh palace anew. Those funds, once collected, instead were spent quelling a provincial uprising, leading the architect to append to his previous comment the words, 'and therefore the palace is as fitting a symbol for the Empire as anything.'

Architectural symbolism aside, this left the palace in some areas full of grand reception halls and elegant apartments, in others a maze of uneven courtyards and twisting passages, and all the more difficult to guard as a result. Exploring the buildings, learning his way around, kept Siebrecht from his thoughts for his first few days on guard. But as the novel quickly became the routine, he found himself brooding again over his friend's troubles. There was little else to distract him; the courtiers, for all Verrakker's warnings concerning their tenacity, had learned from grim experience that arguing with the impassive Reiksguarders was at best a waste of breath, and at worst would find them exiled from court after a short stay in the palace's cells.

The Emperor himself had pared his schedule of public appearances to the bone and made it plain to all that his first, last and only order of business at present was the ongoing conduct of the war, and that he would not entertain any personal applications. Instead, his day was dominated by meetings of the Council of

State; the members of that council quickly became familiar faces to Siebrecht and the other young knights. This merely added to Siebrecht's frustration, however; in the next room from him the most senior members of the government were in discussions that were deciding the future of the Empire, and yet he was stuck outside warding away the unwelcome. The council members themselves treated the knights as little more than pieces of furniture and ignored Siebrecht's presence even as he stepped smartly aside to let them pass. Siebrecht silently nursed a grievance at such treatment; he was not a servant, he was a noble lord and now a knight of the grandest military order. It was all yet another example of Reiklander arrogance. Yet then he overheard something that cast such petty thoughts from his mind.

'But if he should ask about Karak Angazhar, I would not know what to say...'

The speaker was Baron von Stirgau, Chamberlain of the Seal and the Emperor's diplomatic advisor. Karak Angazhar was the name of the dwarfen hold that his uncle had mentioned weeks before. Siebrecht had given it little more thought at the time, however now he found it being discussed at the highest levels. Baron von Stirgau quietened his conversation before entering the council chamber, but he had not cared about speaking before Siebrecht, standing immobile beside the entrance. Perhaps there was an advantage to being treated as part of the furniture after all. The council meetings were held in seclusion with the Emperor and even Reiksguard knights were not privy to them; however, Siebrecht could piece together much from what

the councillors said privately to each other before they
entered and as they left.

'...retreated to the Middle Mountains, our silver
mines there are lost...'

'...still no word from Count Feuerbach, and now this
scandal in a noble family, Talabheim is on the edge...'

'...last we saw them was Krudenwald, but an army
such as that cannot simply disappear...'

'...a dozen more bodies hanging from trees, not that
I'd mourn the loss of such scum, but better human
scum than that which is replacing them...'

'...who is in power down there. Is it anyone?'

'...the Cult of Sigmar have their own problems at
present, I should leave them be...'

Siebrecht absorbed it all, inferred and speculated on
what he could. He was missing many of the specifics,
but he could gather what desperate straits the Empire
was in: three of its grand provinces devastated by the
northern war; two more without clear leadership; their
recent allies increasingly distracted by their own concerns; a canker was left near its heart, defeated but not
destroyed; and money.

'...think the regiments will be disbanded anytime
soon, you are much mistaken...'

'...he cannot afford to do it, he cannot afford not to
do it...'

'...I do not believe that for a moment...'

'...but where is the money to come from?'

Money needed for the troops; money needed to
rebuild walls, roads, cities, farms; and from the sour
look upon the face of Chancellor Hochsvoll and the
way she uneasily toyed with the rings upon her

grasping fingers, it was money the Empire did not have.

But Siebrecht did not hear any further mention of Karak Angazhar until one hot night at the height of summer. Siebrecht was stationed immediately outside the council chamber; council meetings were typically formal, sedate affairs, but this time the voices were raised and Siebrecht could hear them.

'I appreciate the tremendous difficulties of our situation in the north, it only makes it all the more imperative that we secure our border to the south as well.' Siebrecht recognised the voice of Count von Walfen, the Chancellor of Reikland and, it was said, the Emperor's personal spymaster.

'I do not understand why the dwarfs cannot help themselves,' Chancellor Hochsvoll replied, her tone icy even in this heat.

Baron von Stirgau sought to explain in his distinguished intonation. 'The ambassador from the High King has been very open concerning this. Both their strongholds of Barak Varr and Karak Hirn have been besieged; the attackers have been driven off, but at such cost that they cannot send out an expedition to relieve Karak Angazhar.'

'If they do not care sufficiently to defend it, why should we?'

'Because of its location, chancellor,' Walfen repeated. 'It is at the head of the Upper Reik and no more than a few days' march from Black Fire Pass. If it should fall, it would be the perfect staging post for all manner of attacks into Averland, all our defences in the pass itself would be outflanked and rendered useless, and we would forever be under the threat of attacks launched down the Reik river itself. The dwarfs would survive it, but we would not. Our southern lifeline could be cut.'

'You mean the trading routes would be cut,' Hochsvoll retorted. 'Do not think I am unaware of your interests in that area.'

'The Empire's interests, do you mean? Or do you consider that the maintenance of healthy, profitable and above all, taxable trading routes to be of no interest to the Imperial coffers?'

'Future revenues are all well and good, but who is going to pay for it now?' Chancellor Hochsvoll retorted.

'It is not money which is the issue,' the bass voice of the Reiksmarshal Kurt Helborg interrupted, 'it is men. The army is still needed in the north. Despite what you might hear people say in the streets, the war is still being fought.'

'Could you not simply spare a handful of regiments?' Baron von Stirgau asked.

'No.' The Reiksmarshal's tone brooked no refusal.

'Well, what about the mercenary armies?' Stirgau continued.

'And who would pay for those?' Hochsvoll began again.

'There are still troops in Averland, Reiksmarshal,' Walfen interceded.

'Averland's regiments marched north, Wissenland's as well.'

'I was referring to the Reikland garrisons that we have maintained in Averland these last two years. Since the unfortunate death of Elector Count Leitdorf.'

'They are with the army as well.'

'Not all of them.'

This flat refutation provoked Helborg, already hot and tired. 'Do not question my knowledge of the positioning of the Empire's troops.'

'I do not question your *knowledge*,' Walfen's emphasis was slight but noticeable, 'indeed, I rely upon it. I know that you have a sound strategic mind and therefore would not strip our southern provinces entirely of their defences. And I also know that that is where you still send their pay. So, if we may proceed on the basis that there are still men in those garrisons?'

But Kurt Helborg was not to be so easily outflanked. 'There are men left there, but very few. Only enough to ensure that when this current crisis is past, we still have defences in place to ensure we can protect that border. They are not to be frittered away on an ill-judged expedition.'

'They should not be needed to fight, Reiksmarshal, merely to help recruitment.'

'Recruitment of whom?'

'There are still men in Averland. Men able to carry a halberd and march to a drum. The state troops are with the army, that's true, but there are still men there able to fight.'

'Yes, in case of invasion. In case their towns and homes are threatened.'

'If Karak Angazhar is not relieved then that is exactly what will happen.'

'You may convince us here of that,' Helborg intoned, 'but words will not convince the aldermen of Averheim, Streissen or Heideck to allow us to raise their militias, and there is no Elector Count of Averland to aid you.'

* * *

WALFEN WAS READY to play his hand. 'WHICH IS WHY we will need to send one regiment, but only one regiment. But it must be a regiment whose mere presence will inspire the militias to form, who will convince the aldermen of the towns of Averland of the great importance of this expedition to the Empire, that the eyes of the Emperor himself are upon them. And it must be a regiment which is not needed in the north, and indeed has already returned to the city.'

His meaning was clear even to Siebrecht.

'You mean the Reiksguard,' Helborg said.

'Yes, I do.'

'They have only just returned.'

'I am sure they will not be reluctant to fulfil their duty and to march again to war.'

'Soldiers should always be reluctant to march to war, baron. It is amateurs who are eager for it.'

Siebrecht had to imagine the look of distaste and contempt Helborg gave Walfen at that moment. Then someone was talking, but they were quiet and he could not make out their voice. It must be the Emperor, he realised, giving his final verdict on the matter.

'As you command, my lord,' Helborg finally said, 'I will ensure the necessary arrangements are made as quickly as possible.'

THE GRAF VON Falkenhayn did not care for celebratory balls; in his younger days he had used the family ballroom for fencing instruction, and to house his model recreations of the epic battles from the history of the Empire. That usage, however, changed when he married; his wife, the Gravine von Falkenhayn, cared for balls very much. And he cared for her. So out went the swords, armour, miniatures and scenery, and the gravine set to work to make the room a suitable location for her and the graf to celebrate the events of the season. Their ballroom could not compete in size with the grand ballroom of the Imperial Palace, but that did not prevent her from challenging her rival in every other respect. The walls were festooned with golden ornaments and silver mirrors. On the ceiling was an epic mural of the founding of Altdorf, and over each arch, a gilded falcon stood with its wings outstretched. She made the room fit indeed, and this evening there were several hundred of her closest friends there to admire it. For her son, Franz, had been accepted into the Reiksguard and there was absolutely no one of her acquaintance who should not have the opportunity to attend and congratulate her personally.

Everywhere that Siebrecht looked he saw young noblemen and women talking, dancing, drinking and enjoying themselves. Everywhere except right beside him.

'I do not understand why we came.' Bohdan's disaffection caused his heavy Ostermark accent to sound all the harsher.

Beside them, Gausser grunted. His attention was fixed on the delicate wine saucer he held between his big fingers and trying not to snap it in two.

'It's a ball. We were invited,' Siebrecht reminded them cheerfully, trying to raise their spirits and failing.

'And what are we to the Gravine von Falkenhayn that she should invite us, I wonder?' Bohdan mistrusted any large gathering of nobility. There were too many

Ostermarker tales of such evenings where, at the height of the festivities, the outside doors were locked and the hosts, daemons in human form, began a far bloodier feast. He had not yet spotted the wife of the Graf von Falkenhayn, but he was not going to relax his guard an instant.

'Listen,' Siebrecht explained again, 'Falkenhayn wanted his precious Falcons along, of course, but with the delegation from Averland as the guests of honour, the gravine wanted Alptraum here, and Alptraum wanted us, his fellow vigil-brothers, along so he did not have to spend the whole evening with the Reiklanders.'

Alptraum need not have worried, Siebrecht reflected, for as soon as the young knight had arrived he had been swooped upon by the Averland nobles, each eager to update him with news of the latest political manoeuvrings in the province and enrol him in their cause. Behind the scenes in the leaderless province, the families were fighting tooth and nail for every advantage and now that Alptraum was a knight of the Reiksguard, he had become a far more significant piece on their game board.

Gausser grunted again. Bohdan was staring suspiciously at an elderly baroness with pale, withered skin and sunken cheeks who was seated nearby. He glared at her hard until she, rather unsettled, got shakily to her feet and moved away.

Siebrecht rolled his eyes at his comrades' behaviour and, despite his original intention, decided that all their evenings would be best served if he and they parted company. As the next group of revellers swung past, he slipped away and made for the opposite corner of the ballroom. He sashayed around the dancers in the centre of the room, assessing the event with an experienced eye. Ostentatious simplicity was the fashion for the season, Altdorf society's acknowledgement of the deprivation that everyone else in the Empire suffered. The ladies were garbed in simple lines which were all the more expensive to tailor, while the noblemen wore military uniforms, at least all of them who could lay claim to one. The rest made do with clothes cut in a similar fashion. Despite the myriad regimentals on display, Siebrecht was pleased that his own Reiksguard uniform still caught the eye of many of the young ladies waiting for young men to ask them to dance.

Young men, his treacherous mind added, who would otherwise be present if they had not been left behind on the plains of Middenland. Siebrecht quashed the thought instantly; he had had precious few chances of enjoying such occasions since his arrival in Altdorf and he was not going to ruin this one with useless lamentation.

He took a moment's casual repose beside the sculpture of a falcon about to take flight. He had spotted the Reiklanders on his journey: Falkenhayn was holding court as usual to anyone who would listen, his faithful Proktor was by his side ready to confirm all his boasts, Delmar was looking uncomfortable and awkward, and the fair-faced Hardenburg was heavily engaged with a string of soppy-eyed girls. Hardenburg, Siebrecht decided, had the right idea and he was about to introduce himself to a promising noble daughter dallying nearby when another familiar face caused him to forget his original purpose entirely.

'Uncle?'

Herr von Matz turned, glass in hand, and exclaimed: 'Siebrecht, my boy!'

He excused himself from his conversation and unsteadily navigated a path to his nephew.

'Uncle?' Siebrecht asked. 'What are you doing here?'

Herr von Matz looked at him, slightly dazed. 'It is a festivity, is it not? So I am being festive!' he replied, taking another gulp of his drink.

'I cannot believe it. Are you drunk?'

With his free hand, his uncle grabbed him by the shoulder and leaned in close. Siebrecht, no lightweight himself, fair recoiled from the stink of wine emanating from him.

'Not at all, my dear boy,' Herr von Matz whispered, quickly and crisply, all trace of intoxication gone. 'But one finds that drinkers and sots are far more loose-tongued around their own kind than those who maintain a sober disposition, and so one must, alas, adopt all the pretence with none of the pleasure.'

'Your stench is certainly convincing,' Siebrecht muttered, trying not to breathe through his nose.

'Ah, a necessary evil, and the laundry a necessary expense. But what of you? You should be enjoying yourself, a young warrior off to war and all that.'

'You heard of that? *We* only learned of it today!'

'Heard of it? I predicted it, did I not? Karak Angazhar!'

'Aye, uncle, so you did,' Siebrecht acknowledged. 'Does your network of informants now extend to knowing the Emperor's own mind before he does?'

Herr von Matz chortled. 'Nothing of the kind, Siebrecht. There was some inside knowledge, yes, but the rest was merely the comprehensive application of thought and an understanding of the unspoken reasons.'

Siebrecht glanced away at that.

'Ah, I see your mind has begun to work like that as well,' Herr von Matz continued. 'It is not a pleasant path. You will find no heroes or villains upon it, merely fellow travellers like myself. So, Karak Angazhar! You will be marching the day after tomorrow, up alongside the River Reik, I imagine, riding as quickly as you can. Allowing your supplies to be brought up by boat. Recruit what militia you can along the way and then up into the mountains.'

'Taal's teeth, uncle. Did you have a spy in the chapter house today?' Every detail his uncle had told him was exactly the same as the Reiksmarshal had dictated to the assembled order earlier that day.

'Yes, of course,' he replied, bemused.

'Who?'

'You!'

Siebrecht was taken aback. 'Me? I did not tell you a thing.'

'That is because you are not a very good spy! Not yet, at least.' Herr von Matz scoffed. 'You think I need a spy in the chapter house to know the Reiksguard are preparing to leave? You can tell simply by watching the place through the gate! You think the sudden burst of feverish labour that heralds the order's departure goes unnoticed? That your suppliers can magic their goods into your store houses without sending urgent messages around the city to gather what they can?'

Another fact clicked into place in Siebrecht's mind. 'Our suppliers. The guildmarks?'

Herr von Matz smiled encouragingly at his nephew as one would at a puppy who has learnt his first trick.

'That might tell you that we were leaving, perhaps even when we would depart. But not the route we would take, nor that we would be raising troops along the way.'

'Both eminently deducible, my boy. But I will admit that I have had help besides my inference in this matter. The Reiksmarshal did tell you that you would be joined by some Averland worthies who had arrived in the city and would be accompanying you to aid in raising the troops.'

'Yes, as soon as the news went out the gravine tracked them down and made them all the guests of honour tonight,' Siebrecht replied innocently, but his thoughts were catching up with him.

'Well? You did ask what I was doing here?' Herr von Matz reached into his jacket and brought out a feather dyed yellow and black, the colours of Averland.

'You're part of the Averland delegation?' Siebrecht was astonished.

'Correct, and we were given the path of your march, I mean our march, at the same time as you were.'

'What possible reason would they have to…? You're not even from Averland.'

Herr von Matz was affronted. 'I will have you know that I am well known in Averland.'

'I imagine that you are well known in many places.' Siebrecht contained his sarcasm.

'Indeed,' his uncle replied, pleased at himself as much as his nephew. 'It will be pleasant to spend more time with you,' Herr von Matz continued. 'And now our subsequent meeting is established I will allow you to get on and enjoy the evening.'

Siebrecht merely nodded as his uncle turned away.

'One last thing,' Herr von Matz said, turning back. 'A question I perhaps should have asked you before. Karak Angazhar.'

'Yes?'

'Why are you going?'

'The Reiksmarshal said...' Siebrecht recollected, 'that it is the old alliance. They are attacked in Barak Varr and Karak Hirn, and after aiding us in the north they cannot mount an expedition of their own.'

'Hmmm... that was what you were told. Why do *you* think you are going?'

Siebrecht considered it. 'The trading routes. If Karak Angazhar should fall then so would Black Fire Pass and our trading routes with the High King would be cut. Trade we desperately need if we are to rebuild after this war.'

'Good... but let me ask again. Why are *you* going?'

Now Siebrecht knew what his uncle was driving at. 'To serve well. Make my name. So that I will have the privilege to restore our family's fortunes.'

'And...?' Herr von Matz prompted him. 'Resist the urge to plunge your breast onto the enemy's sword.'

'Aye,' Siebrecht replied with good humour.

'And do not forget it.'

SIEBRECHT WANDERED BACK through the white gate. The sergeants there regarded him warily, and he waved at them happily. They would not trouble him tonight, not returning from the Gravine von Falkenhayn's illustrious ball and with a campaign the day after tomorrow. Siebrecht had cheer in his heart. In spite of his uncle's appearance, he had enjoyed himself immensely, and was happily on the other side of the cup. He had sorely missed such evenings since coming to Altdorf.

He made his way into the buildings and threaded his way through the corridors for several minutes before he realised that he was heading back to the novices' dormitory. Since he and his brothers had become full brother-knights, their belongings had been taken from the novices' quarters and into the other wing. He dutifully turned around and tried to find his way to his bed.

On his travels he passed the arming room, and a light inside caught his eye. A single candle flame illuminated the figure inside. It was Krieglitz. The novice was in the middle of strapping himself into armour. It was not the ceremonial plate that they wore as sentries at the palace, it was a full suit of plate. What a Reiksguard knight wore when he went to war.

'Gunther?'

Krieglitz looked up.

'Ah, it's you. Help me on with this, Siebrecht, will you?'

'What are you doing?'

Krieglitz raised the half-fastened elbow cowter. 'What does it look like?'

His smile was there, but it was not the generous expression with which Siebrecht was familiar. It was dark. Bitter.

'Gunther,' he said again slower, 'what are you doing?'

Krieglitz caught the edge in Siebrecht's voice and stopped tying the piece of armour.

'What are you saying, Siebrecht? You can't be thinking that I would…'

'I don't know what to think,' Siebrecht snapped back, his mind quickly clear again. 'You vanish for days. No one sees you. There are all these stories…'

'Stories?' Krieglitz chuckled. 'I would have taken that big lug Gausser to be the gullible one, not you, my friend.'

'Then tell me, what is the truth?' Siebrecht took his brother's arm. 'All I hear of is accusations and trials.'

'Yes, my family are having difficulties.' Krieglitz brushed him away. 'But these allegations, they are all political. How can a son of Nuln, of all people, not recognise politics when he sees it?'

'But the witch hunters are involved, Gunther. If the witch hunters are involved, then this is above politics.'

'Ah, enough gold will turn a witch hunter's head as easily as any other man's,' he dismissed, but without conviction. 'Another one came this morning.'

'What did he say?'

'He said,' Krieglitz mocked, 'that there was evidence enough that my family… my father… has a taint.' He spat the last word.

Siebrecht felt his stomach drop. The witch hunters were strange men, rarely wanted, never liked, but they would pursue any hint of mortal corruption without restraint.

Neither of them spoke for a long moment. Krieglitz's eyes were fixed on the flame of the slowly burning candle.

'What did the constable say?' Siebrecht eventually asked.

'He told the witch hunter… that the order has jurisdiction over the order's affairs. But that as I was not yet a brother of the order…' Krieglitz trailed off. Then he looked away from the candle and straight at Siebrecht. 'I am to return home, and there to share my family's fate.'

'I'm certain you will defend your name. There can be nothing to these charges, but smoke.'

'Aye, smoke, yes.' Krieglitz drifted off again. Siebrecht saw his friend needed help.

'Shouldn't you be packing then? If you are going home?' He wanted to get Krieglitz out of this dark place.

'It's all being taken care of. They told me I need not concern myself.' Krieglitz looked at the cowter afresh. 'I came down here… I wanted to know what it was to wear it all. I wanted to feel what it was like; before I left.'

'You'll be back soon enough,' Siebrecht said, knowing he could only offer cold comfort. 'A crown of mine says you'll be back before the month is out.'

'Hah, I'll take that bet. Still, I would like to know now. Help me on with this, my friend.' Siebrecht did so, and soon Krieglitz stood in the full regalia of a Reiksguard knight.

'How does it feel?' Siebrecht asked.

'Good. It's light. The Reiklanders were right: it is lighter than the practice plate.' Krieglitz inspected himself. 'Do you remember, Siebrecht, when Master Lehrer taught us the meaning of every single piece of this armour?'

Krieglitz lifted his right shoulder pauldron an inch. 'You remember what these stood for?'

Siebrecht did. 'Brotherhood.'

'For a knight stands shoulder to shoulder with his brothers,' Krieglitz recited. 'As the pauldrons defend a knight from the gravest strokes, likewise a knight is defended by his brothers and without them is in peril of death.'

Krieglitz paused for a moment, then continued. 'How do I feel? I feel strong. I feel connected. Like a true brother.'

'I'll help you take it off,' Siebrecht offered.

'Wait, I would take a turn in it. I would like to walk a way, feel how it moves.'

Krieglitz led the way, through the corridors. Siebrecht had expected the armour to make a fearful noise, but it was quiet, so well constructed and maintained that the plates slid over each other with ease.

'Have you heard of the inner circle?' Krieglitz asked as they walked.

'I've heard the name. They are some of the older knights, no?'

'Oh, they are that. But they are much more. You know the power a single Reiksguard knight carries. Imagine the power that those who direct the actions of hundreds of knights have. Knights who serve by the Emperor's side, who guard his rooms in the palace. Knights who campaign with every Imperial general.'

'I can well believe it. What of them?'

'I have a mission from them. I can say no more, not even to you.'

They stepped out of the building. Above them the stars and moons shone in the dark.

'I'm going to walk a little further,' Krieglitz announced.

'Gunther, no.'

'Just once around the walls.'

'Then I will come with you.'

'No, Siebrecht. It is *you* who drag *me* into mischief, remember?'

'You'll get yourself in trouble, Gunther.'

Krieglitz laughed. 'They can hardly do any more to me. Go. Go back. You cause a clamour and they'll find us both. I just need the air.'

Siebrecht hesitated; he thought to insist, but if Krieglitz resented his company then it might push him away still further. If he stayed within the walls, there was little harm he could do; and there were sentries enough to make leaving the citadel difficult even without a full suit of armour. 'You will not leave without saying farewell.'

'You have my oath as a Reiksguard knight,' Krieglitz said lightly.

'I'd rather have your wager. I think you value those greater.'

'If that were true, then I would be a sorry knight indeed.' Krieglitz held out his hand for Siebrecht to shake. 'I must prove to you the contrary, and hereby wager never to collect the crown you so rashly lost to me just now.'

Siebrecht took his hand and smiled. 'How much is the wager?'

'A crown, of course.'

'AND THAT WAS the last you spoke to him.'

'Yes, constable. That was the end of it. He left and I returned to the dormitory,' Siebrecht stated again, but still the scribe wrote it down. The constable leaned back and stared at Siebrecht hard, as though he could strip away falsities and lies simply through his gaze. Siebrecht did not care how he looked at him. A few hours ago Siebrecht would have feigned courage to cover his fear, exercised his wit to prove he was not afraid, but now there was simply no fear to feel. Nothing of anything.

The search for Krieglitz had begun soon after first light, when a sergeant had gone to escort him to morning prayers and discovered that he had not returned. The constable had sent stewards down through the streets to pick up his trail. Before lunch they had returned with a ferryman who had a story to tell. By the afternoon, the order's strongest swimmers were diving into the Reik off the bridge. Before the sun went down, they had dragged poor Krieglitz's body out of the river.

They had not had to search far. The heavy Reiksguard armour had dragged Krieglitz straight down and anchored him to the muddy bottom. Once they pulled his body to the bank, the order stripped the armour off. Sergeants from the Marshal's household had collected it up and returned it to the citadel, for it to be cleaned, oiled and used again. As Siebrecht's uncle had often reminded him, a good set of armour was most expensive and not to be lightly cast aside. The body itself, however, was not returned to the chapter house. There was no place for an unquiet spirit in the Reiksguard's garden of Morr. A priest was found, who mumbled a few words over the body, and it was wrapped in a shroud for transportation.

'You saw no one else on your way back to your quarters.'

'No.'

'And there was nothing else that occurred that night, that you discussed? Think one last time please, Brother Matz.'

He had already told them everything, everything less Krieglitz's mention of the inner circle. Shattered as he was, Siebrecht could sense that such a revelation would make them redouble their questioning. He just wanted to leave, find a corner, find a drink.

He felt himself beginning to shake and saw the constable share a glance with the other knight: Griesmeyer. Siebrecht knew his name. He was the one Delmar had brought back to show off to the rest of the novices that day.

Griesmeyer leaned forwards and entered the conversation. 'We are not looking to place shame on others, Matz. Novice Krieglitz took that with him. You should not have assisted him with the armour, but you cannot blame yourself for his death.'

Siebrecht looked up at that. 'I do not blame myself! I blame the perjurers and the zealots who brought such baseless accusations, with no further cause than their own advancement. Rumours and lies, these are the weapons they wielded to kill my friend!'

Siebrecht felt the anger burn within him, and the constable and Griesmeyer shared another look. Griesmeyer nodded and then dismissed the scribe, who put down his quill and left. The constable followed him out. Griesmeyer turned back to Siebrecht.

'Rumours and lies there may have been, but the accusations were true,' Griesmeyer stated plainly. 'Baron von Krieglitz has been tried and condemned; there was unquestionable evidence of his physical corruption. Amulets imbued with dark power have been discovered in his household, to heal him they claimed. One of his stewards has been exposed as a practitioner of illegal magics and has been burned. The Countess of Talabheim has denounced that line of her family and allowed the Order of Sigmar to seize the baron's estate and possessions. The baron himself has disappeared, as has one of his sons. There can be no doubt. This is the news that we brought Novice Krieglitz last evening before he saw you.'

Siebrecht reeled. All of Krieglitz's behaviour the night before, his protestations that there might be hope, had been pretence. Unlikely as it may have been, Siebrecht had never given up the belief that there might be some other explanation for what had happened to his friend, that there may have been some foul play or accident that had thrown him into the river. But if he had already been told that his father's taint was certain, if the inner circle already knew... In an instant, Siebrecht saw the thread that connected the discrepancies he had noted over the last day. His uncle's admonition rang in his head: understand the unspoken reasons.

'It is all a great tragedy.' Siebrecht straightened up; he found it easy to control himself now. 'But not as great a tragedy as if my unfortunate friend's shame had touched this most noble order. As you said, he has taken all that with him.'

Griesmeyer, noting the young knight's new composure, cautiously agreed. 'It is a great tragedy.'

'It is, in its own way, fortunate then that Novice Krieglitz's actions have allowed us to sever the order's ties with that family so speedily. That he was able to escape his custody last night and then that he, fully armoured, could scale our wall and slip past our keen-eyed sentries without raising the alarm. But then, can we ascribe it all to fortune? For surely there is no way to restrain a man who is determined to meet his end.'

Griesmeyer gave Siebrecht an odd look.

'Novice Krieglitz was never bound here. He was free to leave at will. As you all are. And as you say, a man who longs for death will find his way.'

Siebrecht saw a shadow fall over Griesmeyer's face for a moment, as though he were lost in remembrance. Then he stood to take his leave, but there was one more question Siebrecht wished him to answer.

'My lord Griesmeyer, if I may ask, you are a knight of the inner circle?'

'I am,' he replied. 'Your interest?'

'Just to know your lordship better.'

'There are few secrets here, Brother Matz, though active minds do wilfully perceive them where they are not. If to expunge your grief you must create your villains, then that is your concern; but do not drag your fellows down into your pit. For if you do, then it will no longer be your concern, it will be ours.'

'THAT IS RIDICULOUS, Siebrecht,' Gausser repeated.

'You weren't there. It was written across his face.'

They were out on the practice field, watching Bohdan conclusively trounce Hardenburg with the halberd. They stood apart from the Reiklanders, or perhaps the Reiklanders stood apart from them. It was only a day after Krieglitz's body had been found, and neither faction was eager to share company with the other.

'Was it written across this Griesmeyer's face?' Gausser asked. 'Or was it written across the inside of your eyes?'

Siebrecht was in no mood to be doubted.

'Ulric's teeth, brother, do you even remember Krieglitz? Just a few weeks ago he was standing here with us. Think back then, was there any of us less likely to take his own life? Bohdan over there is as strung as tight as a crossbow, Falkenhayn's so paranoid that he throws down a challenge at the slightest whiff of disrespect, and Reinhardt has such a morbid obsession with his dead father that he named his own horse after him!'

'That I hear, but I also hear your voice when you told me how changed our brother was when you discovered him that night.'

'But don't you see? That was after they got to him. Poured their poisons into his ear and pushed him towards a resolution designed for their own convenience.'

'Only gods may know men's souls, Siebrecht.'

'Then perhaps there are some men here who believe that they are a god's equal. Look, there he is.' Siebrecht indicated off to one side. It was Griesmeyer, riding down towards the white gate. He stopped beside the Reiklander contingent and exchanged salutes. Delmar stepped forwards and the two of them had a warm, comradely exchange, though Siebrecht could not hear the specifics.

'Of course,' Siebrecht spat. Gausser grunted without comment. Siebrecht continued, 'I can't stay confined in here this evening. I'm going over the wall. Will you come with me, brother?'

Gausser considered it for a moment and then stirred. 'Aye, if only to ensure that you come back.'

CHAPTER SEVEN

GAUSSER

Each month the Reiksguard squadrons were in Altdorf, they were subject to inspection. Typically this was performed by the Reiksmarshal and it was his opportunity to ensure his order was fully manned, with its arms and armour in good repair. New knights who had stood their vigil and taken their oaths in the period since the last inspection were given particular attention, a tradition dating back from when the Reiksguard's training and testing was not nearly so formal nor so strict. In more recent times, a new knight's first inspection had become a symbol of his final acceptance into the order, and for the noble families of Altdorf, it was the perfect opportunity for them to attend and bask in the reflected honour.

As the Reiksguard had just returned from the victory at Middenheim, and as it became increasingly known that they would shortly be departing again, the inspection took on a greater significance. And when, a few days before, the palace announced that the Emperor himself would take the inspection, it became a far grander event entirely.

The knights adopted the full Reiksguard battle armour, less the helm, in place of which they wore a cockaded hat bearing the badge of the order and red and white plumes, the colours of the ruling Emperor. They formed up not by the chapter house, but in the grounds of the Imperial Palace, and presented themselves there for the eye of the Emperor.

When Delmar and his brothers awoke that morning, it was clear that Siebrecht and Gausser had not returned from the night before. They eventually appeared, Gausser as upright as ever, Siebrecht ashen-faced and obviously the worse for the night's excesses. They were all full brother-knights now, not novices, and so enjoyed far greater liberty. But that did not mean that the others would make Siebrecht's life the least bit easier for him as a result. It was only Gausser who made sure that the Nulner reported with the rest at the appointed time.

Many of the families of the Reikland knights were in attendance. The Graf and Gravine von Falkenhayn, the Baron and Baroness von Proktor, and, Delmar was overjoyed to see, his mother and grandfather had made the journey to Altdorf as well. Delmar was doubly honoured that day for he had been chosen to carry the standard for the new knights' squadron. The weather proved to be scorching hot and the palace servants ran back and forth with shades and canopies for the nobler sections of the crowds. The new knights slowly boiled in their battle armour, but they would rather be toasted alive than show any sign of discomfort before the Emperor.

Karl Franz himself gave no indication that he felt the heat. He sat calmly on the back of his steed with his champion, Ludwig Schwarzhelm, by his side, as though he would be quite content to remain there for the entire day. When the Reiksguard were ready to begin, Helborg rode to the Emperor, saluted and took his position on his other flank. His eyes flicked to Schwarzhelm, and the two locked gazes for an instant before the Reiksguard began to march.

The Emperor accepted the salutes of the Reiksguard regiments, first the Reiksguard's trumpeters, mounted as cavalry, and then the rest marching on foot. When the time came for the new knights to present themselves, he dismounted and walked up their line. The knights stood at painfully strict attention, eyes forwards, but none of them could resist stealing a glance at the Emperor as he stepped before them. In that split-second, each of them believed that they had discerned some unique insight into the great man. The most mundane moment for him was, for them, a moment of the greatest significance.

As for Karl Franz, he was long accustomed to such curiosity and knew not to dishonour them by catching their eyes as they glanced. There was only a single knight of them whom he truly noticed, and that was one who had a particular look of fierce concentration carved upon his face. He was the only one whose eyes did not flicker as he passed. In truth, Siebrecht von Matz barely noticed the shadow fall across his face. He had begun the morning with a throbbing head and a tongue as dry as the desert. After hours baking in his armour, it was all he could do to endure this new type of damnation.

At length the inspection was over, the audience was duly impressed by another display of the military might of the Empire, and the Reiksguard broke up to make their way back to their chapter house in individual squadrons. The new knights were left until last; some of them were allowed to disperse to greet their families, but Delmar, as standard bearer, had to remain central, to act as their rallying point. He looked over at his own family again and saw the steward taking care of his grandfather. His mother, though, was not with them. Delmar scanned the milling crowd and caught a glimpse of her further along. She was talking with someone, and so Delmar shifted his position to be able to see her better. She was talking with none other than Griesmeyer. Delmar was surprised; he had never seen the two of them utter a word to each other in his company. What had they to talk about now?

The standard from another squadron fluttered through his line of vision as they marched away. When he could see them again Delmar realised that they were not simply talking, they were in the midst of an argument. He could not hear the words, but it was clear his mother was nearly shouting at the knight, she had one hand on her hip and with the other she was yanking a necklace around her own throat. Griesmeyer meanwhile had half-slipped back into a defensive guard, almost as though he expected to be physically attacked. Though Delmar had no idea what had happened, whether he was standard bearer or not, he could not stand apart. He made a move towards them. But then it was over, his mother stormed away leaving Griesmeyer behind.

DELMAR STOOD IN the arming room, fixed upon his thoughts. He had found his mother after the inspection; she had been too upset for him to ask what had happened between her and Griesmeyer. She had merely held him tight and implored him to return home from the campaign alive. Delmar had felt torn; the boy's heart within him was wrenched to see his mother in such a state and did not wish to leave her. Now, however, he discovered that his childhood heart was tempered by a man's spirit. For the first time the display of the emotion itself had made him feel awkward, he had wished to comfort her but found himself holding back, and was relieved when the steward had announced that they were returning to the estate immediately. His secret relief only exacerbated his feelings of guilt. How could he honour his oath to the order, knowing that in doing so he could never make any pledge as to his safety to those he loved, whose lives were rested upon his?

Worse were these new questions about his father and Griesmeyer. Delmar was not a man comfortable with secrets. Secrets, his mother had drilled him as a child, led only to lies, and lies led to damnation. In the countryside, especially as the lord's son, he lived his life in the plain sight of his neighbours, and what one of them saw or heard would inevitably make it back to his mother's ears, so there had been little purpose in trying to conceal anything. But now she was keeping secrets from him, as was Griesmeyer as well.

In the midst of his doubt and uncertainty, though, there was at least one accomplishment of which he could be proud: that he was a knight of the Reiksguard. The order's demands upon him were great, but at least they were plainly put. Even as the other pillars of his life shook, the order would stand firm.

As he brooded on such thoughts, the noise of his comrades' discussions around him began to intrude. None of them could stop talking about the events of the day; those with whom the Emperor had shared a few words repeated them endlessly to anyone who would listen, and everyone spoke of how they now had a far greater insight into the man because of the way he had looked into their eyes. As with all such events, though, there was always one speaker driven more by his personal concerns.

'Here's what I do not comprehend,' Hardenburg grumbled as he pulled his sabatons from his aching feet, 'why are we barracked so far from the palace? I swear I can see the heat shimmer from my foot. Look at this.' Hardenburg pushed his foot at Proktor who scowled and quickly retreated from the offending object. 'They should have built our chapter house right beside it. Then we would not have to trudge there and back for every occasion.'

'If you did not have to gawk at every pair of peaches on display then we could march all the faster,' Proktor snipped.

'Ah,' Hardenburg sighed, 'but how can I resist when in this heat they do swell so delightfully?'

'You're disgusting, Hardenburg.'

'For your opinions, brother, I do not give a fig.'

'I do not give a fig for what *you* think either,' Proktor retorted.

'Keep your fig then, I say. Though I should be heartily surprised if you ever find a lady to accept it.'

Some of the other knights laughed at that and Hardenburg bowed ostentatiously. Flustered, Proktor looked imploringly to Falkenhayn, but his friend was enjoying his embarrassment as well.

'Ya, he makes his point,' said Bohdan, stirring from the other side of the room. 'In case of sudden attack or riot, we should be close to the Emperor's side. In Ostermark, when the night closes in, a guard should be with his master. Out of sight...' Bohdan shook his head. 'One can never be sure what is out there.'

'Who can say?' Falkenhayn spoke up, resenting the Ostermarker's intrusion in their conversation. 'Most likely there was not space in the palace when the order was founded.'

'Perhaps then you do not recall the palace well, brother.' Bohdan's thick accent only added to the contempt in his voice. 'Your many absences from sentry duties must have blunted your recollection.'

Falkenhayn's anger rose at the impertinence, but Hardenburg was quicker.

'More likely the Emperor wanted distance from our stables,' he said, chortling at his own wit. He addressed Delmar, 'Brother Reinhardt will tell you what a noxious place they are, for he spends more time there than anywhere else.'

Delmar did not wish to be drawn into the conversation, but he would not shy from it. He stepped in between them to hang his breastplate upon the rack. 'It does not become you to be so discourteous, my brother,' he admonished Hardenburg lightly. Delmar turned to Bohdan: 'And your concern is proper, my friend, for the protection of the Emperor is our highest duty. What are we if we cannot protect him? But it is not so very far between here and there. We have sentries there to counter smaller threats and, in case of larger, they know to raise the alarm. The whole order then can ride, and any besieger who threatens our Emperor's life will quickly find himself surrounded. So for any such assault to succeed, the foe would have to stop up two locations instead of one, divide and weaken their forces. It is sound doctrine.'

The proud Ostermarker held Delmar's gaze for a few moments, then nodded his approval. That satisfied them all; even Hardenburg had no glib response. Falkenhayn allowed himself to be calmed, and in greater peace they set back to unfastening their armour.

'It is in case the Reiksguard ever turn on their Emperor,' Siebrecht spoke up from the corner. 'So that he will have at least some fortification between him and his guard.'

The room went deathly quiet. Falkenhayn drew breath to erupt, but Delmar stilled him with a gesture.

'Repeat what you said,' Delmar told Siebrecht.

Siebrecht looked up from his half-unfastened greave. He had said it as an off-hand comment. The thought had struck him and gone to his mouth without his mind intervening. He could take the words back easily, but then he saw the expression on Delmar's face: the intense seriousness in the broad, open features, the furrowing of his brow in disapproval. It was all Siebrecht could do not to laugh at how ridiculous he looked.

Instead he stood and readied himself. If this was to happen, then let it happen here.

'Brothers!' Verrakker shouted, appearing at the door. 'What are you all doing still half-armoured? You are all tardy. Wasting your day with talk, no doubt. I should rip your tongues out! Back to your task. In silence! Not another word from any of you. I can't cut your tongues, but I can cut your wine. Yes, Brother Matz, I thought that would catch your attention. Back to it!'

Verrakker glared at them all, his hand twitching as his drummed his non-existent fingers in impatience. The knights quickly bent themselves back to their armour, obedient Delmar amongst them. Siebrecht slowly breathed out, and relaxed his grip on the heavy metal arm-guard he was holding behind his back to knock Delmar senseless.

'DAEMON'S BREATH,' BOHDAN swore as they left, 'what ever possessed you to say such a thing?'

Siebrecht shrugged. 'But am I wrong though?' Siebrecht turned to the Nordlander striding beside them, 'Am I wrong, Gausser?'

'That is not important.'

'It's important to me!'

'Matz! Matz!' The knights heard the steps of someone running up behind them. It was Proktor. He halted in front of them.

'Siebrecht von Matz,' he started formally, 'my brother Delmar von Reinhardt requires an apology from you, for the offence you have caused the order.'

'Tell me, Proktor,' Siebrecht rounded on him, 'is this Reinhardt or is this your precious Falkenhayn speaking through him?'

Proktor looked stricken for a moment and then recovered. 'I do not know what you refer to, I come from Reinhardt as one of his seconds.'

'One of his seconds?' Siebrecht replied in disbelief. 'He wishes to duel over this?'

'No duels, no duels…' Alptraum said, mimicking the long-departed Weisshuber.

Proktor ignored the Averlander. 'He does not wish to, but he is prepared to do so if you refuse.'

'Siebrecht…' Gausser began.

'Damn his blinkered arrogance then!' Siebrecht spat. 'I will not apologise for Reinhardt's propensity for self-deception! As he is so eager to style himself the order's champion then he will have to prove his ability. Tell him I will meet him outside the western city gate.'

Proktor reeled slightly from Siebrecht's fierce response.

'At what time?'

'Now!' Siebrecht growled at him. Proktor hurried away. It was too much. It was all too much. Months of training with these insufferable Reiklanders, enduring their pomposity and righteous belief in their born right to lead. Then Krieglitz and the cold calculating stare of that knight Griesmeyer, with whom Delmar had been so sickeningly proud of having an association. Now this?

'Siebrecht…' Gausser began again, with a tone of warning.

'No, Gausser,' Siebrecht defied him. 'It is enough. You may be with me, or you may walk away, but do not try to stop me. You had your crack at Reinhardt and you couldn't keep him down. But I will have a sword in my hand. Let me see him defy that.'

DUELS BETWEEN BROTHERS of the order were forbidden; discipline was a cornerstone of the Reiksguard's effectiveness and discipline could not be maintained with brothers drawing their swords upon each other in anger. Instead, the order had developed a very formal process to resolve accusations. It was designed particularly to draw the heat from any disagreement and to emphasise the order's fraternity, to ensure that hundreds of proud noblemen, used to their own way, could live together in close quarters without killing each other. The weight and slow deliberation of this system, however, made it all the more attractive for hot-blooded young knights to settle their grievances quickly and physically. Though the order's jurisdiction extended to its knights wherever they were, such combats were always arranged outside the city walls to avoid interruptions and, should injuries result, they could be blamed upon a sudden attack by brigands or a beastkin warband.

'Matz has brought this all upon himself, brother,' Falkenhayn assured Delmar as the Reiklanders pushed their way through the streets, still crowded from the Emperor's inspection earlier in the day. 'From the very beginning he has treated the order with the utmost contempt. The drinking sessions, his rudeness to our masters, and remember Krieglitz and him? As thick as thieves, and look now what we know about *that* family.

'Who is he anyway? He's been a Reiksguard knight a few weeks, never stood in a battle line, and he thinks it's his place to spit on the order's name and drag it through the mud. He thinks it's his place to tell *us*, when our families have served faithfully for generations?' Falkenhayn shook his head in exasperation. 'It is more than a quarrel, brother, it is your duty to teach this wastrel some respect before it is too late.'

Siebrecht and Gausser were waiting for them outside the gate, and the group moved a distance away from the crush of wagons trying to enter or exit the city. Once they were far enough away, Delmar nodded at Proktor.

'Brother Reinhardt gives you one last chance to apologise for your offence,' Proktor announced.

Siebrecht, in reply, held his pinky finger on which he wore his signet ring up at Delmar.

'He knows what he can do,' he smirked. 'Tell Brother Reinhardt he has one last chance to apologise for his idiocy.'

Delmar had not wished to fight before, he had merely wanted Siebrecht to take back his words, but now nothing could divert him from this course. This was not Griesmeyer, this was not his father, this was simple. He was right and Siebrecht was wrong.

They strode away from the western gate in silence until they reached the tree-line and were concealed from the road. They found a suitable clearing and the two parties retired to either side to ready themselves. At one end, Falkenhayn continued to feed Delmar gleeful encouragement: 'He's quick, don't forget, brother. He'll feint most likely; do not allow him to draw your guard.

Keep pressing him back, get him close and you'll have him!'

Delmar heard him, but needed no words to inspire him. The sight of Siebrecht's face and his permanently self-satisfied expression were all the encouragement he required.

At the other end, Gausser was less supportive: 'This is truly what you wish, brother? For your family? For your name? For your life?'

'My life? My life is in no danger. It is Reinhardt's you should concern yourself with, for he can never best me with the blade.'

'That is not my meaning,' Gausser scowled.

As much as he could lie to Gausser, Siebrecht could not lie to himself. Though he felt his body energised for the upcoming fight, he could not deny that, underneath, he was exhausted. The drink from the night before, the lack of sleep, then to spend the whole day at attention, roasting in the sun. His mouth was dry, his hands were clammy; he drew his sword and held it out, and could see the blade shake in his grip. If he could not finish the fight in the first few strokes, then may the gods lend him strength, for he would have none left himself.

On the other side, Delmar drew his own sword and held it ready. He did not nervously practise a few swings, nor fearfully take up a guard before it was time. He was just ready. Watching him, Siebrecht's treacherous mind flicked back to that day before Master Ott, where Delmar had taken all that Gausser could dole out and still refused to give in; and then Siebrecht recalled the story of Delmar and his battle against the beastmen. Siebrecht had assumed that such stories were like those he told of himself, each one consisting of a grain of truth well fermented in bravado. But what if Delmar's stories had all been true? Gods, Siebrecht realised, just how far had he underestimated this Reiklander?

Proktor stepped into the middle of the clearing and asked one last time if Siebrecht would apologise. Siebrecht, focused upon Delmar, curtly shook his head. It didn't matter. It was too late now anyway.

'Then let it begin!' Proktor announced and stepped away.

Siebrecht never even saw the blow. The fist struck him in the side of his face with all the power of a cannon. His vision exploded and went black; he did not even feel himself hit the forest floor. His eyes fluttered open for a moment and he saw his attacker standing over him.

'Gausser?' he mouthed.

Gausser stepped away from him, stretching his fist. On the other side of the clearing Delmar watched, astonished, as the Nordlander then drew his sword and took up a ready stance.

'What trickery is this?' Falkenhayn cried beside him.

'No trickery,' Gausser replied. 'If a fighter cannot fight, then his second takes his place.'

Falkenhayn started to protest again, but Delmar cut him off.

'Step away, Gausser. My quarrel is not with you.'

'That cannot be done, Reinhardt.' The huge Nordlander did not move an inch.

'Our families are linked, Theodericsson. Not by blood, but by battle.'

'That I know.'

'Our fathers fought, side by side, comrades-in-arms against your foe. I ask you... on that bond... step back.'

Siebrecht clambered back to his feet. 'I will be considered no coward, who will not fight for himself. Where did my sword go? Give me that blade, Gausser. I do not need you to stand before me...'

Gausser smoothly turned around and punched him hard above the stomach. Siebrecht's eyes bulged out of their sockets and he slowly folded up into a ball on the ground, struggling for breath.

Delmar stared in disbelief. 'What are you doing? What has he done for you that you protect him so?'

Gausser slowly shook his head. 'You do not understand. Matz is my friend, yes. My brother. I would not see him hurt. But I do not do this for him. I do this for you, Reinhardt. I do this to honour your father, and to honour mine. You do not know it, what I can see. You do not know it, but you are the best of us. You are not the strongest; you are not the fastest; but you are the bravest. Before, you stood up against me for your friend, knowing you would most likely lose. You hold firm in your convictions against those who try to turn you from the true path of the knight. I have seen you with your family and you are the stone that they build themselves upon.'

'But this...' Gausser continued on, gesturing at the swords, at Siebrecht, and everything around them. 'This is not bravery. Your comrade here, your brother, is hurting. Not in his body, but in his mind, in his spirit. You can hurt him more if you wish; you can kill him, easily. But is that a brave act? Is that what a brave man does for his brother in need? I do this for you, Reinhardt. We will fight. You will vent your anger upon me, as you once allowed me to do upon you. We will fight until we drop. Then we will be friends again. And you will go forth from this place without the wound to your soul that you would inflict if you fought your poor brother here. And then, when you see in yourself what I see, you will still have the chance to become the knight you should be.'

No one spoke. No one had ever thought that Gausser could speak for so long, and with such power.

'Theodericsson Gausser,' Delmar finally began, his voice suddenly weak. 'You have shamed me. Your words have… No… I have shamed myself. I cannot fight you. And if you do not stand aside I cannot fight him either. And in this circumstance, I find my anger is now dissolved. All it leaves behind is the lesson you taught me here today.'

Delmar sheathed his sword. With his head bowed, he walked out from the woods. Falkenhayn met Gausser's steady gaze for a moment, then he ran after and Proktor after him.

'That cannot be it,' Falkenhayn exclaimed. 'The savage and the slanderer are standing there and you are just going to run away like a coward?' Falkenhayn took a hold on Delmar's shoulder to stop him.

Delmar halted. Falkenhayn, despite himself, edged away. Delmar looked deep into his eyes and said in final tones: 'Do not touch me again.'

With that he walked out from under the trees and back into the sun.

* * *

THE WILHELM GATE of the citadel opened, and once more the Grand Order of the Reiksguard processed through. There were crowds to see them go, but they were quiet, more respectful, for the knights were marching to campaign. Their route had been cleared for them and so they proceeded without interference through the city, past the Imperial Palace and down to the river. The supplies they would need had been loading aboard their boats since first light; they would travel even quicker than the knights could on land and so would be ready for them when they stopped at night.

As they crossed the bridge, Siebrecht, a welt of a bruise upon his cheek, deftly removed a gold crown from his belt and tossed it high out over the water. Gausser looked in askance at his bizarre behaviour.

'Settlement of a wager,' Siebrecht replied.

Gausser, who understood when words were needed and when words were not, decided not to inquire further. Instead, he checked his distance a fraction from the knight riding in front of him, and returned his attention to the magnificent sight of the Grand Order of the Reiksguard marching to war.

PART TWO

'On this day, I counted how long we have endured the grobi's siege, for I thought we may have reached one hundred days. I searched out our records, their runes freshly marked, but could find no date for its commencement. I spoke to the king, but he said that I should dig for the answer myself.

I stood at the guard post in the western tunnels, but the grobi launched no attack today. When my watch was done I returned to my endeavour. I found the date that Thorntoad first attacked our patrols. I found the date the last trading boat reached us unmolested. I found the date we retreated from the hold of Und Urbaz north of the pass, the date our settlers were recalled from the highland meadows, the date we closed our gates and tunnels against our foes outside. But none of these was called the start of the siege.

I went to the king before my next watch and retold what I had found. I asked him which of these dates he thought was when the siege had begun. He called his oldest counsellor forwards, who placed before him a stone engraved. It was a thousand years old, and it was a copy of records long before that. The king pointed at a single line thereon, the journal of a day when our ancient kingdom was still young. It said that on this day was the kingdom of Karak Angazhar laid siege by the tribes of the grobi.

To my father, to his counsellors, to our ancestors, that was the first day of the grobi's siege. And it will continue until the last drop of blood falls upon our stone, whether it be theirs or ours.'

– Extract from the personal ledger of
Ung Gramsson, son of Gramrik,
King of Karak Angazhar

CHAPTER EIGHT

DANSIG

The foot of the Black Mountains
The Nedrigfluss, border of Averland and
the dwarf kingdom of Karak Angazhar
Autumn 2522 IC

'GAUSSER! ALPTRAUM! BOHDAN! Come in!' Siebrecht shouted, standing barefoot in the shallows on the bank of the Nedrigfluss. His three brothers crouched sceptically on the bank.

'Isn't that glacier water?' Alptraum asked.

'It's invigorating,' Siebrecht replied. 'What's this? Three brother-knights of the Reiksguard afraid of a little water?'

Alptraum, warily, began to take off his boots. Gausser and Bohdan stood aloft.

'He is clearly lying,' Bohdan stated flatly.

'That is certain,' Gausser replied.

Siebrecht rolled his eyes. 'How Nordland and Ostermark must be proud of their native sons, less courageous than two soft southerners.'

Gausser shrugged and shook off his boots. Bohdan followed him. The three of them slid down the bank and splashed into the water together.

'It's freezing!' Alptraum cried, shooting straight back out again and scaling the bank. Siebrecht burst out into great peals of laughter as he fled.

'How can you stand it?' Alptraum asked, sitting on the bank, rubbing his feet warm again.

'Simple! My feet are already numb,' Siebrecht replied. He pulled one of them out of the water for Alptraum to inspect and there was a definite bluish tinge.

'And people say that Averlanders are mad,' Alptraum shot back.

Siebrecht laughed again and clumsily hauled himself out. These past three weeks had been better than he had ever hoped. They rode hard the whole day long, across the magnificent plains of Averland, and at night the boats came up the Reik with food and bedding for them all.

When they had left Altdorf, Siebrecht had been sunk in a misery from which his brothers did not think he would emerge. But his mood had risen with each step he took away. By the time they passed his home of Nuln he was restored completely, and he had regaled his brothers with tales of his adventures in the city's backstreets. As they drew closer to the Black Mountains, they began to break their journey at the towns along the way so that the inhabitants might admire them and join the militias which were marching behind.

Now they had arrived at the border and here the river boats landed armour, barding, rations for both men and horses, camp equipment, even a few field cannon brought from Nuln. Everything too heavy to bring quickly by road, the Reiksmarshal had brought speedily up the river. It was incredible. Siebrecht had served as a pistolier attached to the Wissenland militia before he joined the Reiksguard; in fact he still carried that same pistol, though as a knight he was not supposed to have it. He had seen the Wissenland militia on the march. Six hundred men, trudging ten, fifteen miles a day. Never enough shelter, never enough food. But the Reiksguard, they had gone twice as fast, sometimes more, and done it in comfort. Three weeks since leaving Altdorf at the centre of the Empire, the order was gathered on the southern border, ready to fight.

The feeling returned to Siebrecht's feet and he sat to pull his boots on. Only then did he realise that Gausser and Bohdan had not followed him out of the river. The two of them were still standing in the shallows; both of them had their arms folded as though perfectly willing to stand there until the Nedrigfluss dried up.

'That Nulner says this is cold,' Bohdan scoffed. 'He has never felt the chill of rivers that run from the Worlds Edge Mountains.'

'That is true,' Gausser replied, 'but one does not know cold until one has swum in the Sea of Claws.'

'Indeed,' Bohdan conceded, 'but the Sea of Claws is nothing compared to the frozen lakes of Kislev.'

Siebrecht shook his head and left the two of them to another of their self-imposed endurance trials. They had been competing against each other ever since Altdorf, and if the results of the past were repeated there would be no quick winner.

Beside Siebrecht, Alptraum started and pointed north. 'Another militia's coming in,' he said. 'How many men do you think?'

'Let's go and take a look at them.'

Siebrecht and Alptraum wandered away from the river, back through the makeshift Empire camp. As well as the order's knights and sergeants, there were nearly a thousand militiamen who had arrived already from towns such as Heideck, Grenzstadt, Loningbruck and Streisse ... This new militia, though, came from further afield.

'It's Averheim! It's Averheim!' Alptraum shouted and broke into a trot to greet them.

Siebrecht could not quite fathom it: Alptraum, who had been so withdrawn in Altdorf, had come into his own as soon as they crossed into Averland. In every town they stopped, he introduced himself to those he met. When the militias arrived in camp, he did the same, as though he could learn the name of every single militiaman who was to march with the army. He was doing it again now, right before Siebrecht's eyes, shaking the hands of each man in the militia, asking for all the latest news from Averheim and listening intently to what they said.

The only Averlander in the army that Alptraum had not approached was the commander of the militias, the Graf von Leitdorf. The graf had set his pavilion in the centre of the camp and Siebrecht had noticed that Alptraum would take a significant detour rather than walk past its entrance. The militia captains, who all reported to the graf, also kept a wary distance from Alptraum, as though any association with him might tar them in the eyes of their own commander.

Siebrecht knew the Leitdorf and Alptraum families were old rivals for the title of Elector Count of Averland. The title had been vacant for three years already and still none of the noble families had achieved ascendancy. Siebrecht was no stranger to the political struggles in Nuln and Wissenland, but they at least, after a few days' excitement, were resolved. These Averlanders seemed in no rush to resolve anything, including who should be their lord.

Siebrecht, though, had his own distraction. Amongst the yellow and black colours of the Averheim militia, he saw Herr von Matz dismounting from his horse and, as ever, Twoswords was with him.

Herr von Matz did not join the army alone. He brought a retinue with him. He said they were his travel guards, necessary protection on the dangerous roads. Siebrecht accepted the explanation, but did not believe it. He had seen many bodyguards on the streets of Nuln and they all looked alike: big, imposing men, who could deter casual ruffians with a glance. They dressed smartly, for no noble would retain a bodyguard who looked like a vagabond. But Herr von Matz's dishevelled rogues, to Siebrecht's eye, looked more likely to rob a noble of his coin than defend him. Some were short, some were slight, and all of them wore clothes that looked like they had been dredged up from a cesspit. There was at least one dwarf amongst their number, most likely born and raised in Nuln for he wore an ill-fitting black tunic which aped the human fashion.

Herr von Matz never introduced any of them by name. One of them carried a pair of blades strapped in a cross on his back so Siebrecht had named him Twos-words, and Twoswords never left Herr von Matz's side. He was a swarthy beast; he had a thick, black beard and a shaven head, so that from a distance his face appeared almost upside down. Even with his eye for detail, Siebrecht could not discern the man's origins; his features had everything from Estalia to Kislev about them, and Siebrecht had never heard him talk so there was no accent to decipher.

Herr von Matz waved at his nephew, but did not walk over. Instead, his uncle headed straight for the graf's pavilion. Siebrecht left Alptraum, who was still engaged with the militiamen, and headed back to the river. He had seen boats being prepared to ferry the first knights across the stretch of water where the Nedrigfluss flowed into the Reik, and he did not want to miss the landing on the western bank.

The boats had just pushed off when Siebrecht arrived. The knights onboard anticipated danger, but did not wish to wear full armour in case the boat cap-sized. Instead they carried large shields and wore only their breastplates. The boats were also heavily manned by sergeants carrying their crossbows. Siebrecht doubted whether they could shoot accurately from a moving river boat, but they looked fierce enough. Falkenhayn and the other Reiklanders stood close to Preceptor Jungingen. Their squadron had been assigned to Jungingen's banner for the campaign, and Falkenhayn missed no chance to attend upon the pre-ceptor. Delmar stood on his own. Siebrecht stood apart from the both of them, not wishing to be associated with either.

Delmar had annoyed Siebrecht. Not by anything he had said or done, rather by what he had not done. After the aborted duel, Falkenhayn had cut his ties to Delmar and told his two remaining Falcons to do the same. Siebrecht had hoped that Delmar would challenge him, that the Reiklanders would split between the two. Instead, Delmar had kept himself apart from his former friends, and the Reiklanders had fallen into line with Falkenhayn. Delmar was pushed away. And he had shown no interest in the Provincials. Instead, on the road from Altdorf, whatever cloud had lifted from Siebrecht had gathered over him.

Siebrecht preferred not to think on Delmar too much. He associated him, and his patron Griesmeyer, with too many ill memories. While Siebrecht was not proud of his own behaviour, he felt no desire to make amends. Instead, as Gausser, Bohdan and Alptraum arrived by his side, he turned his attention back to the boats on the river. Beyond them, the Black Mountains loomed, the closer hills covered with dense forest, the further peaks of grey stone with touches of snow. But it was not those for which the Black Mountains were so named; instead it was the dark clouds that were packed overhead. Some were formed in the shape of great anvils, others clumped and tumbled down like avalanches, a few rose as horrific beasts ready to swallow any who dared travel beneath them. The sunny pastures of Averland were behind them, and before them was no realm intended for man.

KURT HELBORG WATCHED the first boat land safely on the western bank of the Reik and disgorge the knights it carried, then the second, then the third. Satisfied, he left the crossing to Knight Commander Sternberg and returned to his tent where the war council was gathering.

Sigmar grant him strength, but he was tired of this. Tired of marching, tired of campaigns, tired of loss. The burden of his office of the Marshal of the Empire had never been so great as it had been this year. Ever since he had returned from Middenheim, he had begun to wonder what his life would be like without the mantle of Reiksmarshal upon him. What a normal day might be if he did not hold the fates of thousands of men in his hand.

Helborg reached the entrance to his tent. There stood Griesmeyer, awaiting his return and deep in thought. For all their years of friendship, Helborg had never been able to read his comrade the way he could so many others. Perhaps that was, perversely, why he valued his advice so highly.

'How is the council today?' Helborg asked.

Griesmeyer's face relaxed. 'They will be all the better for your intervention, Marshal.'

'And the graf?'

'Better than yesterday,' Griesmeyer replied. 'He has brought a new militia captain with him.'

Helborg's face darkened. Graf von Leitdorf had tried to bring two dozen of his staff and captains to the first council and Helborg had had to have undiplomatic words with him afterwards in order to trim his retinue down.

'You may approve of this one, though,' Griesmeyer said.

'Who is he?'

'He is of no title. His name's Ludwig Voll of the berg-jaegers. He has just arrived.'

Helborg's tone lifted at that. 'Does he bring men with him?'

'I do not know, Marshal.'

'Then let us find out.' Helborg quickly stroked his finger across his bushy moustache, pulled back the tent flap and led the way inside.

'Ah, Marshal Helborg…' Graf von Leitdorf declared, looking up from his cluster of staff.

Helborg waited a moment for Leitdorf to finish that sentence, to see if he would dare chide the Marshal of the Empire. Leitdorf thought better of it and stayed silent. Ever since Helborg had become Reiksmarshal, the Leitdorfs of Averland had been a constant source of difficulty. The last head of their family, Marius Leitdorf, the Elector Count of Averland, known popularly as 'the Mad', had been infamous for his erratic behaviour; his moods had been as fickle as an infant's, swinging from contentment to rage to embittered misanthropy in a heartbeat. Helborg could tolerate the existence of such individuals for the most part, so long as he was not obliged to interact with them in any way; but to have such a capricious mind in a position to raise and command armies was beyond his sufferance. It was with mixed feelings indeed that Helborg had heard of Marius's death, valiant as it had been.

Helborg had every expectation that this newly elevated scion of that family, Graf von Leitdorf, would be the same as his predecessor. For all the control that the graf displayed in his public appearance, Helborg could see in the hawkish face and those pinched eyes that same madness lurking within, waiting for its moment to emerge.

'Graf von Leitdorf,' Helborg said simply, 'my thanks for your attendance.'

Leitdorf contented himself with a simple incline of the head as acknowledgement. Helborg nodded at the officers of the order present, Sub-Marshal Zöllner and the senior preceptor, Osterna. He then looked pointedly at the one man he did not recognise.

'Would you introduce yourself, sir?'

Ludwig Voll was a small, rangy man. He wore furs and coarse cloth whilst every other at the council wore armour and silks. Helborg could see that he was somewhat cowed; he was little more than a peasant and he was in the company of lords and the great general of the Empire.

'My name is…' he began, stumbling a little over his words, 'that is, ah, I am Jaeger Ludwig Voll of the bergjaegers.'

'The bergjaegers have a great reputation, Jaeger Voll. I am pleased to see that you have responded to the Emperor's call. How many men have you brought to join us?'

'Well, there's just myself… I've none with me, your lordship,' Voll began. 'I thought it best to see how many you needed and then send for them, rather than…' The jaeger's voice trailed off as he felt the atmosphere in the tent chill. The Reiksmarshal was not impressed.

'How many can you summon?' Helborg asked.

Jaeger Voll, to his credit, did not collapse before the Reiksmarshal's fierce gaze as others had. 'Near two hundred, or thereabouts,' he replied quickly.

'Then summon them all. Have them join us by the end of tomorrow.'

'All of them?' Graf von Leitdorf interjected. 'Is that truly necessary? They are responsible for a great length of these mountains–'

'Yes.' Helborg cut him off. 'It is entirely necessary. We do not know the forces ranged against us, but they must be considerable or they would be no challenge to the dwarfs of Karak Angazhar.'

Helborg unrolled a map over the table in the centre of the tent and addressed the council.

'The cartographers of Altdorf would have us believe these mountains are part of the Empire's realm; they are nothing of the kind. Even before these goblins closed the river, Karak Angazhar has never welcomed visitors to these mountains. Even our traders have not been permitted beyond here.' Helborg pointed to a peak annotated as the Litzbach. 'And so, as you can see, our knowledge of the mountains and of the passes beyond is limited. We do not know where the goblins have their lairs, nor of any of Karak Angazhar's outposts. We must consider these lands as much enemy territory as others a thousand miles from our borders. And we must move quickly through them. The months for campaigns are done and Ulric's wintry breath will descend on us any day. This foe must be defeated before the first snows fall or, if not, we will have to rely on Karak Angazhar to save us!'

The soldiers in the tent duly registered their dismay at such a dishonour.

'We should be across the Nedrigfluss by the end of the day. Tomorrow, we march for the Litzbach. Sub-Marshal Zöllner will detail the marching order.'

'Marshal,' Leitdorf interrupted again, his voice quieter in an attempt to indicate a private aside, 'does this order include the militias?'

'Of course.' Helborg made no attempt to hush his own voice.

'I have not been consulted as to this…'

'You are being consulted now,' Helborg overrode him, watching for the madness to flicker. 'I have no doubt it will meet with your approval. Sub-marshal, continue.'

THE BOAT CREAKED ominously as Siebrecht stepped aboard. Even though the other bank was secure, he felt his heart begin to pound. He had laughed and splashed in the water before, but once they were in the middle of the river, that same water would be their death should they fall in. Even if they survived the cold, his own breastplate would drag him down. Just as Krieglitz's had.

Siebrecht fiddled with the breastplate's straps.

'Keep them loose, let it just hang off your shoulders,' Delmar said beside him. 'Then if you fall in, it will come off.'

Surprised that Delmar had addressed him directly, Siebrecht could only nod his thanks.

'We should be ready to die for the Reik, not drown in it,' Delmar continued, taking his seat.

'Gausser,' Siebrecht whispered to the Nordlander as he stepped aboard. 'Something's very wrong.'

'What?' Gausser replied, seeing the panic in his brother's face.

'I think...' Siebrecht began. 'I think Reinhardt just made a joke.'

ONCE THE COUNCIL was finally concluded, Helborg strode quickly from the tent and back to the river. There, the serious Commander Sternberg was quietly supervising the crossing.

'Which banner is that?' Helborg asked, looking out to the knights in the middle of the river.

'Squadrons from Jungingen's banner,' Sternberg replied, his eyes never leaving the boats on the water.

Helborg nodded and felt his ire lessen; the crossing at least was going to plan. He noticed that Griesmeyer had appeared beside him, politely waiting for his Reiksmarshal's attention.

'You were right, brother.'

'In what way, my lord?'

'The graf was better than yesterday.'

Griesmeyer smiled at that. Helborg, however, did not. The graf would be a problem. With the wars of the last few years these noblemen had grown increasingly full of themselves. The Emperor's own armies were not enough and so he had called upon his nobles ceaselessly for military aid. They knew how much they were needed.

At some point, Helborg would have to disabuse the graf of his notion that he was in joint command, simply because his militias were half the army. Helborg should tell him that a hundred Reiksguard knights were equal to a thousand of his unruly farmhands and cattlemen. But not here, not now. Not while the militias were still within an easy march of their homes, and the salted beef they were providing to feed his knights had not yet arrived.

'I did not think highly of this jaeger,' Helborg continued, recalling Griesmeyer's recommendation. 'I have enough amateurs to deal with in these militia captains, I do not need another. Has he left to fetch his men?'

'I believe he has.'

'There is that at least.'

'Before he left, my lord, he asked me to give you this.' Griesmeyer handed Helborg the map from the meeting and unrolled it. Helborg looked at it closely: there were a slew of corrections and new annotations upon it, marking smaller peaks, passes, elevations and, most importantly, the location of the dwarfen outpost of Und Urbaz and the goblin nests around it.

'He did not say where his knowledge came from,' Griesmeyer continued, 'but he did tell me that he wished his possession of such detail should not be made known to the dwarfs. I believe that, as well as being an Averland mountain guard, Jaeger Voll has also employed himself as an illicit prospector and poacher.'

'Well, he's *our* poacher now,' Helborg smiled, still poring over the map, readjusting his plans. 'Ensure he attends the next council, brother.'

Griesmeyer was about to reply when there was a sudden commotion from the bank. A flight of black shapes had flown from the trees on the far side. For an instant they could almost be mistaken for birds. They were arrows, and they flew straight for the knights crammed on the boats.

THE BOAT ROCKED and swayed as every knight instinctively rose to his feet.

'Shields!' someone cried, but it was far too late. The volley, aimed with time and care at the slow-moving craft, proved deadly accurate. The shafts struck, some hitting the wooden hull, some deflecting off their breastplates, and the rest piercing arms and hands, instinctively raised in protection. A chorus of pained yells rose above the boat.

'Sit down!' the boatmaster screamed as staggering knights made the craft list beyond his control. Delmar and Siebrecht obeyed, keeping their heads low behind the shields now being raised, but the knight beside them stayed standing. Delmar took a hold of the knight's breastplate to encourage him to sit, the boat swayed again and the knight leaned over the edge. Delmar glanced up at his face, and saw the frantic eyes and the hand gripping the arrow sticking out of his throat. The dying knight began to topple over the side and Delmar reached out to grab hold of him. Siebrecht saw Delmar jump up and rose himself to seize him.

'Down! Down! Down!' the boatmaster cried again as the shifting weight tipped the boat even further. Delmar felt someone pull at him and the breastplate slipped from his grip. The stricken knight splashed into the water. Delmar whipped his head back, ready to swear at whoever had held him back, when

Gausser gathered both him and Siebrecht and bore all three of them down to the deck. The boat listed hugely once more, and then the boatmaster regained control and brought it back onto an even keel.

HELBORG SAW THE face of the dead knight as another boat pulled the body from the river. It was Brother Dansig. Helborg did not know him well; he had only been in the order for a few seasons, but he had survived the war and the great charge at Middenheim only to fall here before the campaign even began.

The knights and sergeants on the other bank had reached the dense clump of trees from which the arrows had been shot, but they found nothing except a small tunnel in the earth down which the goblins had escaped. They sent back word that they were unable to follow.

Before them the forest was quiet again, and the peaks beyond remained unmoved. Beneath this veneer of peace, however, Helborg knew a bloody war was being fought.

DEEP BENEATH A mountain, the dwarf grappled for his axe. The leering goblin held tight with one claw, whilst with the other it scratched the dwarf's plated face-mask. It hooked its nails into the mask's eye sockets and, with a screech, broke it from the helmet. It was a screech that swiftly turned into a scream as the dwarf wrested the axe away and brought it down in a final stroke.

Free for a moment, the dwarf fumbled around for his mask. It was an heirloom, it had been passed down from his grandfather, he could not lose it. But then he heard the hiss of more grobi coming down the tunnel towards him. His good sense returned and he left the armour wherever it had fallen. His grandfather would understand.

He hastened away from the grobi, not sure which way to turn. He knew that his comrades were dead. Those of his band who had not been killed outright in the grobi assault would not survive long in their hands. It would be the same for any greenskin captured by his own kind. There was no concept of mercy or surrender; the grobi were vermin, to be hunted and destroyed, though that knowledge gave him little comfort when the vermin were hunting him.

The dwarf also knew that he was trapped. The grobi had been too quick. He had seen the iron hatch close, he had heard the bars drawn across so as to prevent the attackers penetrating any deeper into the hold, even though it meant consigning him and his comrades to their fate. It was a hard choice, but then these were hard times. All his life had been hard times.

This tunnel led him away from the sounds of the grobi, but it led him away from the hold as well. The dwarf knew these tunnels, had walked them often in the years before the siege began. There was no chance to double back; he had to go on. The further he went from the hold, though, the deeper he went into the grobi's territory. The dwarf knew then that he would not be returning home.

But then a tunnel branched away to the side, and through it he heard the sound of distant thunder. He remembered where it led. It would not be pleasant, but it was the only chance remaining to him. He hurried towards the thunder as quickly as he could and, as it became deafening, he emerged out into the cavern.

It was a waterfall, part of the river that flowed from these mountains and down into the Empire of man. It would take him from the grobi, it would take him to the surface. There was danger as well, but it would be day. The grobi of the mountains were dark creatures and abhorred the light. The sounds of pursuers behind settled the dwarf's choice. He was at least young, for everyone knew that old dwarfs did not float. With the greatest reluctance, he lay down his axe, his helmet and his armour, everything about his person that might drag him down. With that, and an oath to his ancestors, he jumped forwards and dived into the water.

THE DWARF AWOKE on the hard bank, pummelled and tenderised by the raging river, but alive. It had worked. He felt the rock beneath his hands; he felt the sun on the back of his head. With an effort he managed to raise himself to his knees and look about. He had washed up in the pass of Bar Kadrin. On each side, all about him, the giant stone heads of his ancestors looked down upon him. If he had been here a year ago, he would have been safe. But how the seams had shifted in that year. The sculptures were now defaced and he was far from home.

A shadow fell across his body. This was no goblin. He looked up, and up, at the monster that stood over him. It was not alone either, for behind it the grobi hunters stood with their nets waiting for the monster to finish with their prize. It sniggered and then brought a meaty fist down upon his head.

Barely conscious, the dwarf felt himself being dragged away in a goblin's net and all he could hear was the same name being chanted over and over again in glee.

'Thorntoad! Thorntoad! Thorntoad!'

CHAPTER NINE

THORNTOAD

THE OGRE KNOWN as Burakk the Craw watched as the mouth of the great stone goblin filled with its lesser, green kin. There were emissaries from each of the ten tribes of the mountains hereabouts; Burakk could see the emblems of the Black Ears, the Stinkhorns, the Splinters, the Biters and all the rest, being waved about the dark-cloaked throng. They were restless, for they did not like being out from under the earth. Even here, at night and on the side of a mountain scooped out so deep that it was never touched by the sun, they felt exposed to the endless sky. But this place was sacred to them, and they had been called here for a reason. They were here to listen to their leader speak.

On a ledge above them, the banners of Thorntoad's tribe, the Death Caps, rose. A hiss of anticipation went through the crowd. He was coming. Thorntoad was coming. Burakk stirred slightly; only two years ago, their reaction would have been very different. The Death Caps had been pariahs, perennial victims of the tribes that had encroached upon their territory on every side, pushing them to the fringes. The name of Thorntoad was unknown outside of one squig herder who kept him as a freakish pet. A year since, after one defeat too many, the Death Caps had turned upon their chieftain. In the chaos that followed, each goblin that attempted to declare himself chief had been quickly deposed, and then disposed of, by another. The other tribes readied themselves to move in, sensing the Death Caps' weakness, waiting for them to exhaust themselves fighting each other. It had been then that Thorntoad the freak had broken free from his cage and, in a night of savagery unparalleled even amongst greenskins, he had seized control. When the other tribes next awoke, it was to a newly united Death Caps. Some of the tribes attacked nevertheless, and the goblins they lost became much-needed food for Thorntoad's hungry fiends. From that day on, Thorntoad's name was known, not as the freak, but as the warlord.

'Thorntoad! Thorntoad! Thorntoad!' the thousand-strong crowd chanted, fever rising. The Great Maw was fickle, Burakk decided, the next bite was never like the last.

Then, with an explosion of excitement, Thorntoad of the Ten Tribes emerged. The goblin warlord was the most wretched specimen of flesh Burakk had ever seen. His body was deformed like a blasted sapling, his legs were thin and crooked, but his arms were powerful. He climbed up the rock with the motion of a spider. He was naked, save for a rag, for the name of Thorntoad was no colourful moniker: there were spines arrayed across the goblin's skin. His thorns, he called them, and they could not bear to be covered with the dark robes the other goblins wore. He vaulted to the top and stood there, bent over, supported as much by his hands as by his withered legs, hideous and triumphant. In this place, he was more than their warlord, he was their totem, he was their connection to their gods.

'Now, my fiends,' Thorntoad began, his screeching, reedy voice music to his goblins' ears, 'now have our starving days turned to nights of glee and gold. Now do we roam free throughout these hills while our foes cower and hide beneath the ground.'

The cloaked goblins howled with delight, shaking helms and weapons captured in battle.

'Now it is our bellies that are full and theirs which are not; our hunger spasms turned to victory dances. Now it is our claws stretched round their throats, and with each moon that rises, our grip grows tighter. Now they are desperate; now they wish they had fled.'

The horde shook their standards and drummed their spearshafts in elation.

'While we dig them out, they dig their graves. While they eat rocks, we eat their bones. Each moon brings us closer, my fiends, each one to the feast we have ahead. But for now, my gift to you all… the trophies we have won!'

At Thorntoad's signal, the Death Caps behind him stepped forwards to the ledge, dragging bundles behind, wrapped up in cloth. They threw them off the cliff, over the crowds below. As the bundles dropped they unravelled, the black cloth streaming behind, one end fastened to the ledge above. Then the cloth ran out and caught its fall. The contents of each bundle was revealed, the bloodied body of a dwarfen warrior, and they hung above the baying crowd like bait upon a fishing pole. Thorntoad revelled in the exultation for a moment more then reached for each body in turn, cut it down and launched it to be swallowed by the ravening horde.

Burakk the Craw grunted and left the greenskins to their petty feeding. Though he began to hunger himself, he knew that Thorntoad would not have dared to forget his cut. Whatever pageantry the freak performed for the benefit of his tribes, the choicest food went to Burakk and his ogres. After all, he would not be known as Thorntoad of the Ten Tribes if it had not been for Burakk. He would not be known at all.

Burakk reached the edge of the mouth of the great stone goblin, the side of a mountain that, the tribes swore, resembled a giant greenskin face shaped there by their gods. Thorntoad was still lauding himself over the sea of black and green. Yes, much had changed in two years. Two years ago, Burakk had been a shadow of his present self. Dazed, without food so long that his gut had shrunk, he had been wandering these mountains without direction when Thorntoad's Death Caps had found him. Near out of his wits, he had lumbered at them on instinct, caught one of the slower ones, but the others had entangled him with nets and kept him at a distance with their spears. Burakk had thought that was his end and he was ready to consign himself to the Great Maw. But the goblins had not eaten him, as he had assumed they would, as he would have done them. Instead, they kept him caged, started feeding him, and once the hunger-dullness had receded, Thorntoad had come to talk.

It had not been easy. It had taken a week for them to start to communicate at the basest level. Burakk, though, was in a cage and had nothing else to do, and Thorntoad concentrated all his time there. Thorntoad wanted the ogre to fight for him, and would feed him in return. He was not the first ogre to have stumbled into this area of the mountains; individuals and small groups had been spotted for months. All of them stunned, confused, many pitted with gunshot or with bones broken by cannonball. They were survivors of some crushing defeat of an ogre tyrant, somewhere in the Empire, and had been chased into the mountains by the victors. When the ogres, maddened with hunger, saw goblins, they attacked; and so the goblins had killed any who appeared. As strong as an ogre was, it could not match a hundred goblins swarming over it. Thorntoad saw in Burakk an opportunity, not simply to add a single ogre to his tribe, but dozens. All Burakk had to do, when they found another ogre, was to convince him to join their cause, by whatever means Burakk could. Burakk readily agreed and their alliance had been struck.

From that day, Thorntoad began to move against the other tribes. Whilst an ogre did not readily fit into all goblin tunnels, he could cause enough destruction on the surface for Thorntoad's Death Caps to triumph beneath the ground. Burakk himself earned his epithet of 'the Craw' after swallowing one Black Ear chieftain whole. Burakk added more ogres to the tribe as well, though not every one they encountered was willing to submit to his authority. Those that did not provided sustenance for the rest. Now, Burakk the Craw was a tyrant himself, with sixty bull-ogres at his command, who each bore a Craw marking upon his cheek. Whatever each bull's origins, they were now a tribe of their own, and Thorntoad paid them in food for lending him their might. First in goblins from the tribes they overwhelmed, and when Burakk had come to find their gristly frames sickening, with dwarfs. Yes, Burakk believed, they would have a grand supper of dwarf-flesh this night.

'THIS IS ALL?' Burakk rumbled, eyeing the paltry few bundled bodies at his feet.

Thorntoad sat on his haunches above his throne-room. The throne had been carved for the chieftain of the Stinkhorn tribe, the former occupiers of the great stone goblin. Once the Death Caps had achieved dominance, however, Thorntoad had made this mountain his lair and kept this throne, though it did not suit him. Those same spines upon his body with which he had impaled the old Stinkhorn chieftain prevented him from finding any comfort on his seat. All he could do was perch upon the top of the throne back, shifting constantly, for even with his spines lowered he was never able to find a position in which he could rest.

Instead, he had stretched ropes across the ceiling and buried metal rings in the walls, so that they formed a web through which Thorntoad's wasted legs were no hindrance. It was amongst these that he lurked, looking down upon his ogre ally.

'That is all,' Thorntoad spoke. 'Yes, Burakk Craw, that is all.'

'What of this one?' Burakk stomped over to a dwarfen warrior tied securely to the wall. Thorntoad scurried from his position, sliding across the surface of his web, and landed directly above Burakk's head.

'It is mine.'

The dwarf's chest sagged a little, blood bubbles forming at its lips as it breathed out.

'It is not dead,' Burakk observed.

'What I do with what is mine, is mine to say alone,' Thorntoad warned, and the ogre stiffly turned away from the prisoner.

'My bulls hunger, they need more than this,' Burakk replied, kicking the bundles in the centre of the room.

'They need? They need? But what do they deserve, Burakk Craw? These were taken by my fiends, not your bulls. Your bulls were not even there. I cannot give the choicest cuts to those who did not fight.'

'We cannot fight in your warrens, goblin. But they hide down there because of my bulls. We stopped them walking the surface. We stopped their caravans travelling down the river. That was our doing.'

'And for which you took your reward and ate most of what was taken, while my fiends scraped their dinners off rocks. Now they have won and taken spoils; they too must be rewarded.'

Thorntoad's logic meant nothing to Burakk. An ogre tyrant commanded the loyalty of his bulls only so long as he ensured their hunger was sated. Thorntoad's goblins could survive on nothing but the fungi that grew in their tunnels; Burakk's ogres needed meat.

'We ate better when the fight was hard than we do when the fight is almost won,' he grumbled.

'Ah, Burakk Craw,' Thorntoad hissed as he climbed the ropes back to the top once more, 'the fight is not done yet.'

An object fell from the darkness around Thorntoad's voice and bounced with a clang. Burakk picked it up. It was a helmet, but this one did not have a finely wrought face-mask as was typical of dwarfen warriors; this one was plain, crudely made by comparison.

'It is from the warriors of the tribes of men. Have you heard of them, Burakk Craw?'

The ogre murmured assent. He remembered these men: the way their flimsy bodies broke, the way their swords and spears bounced off his skin; but he also remembered their guns, their cannon which roared like giants, their iron shot that smashed through gutplates and took an ogre's life from a hundred paces away.

'An army of their warriors has crossed into our mountains, marching to the dwarfs' aid. They are well fed, and they have plump animals with them too. So have patience, ogre, your next feast marches towards you.

'And in the meanwhile, the Snaggle Tooths did not attend this night; you may take your bulls and eat your fill of them.'

Burakk grunted again, then took up the bundles and dragged them away. Thorntoad watched until he had left, and then slithered down his ropes and rings to his prisoner. He pulled on a chain nearby and a goblin was dragged from a hole, the chain connected to a collar around his neck. Thorntoad could not bear to have squig-beasts in his presence; they reminded him too much of his own years of degradation, and in return they detested him, smelling his freakishness upon him. Instead, Thorntoad kept other goblins as his pets, as he had once been kept. This one had been a shaman, and had thought to call down Gork and Mork's judgement upon Thorntoad. Instead the gods had proved who they truly favoured. Thorntoad yanked the shaman's chain again and drew him over to the bound dwarf.

'Wake it up,' Thorntoad ordered.

The miserable shaman took a small pouch of spores and blew them in the dwarf's face. The warrior stirred, mouthing words in the dwarfs' secret tongue. The dwarfs protected their language closer than they protected their gold; they thought if they did so, they could conceal their secrets from their foes. That they could, if the only place their foes looked for knowledge was in their books. Thorntoad preferred to look for knowledge in people; it was far quicker, provided you could hurt them enough. And here the dwarfen language was no protection, for in their greed for wealth and trade, the dwarfs had learned another language, one which had no secrets, one which even a goblin could learn: the language of men.

'What... you... name?' Thorntoad asked the dwarf in broken Reikspiel.

The dwarf gave no reaction, and muttered another few words of his native gibberish. Thorntoad slipped a razor from the rock and held it close beside the dwarf's ear.

'I… cut off… you… beard,' Thorntoad sneered. The dwarf's eye suddenly widened, and Thorntoad grinned in delight. The convenient tribes of men had solved another problem of his. He and the dwarf could understand each other; and that was all that Thorntoad needed. That, and time.

DELMAR SAT AT the base of a tree, the rain drumming on his helmet. The drops poured down the grooves in the metal in tiny rivers, and each time he turned his head a fresh gush of water cascaded off like a waterfall. He clutched his cloak tightly to him, though that had long since grown sodden. Ahead of him, a group of knights and bergjaegers were stepping carefully into a dry cavern, looking for any sign of goblin presence. Every cave, every crevasse, had to be checked in case of ambush.

It had been four days since they crossed the Nedrigfluss, and it had been two days since the rain began. It fell in heavy, packed downpours such as Delmar had never before encountered. The army's progress had stalled. The higher paths had been washed away in muddy slime and the lower submerged beneath the swelling Reik. On the first day they had tried to carry on and made a little progress, but by the second it was fruitless; it took no more than a few dozen horses upon a fresh track to turn it into a morass.

Around Delmar, the other knights of Jungingen's banner did what they could to keep both themselves and their equipment dry. Some sat under trees like Delmar, some even under their horses; they had stored their bright plumes, and their scarlet cloaks were so waterlogged that they were nearly black. It was a picture of misery, and Delmar felt the most miserable of all.

This campaign was not as he had hoped his first would be. He had not even seen the enemy. The goblins knew they stood little chance against the knights at close quarters and so they gave ground, harassing them from a distance. The only proof Delmar even had of their existence had been the occasional shower of black arrows from the depths of the woods and the tops of cliffs. They caused little harm to the knights in their thick armour, but each time the column was attacked, it came to a halt while the site of the attack was investigated and secured.

Delmar's investigations concerning Griesmeyer and his father were equally unsuccessful. He had spoken to every knight in his banner, but none had been with the order twenty years before. Preceptor Jungingen himself had only served for ten. He was ambitious as well, and was determined to reach one of the senior offices within the order, and so only had praise for the influential Griesmeyer.

Though Delmar was surrounded now by nearly a thousand men whom he called brother, there was not one of them whom he trusted enough to confide in. For all the talk of brotherhood during their training, of the connection that ran through each knight of the Reiksguard, here he was on campaign and he felt nothing. The older knights of the banner had drawn close during the war in the north, but he had not been a part of that. Amongst the knights of his vigil, Siebrecht,

Gausser, Falkenhayn and the rest, those brothers to whom he should be closest, there was still that division.

Delmar had thought, had hoped, that the rivalry between the Reiklanders and the Provincials would have fallen away on campaign, that they would be united in the face of the common foe, but it had not happened. The distance between the two factions was still there, and Delmar no longer fit with either. He could not stand Falkenhayn's superiority and posturing, and yet there was no place for him amongst the Provincials.

For all of Gausser's words the day of the aborted duel, he and Siebrecht had never been out of each other's company, and yet Delmar could not make his peace with the knight from Nuln. Gausser had shamed Delmar into withdrawing his challenge, but Siebrecht had never withdrawn his own injurious comments. His mind may have been sick with grief at the time, but it was no longer. He therefore either meant what he had said, in which case he denigrated everything that Delmar believed in, or he did not and it was sheer pride and arrogance that prevented him apologising. If that was the case then he was just as bad as Falkenhayn, and Delmar wanted nothing to do with either of them.

A bergjaeger emerged from the cavern and declared it clear. Delmar and the knights around him wearily clambered back to their feet, brushing off the mud as best they could, and led their horses inside.

SOME WAY AHEAD, Kurt Helborg led his own horse into the shelter beneath a ledge. Ahead of him a crew of a light cannon had blocked the path, struggling to lever their burden upwards. It was too wet to bring out the map, but Helborg did not need it in any case. This territory was burnt into his brain and he saw the pattern of mountains and rivers every time he closed his eyes. For all the care and attention to detail that had gone into its creation, though, the map did not tell him what he most desperately needed to know. Where, in Sigmar's name, was his enemy?

Councillors of state like Count von Walfen and the Baron von Stirgau thought they knew what war was because they read dispatches and watched it happen from a distance. Helborg had heard of a game that was becoming increasingly popular amongst the noblemen of Altdorf and the palace courtiers. They used models as fighting men, and they played on a board to represent a battlefield, standing over it as gods. They thought it taught them strategy, generalship, the qualities of a Reiksmarshal. Helborg had had Preceptor Trier sit down with him for an hour and teach him the basics of the game; Helborg had then vowed never to play it again. It was a toy, an exercise in fantasy. Nothing more. Had the players been blindfolded, kept in separate rooms, only been told once an hour of the positions of their forces and been required to feed their models each day or have them disappear, then, perhaps, they might acquire the merest inkling of command.

The army had progressed nearly five miles up the western bank of the Reik, passing the lower peak of the Litzbach and crossing another smaller tributary, known as the Sonnfluss. The vanguard of the army had reached the next tributary along, the Unkenfluss, and there it had paused; for on the other side of the Unkenfluss was Und Urbaz.

UND URBAZ WAS little more than an outpost, a walled watchtower and storerooms for trade. But nothing constructed by the dwarfs was ever less than sturdy and as a race they could not help but build with a touch of grandeur. Und Urbaz was as strong as any Empire fort, and its walls and towers were sculpted with the faces of dwarfen warriors and the anvil and fire totems of Karak Angazhar.

The dwarfs, though, were nowhere to be seen. The grey walls were blackened with smoke, and the lower sculptures had been attacked and chiselled away. Whether the place had been captured or whether the dwarfs had left of their own accord, Helborg could not discern. Goblins had certainly been there since, and if they hid there still then they could wreak havoc upon the army as it tried to cross the Unkenfluss.

Jaegar Voll assured Helborg that the Unkenfluss could be forded an hour or so to the west and, for once, Helborg had relented in his pursuit of speed. He sent Sub-Marshal Zöllner and Wallenrode's banner up the tributary. They were to cross where they could, then take Und Urbaz from the flank. And if they failed, Helborg had deployed the cannon ready to pound Und Urbaz to dust.

Zöllner's knights were harassed by goblin archers from the heights every step of the way, but their casualties were light, their armour protecting them from the goblins' barbs. It took them half a day, though, to reach the ford in the Unkenfluss and then circle back.

As the rain began again, Helborg watched Zöllner's assault from across the river. As he expected, Zöllner orchestrated an expert assault with his knights both mounted and on foot. They quickly surmounted the undefended walls and disappeared inside. All a general's skill, though, could not protect his men from the unknown, and Helborg waited impatiently for them to re-emerge. Half an hour passed, and Helborg watched Zöllner himself head into the outpost. Whether it meant that they had encountered the enemy or not, Helborg did not know. He did not, though, try to call over or send one of his guard to check. He had trained Zöllner, he had trained all his preceptors personally. They trusted his orders, and he trusted them to carry them out.

After an hour, Zöllner's knights re-emerged. There had been no goblins. The chambers under Und Urbaz had been cut deep and had taken time to explore. But Helborg's hope that Und Urbaz might hold some means of communicating with the dwarfs was in vain. The tunnels which stretched further into the mountains had been collapsed, deliberately.

With Zöllner's knights standing watch, the rest of the army crossed behind them. The soldiers hoping to spend a few dry days inside the outpost were to be disappointed, however. The storerooms were full to their low ceilings with the charred remains of barrels and crates, and the stench the goblins had left behind was unbearable.

Even the watchtower was no use, for its insides had been gutted and it floors broken apart. And so it was left there, unclaimed by either side, looming over the army as the rain poured down.

Und Urbaz was the gate to Karak Angazhar, keeping all the unwelcome, men included, from trespassing too deep into the dwarfen kingdom. For beyond Und Urbaz lay the great mountain bastion known as the Stadelhorn, which dipped at only one place for the route of the Reik. Voll said the dwarfs called it Bar Kadrin, but the bergjaegers called it the Dragon's Jaw.

It was there, Helborg predicted, that the goblins would attack. And it was there, he knew, that they might be destroyed.

THE DRAGON'S JAW, just as Und Urbaz, bore the marks of its previous owners. The dwarfs, in more prosperous times, had carved giant faces of their ancestors into the rocky outcrops on each side, in the hope that they would watch over the river below them and the dwarfs' enterprise. When the greenskins had taken control, they too had put their own touch upon the landscape and smashed the faces into grotesque parodies more akin to their own features.

The Jaw cut through the Stadelhorn bastion, leaving the heights to the west and the peak known as the Predigtstuhl to the east. It sides were steep and what little level ground there was at the base of the pass was filled with the raging Reik. Helborg's army would be horribly exposed as it marched through, for only three or four men could walk abreast on either bank. For all that the goblins may have abandoned Und Urbaz, they would not, they could not, leave them to travel through the pass unopposed.

Helborg sheltered against the thundering rain in the lee of the watchtower and looked out into the Jaw. He could not simply entrust his fate to Sigmar and advance blindly into that. In the first two days since they entered the mountains, he had sent out scouting parties spread on either side of the army's line of advance to look for the enemy. They had found them. None of his scouts had managed to travel more than a mile from the main body before being attacked and driven back. If they could not venture even that far without the protection of armoured knights, there was no chance that a single rider might slip past and make it all the way to Karak Angazhar. The dwarfs, Helborg assumed, must be in similar straits for if they had sent a messenger, by boat or foot, then it had not reached him.

It had been Jaeger Voll who found the solution, and on the third day he had left the army to make the arrangements. He had only just returned.

'Did you get them?' Helborg asked the smaller man.

'Aye, my lord. They're outside.'

'Good,' Helborg said. 'Where would be best for them?'

'Normally,' the bergjaeger said, 'we would use them from the Litzbach, from there they could reach Und Urbaz. But now the dwarfs are no longer here, the Litzbach will be no good.'

'Then where?'

The bergjaeger brought out his own small map, painted with black oil on calfskin and quite waterproof. 'The only place then is here.' A dirty finger pointed at a spot. Helborg peered down. The bergjaeger's finger was pointed at the Predigtstuhl.

'That mountain, jaeger, is huge, and the western face is infested with goblins. I have had more and more reports of sightings every hour.'

'Aye,' the bergjaeger muttered patiently, 'but we will not need to be at the peak. On the eastern face, there is a ridge. If we go around the Predigtstuhl and up onto that ridge, then we will reach Karak Angazhar itself.'

'Brother Sternberg?' Helborg called for the knight further down the wall.

'Yes, Marshal?'

'Who is there left to cross the Unkenfluss?'

'The sergeants' rearguard, Marshal, and Preceptor Jungingen and his banner.'

'Very well. We will divert Jungingen and his knights to the eastern bank of the Reik. You can meet them there, Jaeger Voll.'

'Aye,' the bergjaeger replied, but did not move. Above them, the rain continued to fall.

Helborg considered the man for a moment. He was often dubious about these kinds of local irregular troops: their loyalties were divided between the Empire and their home; they were unused to direct command and often proved stubbornly independent. They had no understanding of the brutal choices that war put upon commanders and their men. This wiry bergjaeger with his pointed face had proved himself motivated and ingenious, but his obedience had yet to be tested.

'I will have a message sent to Preceptor Jungingen to expect you and your men. You leave at once.'

'Aye, my lord. We will set out as soon as the storm breaks.'

Here was the moment, Helborg knew, where the true extent of the bergjaeger's loyalty would emerge.

'No, Jaeger Voll. At once. You must be in position to act as soon as the rain clears; we cannot wait and hope that it holds off long enough for you to circumvent the Predigtstuhl as well.'

The bergjaeger paused and sucked air through his teeth in thought. He knew, far better even than the great Reiksmarshal, the danger in that order, in climbing even part way up the Predigtstuhl in such weather, not knowing what forces might oppose them. But then, the Reiksmarshal knew that he knew better, and yet still it had to be done.

'Aye, Marshal,' Voll said slowly. 'At once.'

Helborg dismissed the bergjaeger with a nod. This mountain hunter was indeed proving to be quite exceptional.

As HIS BOAT approached, Siebrecht sat and eyed the eastern bank of the Reik warily. The water had risen to the forest's edge and the trees cloaked the ground in shadow. He could not help but be reminded of their crossing of the Nedrigfluss and of the arrows that had shot from the darkness to kill them. The leading elements of Jungingen's banner had already landed and cleared the bank, but still Siebrecht could not quiet his trepidation. Gausser and Bohdan behind him were speaking of their new companions, Jaeger Voll and his men. Five of them had caught the knights' attention, for instead of carrying a bow they each had a long pipe, twice the height of a man and curved and splayed at the bottom end, strapped in a harness on their backs. The tubes were wrapped up tight against the rain.

Siebrecht turned to his brothers. 'Standard bearers, do you think?'

'Amidst the woods?' Gausser shook his head.

'They look like winged lancers, down on their luck,' Bohdan remarked dryly.

Ahead of them, Delmar turned about in his seat. 'I have seen longrifles that length in the hands of hunters in Hochland.'

'Perhaps,' Siebrecht carefully replied. He felt the eyes of the other young knights upon them, watching what would happen between the two, and suddenly could not think of anything else to say.

No one else had any other suggestions to make and so Delmar turned back around.

'Ready for landing,' the boatman announced, and the knights took hold of the side of the boat with one hand and the hilt of their swords with the other.

THE KNIGHTS LEFT their boat as soon as it hit the bank, and made for the cover of the trees. They had left their horses behind; they carried all they needed. The sergeants took the boats back across the river so as to leave no trace of them for a goblin scout to see.

Led by the bergjaegers, the knights cut directly away from the bank, straight into the forest. They kept to the low ground, where the tree canopy was thickest, and skirted around the lower slopes of the Predigtstuhl. The rain over the previous few days had made the forest floor treacherous; dips in the ground that had filled with water slowed their progress, but threatened no more than the dignity of any knight who slipped into them. Siebrecht was thankful that they were not fully armoured. The knights wore only partial plate, as with such a trek before them, the weight was not worth the protection. As ever, the bergjaegers led the way, searching out the driest paths, but the five pipebearers stayed in the middle of the column. The orders were that these men were there to be protected.

Siebrecht, never at home in woodland, quickly lost his bearings. There was nothing to see but the trees ahead, which looked remarkably similar to the trees behind. The grey light that filtered through the clouds and the leaves did little to help him distinguish between them. All the knights stuck close together, hemmed in by the forest on either side. At some arbitrary moment, about an hour or so into their trek, Jaeger Voll called them to a halt, then led them off again sharply to the right.

'I am glad someone has a clue where we are going,' Siebrecht muttered under his breath.

'We're to the north-east of the Predigtstuhl, we're about to climb the eastern face,' Delmar supplied.

Siebrecht had not meant his idle thought to be overheard, and felt a touch of resentment at

Delmar's presumption. 'You sound pretty certain of yourself, Reinhardt.'

Delmar shrugged. 'I am.'

Sure enough, not ten minutes passed before the ground started to rise, the mud giving way to stone. The canopy began to thin and, in a gap, the knights saw the eastern side of the peak of the Predigtstuhl. Siebrecht forwent comment.

The forest of the lower slopes had been dark and gloomy, but as they climbed, the woods took on an added air of malevolence. The trees were thinner, their bark as black as cannon metal. Their lower branches had been hacked away; a few even had crude glyphs daubed upon them, though they were old and faded. Marks of their goblin owners, Siebrecht guessed, and realised for the first time how deep into enemy territory the knights had come. No one unsheathed a weapon, though, as they needed both of their hands free for the difficult path ahead. They had left the mud behind, but now the knights had to clamber up rocks, slick with the rain. The bergjaegers took turns standing watch over each obstacle, ensuring every knight made it safely up. Jaeger Voll somehow managed to be everywhere at once, climbing up and down the side of the path with the ease of one born to it.

The sound of the rain was soon drowned by the ragged breathing of the knights. Gausser, to Siebrecht's surprise, was the first of the squadron to start to lag behind. Siebrecht dropped back to help him, but the Nordlander swatted him away, ashamed of his own weakness. Siebrecht himself, though, could not maintain the pace for much longer, and he and Alptraum gradually slowed and watched Delmar obstinately pull ahead, keeping up with the leaders. Inexorably, and despite Voll's best efforts, the column began to stretch out back along its path.

Finally, Siebrecht rounded a tight corner and saw the lead knights leaning against the boulders ahead of him. He flopped down beside Delmar, chest heaving.

'Thank Shallya you stopped,' Siebrecht gasped, then realised Delmar was staring at him with urgent warning.

'What?' Siebrecht asked. Delmar urgently put his finger to his mouth. Siebrecht peered over Delmar's head. There was a deep cavern, hidden behind a great flat stone. Voll had crept towards its entrance, his pick ready in his hand, and was preparing to go inside.

'What is it?' Siebrecht whispered. 'Is it goblins?'

'We don't know,' Delmar replied. 'But the bergjaegers don't think so. There are no markings, no totems around the sides.'

'What is it then?'

'Maybe trolls, something wild for certain. Maybe it's the reason the goblins don't come here any more.' Delmar shifted so as to have easier access to his sword. 'Maybe Dragon's Jaw isn't just a name.'

'You are so great a comfort to me, Reinhardt.'

One of the knights ahead of them shot them both an angry look and they quietened. Voll disappeared into the cavern's mouth. *And what if he doesn't come out again,* Siebrecht found himself thinking, *what then?*

But Voll did come out again, his weapon stored back in his pack. He gave the knights a brief shake of the head and then led them on. The bergjaegers began to range further ahead of the knights, determined to discover any further threats before the column chanced upon them. Siebrecht kept close to the vanguard now, and saw the bergjaegers appear and disappear amongst the trees. The knights passed a few more caves, these ones clearly goblin dens, though long abandoned.

Then, the trees thinned and the knights emerged onto the crest of a ridge. The storm had finally moved on and Siebrecht could see the dark thunderhead clouds slide east in the direction of Black Fire Pass. To the south, there was the distinctive crater of a dormant volcano and beyond that a tantalising glimpse of the corner of some great lake from which the highest reaches of the River Reik flowed.

Preceptor Jungingen wasted no time admiring the view; even while the rest of the banner arrived he began addressing his knights.

'Brothers, we hold here. I cannot tell you how long, only that in the next few hours we may have every single foe upon this mountain at our throats. The Reiksmarshal himself told me that the fate of our campaign relies upon us keeping them back until we are finished. Prepare yourselves, my brothers, for today we prove our Marshal's trust.'

The other knights solemnly concurred, but Siebrecht had already begun looking past his preceptor at the pipebearers who were now carefully unwrapping their strange burdens.

'Are they horns?' Siebrecht asked, approaching the berg-jaegers after Jungingen had finished speaking.

'If horns can be twelve feet long,' Gausser said, 'then that they can be.'

'Aye,' Jaeger Voll answered them. 'The sighorns of the Black Mountains they are.'

'And what can they do?' Siebrecht continued. 'Will they bring the mountains crashing down upon the goblins' heads?'

'Perhaps,' Voll replied. 'In their way.'

LIKE MANY OF the devices of man, the sighorns of the Black Mountains had their origins in war. The human tribes of the region, aping their dwarfen betters, blew horns as they charged into battle to frighten their enemies. It was the Averlanders' great hero Siggurd, according to their legends at least, who fashioned a warhorn so long that he could sound the news of the great victory at Black Fire Pass to all the tribes of the mountains at once.

Other legends, however, say that the language of the sighorns came from the dwarfs of Karak Angazhar who, notorious for their isolationism, gave the mountain men a means by which messages could be passed without the need for physical meeting or revealing the location of their hold.

Whatever the truth of its creation, and though Averland soldiers now marched to the drum and the trumpet, the tradition of the sighorn messages to the dwarfs of Karak Angazhar had survived. Voll merely hoped the dwarfs would be listening.

Delmar heard the low, mournful notes of the sighorns doled out in careful measure down the slope of the

Predigtstuhl, through the valley of the Upper Reik and towards the peaks where, somewhere, Karak Angazhar was hidden. Now he understood Jungingen's words. Before they reached dwarfen ears, those notes would be heard by every goblin in between. The knights were exposed there on the wrong side of the mountain, waiting for a reply, and they had just announced their presence to anyone who cared to listen.

Delmar stood on sentry, expecting for a goblin horde to surge over the peak above or burst from the trees below. He kept his hand ready by his sword, his father's sword, which would once more be wielded against the Empire's foes, and waited.

THE SOUND OF the horns reached even the great stone goblin, and the ears of the Death Caps there. They reached for their weapons, the strongest of them bearing swords and axes taken from the dwarfs, and looked to Thorntoad in anticipation. Thorntoad, however, snapped at them to stay still, and disappeared into his lair.

His prisoner was still there; the shaman had kept the dwarf alive these past days, forcing him to eat scraps of meat, stolen bread and a very specific type of toadstool of Thorntoad's own cultivation. The poisons in the toadstool were not fatal, but they attacked the mind, fuddling the senses and churning its memories. The dwarf's beard was ragged and damp with its own sweat, for it laboured within a fever-dream, not awake, not asleep, not in the present, not in the past, but somewhere in between.

Thorntoad used one of his nails to open the dwarf's eye. Its pupil was as small as a pinhead. It was ready. Thorntoad hung from a hoop, so that his lips were an inch from the dwarf's ear.

'Hear me... Gramsson...' The prisoner's name was the first thing he had discovered. 'Hear me...'

Thorntoad could see the dwarf struggling to wake, but failing.

'Eye... close... Gramsson...' Thorntoad reassured him. 'Speak...'

The dwarf began to talk in its native language once again.

'No... Man tongue... speak... man tongue...'

The dwarf's eyes opened and crossed for an instant. New beads of sweat formed above its eyebrows.

'Aye, my king,' the dwarf replied. Thorntoad nodded. For some reason his prisoner's mind had fixated upon the dwarfen king and it had addressed Thorntoad as such during their previous interrogation. Thorntoad was only too happy to encourage the drugged misconception.

'Hear... the noise... hear the horns?'

'Aye, my king.'

'It is... message... from men...'

The dwarf paused and Thorntoad feared its mind had slipped away again. But it had not, it was listening.

'Aye, they call to Karak Angazhar.' The dwarf paused again as it translated the horn's notes. 'They wish a response.'

Thorntoad's spines bristled with excitement. 'Hear... Gramsson... tell me more...'

* * *

THE SIGHORNS BLEW for an hour and still no goblins had been seen. Some of the knights began to relax, considering that if the goblins were to attack then they would have done so already. Others grew more concerned, believing instead that the delay gave the goblins a chance to mass together, making it all the more likely that when they did attack, Jungingen's knights would be overwhelmed.

Siebrecht, for the first time since leaving Altdorf, began to feel that old nervous buzz that meant his body was craving a drink. If he just had a single cup of wine, he would quite happily wait for these greenskins until the winter came. He glanced around at his companions. Gausser was like a boulder, solid, unmoving; Alptraum was humming along with the sighorns. Over with the Reiklanders, Hardenburg appeared to be in an even worse way than Siebrecht; and Delmar... Delmar was relaxed but alert, at rest but ready for action. It was the look of a hunter.

Voll patrolled the sentries' positions and stopped by Siebrecht. He looked up at the clouds warily. It was too early for dusk, Siebrecht knew, it was another rainstorm brewing.

'If we are here much longer,' Siebrecht said to the berg-jaeger quietly, 'we shall not need the greenskins. The rain will wash us off this mountain before they will.'

'The rain is good and the rain is bad,' Voll replied. 'The goblins don't like it. While it rains, we're safe. Mostly.'

'And the bad?' Siebrecht had to ask.

'Can't use the horns. We have to keep them covered. And even if we played on, the storm would drown them out.'

'But then we will head home, won't we? We cannot be meant to stay here the night.' Siebrecht felt himself give a tiny shake. He put it down to the cold.

'It's not my place to say,' Voll said evenly. 'But I heard your leader's words. Didn't sound to me as though he planned on leaving until the job was done.'

Just then, the sighorns quietened and the players did not start the measure again. Alptraum stopped humming and started listening. From somewhere in the mountains, a dwarfen horn was replying.

CHAPTER TEN

GRAMRIK

'KING GRAMRIK THUNDERHEAD?' Kurt Helborg asked ceremonially.

'Aye,' the imposing ruler of Karak Angazhar replied in formal Reikspiel. 'We have kept our oath to answer the call of the hunters' horns, just as we have upheld our ancient oaths to defend the mouth of the great river.' The dwarfen lord planted the bottom of the long shaft of his axe-hammer firmly on the ground. 'We are glad that the sons of Sigmar have come to destroy the grobi by our side.'

The Reiksmarshal and the dwarfen king met on the lower reaches of the Achhorn, a razor-thin ridge on the far western side of the Stadelhorn Heights that stood apart from the mountains around. Helborg had had his wish granted. More than he had wished. The king himself had answered his call to meet. There had been a price, however. The dwarfs had opened up a new tunnel, outside the goblins' siege lines, one whose existence they had so far kept secret. Now they had revealed it, the tunnel would have to be collapsed lest it allow the goblins back into Karak Angazhar. Preceptor Jungingen was a capable man and he had sent a squadron of his knights ahead of the rest of the banner to bring the dwarfen message back to the army as quickly as they could. But even then it had allowed Helborg precious little time. Griesmeyer had the Reiksmarshal's personal guard to arms at once and they sent word ahead so that, as they raced west, Osterna's banner was primed to escort them.

It should be enough; Helborg knew that the unruly goblins needed time to gather their forces together. A hundred and fifty Reiksguard knights would be enough to brush aside any goblin warband that stumbled across their path. Helborg left orders for the rest of the army to ready themselves, but to remain where they were. It would not do to have dribs and drabs of men come after them, nor was he willing to weaken the main force so greatly that they might be assaulted in his absence.

They rode hard. For the first time since entering the mountains each knight gave his steed its head. They journeyed up the Unkenfluss and around the goblin tribes that inhabited the Stadelhorn Heights and up onto the Achhorn. With surprise on their side, his knights had arrived at the meeting place unchallenged. Helborg doubted, though, that the journey back would be so easy.

'Now let us talk,' King Gramrik declared.

* * *

DELMAR AND SIEBRECHT held the reins of the horses of the Marshal's guard. They were most fortunate to be there: it had been the two of them who had been first to reach the Reiksmarshal with the dwarf's message and so, when his guard had mounted up, Griesmeyer had beckoned them on as well. Now, they were present when the two commanders, one human, one dwarf, met for the first time. Their two personal guards, Griesmeyer's knights and Gramrik's dwarfen veterans, stayed a few paces back; this was a meeting of equal allies, after all, and neither side wished to appear that they were imposing their will.

Delmar stared at the dwarf veterans standing rigidly behind their lord. They wore plate armour similar to the Reiksguard's; unsurprising, Delmar realised, as the order's plate was forged by dwarfen armourers in Altdorf. But the knights' armour was, for the most part, shining and new; the dwarfs' plate bore the scars and dents of hundreds of battles and skirmishes. Their axes were notched from use, yet still carried a razor-keen edge. The warriors' faces were covered with fearsome warmasks of plate and mail, and the eyes behind them glared out with an indomitable determination. These were warriors indeed.

The sky was still dark. The storm which had begun to threaten whilst they were on the Predigtstuhl still had not erupted. The clouds hung low, bulging as though filled with water and ready to burst. The wind had also picked up and maverick gusts blew up and down the slope.

'That is our position, King Thunderhead,' Helborg concluded. 'We can advance to you but the bank on either side of the river through the valley is too narrow. We cannot get through without support, not without great cost at least.'

The dwarf lord ruminated deeply and then spoke: 'We will honour our ancestors, and hope that they will provide.'

Helborg was taken aback by the curtness of the response, but then he sensed something in the king's tone. Honouring their ancestors nothing. The dwarfs of Karak Angazhar had something, some scheme or device, of which they did not wish him to know. He struggled for a moment between relief and annoyance. How could he plan effectively, form a strategy, how could he command an army if his own allies would not tell him what they were to do?

'Well, Reiksmarshal?' Gramrik prompted. The King of Karak Angazhar stamped the shaft of his axe-hammer on the rocky ground again and, as if in response, the clouds above them crashed with thunder.

'Grobi!' the alarm went up around them. A dwarf hurried up to Gramrik: 'Grobi, my king. There are grobi warbands in the heights to the east.'

'How many?' Gramrik demanded.

'Two, three hundred, coming up from the ground,' the dwarf replied.

'We are out of time, Reiksmarshal. I must return to the tunnel before my miners bring it down…'

'Goblins! Goblins! Reiksguard to your horses!' the bellicose Osterna cried as he galloped through his men.

'Osterna!' Helborg bellowed, meaning to quieten his subordinate. Gramrik was already making to leave.

'Goblins, Marshal! Goblins to the north!'

'I…' Helborg began, and then realised what Osterna had said. 'To the north?'

'Yes, Marshal.' Osterna pointed back the way the knights had come. 'A few hundred to the north, blocking our path.'

'Grobi!' the call came again, but not from the north or the east. This time it came from the south, and at that Helborg realised that surprise had never been on his side at all.

'Treachery!' Gramrik boomed, clutching his axe-hammer in both hands.

'Never!' Helborg snapped back. 'No knight of mine…'

'No dwarf would ever…'

The sky crashed again, echoing the two generals' anger. Helborg's guard and Gramrik's warriors were tense, each eyeing the other, waiting to follow their commander's lead. Preceptor Osterna, meanwhile, was organising his mounted knights into their squadrons, ready to attempt a break-out through the green horde.

'Get on your horses, manling, and run,' Gramrik boomed. 'I was a *skrati* to allow myself to be lured from the hold. Angazhar will stand, as it always has, alone!'

Helborg looked at the furious dwarfen king, at the readied dwarfen warriors behind him, at the goblins advancing, surrounding his knights, and came to his decision.

He drew the runefang sword from its gilded scabbard at his side. The dwarfen warriors hefted their hammers and the Reiksguard went for their weapons in reply. Helborg prepared no blow, however, instead he reversed his blade and held it out to Gramrik. Even in the grim half-light the runefang still shone brilliantly.

'King Gramrik. Do you know what this is?' He indicated the runes etched deep into the metal. 'Do you know what they mean?'

Gramrik did not need to read them. 'Aye, there's none of my kind that doesn't.'

'They were a gift; from your High King to my Emperor. A gift of thanks for when Sigmar stood beside Kurgan Ironbeard in battle at the birth of my Empire. We stood together then. We shall stand together now,' Helborg stated calmly. 'My brothers and I came to defend your hold and all within it. If you doubt me, then here, here is your gift returned. You may take it back.'

Gramrik's thunder faded, and he held up his hand to refuse the ancient sword.

'I know why you truly come, Kurt Helborg of the manling Empire, but you have spoken well nonetheless. We shall stand together then, as Sigmar and great King Kurgan did. But it matters little unless one of us survives. They have surrounded us, and if my tunnel still stands it shall not for long. Your horses though, can carry you out. I shall make my stand here and buy you the time to escape.'

'If you do not return, King Thunderhead, then none of your kin will answer my calls.'

'Aye,' Gramrik admitted.

'Then you must return to your hold, no matter what the cost. We must make for the tunnel, as fast as we can. And if that is lost, we make our stand where there is something solid which may protect our backs.'

'Then put your backs to ours, manling. For you'll find there's nothing more solid than a dwarf with an oath to keep.'

Gramrik turned to order his warriors, and Helborg called Griesmeyer over. 'Tell Osterna, forget our path back; we follow the dwarfs.' Griesmeyer nodded and went to obey, when Helborg caught his arm and brought him close.

'Find a horse yourself,' the Reiksmarshal ordered, his eyes fierce. 'Get through their lines, however you can, and bring my army back to me.'

'DELMAR!' GRIESMEYER SHOUTED through the storm, riding up beside him. 'Keep your steed!'

Delmar looked about, confused; he raised his visor and a flurry of rain splashed against his face. 'My lord?'

'The Marshal needs us to gather the army and bring it here. Dump anything from your saddle that you do not need to fight,' Griesmeyer replied. 'We shall need the space, for we carry the life of our Reiksmarshal and the King of Karak Angazhar with us.'

Griesmeyer spurred his horse and Delmar followed. The two riders raced for the thinner section of the goblin encirclement. Against such determination, the few goblins in their path scurried to the side, and Delmar saw the path through was clear. But then the black arrows whistled through the air and plunged down upon them. Delmar felt their impact against his back and side and hunched over the saddle so as to protect his horse. He galloped clear, but Griesmeyer was not so fortunate. With a screeching whinny, the old knight's mount fell.

Delmar heard the sound and checked his horse to glance back.

'On! On!' Griesmeyer shouted, already on his feet from his stricken mount. 'Your duty first!'

Griesmeyer began to run from the eager goblins and their spears, and Delmar turned his horse and spurred it again.

THORNTOAD SQUATTED UPON his palanquin as he watched the men and dwarfs panic before him. Seeing them squirm and struggle warmed him against the driving rain.

'See, Burakk Craw!' he said to the ogre pacing beside him. 'The horns were not a trick. They are exactly where the prisoner said they would be!' Thorntoad watched to see in which direction the dwarfs were forming. 'And now they show their path. Go to it!'

Burakk licked his lips in anticipation and loped away. Thorntoad hopped back and forth in his excitement. Even with forewarning, he had only time to gather a portion of his own Death Caps from their warrens, but the Biters in the north and the Stinkhorns to the south had been closer. He had run to death a dozen of his bearers rousting the two tribes, but it had been worth it. No matter what the dwarfs and the men did, in a few minutes they would be overwhelmed.

'MY MEN ARE mounted, Marshal,' Osterna reported back.

'Good. The king is ready, you must clear his path.' Helborg pointed down the ridge to the south in the direction Gramrik was already marching. 'Charge, break through, circle back and...'

Helborg's voice trailed away. 'Marshal?' Osterna asked, but Helborg was looking past him. There, in the north, a single knight was fighting alone against the tide of goblins rising against him.

'Griesmeyer,' Helborg said.

Osterna turned and saw it too. 'I'll bring my men around, Marshal. We will save him.'

'No,' Helborg countermanded. 'Follow my orders. Protect the king.'

Helborg spurred away leaving Osterna no chance to argue.

GRIESMEYER FELT THE goblin leap upon his back and scratch its nails across his visor, grasping for his eyes. He switched his grip on his sword and then swung it back over his shoulder as though he were a flagellant absolving himself with a whip. The sword cut through the goblin's shoulder and into its back. Its grip loosened and Griesmeyer hauled it off him with his free hand.

He heard the goblins closing behind him again; with his next step he planted his foot and twisted, whipping his sword around in a rising stroke. One grasping goblin lost an arm, the second had his face cut in two. They fell back and tripped the others behind them. Griesmeyer did not stop to see the results, but struggled on. The mud beneath his foot shifted and, off-balance, he slipped. Desperately, he caught his fall, and his knee twisted and screamed as the weight fell badly upon it.

Through the drumming of the rain upon his helmet, he heard Reiksguard trumpets sound the charge ahead. For a moment, he thought he was saved, but the thunder of their hooves receded. Wherever they were charging, it was not for him.

He took another step and his knee near collapsed beneath him. He realised he could no longer run. This was the end, then. He turned and faced the horde behind him, and the goblins crowed as their prey stood at bay. He would see how many he could take with him. A dozen sounded fair. He had a bad leg, after all.

But then the thunder rose again.

'Reiksguard!' Helborg roared as he charged in. His mighty steed barrelled into the goblin warband and sent the closest goblins flying. He swept the deadly runefang around in a great arc and ended five more greenskin lives. His horse leapt forwards, trampling more beneath its hooves, and the blade scythed down again.

With a nudge of his heel, Helborg turned his horse from the goblins as they reeled back and spurred it towards Griesmeyer.

'Brother!'

Griesmeyer reached up his hand to grasp Helborg's as he passed, but Helborg leaned out, lifted Griesmeyer bodily from the ground and swung him into the saddle.

'The army... the message...?' Helborg shouted without ceremony as they raced away.

'Delmar got through,' Griesmeyer gasped back, 'Delmar got through.'

SIEBRECHT ROARED AS he rode amongst Osterna's knights. The goblins did not even stand, but broke before the knights struck. The knights followed through, stabbing at the backs of the dark-clothed goblins as they scrambled away. Gods, Siebrecht exulted, such a feeling of power! Of unstoppable force! His heart raced. He felt sick. He felt magnificent. He struck down again and another black shape collapsed with a shriek, but he could hear nothing but the pounding of his blood in his ears.

'Turn!' Osterna roared. 'Turn and reform!' Siebrecht did not even hear it until another knight smacked his helmet with the flat of his blade. Siebrecht caught himself and turned.

Behind them, in the gloom of the storm and the closing day, Siebrecht could barely make out the battle behind him. The king had led his warriors into the knights' path, but the goblins to the east were moving in too quickly. Osterna had reformed, but Siebrecht's distraction had left him far behind when the knights charged again. Siebrecht was thirty paces behind them, and so was the first to see the ogres.

OSTERNA'S MEN CHARGED, but these goblins held. The horses kicked and the knights hacked away at their foe below them. Burakk and his ogres had run around the lower level of the ridge, out of sight of the Reiksguard, and then climbed up. They held their warcry back until they were only a few paces away. Preceptor Osterna, closest to them, whirled around in his saddle just in time to see Burakk's mace smash into his face.

The blow was so powerful that it knocked Osterna's head off his shoulders and sent it spiralling into the air. The knights' armour, which had proved so invulnerable against the goblins' weapons, was little defence against the strength of an ogre. The next knight was knocked from his mount by a mallet, his ribs broken. Another dodged away from the swing of a cutlass the length of a man, only to have it decapitate his panicking horse. More knights were culled as the hefty clubs and bludgeons broke skulls and snapped necks.

'Back! Back!' the order went up amongst the knights, and their steeds needed no encouragement. The ogres launched themselves forwards and tackled their horses to the ground, sending the knights sprawling into the waiting clutches of the triumphant goblins.

Just then a single cry rose above the ogres' roars. It was Siebrecht charging in. He had not thought to hold back; he had just seen his brothers in peril and so gone to intervene. It was only when the ogres turned to look at him, that he realised he was about to die, and that it would be his own stupid fault.

He rode down the edge of the ridge, where the path was clear of Osterna's men, and held his sword out before him as though it were a lance. He picked his target, an ogre holding the severed arm of a knight dead at its feet, and aimed for above its armoured gut-plate, straight for the heart. Siebrecht's sword struck true, the impact near knocking him out of his saddle, and he plunged the blade deep into the ogre's heart.

The ogre looked down in surprise at the blade embedded in his chest. And then he started to snigger.

'Morr have mercy,' Siebrecht whispered to himself, as he reached in his saddle for his pistol. The ogre seized him with both hands and lifted him bodily from his terrified mount. The ogre's mouth opened wide, intending to bite Siebrecht's head off. Siebrecht's pistol was in his hand, but the ogre had his arm pinned by his side.

Siebrecht twisted his hand until the muzzle pointed straight up. As the ogre's mouth came down from above him, he pulled the trigger with his thumb and prayed the powder had kept dry. The ignition burnt his wrist, the bullet whipped past his face and shot through the roof of the ogre's mouth.

Siebrecht tried to break free from the ogre's grip, but even as it died, its brain shot through, it was too strong. The ogre toppled backwards, off the ridge, out into the blackness, taking Siebrecht with him.

DELMAR SAW THE body in the grey light of the next morning.

He had ridden as hard as he could with the Reiks-marshal's message, but night had closed in before he had made half the distance back and he had to find his way back in the rain and the pitch darkness. Eventually, he had reached the camp and found Sub-Marshal Zöllner. Zöllner, though, much as the decision pained him, could not send his men out into the night, and so they had had to wait. At the first hint of light his banner had set out with Delmar riding ahead of them.

Following the route back, Delmar had spied a herd of horses in the distance, a strange sight amongst these mountains. He had ridden to them and seen the Reiksguard markings upon them. Their riders were nowhere to be seen. It was an ill omen. The Reiksguard would only loose their horses in the direst straits, where escape was no longer possible.

He had reached the site of the battle to see his worst fears confirmed. Though it was clear from the blood and broken weapons that men and goblins had fought and died in that place, there were no bodies. They had all been dragged away as food, and that meant the goblins had won.

It was then that he had looked down over the ridge's edge and seen the corpse below. It was an ogre, half-sunken into a mire. It had obviously fallen during the fight to the bottom of the slope and had then been overlooked by the goblin scavengers.

Then it moved.

Delmar looked closer in the half-light. It was definitely moving. Only a fraction, but it was enough. It was still alive. Delmar climbed down to it. His mission of rescue had been a failure. He had not been here to defend his brothers, but dispatching this one beast might bring the dead some small satisfaction.

He drew close, stepping carefully around the swampy ground, and unsheathed his sword. The ogre spasmed again, except that here, closer, Delmar could see that it was not the ogre. It was something beneath it.

'Siebrecht!' Delmar called. 'Siebrecht, can you hear me?'

Siebrecht, unconscious beneath the ogre's corpse, shifted a little. At his motion, the thick mud sucked him down further.

'Sigmar preserve us.' Delmar waded into the mud and tried to heave the ogre's body off. 'Siebrecht, wake up!'

Siebrecht did so, felt the suffocating mud all around him, felt the pressure pushing him down, and panicked. He tried to take great gulping breaths and swallowed mud instead, which made him choke and panic all the more.

'Take hold, brother.' Delmar strained as he lifted the ogre's body a fraction.

'Siebrecht!' he shouted again to get his attention. 'Take hold of me and pull yourself out.'

Siebrecht did so, grabbing Delmar and dragging himself onto firmer ground, coughing up the mud. When he was clear, Delmar collapsed and let the ogre sink.

'Siebrecht, can you talk? Did any others survive?'

Siebrecht shook his head. 'I don't know,' he gasped. 'I fell with this...' He waved a hand at the submerged ogre. 'Is it over?'

'Yes. Yes, it is.' Delmar sighed, and looked back up the slope.

'Did we win?'

'I do not think so.'

But Delmar was mistaken. Another of Zöllner's scouts had seen a section of the ridge suddenly cave in upon itself. Fearing another goblin attack, Zöllner led a squadron of knights ahead to investigate, only to discover the Reiksmarshal and the dwarfen king stepping calmly out into the dawn. Zöllner's joy at seeing Helborg alive was tempered, though, when he saw the number of his brothers laid out behind. Fully half of Osterna's men were dead, or injured so that they would never ride again. Of Osterna himself, they had only his body. His head was not recovered.

It had only been by the Reiksmarshal's own heroism that the dead had not been taken by the goblins and the ogres. Siebrecht's lone charge had bought Osterna's knights the chance to escape, but it had been the Reiksmarshal who had then ridden up and rallied them. And rather than fleeing with the dwarfs, he had led the charge back against the ogres, slaying several of them, and knocking them back long enough for his knights to gather their fallen brothers. When Gramrik saw his aim, the dwarfen king could not help but return as well and help the Reiksguard, both the living and the dead, to the safety of the tunnel.

Gramrik's miners had then collapsed the tunnel entrance behind them, and the goblins picked the battlefield clean, before they too trudged back to their warrens. The dwarfs though, had not returned to Karak Angazhar. Instead they had waited out the night with the knights beneath the ground. And when morning came, the miners dug a new tunnel to return them to the surface.

During the long night, Gramrik had revealed the truth of his scheme to aid the Empire through the Dragon's Jaw. Now, Helborg looked into the dwarf's aged face in the morning light. He saw the deep furrows in the king's brow, the scars on his cheek where his white beard no longer grew and the flint in his eyes. Helborg had spent his life fighting for the Empire, but his life was but a single season to this warrior. The success of the campaign rested upon whether these two old soldiers could trust one another.

Helborg decided they could.

'I will lead my army into the Jaw,' he said.

'Aye,' Gramrik replied solemnly. 'Be ready tomorrow morning. That'll give us time enough.'

'Time enough for you to consult your ancestors?' Helborg asked lightly.

'Aye,' Gramrik said. Helborg thought he saw the trace of a smile beneath the thick beard. 'That's about right.'

'TEN OF MY bulls. Ten!' Burakk the Craw waved his hands, five fingers splayed as though each one was named for one of his lost ogres.

Burakk rampaged back and forth, waiting for Thorntoad to reply. He had said nothing in front of those who had returned from the battle; to do so would have been a public challenge against Thorntoad and it was not the time to do that, not while the goblins still outnumbered Burakk's bulls three hundred to one. No, he had stayed silent out there; but in here, in private, Thorntoad owed him answers.

'Ten bulls lost,' Burakk continued, bellowing even louder. 'And what to show for it? Nothing! The Empire men, they took their fallen with them. The dwarfs the same! They left nothing. Nothing but your goblins and ten of my bulls.'

'I am certain they tasted well enough.' Thorntoad prodded Osterna's severed head with his nail, idly testing how much pressure its eyeballs could take.

'We will not win by eating our own kind, goblin. You promised me the flesh of the men and their animals. But you do not take it!' Burakk pounded the rock wall for emphasis. 'You shoot your arrows at them from afar. You snatch one or two in the night and then run when the men in armour come after you. Their army marches unchallenged. This night is the only time we have been close enough to spit upon them. When are we to attack in strength? Bring the tribes together? Drive the men back; leave their dead so we may eat? Eat!'

Thorntoad dropped from the ceiling and landed, hunched, upon the throne's back. 'Soon, Burakk Craw, soon. They are stopped already at the mouth of the valley between the mountains of the Black Ears and Biter Peak. The river runs fast, the banks are steep and narrow, and there is no path around, save that which will take them a week out of their way. We will crush their armour beneath our boulders, and when they can fight no more we will descend upon them and feed.'

'And what if the dwarfs interfere again?'

'They are captives behind our siege lines. Trapped in their hold. They cannot interfere.'

'They did so last night! What use is your siege if the dwarfs come and go at will? Give me the name of the tribe to punish and we shall feast upon them.'

'They used a secret way, and in doing so exposed it to us. We have discovered their path and the dwarfs have been forced to seal it off. They cannot use it again.' The warlord climbed the wall behind the throne and crawled, upside down, across the roof until they were so close that the ogre's rancid breath made the goblin's thorns rise. 'And as we are at war with these tribes of men, I cannot allow you to feed on the fiends I need for the fight. As you say, Burakk Craw, we will not win eating our own kind. Either of our kinds.'

ANOTHER KNIGHT THAT Siebrecht did not recognise shook his hand to congratulate him. Word had spread since the night before. By the time Delmar and Siebrecht had returned to Jungingen's banner, the preceptor had heard all about Siebrecht's triumph against the ogre champion. It had been a glint of heroism in what had otherwise been a bloody night of loss.

Jungingen knew that his knights' successes reflected well upon him and so he ensured that the whole banner was turned out to give Siebrecht a worthy welcome. Siebrecht had quickly lost sight of Delmar amongst the press of his brother-knights and their commendations. As unexpected as the reception was, Siebrecht had adored it. It was just as it had been back amidst the gangs of noble youths in Nuln, where each victory over their rivals was cause for celebration. He had been the fastest blade amongst them and they had been so proud of him. Now, for the first time, the Reiksguard were proud of him as well.

Siebrecht woke that afternoon in a different humour. His brow was hot, his head was stuffed and his throat felt as though a stone were lodged within it. After the alarms of the day and night before, the Reiksmarshal had few orders for the army, but to rest and take care of the wounded and the dead, and to be ready to attack the Jaw the day after. Siebrecht could not imagine how he would be ready to fight tomorrow if he still felt as bad as this, or worse.

The sergeants had built a small cooking fire nearby for the knights' morning meal. These sergeants were strange men, Siebrecht decided. As a novice, he had thought the sergeants were little more than sentries, the tutors' muscle and, occasionally, his gaolers. But out on campaign, they were very different. They were careful, protective even, of the brother-knights. They marched all day with the army, in the evening they lit the fires and cooked, and at night they stood guard. All to ensure that when their knights went into the fray, they would fight at their best. They took their pride in carrying their knights to battle, and carrying them home again.

One of the older sergeants brought over two cups, one for Siebrecht and the other for Gausser who sat by his side. Siebrecht accepted the cup gratefully, but then smelt the horrible stench coming from it and pushed it away.

'Drink it, my lord,' the sergeant insisted.

'Damned if I will,' Siebrecht replied. 'It smells terrible. How did you make it? By washing out a cannon?'

The sergeant chuckled, and Siebrecht realised that he was not laughing with him, the sergeant was laughing at him. Siebrecht felt suddenly quite patronised. Beside him, Gausser downed his at a stroke.

'Drink it, brother,' he said. 'It is not so bad.'

Siebrecht tried to ignore the sergeant's encouraging smile and raised the cup again. He gave it a sniff in case its odour had improved. It hadn't. Instead, he held his breath as he swigged it down. As Gausser said, it did not taste as bad as it smelt. The first taste was very bitter, almost acrid, but it was quickly washed away. The sergeant nodded approvingly at him, as though he were a child who had taken his own medicine for the first time.

'You will feel better soon, my lord.'

'Will I, by the gods?' Siebrecht stared at the thick, black residue left at the bottom.

The sergeant took the cups back. 'I have served the order on campaign for nearly forty years, my lord. We know how to keep fighting men ready.'

'And how many did you poison along the way?' Siebrecht muttered, as the sergeant pottered back to the fire and to his fellows. He was being a mite uncharitable, but he was not well and the sergeants were grinning at him with patronising indulgence. Siebrecht pointedly turned away from them as another knight came over to shake his hand.

DELMAR WATCHED FROM the shade of the trees as Siebrecht modestly accepted another knight's compliments.

'Thinking that should have been you?' a familiar voice interrupted.

Delmar instantly stood. 'My lord Griesmeyer,' he said formally. 'How are you?'

The older knight was only half-armoured, wearing a blue doublet in place of his breastplate. He leaned casually against the tree trunk and scratched the short red beard on his chin.

'Better than when you saw me this morning. And please, Delmar, we have fought together now; surely you may call me brother.'

'Yes, my lord, I will.'

Griesmeyer laughed lightly at the young knight's intractability. 'Your brother over there, Matz, he did well yesterday.'

'Yes, he did.'

'You did well also, Delmar.'

Delmar felt his throat tighten. 'I was not the first to best an ogre. I did not pull you from the horde. I did not charge with the Reiksmarshal and defend my fallen brothers.'

'Those were not your orders. Your orders were to give the Reiksmarshal the message from Karak Angazhar, which you did. And then your orders were to bring the army, which you did as well. The Reiksmarshal trusted you with his life and those of all the rest of us; that is a far greater commendation than the ones that Brother Matz has been receiving.'

Delmar hated this. He hated that Griesmeyer was saying exactly what he wanted to hear, and yet his suspicions ensured he could take no comfort from it. He hated Griesmeyer's easy familiarity; that the knight had not even noticed the distance that had arisen between them. Most of all Delmar hated himself; that he knew Griesmeyer had lied to him, and yet he still wanted to believe.

'Yes, my lord,' he replied without emotion.

'Please, Delmar,' the older knight chided him, 'call me brother.'

'I would, my lord, if you would do the same.'

'Call you brother?' Griesmeyer said, surprised. 'I do already.'

'No, my lord, you call me Delmar,' he corrected softly. 'Would you call me Brother Reinhardt?'

Griesmeyer paused at that. He pushed himself away from the tree and regarded Delmar thoughtfully.

'You hesitate,' Delmar said, 'because that is what you called my father. Am I correct?'

Griesmeyer stroked his short beard. 'You took me off guard for a moment. That is all. Of course I shall call you Brother Reinhardt if that is your wish.'

'It is, my lord.'

'Very well then,' Griesmeyer replied, speaking slowly to emphasise his words. 'Brother Reinhardt.'

'Brother Griesmeyer.' This was it then, Delmar knew, the time to ask the question that was eating away inside him. 'Brother Griesmeyer, how did my father die?'

'Is that it, Brother Reinhardt?' the old knight said with compassion. 'Is that what has been worrying you so?'

Griesmeyer looked out over the knights encamped.

'I suppose it is only to be expected that you should think of it now, on your first campaign,' he said. 'But I have told you already of all the circumstances of that day.'

Delmar considered his words carefully.

'My mother blames you for his death, does she not? You have not told me why she does that.'

'Of course your mother blames me. She felt her world end when I brought her the news, she had to blame someone. And she knew I was his friend, that I should have kept him safe.'

'You were not friends on that day, were you? I know of the arguments you and he had. Gods, the whole order knew. Were you even speaking to him that day?'

'I would have given my life for his, if I could.' But Griesmeyer did not answer the question.

'How did my father die, Brother Griesmeyer?' Delmar demanded.

'He died...' the knight snapped back, but then checked himself. 'He died with honour.' At that, Griesmeyer turned his back on Delmar and walked away.

* * *

THE MORNING BROKE gloriously over the Dragon's Jaw. The rain that had pelted down over the last few days and swollen the river, the rain that the men begrudged and the goblins despised, held off. The dark clouds had moved east to threaten the mountains around Black Fire Pass and, for once, the sky was clear. The gods, both of men and greenskins, had decreed this day for battle.

It was to be a battle where the Reiksguard would force their way through the Dragon's Jaw or their campaign would be at an end. The army would have to endure a harrowing retreat back to Averland with the goblins at their heels, and Karak Angazhar would truly have to stand alone.

The Dragon's Jaw was well named. The cliffs on either side rose sharply like the sides of that creature's mouth. The rocky outcrops that jutted out of the slope were its jagged teeth, and the fast-flowing Reik at its base, its fat, lashing tongue.

It was a landscape that threatened to close and swallow them whole.

The trumpets roused the Empire camp once the sun had risen. The bergjaegers that had been sentry pickets for the last few hours of the night gratefully yawned, their duty done. They returned to their regiment and there found a comfy piece of dirt to lie upon. The men, whether knight or militiaman or bergjaeger, arose. Their officers did not hurry them; they did not need to. The men had had the entire day before to prepare and to dwell upon the battle ahead; to reflect upon the chaos of combat, the injuries they might suffer, the killing blow they might receive. They did not rise eagerly, but at least with relief that the waiting would soon be over.

Helborg rode back towards the camp with his guard. As was his habit, he had risen as early as he could to test the ground ahead. He had given his orders for battle yesterday, and nothing that he had seen warranted their alteration. His legs and his horse's flanks were soaked through with river water, though, and he wished to dry off before the chill got to him. He had long ago learned that part of taking care of his army, was taking care of himself. He did not have to look too far back in the Empire's history to find battles that had been lost because of their general's indisposition.

He rode past the army as it assembled. Twelve hundred knights, nearly the Reiksguard's full strength, were in the field, wearing their laurel crests and plumes. There was Preceptor Wallenrode, whose knights had made their name battling the horde of the orc warlord Vorgaz Ironjaw, and wore the badge of their victory in each of their standards. There was Preceptor Trier, who commanded in his banner three more of his own name, two cousins and his own son. There was Preceptor Jungingen, whose keen mind and drive to succeed had made him invaluable despite his youth. And there, at the front, was Osterna's banner. Even though their preceptor was dead, his knights had refused to fight under any other name.

Beyond them assembled the militia. There were cattlemen from Heideck, vintners from Loningbruck, slaughtermen and their apprentices from Averheim, burghers from Streissen, and the citizen-guard of Grenzstadt, many of whom were dwarfs themselves. Dwarfs of the Empire, though, and distant from their cousins in Karak Angazhar, though no less keen to fight for them. They were all citizens of Averland, far from their homes, but still defending them.

Siebrecht sat, armed and armoured, waiting on his mount. He patted the animal's neck, though in truth he was trying to calm himself. He did not look at the great force of knights around him; instead his focus was on their path ahead. He had begun the day well, miraculously restored from his sickness. When he joined his squadron, all of them, Reiklander and Provincial alike, had deferred to him.

'There they are.' Gausser's voice shook Siebrecht from his reverie. A tribe of the goblins had emerged from the slope of the Predigtstuhl on the other bank of the river.

'That will not do them much good,' Bohdan said. 'They are on the wrong bank if they think to halt our march.'

'Is that all of them?' Alptraum asked. 'I see only a few hundred.'

'Of course it is not all of them,' Siebrecht bit back, harsher than he intended. 'The rest of them will be before us. Look how many of them carry bows; they are not there to stop us, they are there to bleed us as we pass.'

And with the Reik between them, only Voll and the bergjaegers could respond, the knights could not touch them.

Evidently, however, the Reiksmarshal disagreed. With the sound of a trumpet, Osterna's knights began to advance towards the goblins, heading straight towards the river.

DELMAR LEANED UP in his saddle in order to see. This was strange indeed. Every story he had ever heard of Kurt Helborg had told of his generalship, his tactical mastery that had brought the Empire's armies victory after victory. Yet, once Delmar had seen the army's deployment as the sun rose, he could not help but wonder if the rumours of Helborg's exhaustion after his return from the north had truth behind them.

Delmar saw that Hardenburg had taken the place beside him. That was odd. As genial as the Reiklander was, he always fell in line with Falkenhayn, and had not spoken to Delmar since Altdorf.

'Are you well this morning, brother?' asked Hardenburg .

'I am vexed, Tomas.'

'Oh?' Hardenburg sounded surprised. 'In what way?'

'Our deployment, it makes no sense.'

'What do you mean?'

'Why are we mounted? Look at the valley sides, look at those cliffs. You think a horse could even walk along that incline, let alone charge? It's only flat enough for us to ride right beside the river and there only enough for us to go three or four abreast. If a few of our knights should fall at the front, the rest of us would be trapped. The goblins need only sweep down from the slopes and drive us into the river.'

Hardenburg nodded, but his mind was elsewhere.

'And now he has ordered Osterna's knights against those goblins across the river?' Delmar continued.

'What, does he think that their armour will help them swim?'

Others, too had taken an interest in their hushed conversation. 'What's that you're whispering there?' Falkenhayn called.

Hardenburg looked guilty, as though he had been discovered betraying his friend's trust.

'The line of battle makes no sense, Reinhardt says,' he replied.

'Does he? And does Brother Reinhardt think he knows better than the Reiksmarshal?' Falkenhayn snorted. 'Brothers, listen to this: Reinhardt thinks he knows better than our Reiksmarshal! Perhaps, Reinhardt, he should be submitting the order of battle for your approval, do you think?'

Falkenhayn nudged his horse forwards a step. 'Here, let us apply to the preceptor at once and get you permission to ride to him, so you can show him how grievously he has erred. For surely it is every loyal knight's duty to question his general's orders.'

Delmar felt the eyes of the squadron upon him, Reiklander and Provincial alike. Falkenhayn was baiting him, trying to make him flustered and back down. On another day, back in the sophisticated noble circles of Altdorf, Falkenhayn might have succeeded; but here, upon the field of battle, there was no chance at all.

'Put a thought in your head before you put words in my mouth, Falkenhayn,' Delmar replied, his voice calm and measured with that same tone of command that had come to him at Edenburg. 'And should you question my loyalty again, you had best be ready to draw your sword and have your second ready to return your body home.'

Delmar held Falkenhayn's stare until a short trumpet note alerted the squadron. The standards were raised; the battle was about to begin.

HAD THE REIKSMARSHAL overheard Delmar's concerns, he would not have disagreed. The floor of the valley was covered by the fast-flowing Reik, swelled with rain; the narrow banks were too steep for cavalry, and any man who climbed the slope would be easy pickings for any archers upon the cliffs. The Dragon's Jaw was no place for an army of the Empire to fight. Yet fight they must.

War was ever the reconciliation of the ideal to the real, with the difference paid in soldiers' lives. The key for any general, at least for any general who wished to command an army more than once, was to ensure that difference was as slight as victory would allow. Sometimes that required caution, sometimes that required courage, and sometimes the gods provided a weary general with a boon for his service. The gods... though today the dwarfs were ample substitute.

A cry went up from the bergjaegers, a shout picked up by the knights, then the militia and carried all the way back to the Reiksmarshal, but Helborg had already seen it. King Gramrik had provided his miracle.

The Reik had stopped flowing.

CHAPTER ELEVEN

DRAGON'S JAW

'It is done, my king,' the dwarfen engineer reported. 'The lower tunnels are flooding and the level of the lake has dropped enough that it is too low to flow out of the basin. The river is halted.'

'For how long?' King Gramrik asked.

'I cannot say for certain, my king. But I would judge a few hours, maybe a little more, before the tunnels fill and the river flows again.'

A few hours, Gramrik brooded; it had taken them ten years to clear those mines. Given a few more years the machinery might have been in place to make it simple to pump them clear, but now that effort had been lost and who knew if they would ever have a chance to try again.

And, as much as the manlings of the Empire had begged for his help, when word got back to their masters there would be some amongst them who would decide that they could not trust their oldest allies with such control over the river they considered their own. It was ever thus, dealing with the manlings, the memory of their fears lasted far longer than that of the favours they owed.

THE REIK HAD drained away, but only upstream of the pass. Behind the Empire army, the Unkenfluss continued to flow into the Reik's channel, and the other, lower, tributaries merged with it downstream. As the waters had receded in the valley, the riverbed was exposed. Helborg had inspected the ground himself the day before: the Reik ran fast through the narrow pass, and any loose soil was carried further downstream. The riverbed was not mud but rather rock smoothed by the river's passage. It was not ideal, Helborg knew, but it should be enough.

As the waters dropped, Osterna's knights urged their horses from the walk to the trot and splashed down the bank into the remains of the Reik with as little trouble as they would cross a stream. Had the Snaggle Tooths made a stand upon the far bank, then they might have had a chance. They were still hundreds against only sixty. But the goblins of the wretched Snaggle Tooth tribe only stared, their red eyes wide in horror, as the barrier they had thought to protect them from harm poured away. They were transfixed by the sight of the knights approaching, the sharp swords, their iron skin, their giant warhorses with heavy hooves that would crush their bones. Only a few had the presence of mind to fire their bows, and those few shots were aimed in such fear that they spiralled harmlessly away.

Osterna's knights had not even reached the other bank before the Snaggle Tooths broke, fighting and clawing at each other in the flight to their warrens in the mountain. Then the knights climbed the bank, spurred their horses hard and raced forwards into the green panicking mass, roaring with bloodlust, as they cut down and avenged the brothers they had lost.

Delmar and his squadron cheered at the sight of Osterna's victory, but already the rest of the army was moving. Helborg had used the distraction of Osterna's charge to cover his new deployment. The Averland drummers had taken up the beat, and the militias were traversing the riverbed and were forming up in a column on the other side.

In the few minutes of Osterna's charge, the Reiksmarshal's army had gone from rest to full march. Now, Delmar saw the sense of the Reiksmarshal's plan and shook his head in wonder.

ON THE CLIFFS of the Stadelhorn Heights, Thorntoad saw it too. His scouts had kept a beady eye on the Empire army the whole day and night before, just in case they made an attempt to cross onto the eastern bank. They had not, and so Thorntoad had brought the bulk of his warriors; the Black Ears, the Splinters and his own Death Caps, onto the west side leaving only Nardy and his Snaggle Tooths there to harass from a distance. Together they would have swarmed their foe and forced them back into the river. But now the river was gone. The Snaggle Tooths had run, and the enemy had crossed to the other bank and were out of range of his archers on the western cliffs.

A column of their soldiers was already marching into the pass. It was not the armoured men, but the lesser ones, the militias. They were marching quickly down the eastern bank. The human general obviously hoped that Thorntoad had been so stunned by the attack on the Snaggle Tooths, that the militias might pass unhindered. Well, that general had much to learn of Thorntoad, if it thought that he would even blink at their loss. They were the lowest fraction of his tribes.

'Gigit!' He called to the tribe he had placed at the northern end of the pass. Warboss Gigit of the Splinters acknowledged the order and strapped the ill-fitting dwarfen helm to his head. With a cry, he ordered his warriors down the slope.

THE SPLINTERS POURED down the mountainside towards the riverbed and the militia column beyond. Those in the lead chewed the fungi that made them feel fearless and strong, and the rest followed their example, emboldened by the power of the mob.

Behind them came their bosses with their whips and their prods. Thorntoad understood that, so long as a goblin feared what was behind him more than what was before him, it gave him that same kind of madness that nobler creatures called bravery, and the thousand Splinters ran down the slope, slipping, skidding, falling, whooping and shrieking in their excitement.

Helborg watched them come. The enemy's first charge, it was a sight he had seen many times before. It told him much about the opponent. For instance, here, it told him that Thorntoad had never faced an army of the Empire before, and did not know how fast his knights could ride.

He gave the order, and Wallenrode's knights raised their standards with the orc-head badge.

'Charge!'

THE SPLINTERS' ATTACK was reduced to tatters and, their horses wearied, Wallenrode's knights reformed behind the safety of the marching militia column before trotting back, triumphantly holding their bloody blades aloft. Those goblins who had survived the charge by Wallenrode's banner milled about in confusion, some were already turning their backs, sensing the opportunity to slip away. Gigit stormed down to them, smashing heads together as he went. He loomed over them all and bellowed for order. His goblins stared, waiting for his command. Gigit opened his mouth to speak and an arrow ripped through the back of his throat.

From across the riverbed, Jaegar Voll strung another arrow to his bow. The rest of the bergjaegers fired and showed the goblin archers the true power of the bow when used at close range in the hands of men whose lives daily depended upon their ability. The bergjaegers fired and sixty goblins fell, some with two or more shafts embedded within them.

Burakk watched the remnants of the Splinters scrabble their way back up the slope. More had survived than they deserved. The knights on their horses, who had broken them so easily, could not climb the slope in pursuit. The militias, once the

Splinters had fled, had blithely continued their march. Even their bowmen did not fire after them, preferring to conserve their arrows for the long battle ahead.

'Herd those together, I shall have use for them later,' Thorntoad ordered of the returning Splinters. 'Do not look so concerned, Burakk Craw.'

'It was a thousand of your creatures.'

'And I have ten thousand more.'

DELMAR WATCHED AS another tribe of goblins was sent down into pass. This time, the honour went to Trier's banner. The knights charged down the riverbed, but this time the goblins were more wary. They did not strive so hard to reach the militia column on the other side; instead they braced for the knights' impact.

Trier's knights were ready and stayed in close order so as to bring the full weight of their charge upon the goblin tribe. But as they closed, breaks appeared in the goblin ranks. The prodders were shoving some of their kin to the front. These goblins laughed and bawled in delirium, their eyes rolling, their mouths frothing as they chewed their maddening mushrooms. Each one dragged behind them on a long chain an iron ball, bigger than cannon-shot.

To the charging knights' horror, these mad greenskins began to twirl and dance. Their muscles bulged with unnatural strength, and they lifted their chains and whirled them about like morning stars, as their fellow goblins unleashed them in the knights' direction and retreated away cackling with laughter.

The bergjaegers near the militia sprinted forwards, nocking arrows to their bows. They stood and fired. The nearest of these fanatics fell, shot through like pin-cushions, but not all.

The fanatics were still shrieking and spinning as the charge hit. With no room to manoeuvre, Trier's knights could only pray as the whirling balls flew at them.

Holes appeared in the knights' first line as the bone-crushing weights smacked into the flanks of horses and their riders, smashing legs, chests and heads. The first men of the battle died, and a band of sergeants and went to try and recover them. The stricken knights though, bore forwards. Even in death, they collapsed upon their foe, and the remaining fanatics were buried beneath the bodies of the horses and men that they had killed.

The rest of the charge hit home, knocking the green-skins aside once more, leaving untouched only those goblin warbands who had sheltered directly behind the fanatics. These goblins, though, had only a few seconds to count their blessings, before the second wave, guiding their horses around the carnage, struck and cut them apart.

The goblin warlord appeared unconcerned and ordered even more down from the heights.

Delmar heard his banner's trumpeter call them to form up. It was their turn at last.

'We charge in two lines,' Jungingen commanded. 'Charge. Cut free by the squadron. Reform around my standard.'

At the trumpeter's note, the knights nudged their horses to the trot. Jungingen led them down the bank onto the riverbed. Delmar and the others were in the second line, unable to see their foe clearly past the first line, and so Delmar watched the knights ahead of him, to gain forewarning of obstacles ahead.

The trumpeter blew again and the knights urged their mounts to the gallop. The danger of the uneven ground was aggravated by the slumped greenskin bodies that impeded their path; however, the experienced knights of the first line maintained their formation.

Then, at last, Jungingen raised his lance and the trumpeter blew the charge. The knights spurred their horses as one. Delmar could hear the cries of alarm from the goblins ahead. In the last few seconds, the first line lowered their lances. The charge struck and Delmar saw the lance arms of the knights ahead jolt back as the lances plunged and the knights impaled the closest goblins.

The knights dropped their spent lances and drew their swords; the line slowed, but it did not stop, and the knights held together. The greenskins in the centre were running, but those to either side were not. Delmar saw the goblins clearly for the first time, hooded in their dark cloaks against the sun, desperation in their eyes, spears and blades clutched tight.

'Second line, to the flanks!' Jungingen ordered.

'To the right!' Falkenhayn shouted to the squadron, and the knights turned to strike beside the first line, their own formation loosening. Delmar readied his lance and picked his target, one of the few goblins that stood its ground. The goblin had braced itself with a short spear, but too short, for

Delmar's lance had the range. Delmar let his lance tip drop, aimed it square at the goblin's belly, braced against his stirrups and let the weight of his charge run the goblin through. With the impact, he knocked the spearhead aside with his shield, then dropped the broken lance and drew his sword.

All about him, his brothers were charging home, some equalling Delmar's success, others having less effect as their targets ran or dived to the ground between the horses' hooves.

'Cut free!' Falkenhayn ordered. The greenskins were running well now, easy kills for the knights' swords. But as the greenskins broke, a second tribe appeared behind them, carrying standards of a diseased toadstool. Their spears were ready, and pointed at Jungingen's knights whose charge was spent. In there as well, Delmar saw, were goblins carrying heavy nets, ready to launch them on the knights as soon as they ploughed through.

The fleeing goblins were halted and, for a moment, the tide flowed back against the knights. They were suddenly engulfed by panicking goblins, screeching, tearing and biting at anything in their way. The knights in the centre were boxed in, the goblins before and their brothers to either side. Out on the right, Delmar saw the chance to break out. He glanced at Falkenhayn, but the Reiklander was too busy stabbing down at the goblins cowering beneath his horse.

'Break right!' Delmar bellowed, cutting the way through. 'Break right, go around!'

Falkenhayn looked up, 'What? No! On! On!' he shouted, but the rest of the squadron was already following Delmar. First the squadron, then as the knights in the centre got space, the whole banner followed Delmar out and around the trap Thorntoad had lain for them.

THIS THORNTOAD HAD never fought the Empire before, Helborg reflected, but it learned quickly, and it had no compunction in sacrificing a score of more of its own kind to bring down a single knight, herding its weaker kin to act as buffers, to slow each banner's charge, then counter with its own. And the knights were beginning to fall; no longer when the banners returned did they do so eagerly, with only their swords bloodied. The sheer numbers of Thorntoad's tribes were beginning to tell, and he had still not unleashed his ogres yet.

SIEBRECHT REINED HIS horse in around the squadron's standard and tried not to let his exhaustion show. His thighs ached from controlling his mount, and his sword arm burned with the strain of constantly hacking; down at these low targets. That's all that was required, hacking; no thrusts, no parries, no finesse, just chopping down with all his might. The stains of goblin blood upon his sword and his horse's flanks were evidence of his success.

They had a moment's respite and he shakily raised his visor. He was the last of the squadron to reform again, but at least the margin was getting smaller as the other knights and horses wore out as well. Siebrecht had always considered himself a good horseman, not the best, but good enough to ride for a day without complaint. But this was something else entirely: the short bursts, the quick turns, to be watching your horse's step, watching your enemy, watching all about you as to where your brothers were going. More than once he had heard the order to cut free, only to look about and realise his brothers had already wheeled away. It was thanks only to his horse's herd instincts that he stayed with them.

He did not know how the others were doing it. Delmar and his horse, especially, moved as though they had been born together. Their squadron had charged half a dozen times in the last hour. Each time Delmar had been the first to strike, the first to the turn, the first to reform. He might as well be a bloody centaur in disguise.

The goblins were all along the riverbed now, the dead and the living. There were nearly two thousand of the creatures together, too many for the cavalry to clear away in a simple charge. A courageous squadron from Osterna's banner that had tried was swiftly bogged down amongst the mass, their horses hamstrung and the knights toppled onto the floor and swarmed.

The militia still advanced steadily, but they were still only halfway through the Dragon's Jaw, and Siebrecht could feel the momentum of the battle shifting in the goblins' favour. Few of the Empire had fallen, but if the column stalled and wavered those losses would quickly multiply.

The Reiksguard were fighting by the squadron now, each band of knights trying to contain the goblins as best they could, without getting caught in their horde.

Falkenhayn was still calling their squadron's orders, but it was Delmar's lead that the knights now followed. There had been a moment two charges before; their squadron had just reformed. 'Beware right!' Delmar had shouted: a goblin warband with nets and spears had broken from the horde, looking to snare the knights while they were resting. Falkenhayn, already irritated by Delmar pre-empting his orders, had seen the danger as well and had snapped, 'To the right!'

Some knights in the squadron had listened to Delmar and wheeled left, the others had listened to Falkenhayn and thought his words were a command and wheeled right. The moment of confusion that resulted gave the goblins their chance and they had rushed forwards, hurling their nets to entangle the horses' heads and legs.

The Reiksmarshal's own guard had been close by and had cut them free, but it had been a damned near thing.

'ON! ON!' FALKENHAYN called to the squadron. 'The standard, take the standard!'

One of the mobs of Death Caps had finally broken and their standard was exposed. The knights could see the horrible thing, being passed frantically back to the rear of the goblin tribe. It was almost within their grasp, and they all knew the glory that went with it. Their fatigue disappeared and they spurred their horses on to charge after the running bearers, ignoring the rest of the goblins cowering to either side. A few of the greenskins who had bows had the instinct to fire an arrow at the passing knights. Most of the arrows, fired in haste, spiralled wildly; some hit Reiksguard armour and skimmed uselessly off; others flew past the knights and struck goblins on the other side. One, however, hit its mark.

Delmar's horse had just pushed off with its hind legs when the point of the arrow burst through its eye and stuck in its brain. The hind legs had pushed, but the front then simply failed to move. Delmar felt the animal beneath him die and readied himself for the fall; as the horse crashed down he was thrown over its head. He curled himself up as tight as his armour allowed and hit the ground rolling. He blinked away the dirt that had been driven through his visor into his eye and levered himself up from the ground. He had no thought but that he was in danger and he must escape.

Only two of the other knights saw his horse collapse. Falkenhayn, though, considered a single knight an acceptable loss for this chance at glory. The other knight did not even think of glory; he saw Delmar fall and, in an instant, reined his horse in to turn back.

'Delmar! Delmar!' he called. 'Give me your hand!'

Delmar looked ahead and there saw Siebrecht galloping back towards him, hand outstretched.

'No, Siebrecht,' he tried to shout. 'You can't...'

He held up his arms to ward his brother off, but instead Siebrecht grabbed one of them and heaved to swing Delmar onto the back of his saddle. Siebrecht, though, as he quickly learned, was no Helborg, and found himself dragged from the saddle and onto the ground.

'Taal's teats, Delmar,' Siebrecht spluttered from the mud, 'you never do make anything easy for yourself.'

Delmar hauled him up, 'What kind of fool…'

'Apparently, my kind of fool, Delmar. I assure you I will berate myself…' Siebrecht trailed off. The goblins had reformed and now there were dozens of them, maybe a hundred, and they were all staring back at Siebrecht.

'Delmar,' he whispered, 'get your sword. I'll be damned if I'm going to fight here alone.'

The massed ranks of the goblins hissed and edged forwards. The odds were impossible, Siebrecht knew, but then he did not have to win, he merely had to delay the inevitable long enough for his brothers to come.

'Hear me!' he bellowed at them. 'For I am the great Siebrecht von Matz, the finest swordsman of the Empire!' He swept his blade through the air, its edge making a threatening swish. The goblins paused. Good work, Siebrecht told himself, now keep it going. 'You may feel brave because you are a multitude, but I tell you now: I may not kill you all, but I shall cut in two the first of you who approaches, and the second, and the third!'

Siebrecht paused for dramatic effect. 'So! Whichever of you wishes to be the first to die, step forwards!' He spun his deadly sword twice around his body for emphasis.

'A brilliant ploy,' Delmar muttered, standing at his back, sword in his hand.

'Thank you,' Siebrecht replied, his gaze never wavering from the beady red eyes of his adversaries.

'It might have worked as well,' Delmar replied, 'if only goblins understood a single word of our Imperial tongue.'

'Ah...' Siebrecht began, and then the goblins charged.

'HAAAAA!' SIEBRECHT YELLED, and charged right back at them. He whipped his sword at them, moving it faster than any of them had ever seen. Sheer speed! Being faster than the rest, this was what true swordplay was about!

Siebrecht lunged at the first goblin in his path and, as it went to defend itself, he turned the lunge into a cut that took its head off. The goblin beside it blocked the blow as Siebrecht followed through, but Siebrecht spun the blade about its head and cut straight down through its shoulder. He felt something strike his side, but his armour held and Delmar, behind him, hacked the attacker down. Siebrecht flicked his point up and ran the next goblin through. He quickly pushed it back to pull his blade free, and brought it up and around like a windmill's sail and cut a greenskin behind Delmar in two.

Delmar bashed another goblin's nose in with his hilt, lifted it up bodily and threw it back upon the spear-points of its fellows. Delmar and Siebrecht fought back to back, shoulder to shoulder, brother to brother. Siebrecht's heart raced; he glanced this way and that, looking for the next threat.

'Step back, foul fiend,' Siebrecht found himself exulting at the next goblin who approached them. Foul fiend, Siebrecht madly wondered at his own turn of phrase, where did that come from?

'I have grim news, Delmar,' Siebrecht shouted as he changed a high thrust into a low cut and took the goblin's leg. 'I'm beginning to talk like you.'

'Just shut up and fight!' Delmar snapped back as he drove his blade through a goblin's belly.

The goblin, though, was not finished. Its claws scrabbled at Delmar's visor and its fingers took grip, dragging Delmar down with it in its death throes. Siebrecht whirled his blade around to keep the goblins at bay for a moment and reached down to Delmar.

'Here,' Siebrecht ordered. 'Quick. Get up.'

'Quick! Get down!' That same hand shoved him hard and Delmar fell flat in the dirt. The sounds of charging knights thundered over their heads.

'Siebrecht!' Alptraum called from atop his steed. 'Take heart!'

'Your brothers are with you!' Bohdan cried.

'That is certain,' Gausser finished.

They and a squadron of Wallenrode's knights carved their path clear. Delmar and Siebrecht hauled themselves up, ready to stumble after, but as they did so they realised that the goblins were falling back, not in flight. Thorntoad had descended to the floor of the Dragon's Jaw and had recalled all his warriors. When they looked at the conglomeration of tribes before them, both Delmar and Siebrecht knew they could not pass.

FOR TWO HOURS now, the armies of the Empire and of the Ten Tribes of Thorntoad had hammered against each other in the Dragon's Jaw. The battle left a trail of its dead behind on the banks of the riverbed as it staggered onwards through the pass: mostly greenskins, but some Reiksguard as well. The sergeants had done their best to recover those fallen, but the goblins swarmed each knight that fell and so precious few still lived to be rescued. Helborg could feel his army's exhaustion, and as his brothers grew weaker so their losses would mount. Thorntoad had succeeded. The cost had been great: eleven thousand goblins began in his great horde and half of those now lay upon the field, and more had scattered, taking their chance to run into the mountains and escape both the Death Cap prods and the knights' lances. But in throwing the goblin warriors' lives into the grinder, Thorntoad had managed to wear the knights down to the point where the day was in its grasp. And now standing at the very end of the pass, in the throat of the Dragon's Jaw, he had gathered the full Black Ear tribe and, at their centre, the ogres of Burakk the Craw. The ogres roared that the battle might continue, that they might fill their bellies to bursting, and the horde advanced to drive the Reiksguard from the pass and, perhaps, wipe them from this earth.

If the circumstances had been ideal, Helborg would have retreated. Their achievements that day should have been enough for any army. But the truth of this day was that they had to pass through the Dragon's Jaw, or retreat and be harried all the way to Averland. Helborg had known retreats before; they were terrible things, far costlier in lives than the fighting itself. A generation of the Empire's eldest sons might be lost in these mountains if he turned his back upon this foe. Helborg arranged his own forces to make his stand. Most of his knights were dismounted, their horses too weak to carry them. These wearied foot-knights held the right, the militias the left, and in the centre all the cavalry that remained to him. His own guard and, perhaps, five score knights from a mix of banners.

Burakk watched as his enemy stood before him, waiting to be ended. He had seen it before many times: the foe, so exhausted that he accepts his own death. Well, Burakk would oblige. Before him, the men had placed their horses; perhaps they would have one last charge in them, but it would be slow, and once they did, his ogres were ready to take their lives.

As they closed, he heard the man general shout an order, and then suddenly the knights turned their horses around and walked back. That will not save you! Burakk thought to himself with glee.

But as the knights retreated, they stepped around something else behind them. It was a sight he had seen before, and wished he would never see again. As the knights stepped back, they revealed a line of cannon. Cannon, whose black mouths gaped like death.

'Fire!'

The cannon roared louder than any man, than any ogre could. The cannonballs whipped past Burakk and through his ranks of bulls, ripping limbs from their sockets, smashing through gut-plates. Three of his bulls died in that instant. Burakk heard Thorntoad shouting: 'On! On! Charge them down.'

But Burakk could not. The cannon fired again and this time Burakk did not even look to see how many he lost. He turned his back and ran for safety back at the Stadelhorn Heights that reminded him of his home.

His ogres ran with him, and following their example, the Black Ears broke as well. Facing defeat, Thorntoad had no choice but to escape as well, though as he went he swore vengeance against the ogres who had snatched such a victory from his grasp.

THE DRAGON'S JAW was forced, and the flowing Reik washed away the battlefield of the day. Tired but victorious, the Reiksguard made camp on the flat beyond. The sergeants and the bergjaegers stood guard, but all knew that after such a defeat, the goblins would not attack that night.

Fires were lit against the plunging temperatures, and soldiers across the army gathered around them, trading tales of their day and alcohol with which to celebrate.

'Keep that away from me,' Alptraum said to the wineskin Bohdan offered. The other Provincials sitting around the fire voiced their dismay.

'Brother Matz,' a voice sounded from outside the circle. The conversation stopped and all the young knights turned to look at the newcomer.

'Brother Reinhardt,' Siebrecht said. 'I am glad to see you well recovered.'

Delmar tried to smile through his split lip and bruised cheek. 'A few scrapes only. I have fallen off horses enough to know how to bounce.'

The knights laughed, but then there was that silence again. Siebrecht glanced at Gausser and he could read the Nordlander's thoughts clear upon his face, but Siebrecht knew that his friend would not intervene to impose a settlement. No, Siebrecht knew, Gausser wanted he and Delmar to put the rivalry behind them themselves.

'What are you doing standing there, Delmar?' Siebrecht said. 'Come, you must help. The heroes of the Dragon's Jaw here,' Siebrecht waved his cup at his friends across the fire, 'have exhausted me with tales of their victory. I need reinforcement! Sit down. Sit down.' Delmar sat, easing his injured leg to the ground. 'Bohdan,' Siebrecht continued, 'another cup of that fine wine.'

Delmar noticed Siebrecht give the Ostermarker a sly wink.

'Oh yah,' Bohdan replied. He poured a large measure from the wineskin into a cup and handed it around the fire. Alptraum's eyes flashed with mischief and only Gausser maintained his usual solemn demeanour. Delmar took the cup and went to taste it.

'No, no, no,' Siebrecht interrupted, 'you cannot sip it. Sipping is disrespectful to the wine, and disrespectful to the one who gave it.' He nodded pointedly at Bohdan.

Bohdan took his cue and chimed in: 'Yah, most disrespectful.'

'You must be bold, Delmar,' Siebrecht continued. 'As you were in battle today, unwavering. Seize the cup and drink it bravely.'

Delmar ignored Siebrecht and instead swirled the wine thoughtfully. He did not much care for wine, and the concealed glee in Siebrecht's face told him that this brew would be especially potent or vile. He could tip it out on the ground and walk away. That's what the old Delmar would have done back in Altdorf; his mother had always told him to chart his own path and not play the games of others. But Delmar was learning that life was not so simple.

This ploy of theirs was designed to embarrass him. If it had been Falkenhayn running the scheme then Delmar would know his motivation, for Falkenhayn raised himself up by pushing others down. But Siebrecht had saved his life today, why did he now want to make him look a fool?

Delmar thought back to the day of their duel, his shock when Gausser had knocked his friend to the ground and refused to let him rise. Delmar had thought the Nordlander was saving his friend when in fact he had been saving Delmar. The truth was that only through a man's intentions can one discern the real nature of his actions. The only question he had to answer was whether he thought, after all they had been through, he could trust this knight of Nuln.

Delmar took a firm grip on the cup and then swigged the wine down. The other knights watched with baited breath. Delmar licked his lips; it had not been unpleasant, more savoury than sweet. But then he felt the inside of his mouth begin to hotten, his gums were on fire and his teeth about to melt.

'Well?' Siebrecht asked. 'What do you think?'

Delmar maintained his composure as much as he was able; he sucked in cold air but that gave him only a moment's respite from the inferno. Summoning every ounce of his self-control he answered: 'Palatable... An acquired taste perhaps,' and then collapsed into a coughing fit.

The knights around the fire fell about laughing and Siebrecht slapped Delmar heartily on the back.

'What is it?' Delmar gasped.

'Ostermark pepper wine,' Siebrecht replied. 'Dreadful gunk, but Bohdan seems to like it.'

Through his watering eyes, Delmar saw Bohdan pour himself another cup and raise it to him in salute.

'He lasted longer than you, Siebrecht,' Bohdan called.

'He is more used to having fire in his belly,' Gausser stated.

Siebrecht took mock offence. 'I am simply more accustomed to the best,' he declared grandly, and the laughter continued.

'Brothers!' A group of knights appeared around them. It was Falkenhayn, Proktor and Hardenburg. The laughter stopped. 'This is where you have been hiding.'

Falkenhayn looked around the circle at Bohdan, Alptraum and Gausser, and very deliberately ignored Delmar and Siebrecht. 'Preceptor Jungingen sent us to find you. He wants to congratulate all the brothers who carried off the Death Cap standard, all together.'

None of the Provincials moved. 'Come on,' Falkenhayn insisted, 'stand up, stand up. The preceptor's orders.'

Alptraum and Bohdan got to their feet at that. Gausser glanced at Siebrecht, but then did likewise. The Reiklanders welcomed them and Falkenhayn led them off. One of them, however, lingered at the fire.

'What wine is that you're drinking?' Hardenburg asked.

'Ostermark pepper wine,' Delmar replied. He held his cup up to his brother-knight. 'Come sit with us, Tomas, and try some.'

Hardenburg hesitated. Delmar saw the indecision in his eyes. Hardenburg was a good man, but the privilege of his birth, his handsome face and his protective elder sisters had led him to sail through life, never having to make a decision of his own. And when he had joined the pistolkorps and then the Reiksguard, he had had Falkenhayn's lead to follow.

Now, though, he was troubled. Troubled by something he could not confide to his exacting and ambitious friend. He was beginning to realise what he had been missing: true brotherhood. It was not the wine he desired, it was the confidence of another troubled spirit that he saw in Delmar. But Hardenburg found it was harder than he thought to defy the expectations of one he had followed for so long.

'Another evening, Reinhardt,' Hardenburg said, his courage failing him. 'Honour awaits.'

And so he too went.

Delmar and Siebrecht were the only ones left. It had only been seven days since the army had marched into the mountains, but Delmar felt so much had changed. Siebrecht most of all: the sly, fool-tongued wastrel that Delmar had challenged back in Altdorf was not the same man as the knight who had returned for him this day, shielding him when he was at the foe's mercy, and giving up his own chance of glory at the same time.

'I am sorry you cannot be with your friends,' Delmar said.

Siebrecht turned back and looked deep into the fire. 'It is no matter.'

'It was a great service to me, and one I will strive to repay.'

'No, no.' Siebrecht waved his finger. 'You saved me once already. I have merely repaid you.'

Delmar hesitated, but he could not accept any honour that was not rightfully his. 'I should tell you, Siebrecht. I was not searching for you that morning. In truth, I did not even think of you until I saw you there. I was searching for another.'

Siebrecht looked from the fire and stared at Delmar's downcast, penitent face.

'Yes. Griesmeyer. Of course you were,' Siebrecht said.

Delmar looked up, confused.

'Why,' Siebrecht continued, 'in Sigmar's name, would you have been searching for me? For me, more than any other knight? I was hiding under an ogre from goblins eating their dead!'

Siebrecht threw up his hands. 'But that does not impair my debt to you in the slightest. Why you were there does not matter. How you came across me does not matter. It is what you did when you found me that was your service.'

'But, brother, a knight cannot take credit for an act he did not intend–'

'Pah!' Siebrecht exclaimed. 'Intention is overrated. My uncle told me years ago, "If you reward a man for good intentions, then good intentions are all you shall ever receive." No. Reward a man for good actions. No matter your intention, your action when you saw me was to come to my aid.'

Delmar shook his head. 'I cannot accept that.'

'Very well,' Siebrecht countered, folding his arms. 'In that case, consider this if it gives you comfort. I did myself no harm today in defending you. I did not share the "glory" in taking some ragged, rotting standard, but still I hear my name mentioned.'

Siebrecht got to his feet so as to make his gestures all the grander. 'A single knight, standing above his fallen brother, defending him against every foe that approaches; to these Reiksguarders it is the greatest symbol of their noble ideals of brotherhood. Glory is one thing, any knight can gain glory. But brotherhood... that is what they hold as the true virtue of this order. Think of it this way, Delmar; that I knew I would garner far greater renown for myself defending you than I would with the others. And so, though my actions were good, you may disregard my service for my intentions were all for my own reward.'

Siebrecht bowed theatrically and stood over Delmar, willing him to agree. Agree, Delmar, he thought, compromise your precious duty and admit your own self-interest. Prove yourself no better than my uncle, no better than me.

Delmar spoke: 'I cannot think that way, brother.'

'I can,' Siebrecht flopped down again, 'but sometimes I wish I did not.'

They shared a moment's peace, broken only by the sound of their friends' revelry around the preceptor's fire.

'It sounds to me,' Delmar began, 'that your uncle has had great influence over you.'

'As much as your father has had over you.' Siebrecht flicked a rock idly into the flames.

'Perhaps that is true,' Delmar conceded.

'And we cannot escape them. I cannot escape mine because he seems to be wherever I go; and you cannot escape yours because you carry him with you. And everyone who knew him sees him in you.'

'You did not know him though,' Delmar said.

'No. But at times I feel as though I am the only one who does not. Even Gausser has stories of the Reiksguard knight who saved his father's life. And just this evening, in fact, another knight told me that my rushing to your defence reminded him of Griesmeyer galloping to your father, and that you must inspire the same devotion in your friends that your father did.'

Siebrecht gave a hollow laugh. 'It is just my luck, that it is *my* most noble act that inspired him to think the best of *you*!'

'What knight was this?' Delmar asked.

'What?'

'The knight who said I reminded him of my father.'

'I don't know his name,' Siebrecht replied, a little irked at Delmar's failure to appreciate Siebrecht's woes. 'But you know him, we saw him today. The one with the long beard and the broken nose. He was in Wallenrode's banner. Wolfsenberger, that is his name.'

'Yes, I remember.' Delmar quickly got to his feet.

'You're not retiring are you?' Siebrecht asked.

'Yes,' Delmar lied instinctively, but then reconsidered. He would not fool Siebrecht in any case. 'I mean, not yet. I am going to look for him.'

'Of course you are,' Siebrecht muttered. 'You can carry your father with you as long as wish, Delmar. But sooner or later you will have to accept that the man he was is not the man you are.'

'It is not that. It is…'

'It is what?'

No, Delmar considered, he would not tell Siebrecht of his doubts of his father and Griesmeyer. There were some things that could not be said. They could barely be thought.

'Good night, Siebrecht. Thank you for the wine.'

Siebrecht scoffed and Delmar left. Siebrecht threw another stone on the fire. The noise from around the preceptor had quietened, but there was still no sign of Gausser or the others. His thoughts returned to Delmar and his father. He simply did not understand Delmar's obsession with one who had died so long ago. Siebrecht could tell him that no matter what he learnt, he would discover nothing about himself that he did not already know.

Taal's teeth, Siebrecht swore to himself, he could tell Delmar from the bitter experience of knowing his own father that there was no insight to be had there. No, there was no one in his family to whom Siebrecht thought he bore any true resemblance. Not his father, not his younger brother or sisters, and most definitely not his uncle.

'I am encouraged to see that you are making new friends, Siebrecht.' Herr von Matz stepped into the circle around the fire.

Of course, Siebrecht sighed to himself. If you even think his name he shall appear. For once, however, his uncle was alone.

'So where is Twoswords?'

'Twoswords?'

'Your bodyguard. Your escort. Your sentinel. Your chaperone. The one with the face only fit for the circus or the zoo.'

'Yes, I understand,' Herr von Matz said, amused. 'Twoswords, you call him? How interesting.'

'Not really.' It had been a long, bloody day and Siebrecht was not in the mood for his uncle's diversions. 'What's his real name?'

'I don't know.'

Siebrecht blinked. 'You don't know his name?'

'No, you asked if I knew his real name, which I do not. I know the name by which he was introduced to me and how I think of him. But now you say it, Twoswords has a certain ring. I think I shall use it in the future.'

Siebrecht was weary. 'Whatever you wish, uncle.' He waved him away, but Herr von Matz instead took it as an invitation to sit.

'I hear you have made something of a name for yourself in the last few days. Besting an ogre single-handed.'

'I was lucky, that was all.'

Herr von Matz peered at his nephew, unimpressed.

'I am not here to praise you, Siebrecht. Risking your life for so little consequence? When I heard of your exploits I could scarce believe my ears.'

Siebrecht could scarce believe his own ears. 'What are you saying? That I should not have killed it?'

'I am saying that you should never have put yourself in a position where you had to best an ogre single-handed in the first place. What were there? Near a hundred knights with you? As many dwarfs again?'

Herr von Matz shook his head in dismay at his nephew's thick-headedness. 'I told you before, resist the urge to plunge your chest upon the enemy's swords. You thought I was a fool back then, didn't you? But I know better than you think. I've seen how these knightly orders instil their doctrine within impressionable young men: the blind devotion to fraternity, the passion for self-sacrifice. That is not to be your destiny, Siebrecht.'

'If that is the case then I find it all the harder to understand why you have placed me with them.'

'Because I believe better of you than you do yourself. I believe you are sharp-witted enough to see past the fiction that entrances the rest.'

'But if I am so important to you, to the family,' Siebrecht exclaimed, giving vent to his bewilderment, 'then why expose me to such danger?'

'All life is risk and danger. If you listen to me and do as I say, but still Morr takes you, then I shall weep for you. But if you die because you have stood forwards and taken a blow meant for another, because you have been convinced that your brother's life is worth more than your own, then I shall not shed a single tear. Let those that crave honour in death seize it; do not let their example blind you as well.'

Siebrecht could not make out his uncle at all. Herr von Matz berated him with concern, bludgeoned him with kindness, to keep him safe.

'Is this all you came for, uncle?'

'No, I have something more interesting for you.' Herr von Matz smiled. All trace of his previous censure dropped away and Siebrecht felt the tendrils of his uncle's ingenious charm reach out towards him. 'It is something of great opportunity for us.'

'By which you mean, of great opportunity for yourself.'

Herr von Matz leaned in close and whispered: 'Not at all. Not at all. It is an opportunity for those who would see this campaign concluded in victory and Karak Angazhar freed. Not in weeks, but in days!'

The reflection of the fire danced in his eyes. 'Are you one of those, Siebrecht?'

'Of course. What must I do?'

'Not here. Come with me.'

Siebrecht followed his uncle to the northern edges of the camp and the pickets stationed there. Siebrecht thought that his uncle would stop there, for they were far enough out of earshot of any casual eavesdropper, but he did not.

They were challenged from the darkness. Herr von Matz identified himself and the bergjaeger emerged, greeting him like an old friend. Siebrecht saw the glint of the coin pass from his uncle to the sentry. The bergjaeger disappeared back to his hiding place and Herr von Matz beckoned him on.

'Wait, uncle. You cannot mean to go out there now.' He peered warily back down the Dragon's Jaw. The Reik had returned to its old course and the night made it as black as pitch. It had washed away much of the remnants of the day's carnage, but only the gods knew what else might be out there, picking over the remains. Only the gods, Siebrecht reflected, and maybe his uncle.

'Come on, Siebrecht. Not much further.'

He felt his uncle's urging; he should follow him as he wished. After all, he surely had Siebrecht's best interests at heart. He should just say yes and follow him.

'No,' he said. 'No, uncle, I go no further. You see I have learnt one lesson from you at least: I shall not follow any man blindly. Any man, including you.'

Herr von Matz regarded the young knight without expression; his attitude of easy geniality had evaporated. Siebrecht waited. For the first time he found that his uncle could neither fluster nor infuriate him. He felt calm, perfectly calm.

'Very well then,' Herr von Matz began, 'I shall attempt to open your eyes.'

'The truth, uncle,' Siebrecht warned.

'Yes. The truth.' Herr von Matz stepped towards his nephew. 'Ever since we entered these mountains, my guards and I have been searching for a single piece of information. One fact that will allow the Reiksguard to end this campaign at a stroke. I will not toy with you and ask you to guess what it is.'

'I do not need to guess, uncle. I know. It is the location of Thorntoad's lair.'

'That it is.' Herr von Matz was impressed. 'The Reiksguard does not face a single army of goblins; it faces ten tribes of them, far more used to battling between themselves than cooperating. It is only the sheer force of their leader's will that keeps their claws from each others' throats. Remove Thorntoad and you will not need to kill the rest, they will tear each other apart to choose a new leader. And by the time they're finished, what horde remains will not be worthy of the name and it will be years before they will threaten Karak Angazhar or the Empire again.'

'And you know where it is?' Siebrecht felt his heart pound; his uncle had not lied, this was a great opportunity indeed.

'I am close. I have the name of one who can tell me and, an hour ago, we made contact. I am to go and meet him now, though I do not know what to expect, and so I want you to come with me.'

'What of your men? Won't they protect you?'

'They will go. They are not far from here.' His uncle leaned in very close to whisper. 'But they are not what you think. They are not my protectors, they are my keepers. They serve another master, not me. I cannot be sure what their true orders are. There is no man within a hundred miles of here whom I trust more than I trust you. And so I ask you, my nephew: come with me.'

Faced with such a plea, Siebrecht did not deny him. 'I will come.'

Twoswords and the other keepers were, as his uncle had said, close by. They were hidden, quiet, amongst the talus and scree at the base of the Stadelhorn Heights, waiting and watching. Without a word, they fell into step with the knight and his uncle. They were dragging two loads behind them, wrapped in canvas. None of them carried torches or lanterns; instead their compliant dwarf led the way, the starlight more than enough for him.

They struck suddenly into a tunnel burrowed into the heights and emerged in a dry crater. One of the keepers lit a fire at the bottom. It would not be seen far. The keepers shrank away from the light. They were on edge; they knew how exposed they were here and they did not like it.

Herr von Matz, though, stood in the light and Siebrecht stayed with him, though he kept his hand near his weapon. He did not know what kind of man they were to meet out here, but he would have to be exceptional indeed to meet so close to the foe. A foul wind gusted down into the crater for a moment, and then a new range of boulders appeared above them at the crater's lip. One of them stepped forwards.

It was an ogre. Siebrecht went for his sword.

CHAPTER TWELVE

WOLFSENBERGER

'I DO WISH you hadn't done that,' Herr von Matz remarked.

The ogre thundered at them; its folds of muscled flesh, mottled and embedded with hooks and skinning knives, rippled in outrage. Its two meaty hands, each as big as a cannonball, grabbed a pair of wicked blades from the armour plate covering its gut and its huge mouth opened wider and wider as if to swallow them all. A dozen more of its kind rose from the crater's lip, as if the boulders had stood and were readying to charge.

The keepers drew an assortment of weapons as well, but Herr von Matz stepped in front of them. He stared the ogre in the eye and bawled right back in its face.

The ogre paused; it opened its mouth again and a lower rumble emerged. Herr von Matz replied in a series of grunts, smacking his fist on the ground and on his belly. He turned to his men and indicated for them to lower their weapons. He gave Siebrecht a pointed look and the knight grudgingly sheathed his sword.

Siebrecht watched his uncle and the ogre communicate. The ogre growled, making a noise like an avalanche, and Herr von Matz did the same. He made savage gestures with his hands, just like the ogre. It looked bizarre, the diminutive figure of his uncle 'speaking' the ogre's own language, but it was working. Herr von Matz was making himself understood. He waved at his men and four of them dragged up the heavy sacks. They loosened the threads and opened the canvas, revealing two dead Averland longhorn cattle, taken from the army's herd.

The ogre peered at the meat and Siebrecht could see it start to salivate. It ripped a leg off one of the cattle and tore into the dripping flesh with its teeth. The other ogres moved into the light, their bodies daubed with warpaint in a variety of different colours. They clustered in behind, sniffing the air and drooling. Their chieftain finished with the leg and threw the remains, still with a fair bit of meat on, over his shoulder, and there was a scuffle to catch it.

The ogre chieftain lifted the carcass and began to chew upon the torso. Though its mouth was full, Herr von Matz began to speak again in that crude language. The ogre initially ignored him, its gaping maw feasting on the first longhorn, then throwing what was left to the others, before starting on the second. As Herr von Matz continued, however, the ogre began to respond. Its voice still rumbled, but it was quieter than before, its actions less violent; the beast was actually listening to what Herr von Matz was saying. The atmosphere of hostile encounter had dissipated, to be replaced by one of negotiation.

BURAKK THE CRAW led his ogres back to their stronghold further up the heights. The human had surprised him. He had simply gone there to eat. They had eaten the scout the human had sent to find the ogres, cutting it up even as it screamed out its message. It had said that more of its kind would be at that place and so Burakk had gone to add them to his gut.

But while he had been eating the cattle, the humans' words had sunk into him. The deal was simple. Burakk liked simple. Thorntoad made things too complicated. The goblins did not understand how the world worked. Burakk was strong, his ogres were strong. They would take what they wished, and the goblins could fight over what remained.

Burakk had no desire for a dwarfen hole in the ground. That was what the goblins wanted, not he. No, it was time to set the world back to how it should be. And the human's deal was tempting indeed.

HERR VON MATZ and his keepers retraced their path to the camp. The sad dwarf, who, Siebrecht had noticed, had made himself scarce during the encounter with the ogres, was once more leading the way.

'You must manage your instincts better in future,' Herr von Matz chided his nephew. 'We are lucky the Craw did not think you were a real threat otherwise he would have killed us both where we stood. And then where would we be?'

'Dead?' Siebrecht glibly replied. His thoughts were still tangled in confusion and fear, and in such instances his quick tongue answered without him.

'Do not make light of such things,' his uncle warned. 'I lost two of my men just trying to get this ogre's name.'

'Burakk.' Siebrecht had heard his uncle already mention it, though he could barely conceive honouring such a monstrosity with a name of its own.

'Yes, Burakk the Craw. Aptly titled as well. I've never seen any creature eat so, but I suppose it is no stranger way of choosing their leaders than ours. I feared that even two full-grown longhorns might not keep his attention for time enough.'

'How can you speak so casually about them, uncle? They're the enemy,' Siebrecht stated.

'To mercenaries, the only difference between enemy and ally is simply who pays them the most,' Herr von Matz replied.

'They are mercenaries?' Siebrecht had seen mercenaries before, Tileans mainly, in Nuln to sell their services. They typically wore colourful uniforms with outrageous plumes and boasted of their great victories; they were a far cry from the ogres they had just left.

'They were not, but they are now.' Herr von Matz looked at Siebrecht. 'Can you work it out? Who they are? Or do I have to spoon-feed you again?'

'Who they are, uncle? They're ogres! What more is there to know?'

'What of their markings? Tell me about those, or did you spend the entire time thinking up your clever jokes?'

Siebrecht sighed and tried to remember. 'Their markings… They each had the same mark on their right cheek.'

'Yes, the Craw's own mark most likely. What of their other markings?'

'It was just warpaint, like every savage. There was no consistency to it.'

'Now what if I told you that that warpaint was their tribal markings? What could you then conclude?'

'Obviously, that none of them were of the same tribe.' It was only when he said it that Siebrecht realised how wrong that sounded. 'Why should that be the case though?'

'You tell me.'

Siebrecht was thinking now. 'Outcasts, banding together?'

'A good thought. But let me remind you of something you already know. Have you heard of a battle, about three years ago, on the River Aver where the army of Nuln fought an ogre horde, a conglomeration of tribes, and triumphed?'

'The Battle of a Hundred Cannons? I remember I thought it was a ridiculous name,' Siebrecht replied, irritated at how his uncle was dragging this out. 'Of course I've heard of it, the whole city went mad with celebration. There was a parade. When I joined the pistolkorps at Nuln they wouldn't stop talking about it.'

'Those ogres we saw were all members of tribes that fought and were destroyed at that battle.'

'They are the survivors then.'

'Yes, survivors of a battle where their tribes were destroyed by the massed cannon batteries of Nuln and the dwarfen guns of Karaz-a-Karak.'

The insight struck Siebrecht. 'Then that is why they ran at the Dragon's Jaw when the cannon fired upon them.' Siebrecht stared at his uncle. 'Was that your doing?'

Herr von Matz scoffed. 'The Reiksmarshal does not need me to tell him to point a cannon at an ogre and shoot. But he did need to have the cannon with him. Bringing cannon into the mountains does not make a great deal of sense otherwise. But once he had them given to him, he found the best way to use them.'

Then his uncle had had his hand in this campaign all along, Siebrecht thought, even the victory at the Jaw. Or alternatively, he reconsidered, none of this is true. And his uncle was concocting a story that gave him credit due to others.

Siebrecht shook his head to clear his fatigue. This was what his uncle did; this was what he always did for as long as Siebrecht could remember. When his uncle returned to the family estates for one of his visits, he filled your head with stories and fantasies, pretended to speak with authority on topics of which he knew nothing. He drew no line between fact and fiction, using either or both as he required at any one time. He had not changed. But Siebrecht had. He was not the same wide-eyed cub, suffocated at home and eager for any glimpse of the world beyond the estate wall. He was a Reiksguarder now, he had sworn his oaths to the order, and the order was here in these mountains for a purpose.

'Did you get what we were after? Did it tell you where we may trap Thorntoad?'

'Oh yes, he told me that.'

'And we're going to tell the Reiksmarshal?'

'Yes… in our own way.'

SEARCHING THROUGH THE standards and tents of the dark camp, Delmar found Wolfsenberger. He was sitting before a fire, in a chosen circle of comrades, talking of the events of the day before and the day to come. Delmar watched them for a moment before he approached and he was struck by the resemblance of this band of older knights to Siebrecht and the others, clustered around a fire. Their faces bore the lines of age, their movements were stiffer, but the easy familiarity between them was just the same. Delmar could hear the accents in their voices, from Middenland, Stirland and across the rest of the Empire. A Hochlander with a monocle and a pinched moustache was relating a story to his assembled fellows, Wolfsenberger, listening, sat on the far side of the fire. His face was long, his cheeks sunken, his skin pale; he wore a beard, but he wore it carelessly, leaving its grey hairs straggling around the sides of his face. His nose was bent below its bridge, evidence of a break that had never properly healed.

'Brother Wolfsenberger?' Delmar asked.

Wolfsenberger and his band of brothers turned to look at Delmar.

'Yah, what is it you want?' Wolfsenberger replied, the words flattened with the distinctive accent of an Ostlander. 'It is Brother Reinhardt, yah? We saw each other today.'

'That we did, brother. Brother Matz and I have much to thank you for.'

'Yah,' Wolfsenberger nodded. 'But it was our pleasure. You and your friend made quite a stand. No thanks are needed.' A murmur of agreement went around Wolfsenberger's comrades.

'Well, you have them in any case,' Delmar said. 'But I had another reason for troubling you.'

'Go on.'

'You knew my father? Heinrich von Reinhardt? You were in the order with him?'

'We all were. Our first campaign,' Wolfsenberger indicated his fellows, 'was his last.'

'I have questions. About his death.'

'Ah, then that would be for me. For I was the only one of us there,' Wolfsenberger said. 'But you should ask your questions of Brother Griesmeyer, he was senior to me; I had only just taken my oaths, and he was closest to it all.' The knight turned back to the fire, dismissing Delmar, and his comrades did the same.

'I would rather ask you, brother.'

Wolfsenberger paused for a long while. 'It was a tragedy. But it was a noble death. He saved the elector count's son, but he could not save himself. And there was nothing anyone could have done.'

'Oh,' Delmar murmured.

'You sound disappointed. Is that not what you came to hear? Is that not what Griesmeyer told you?'

'It was what he said, brother. But it is not what I came to hear, for I do not believe him.'

Wolfsenberger stared at Delmar hard and then exchanged glances with his comrades. One by one, they rose and took their conversation to another fire, leaving just Wolfsenberger there alone.

'Sit with me, Brother Reinhardt,' Wolfsenberger quietly ordered. Delmar obeyed him, his breath shallow, his chest tight in nervous excitement. He had been right, there was more to learn, but he almost feared what he might discover.

'Sit with me, Delmar, and listen to my words.' The faded knight beckoned Delmar down. 'You were right to disbelieve, for what you have been told is a lie. I was there at the end, and I have never forgotten what I saw.'

'Reinhardt!' the young Griesmeyer cried, as the knight charged against the Norscan warriors. The Skaelings had been too focused upon their prey, the young noblemen trapped in their midst, and the sounds of the battle had drowned the drumming hooves of the lone knight's charge. The first few managed to dive out of his path. Let others be the ones to use their bodies to halt the mighty warhorse, not them. The next few were slower to see Reinhardt and were slammed aside, bones broken. Reinhardt, with an expert touch, sighted his steed at the gaps as they formed within the mass of Skaeling warriors. Then he tapped his heels and the horse slowed, bunched its powerful hind legs and shot from the earth, leaping the final barrier of men that kept the knight from his goal.

The horse burst into the circle of those few Nordland nobles who still lived, surrounding the elector count's son, still dazed from his fall. Reinhardt pulled back on the reins and his steed reared on the very edge of the bank over the thawing, bloody bog. Reinhardt pulled his sword from its sheath and raised it high, so that all of his enemies could see the fate that awaited them.

Just for a moment, the Skaelings fell back, slipping down the bank where they knew the horse could not follow. The nobles took their chance and fled, leaving their lord and the knight behind. Their flight broke the Skaelings' hesitation; like hunting dogs they chased whatever ran from them. Reinhardt leant down to pull the elector count's son to his feet, but a thrown axe ended the life of Reinhardt's horse. It bucked and twisted in its death throes and Reinhardt tumbled from the saddle.

The Skaelings pounced upon their fallen foe, expecting an easy kill, only to find death themselves as his sword lashed out and cut the first attackers down.

A warrior swung down, using a captured Nordland halberd like a mallet. Reinhardt spun away and took the man's arm with a circular cut. Another threw a blow with an axe; Reinhardt caught the shaft with the flat, then ran his sword down and skinned the Skaeling's knuckles to the bone. A daubed, frenzied youth lunged, and Reinhardt trapped the seax beneath his arm, shattered the elbow and let the youth fall wailing back.

The attack paused for a moment as a Skaeling champion in black plate armour forced his way to the front and slashed at the knight. Reinhardt let the strike connect, his shoulder pauldron absorbing the blow, the wicked serrated edge designed to tear into flesh glancing uselessly off the knight's metal shell. Reinhardt smoothly reversed his sword and smashed in the side of the champion's helm with a two-handed murder stroke. The champion stumbled and did not rise again.

Then there were shouts, oaths roared in the Imperial tongue. Two knights were with him. Two of his brothers cutting a bloody path through the Skaelings towards him. The *first, Reinhardt knew, was his old friend Griesmeyer. The other, that new knight who proudly wove Ostland colours into his crest wreath: Brother Wolfsenberger.*

'YOUR FATHER TOLD me to take the elector count's son,' Wolfsenberger continued to Delmar. 'So I did. I hauled the frightened youth over my saddle and spurred my horse away. I was exhilarated, so young myself, my first campaign, such a daring venture and we had succeeded!

'I had thought that Griesmeyer and Reinhardt would be a few steps behind me, but when I reached the edge of the horde I saw they had not followed. I glanced back. Griesmeyer was mounted, but your father remained on foot. His sword was still inverted, the hilt high, ready for another murder stroke.

'And then I saw an act that scorched my spirit.' Wolfsenberger paused, as though the power of the old memory was still too much to bear.

'As the hilt of your father's sword swung up high, Griesmeyer reached down from his saddle and caught it in his hand. He pulled and the blade slipped from your father's fingers. He took his sword from him. He took his sword from him!' Wolfsenberger repeated in his astonishment. 'That same sword you carry at your belt.

'Griesmeyer turned his back and galloped away, leaving your father defenceless. And then those savages were on him again. Their attack redoubled in rage at being denied their victim. I could barely save myself and the elector count's son.'

Delmar could bear it no more, and he shot to his feet. 'It is beneath contempt! It is beyond excuse!'

'Sit down, brother,' Wolfsenberger said, regaining his calm. 'You will cause a scene.'

'A scene? I swear to you now, I will cause far more than that!' Delmar's hand gripped the hilt of his sword. Gods, he had known that something had been withheld. Something hidden. But he could never have guessed this! His sword was ready. He would find Griesmeyer this instant and, in the goddess Verena's name, he would have justice!

The occasions Delmar had spent with Griesmeyer, the adulation he had given him, the pride he had taken in his association with this murderer. It sickened him.

'And you,' Delmar rounded on the knight. 'You were his brother. How can you tell me this now when you stayed silent that day? How could you let this man walk free for twenty years when he deserves to hang for his crime?'

Delmar was a moment away from lashing out at Wolfsenberger himself. However, the faded knight sat unperturbed. He raised his hand to Delmar. 'Here, help me up.'

Delmar, fuming, grudgingly took hold of Wolfsenberger's hand and pulled him up. The knight got to his feet and then, in the blink of an eye, kicked Delmar's knee out from under him. Delmar landed hard and swiftly found himself pinned to the ground, Wolfsenberger's knee lodged in the small of his back.

'There!' Wolfsenberger whispered harshly. 'Now you know the feeling of being betrayed by one you trusted. You think to threaten me? You are a cub, a Reikland infant. You whine for the food the adults eat, and then you cry when you find it does not suit your taste, and blame the one who gave it you!'

'You are a knight!' Delmar replied, though the weight pressing upon his back made it hard for him to speak. 'You swore an oath and you said nothing!'

'I said nothing, yes. You think I am mad enough to charge one of the inner circle? Even then he was one of Helborg's favourites, and I was just an Ostlander, little more than a novice. They would have ruined me. If you are searching for justice within this order then you will search in vain. It was my word against his and it would have ruined me. A knight who charges another without proof puts himself at risk of the same punishment.'

'But Heinrich was your brother,' Delmar gasped.

'What do I care if one Reiklander kills another? How many years have those of Reikland eaten well and lived warm, whilst Ostlanders have gone cold and hungry in the fields? No, Delmar von Reinhardt, it is no business of mine. And I say, if you value your life or your future, then make it no business of yours.'

'I could never…'

'Then go,' Wolfsenberger interrupted him. 'And let there be one fewer Reiklander in this world.' There was an alarm running through the camp, men were waking, gathering their weapons. Even though darkness was still upon them, they were being ordered to battle. The knight released the pressure on Delmar's back and stepped away. 'Go, Delmar von Reinhardt, find your justice or find your death.'

SIEBRECHT, HIS UNCLE and the rest arrived back at the Empire camp at the exact same spot that they had left. The pickets ignored them as though they were ghosts.

Herr von Matz's keepers dispersed on errands of their own, except for Twoswords of course, who did not let Siebrecht out of his sight. They did not march straight to the Reiksmarshal's tent as Siebrecht had assumed they would; instead Herr von Matz led them to the militia's part of the camp and the pavilion of the Graf von Leitdorf.

The capricious graf did not take kindly to being awoken at such an hour, but once he heard what news he had been brought he granted an interview at once. The graf was not a man who easily trusted others; if he had not been born naturally suspicious, then three years of political manoeuvring between the Averland nobility for the vacant title of elector count would have made him so. Despite that, Herr von Matz came to him with recommendations from high places, and he had a Reiksguard knight with him as well, which lent credence to his information.

Once he had heard what this Matz character had to say, he knew he had to inform the Reiksmarshal. That obligation, however, did not go so far as to require him to blunder out into the night half-dressed. He called for his stewards to dress him properly, and sent a man to alert the Reiksmarshal and afford him the same opportunity. The two commanders of the army would meet, but they would do so in a manner befitting their rank and position.

After half an hour, the graf was ready and attended the Reiksmarshal. This time, Siebrecht and Herr von Matz were not invited inside. Helborg was less concerned with ceremony, and within a few minutes of the graf arriving Helborg's sergeants hurried from the tent to fetch Sub-Marshal Zöllner, Knight Commander Sternberg and, at the Reiksmarshal's specific request, Jaeger Voll. Ten minutes after they entered the tent, the sergeants left again and this time brought back the five remaining preceptors. The graf, feeling a little over-whelmed, called for his own militia captains and quickly the tent became full to bursting with tired, excited officers.

The men in the camp still awake sensed their leaders' agitation and the few impromptu victory celebrations still proceeding petered out as the men watched the shadows on the canvas of the Reiksmarshal's tent. At one instant they danced back and forth in heated dis-cussion, the next they flew as the officers strode out. Squadrons of knights were dispatched to confirm the information the graf had presented, but the Reiksmar-shal's instincts told him it was true. It was time to wake the army.

The word rippled out from the centre of the camp: every man was to stand to, ready to march as soon as there was a hint of grey light. The militia, thinking that after the trials of the previous day they might be allowed a chance to rest, grumbled and groaned at being disturbed. But then they saw the Reiksguard, already armoured, quiet, disciplined, and the militia stilled their complaints. Helborg looked over his order's swift preparations with a sense of pride. All through his youth he had studied campaigns; time and again he had read tales of brilliant generals who had won battle after battle, but lost the war because their armies, even in victory, had been expended and unable to seize the advantage bought with soldiers' blood. So instead their grand armies were ground down by foes with mediocre ability but inexhaustible tenacity.

The Empire needed a force that could march and fight, die and win, and the next day do it all again, and again, until the final victory was achieved. And that force was what he had created with the Reiksguard. Watching his knights now, bloodied, exhausted, but ready to ride to battle once more on his command, he felt the connection. He felt their tirelessness flow through his brothers and into him, and the weight he had carried in his soul ever since Middenheim finally lifted.

He was their inspiration, and they were his.

THE MORNING CHILL of the mountains was nothing to Delmar; his fury kept him hot. He forced his way through the crowds of men. Knights, militia, berg-jaegers, all blocked his path, all kept him from the one he sought. The army was rousing, its soldiers buzzing within the confines of the camp, each one looking for food, for a weapon, for a friend, for his regiment. There was order to it; within half an hour each one would be back with his banner, waiting for his general's instructions, but right now to Delmar's eyes it was little better than chaos. The entire landscape of the camp had changed: the regimental standards that had been embedded into the ground had all been uprooted in preparation to march. Tents he had used as landmarks finding his way to Wolfsenberger were being hurriedly dismantled and packed away. The army was sweeping clear every trace of its presence on this ground. Finally,

Delmar spotted a banner, the Reiksmarshal's standard, fluttering in the pre-dawn near the graf's pavilion. Delmar headed towards it. Wherever the Reiksmarshal was, Griesmeyer was never far from his side.

Delmar pushed towards it, his determination such that the soldiers around him gave him a wide berth. His hand was ready on the pommel of his sword, that same sword he had been so honoured to receive when Griesmeyer presented it to him, now only a reminder of his shame at being so completely duped. Griesmeyer had bought his devotion with the very instrument by which the knight had ensured his father's death.

The Reiksmarshal's guard were already mounted. Helborg, as ever, was eager to check the battleground ahead of the fight. Their horses shivered in the cold, snorting smoke through their nostrils as though ready to breathe fire. There his father's murderer was, Delmar saw him, sitting upon his mount, talking amiably with a sergeant beside him.

'Delmar!' Siebrecht cried, appearing beside him. 'What are you doing here?'

'Siebrecht? I...'

'Come, we must get to our banner. You will not believe the tale I have to tell you.' The excitement shone in Siebrecht's eyes. 'Come on, quickly, they'll ride out without us.'

Delmar could see the Reiksmarshal's guard readying to leave, and when they did Griesmeyer would be gone.

'Wait a moment. I have to...'

Siebrecht saw the object of his brother-knight's fixation and let him advance.

'Griesmeyer,' Delmar stated.

The knight of the inner circle turned from his conversation with the sergeant beside him and regarded Delmar calmly.

'What is the matter, Brother Reinhardt?'

'Do not call me that,' Delmar snapped. 'You have no right to say that name.'

That surprised the knight; but Delmar wanted it clear that he was not Griesmeyer's pet novice any longer. The knight turned his horse and looked down upon him.

'Be careful of your tone, Delmar. It takes liberties that I cannot believe you intend.'

'I spoke to Brother Wolfsenberger.'

The words hung in the frosty mountain air between them. For all his anger, Delmar still clutched a tiny thread of hope that Wolfsenberger had been wrong. That the faded knight had some personal vendetta against Griesmeyer and wished to slur his name. But the look Delmar saw in the older knight's face at the mention of the name was all the confirmation Delmar needed.

Delmar gripped his father's sword and tried to drag it free. He found his arm restrained, however; Siebrecht had grasped his arm and was holding tight.

'Delmar! In Sigmar's name, what do you think you are doing?'

Griesmeyer was even more outraged. 'Delmar, you dare…?'

Delmar tried to wrestle his weapon free, but Siebrecht was equally determined that he should not destroy his career and perhaps end his life. While they struggled, the Reiksmarshal's standard was raised and a trumpet blared. As one, the knights around them spurred their horses. Griesmeyer had no choice but to follow.

'Brother Matz!' Griesmeyer shouted back. 'Take care of your friend; he suffers like the last, but do not allow him the same fate. On your honour. On your name, Matz.'

Siebrecht thought of Krieglitz's body being dragged from the water. The Reiksmarshal's guard rode out, and Siebrecht released his grip upon his brother. Delmar shoved him away.

'I shall kill him when I meet him again, Siebrecht. I shall kill him.'

Siebrecht took hold of him and dragged him off in the direction of their banner. Siebrecht knew he had failed Krieglitz, but he also knew he would not fail another.

'Kill him tomorrow, Delmar,' Siebrecht told his friend, as he pulled him away from his insanity. 'Today, just do not kill yourself.'

CHAPTER THIRTEEN

REINHARDT

THE CLOUDS HUNG low that morning, blanketing the valley below the Karlkopf. The Reiksguard knights had ridden ahead to surround the mountain on the southwest and east faces, leaving the militia behind.

The bergjaegers had stayed to bring them along, and the militias followed them through the mist. These ordinary men of Averland had weathered a battle, frozen during the night and had been disturbed from their sleep before the sun had risen, and yet once they were marching they did not grumble. They saw their officers' excitement; they sensed their advantage, that this time it was they who had the upper hand. They had seen the foe beaten once, and now they were going to finish them. Yesterday, they had been burghers, cattlemen, vintners and apprentices; this morning, though, they were hunters.

Helborg watched them from above as they advanced into the valley. He did not like to have militias under his command. Each man ate the same as one of his knights, yet they were worth far less in a fight. It was more than that, though. They were not soldiers. They were workers. They were the ones who would rebuild each time soldiers trampled across their lands. They produced, whereas soldiers only destroyed. They were the men that their towns could not survive without. To lose them here would devastate their communities in a way an invader could not.

And yet, as great as their worth to others, as little as their worth to him, he could not win this battle without them.

He regarded their target again. Voll had called it the Karlkopf. What he had not known, and what Helborg now knew, was that the mountain the Averlanders called the Karlkopf was also called the great stone goblin by the tribes of the Black Mountains. That was Thorntoad's lair.

The Ten Tribes of Thorntoad were so called for a reason. They were not a single force: they were ten forces, cobbled together by the iron will of a single leader. That was how these greenskin hordes functioned; Helborg had fought enough of them to know that. A strike at the head, that was the surest way to halt them. Thorntoad had had its chance to eliminate the Reiksmarshal on the Achhorn, and the blow had been parried. The goblin warlord would find Helborg's counterstroke far harder to evade.

THORNTOAD SAT PERCHED upon his palanquin as he was carried amongst his Death Caps through the tunnels behind the great stone goblin. After a defeat such as this, any warlord was vulnerable. If he locked himself away, as he might wish, then his fiends would whisper to each other. Bargains would be struck, one would rise and declare that their gods' judgement was upon their warlord, and then they would come for him. Thorntoad knew this, for it was how he had seized control of the Death Caps two years ago.

As much as he longed for the peace of his web, he had to stay out. Keep each one of his Death Caps in his eye. Have each of them know that he was watching them, and that if they stood against him, then they would stand alone.

If he held his Death Caps, he would hold the great stone goblin. If he held the great stone goblin, he would hold the Ten Tribes still. Yes, he had taken losses, but he had left five of his tribes to maintain the sieges of Karak Angazhar and those were untouched.

He would not look to meet the armoured men in battle again and fight as they wished. No, he had learned that lesson well. He was a goblin. He would fight as goblins should. Run when the enemy isstrong, hide when they search, then strike when they show weakness. He would let the men march on, if they so wished. They could parade into the dwarfen kingdom with standards unfurled for all he cared. Then he would close the path behind them and they would be trapped there by the winter, with all the more mouths to feed.

These mountains would be his again, and then he would turn his attention to those who had betrayed him. He would make himself a new throne, and there he would sit upon the skull of Burakk Craw.

JUNGINGEN'S BANNER RODE quickly. The low cloud gave them some cover, but there was little chance goblins infesting the Karlkopf would not see them nor hear the thundering hooves. Speed then, speed was what they had. While the army of the Empire had been able to gather and move within half an hour of the orders being given, the goblin tribes had dispersed back to their warrens across the heights, the Predigtstuhl and the mountains around. And it took time for a goblin chieftain to kick and prod his warriors into action. But once they did, they would come and the Reiksguard itself would be surrounded. So, speed was the knights' weapon for now, and the knights pushed their horses as hard as they could.

Falkenhayn, carrying the squadron's banner, and his falcons rode at the head of their squadron. Delmar was behind them, speaking to no one and listening only to his daemons. At the rear Gausser and Siebrecht kept up as best they could.

Siebrecht thumped up and down in his saddle as he rode the uneven path around the mountain. Though it did his bones few favours, at least it kept him awake. The fight at the Achhorn, the hours he had spent beneath that rotting ogre corpse, his sickness, the battle at the Dragon's Jaw, his uncle's late-night escapade and now Delmar losing all sanity moments before another fight, it was too much!

Or at least, Siebrecht smirked to himself, it would be too much for a lesser man. But for Siebrecht von

Matz, who had trained at the taphouses of Nuln, who had drunk and danced for two days straight without releasing his partner or his glass, who had paraded in the burning sun before the Emperor whilst his brain pooled in his boots, this was nothing!

With a kick, he spurred his horse faster up the slope. He was Siebrecht von Matz, and he would sleep when he was dead!

'That look upon Delmar's face,' Gausser said beside him. 'I have seen it before. In your face, brother.'

'And I have seen it too, in another,' Siebrecht replied. 'Are we agreed then, in our wager?'

'I do not need to gamble on a brother's life,' Gausser said. 'My oaths are enough.'

Siebrecht shook his head. 'My family does not have your honour, Theodericsson. We do not understand brotherhood. My father does not, my uncle does not, and, in my heart, I know I am the same. We are driven only by grasping self-interest, and so it must be my interest that Delmar von Reinhardt lives to see another morning.'

'Then in this case I accept.' A trace of amusement showed in the Nordlander's strong face. 'I shall owe you a crown if Delmar survives the day...'

'And I shall owe you ten thousand if he does not,' Siebrecht finished with a flourish.

Gausser smiled with a big, open grin. 'You are a strange man, Siebrecht.'

'At last, brother, you understand me!' Siebrecht cried as they rode on.

* * *

TRIER'S BANNER, CROSSING the valley directly to the Karlkopf's northern face, reached its positions first. The knights rode as high as they could up the slope, and then dismounted, handing their reins over to the sergeants who would stay behind and wait for the casualties. In the northern war, Trier's knights had fought together in the Middle Mountains. They knew their objective, and they knew what to do without further instruction. Reiksguard armour was strong, but so fine was its construction that its weight was no greater than that carried by a fully laden mountaineer. Trier's veterans knew that even a mountain could be conquered, with time and a steady pace.

Helborg ordered his personal guard to go with them, for this northern face would be the hardest-fought assault. It looked towards the Dragon's Jaw and it was the gentler slope, so Helborg expected Thorntoad to send every one of its Death Caps to defend it. Once Trier had broken through, Jungingen was beyond the valley to the south-west, and Zöllner and Wallenrode were riding around to the eastern slopes, to cut off the goblins' escape in those directions. The goblins would be forced down into the depths, and there they would meet the dwarfs coming up.

Somewhere between the Reiksguard's hammer and Gramrik's anvil, Helborg prayed, Thorntoad would be caught.

And then there was the militia. Helborg had had them bring the entire supply train with them. The wagons were dragged to an exact position that he had specified to make a rudimentary fort. It was nothing like the mighty wagenburgs of Kislev or the armoured caravan trains that made the perilous journey east, but it was a barrier. It was a boundary. It said to the men of the militia, that whilst the land beyond might belong to the goblins, inside it was the Empire. Helborg looked over the ragged but proud militia regiments as they cut the draught teams loose and chained the wagons together to build their fort in between the heights and the Karlkopf. They, Helborg knew, were soon to be caught on an anvil all of their own.

'BROTHER-KNIGHTS,' PRECEPTOR Jungingen told his knights as they dismounted, 'goblins are cowardly creatures, but even cowards will stand and fight to protect their homes. No mercy! No prisoners! Remember, *they* do not take prisoners; they take food for their pets and sport for their blades. We are not here to defeat them. We are here to *eradicate* them. In Sigmar's name!'

The preceptor's tone shifted as he moved onto more practical matters. Jungingen knew that the Reiksmarshal did not expect much from his attack. Their slope was the steepest, his knights less experienced, but Jungingen had no intention of simply meeting the Reiksmarshal's expectations.

'There is no room for regiments, for grand manoeuvres. You cannot wait for orders; you must advance up wherever you can find purchase. You must look to the brothers in your squadron. They are your regiment, they are your banner today. Follow your standard, and if you should lose that, follow another.

If you keep climbing, you will not go wrong. The dwarfs will be attacking from below, we from above; make for the summit for there we believe we shall find Thorntoad, and it is that creature's death which is our goal.'

As the banner stood ready, Siebrecht and Gausser stood close beside Delmar. Unlike the other knights who looked up the slope, Delmar stared straight ahead, unmoving, his mind a thousand miles away.

The clouds had risen and the sun had broken over the peak of Karak Angazhar to the east. The Empire army in the valley would now be in plain sight.

THE DEATH CAPS on the lower slopes squawked their alarm back up to their fellows above. Thorntoad climbed up his web and out a hole near the very peak. The men were here! Their army covered his valley; the armoured ones were already slaughtering his fiends that were too slow to get out of their way down below. They were coming straight for him! How did they know? Traitors, again. Everywhere he looked, there were traitors.

Thorntoad dropped, and swung down to the throne room's floor. He pulled his shaman from his hole. The goblin growled at him and Thorntoad smacked him twice about the head to remind him of his obedience. The warlord snapped two of the toadstools growing on the cavern wall and then climbed back up again, dragging the shaman with him. He shoved the shaman through the hole and out onto the mountain. The goblin hissed and recoiled at the early morning sun. Thorntoad twisted the chain around his neck and pulled him against the rock. The shaman yelped in pain and the warlord shoved the two toadstools in his mouth, then held him down and forced him to swallow.

The shaman kicked a little, and lay still. Then he began twisting and writhing under Thorntoad's strong arms. Thorntoad pulled him up, the shaman's eyes burning green with power.

'Call them...' Thorntoad hissed in his ear. 'Call them all!'

The shaman struggled free, body popping and spluttering with each step. Then he curled down into a ball, hugging his bony knees. The green glow expanded from his centre until it enveloped him completely. The shaman threw his body back, reaching up to the sky. The power shot upwards, keeping the goblin's shape and growing until, for an instant, a greenskin god appeared above the mountain, roaring its call, its arms outstretched and beckoning.

Within every mountain around, the goblins heard. They grabbed their weapons and obeyed.

ALL IN THE Empire army heard the greenskin god's call. The militiamen each took a step back in fear. The knights each took a step forwards; they had been shown where their enemy was.

Helborg had been expecting it ever since he had led his army into the valley. Every goblin would be on the march now. They would surround the knights on the Karlkopf and there they would trap the Reiksguard and slowly destroy them. Unless, that was, a more tempting target lay in their path.

Fourteen hundred militiamen sat in the valley, guarding the wagons and tending the herd, and lying across the path from the goblin warrens in the heights and the Predigtstuhl. Six thousand goblins and three dozen ogres would now be heading towards them.

This was the role that the militia would play, the purpose they had marched all the way from Averheim and Streissen and Loningbruck to serve. They were there to hold their ground, to stand and die, to give his knights the time to finish their task.

Helborg rode amongst them, and they cheered him as he passed. He told his gonfanonier to fly the order standard as high as he could. Helborg wanted to be seen, not only by the militiamen but also by the red eyes in the hills. He wanted to draw the goblins all into this valley and hurl themselves at the militia. And when they did, they would find Helborg waiting for them here.

Helborg wanted to be fighting alongside his brothers and conquering the Karlkopf, but they did not need him to accomplish their task. As he saw the ordinary men of Averland, far from home, look up with hope, confident that their Reiksmarshal would assure them victory, Helborg knew that this was where he was needed.

'COVER, FALCONS. FALCONS, take cover!' Falkenhayn shouted with the last of his breath, as he scrabbled up the steep mountain path into the safety of an overhang. Black arrows and rocks bounced harmlessly down either side of his hiding place. His Falcons, Proktor and Hardenburg, were with him, and he was sure his squadron had surged ahead of every other. He had sprinted ahead lower down, where his effort would be seen by the preceptor. Now, higher up, he could take his time to recover. The goblins had rolled a pair of boulders into the path ahead in any case, and were defending them like a barricade. He would have to find another way around.

He sat, cradling the squadron's standard, and gasped to regain his breath. The ungainly Provincials were struggling up behind him, the intolerable Delmar in the lead. Some of them still had worth, that Alptraum, maybe Bohdan as well. They had shown proper deference and appreciation at the preceptor's fire last night. Once Falkenhayn had planted the squadron's banner upon this mountain's peak, they would fall into line and join his Falcons. Even Gausser, perhaps, for though he was an ill-mannered brute, he was the grandson of an elector count, and so there must be something to him.

Gausser, though, was following Delmar and Siebrecht like their shadow. The three of them were approaching now, and Siebrecht had raised his shield to ward away the missiles from above.

'Cover! To cover!' Falkenhayn stood up and ordered them over. Delmar, the first to arrive, walked up to him. Falkenhayn pointed Delmar to a spot further down, but then Delmar strode past. He was heading straight to the rock barricade, even breaking into a run. Siebrecht was behind him.

'Hey!' Falkenhayn panted after them, outraged, but then he felt a sudden tug as the standard was plucked from his hand.

'Thank you, brother!' Gausser shouted, took a proper grip upon the standard, and then he followed the charge.

DELMAR HELD UP his arm and the hastily aimed arrow stuck his gauntlet and skittered away. The pain of the impact flashed up his shoulder, but it was not enough to block out the rage within him. A goblin standing upon the barricade heaved a rock at him, but it flew wide and bounced off Siebrecht's shield. It was not enough. He ran full-tilt at the boulders in his path; his chest burned, his legs ached. It was not enough. He drew his sword and cut the leg from that goblin even as it tried to jump away. Its blood spurted out. It was not enough. He smashed himself against the stone and heaved to shove them out of their way, straining every muscle with effort. It was not enough. His brothers were with him, Gausser pushing with him, Siebrecht protecting them both with sword and shield. They were not enough. The boulder shifted and the path was clear; the goblins ran from him, ran back up the slope towards that strange formation that resembled a greenskin face carved into the hillside. They had run from him. It was not enough.

IN THE DIM light of the throne room, Thorntoad levered a stone from the wall. Beneath it a narrow shaft went straight down. Rungs were hammered into the sides; it had taken him days, but no goblin was ever forced into a corner from which he could not escape. He tossed a few more toadstools to the shaman, lying dripping on the ground. He would provide a useful distraction. The great Warlord Thorntoad of the Ten Tribes lowered his spines and slid down into the bowels of the great stone goblin.

HELBORG'S EXPERIENCED EYE looked across the advancing goblin horde. In the tribes' rush they had not had time to work any of their goblins up into the frothy-mouthed fanatics that had caused such carnage in the Dragon's Jaw. It was only small relief, for each of the goblins within the horde strode towards the wagon fort with an intensity of purpose that Helborg had never seen in their kind before.

Voll and the bergjaegers who had gone out to stall the horde were now running back again. Their shots were pinpricks to the goblin mass; they could not even slow them, let alone stop them.

The bergjaegers ran into the fort and climbed up to their new firing posts on the roofs of the wagons of the central enclosure. Within that central enclosure, the longhorn cattle began to stamp, smelling the approach of the goblins. If all else failed, Helborg would stampede the longhorns into the goblins to cover a retreat up the mountainside. But all else would have to fail for a general such as he to fall back upon such an erratic and unpredictable ploy.

As the horde drew closer, a ripple of unease went through the militiamen.

'Stay in your ranks. Hold your lines and you will be victorious,' Helborg reassured them. His voice echoed with confidence, and in spite of the odds it gave the men hope. It was a hope that Helborg did not share.

Once the ogres reached them, the wagons would be no defence at all.

SIEBRECHT PULLED HIMSELF over the ledge and tried not to throw up inside his helmet. In this brief moment of peace, he reflected unfavourably on his former confidence. It struck him that in the past, after he had drunk and danced for two days straight, he had tended to go and get some sleep. The one thing he did not do was try to run up a mountain after a doomseeking madman.

Gausser, in little better shape, helped him up and the two knights struggled not to gasp at what they saw. It was a veritable city, a goblin shanty town of dens and burrows dug into the ground and roofed with moss and lichen. They bulged like spores so that the earth itself appeared diseased. The sprawling town lay concealed within the shade of the cliffs above, which arched overhead casting the dwellings in the creatures' beloved shadow. It was as though the mountainside itself was split open with a leering goblin grin, the rocks its teeth and the shanty town its wide, sickly tongue.

The remaining goblins had fled. They ran, not up the steep slopes either side of the giant mouth but instead into a wide cavern that lay at the base of the overhang: the mountain's throat. Delmar, Siebrecht and Gausser paused there, while Alptraum and Bohdan caught up behind them. The knights had been told not to enter the tunnels; they had been warned of the devious traps the foe might lay. They were tired, but their blood was high. Surely only a coward would let his enemy flee without pursuit?

Siebrecht wiped his bloodied sword blade on the roof of a goblin dirt-den, dislodging the toadstools growing there. Gausser leaned wearily on another and it moaned under his weight. Delmar just stood where he was, unmoving. Siebrecht saw Preceptor Jungingen crest the ledge. In spite of Jungingen's hunger for glory, even he regarded the deep cavern with a wary eye. He called his second to him: 'How many have we lost so far?'

The preceptor's gonfanonier picked his way through the greenskin corpses. 'Four, I think, preceptor. Some of the sergeants are carrying them down now. Three, I believe, will recover, but I fear Brother Verlutz will not.'

'The priests of Shallya will not fail him, brother,' Jungingen replied. The thought struck Siebrecht that the preceptor could have no knowledge of his brother's injuries, could not know whether the injured man would live or not; yet Jungingen's confidence was such that even the knights who had seen Verlutz's death-white face half-believed that he would survive. Now was not the time to allow men to linger over the lost.

Deep in the shadow cast by the wide overhang towering above them, Jungingen paused at the entrance to the mountain's throat and peered inside. His brother-knights closed in behind him, staring into the depths. Nearly the whole banner had reformed here, waiting for their preceptor's orders. Siebrecht could see Jungingen's mind working, weighing the decision of whether to follow the goblins and enter the mountain or stay to their original course. Siebrecht could not decide himself what the right choice was; there was simply not enough information to be sure one made the right choice, and yet if one did not then the lives of all his brothers might be forfeit. This was what it was to be a leader, Siebrecht realised: to choose without fear, and then bear the consequences without regret.

'Keep climbing, and we will not go wrong,' a knight announced.

Jungingen looked around to see who had repeated his own words back to him.

'Brother Reinhardt. You speak out of turn.' Jungingen paused for a moment. 'But you speak well. Brothers, back to your squadrons. Look for paths on either side. The summit is our goal, remember. That is what we promised our Reiksmarshal.'

The knights moved, following his orders.

'And if they should return to retake their hovels, preceptor?' the gonfanonier asked.

'Then we shall have the advantage of height over them. Or, over these stunted wretches, even greater height than we did before!'

The knights who heard raised a low chuckle at that. But that brief merriment was cut short by an inhuman screech from above their heads. The savage noise began high, piercing, but then dropped low, and Siebrecht felt it move down his chest, through his gut and lower still, until it burrowed deep into the ground at his feet. The sound became a rumble that rattled the earth then rose again over their heads as it grew louder and louder. Siebrecht looked up and saw the rocks above them shake, then drop. The heavy overhang was falling down upon them all.

The jaws of the great stone goblin of the mountainside closed shut and swallowed the knights whole.

* * *

THE ROAR OF the avalanche on the south side of the Kar-lkopf echoed around the armies. The militias in the valley and the knights of the other banners paused, their faces raised, fearful that the mountain would fall upon them all. Those goblin tribes advancing from the north fell back at the anger of their god and the dwarfs in their tunnels each whispered an oath. The thunder quietened and there was a moment's hush across the battlefields, then sword and spear struck out once more and the struggle recommenced.

Kurt Helborg swore by every god he knew, and then sent two of his riders to learn what had happened. He prayed for the best and prepared for the worst, for he knew his prayers were rarely answered.

One wish, though, the gods had granted him. The ogres were not to be seen.

THE GOBLIN SCAVENGER skittered down the talus slope left by the rockfall, a curved skinning knife in his hand. The humans in their metal skin had thought them-selves invulnerable to the goblin weapons, had grown complacent, but they had not counted on the power of the greenskin gods and their shaman. The scavenger grinned; he would unearth one of these humans and take himself a nice trophy, and a good meal into the bargain. He scrambled to the edge of the scree; the humans there were less buried and easier to reach. He chose his prize and landed on its chest. He put the tip of his blade into a gap between the armour plate at the neck and made ready to take the kill.

A gauntleted fist burst up through the dirt beside him and grabbed the hand with the knife. The scavenger shrieked and jumped away, but the hand would not let go. The scavenger tried to pull himself free and, with a jerk, the knife came back up, guided by the gauntlet, straight into the goblin's chest.

DELMAR THREW THE dying goblin to one side, pulled himself out from under the loose rocks and clambered unsteadily to his feet. The goblin's cry had alerted its kin, and a dozen more scavengers started scrabbling towards him. He looked for his sword; his scabbard had been ripped from his belt. He dug down into the dirt. The first goblin had already reached him, charging with its weapon raised. Delmar's questing hand felt a hilt, took hold and pulled hard. His sword came free and he whipped it round, slicing the top of the goblin's head clean off. The other goblins saw their comrade's fate and caught their step, wanting to be sure they could strike all together. Delmar saw them begin to gather and, without a moment's hesitation, he attacked.

He ran at them, his sword high, held double-handed, ready to smash down with a crushing blow. The first goblin hissed in defiance and raised its spear to knock the sword away. Delmar shifted his grip and instead swung his sword back and around like a windmill's sail, cutting up below the goblin's guard and embedding itself between the goblin's legs. The greenskin howled and Delmar shoved it back, cutting the blade free. He spun his sword back around again and cleaved the goblin's head straight down the middle. Without pause, he struck left and right, knocking another goblin back with the pommel and running a third through.

The other goblins began to scramble away, up the slope, back towards their line of archers, unwilling to face this crazed warrior. As they turned, two more fell, their backs cut through by Delmar's sword; but his blood-rage was interrupted by the sound of shifting rock beside him. Another gauntlet broke free. Delmar stared at it for an instant, then dropped his sword, fell to his knees and dug with both hands. He pushed the rocks aside and pulled Siebrecht free.

'Brother? Brother? Can you hear me?' Delmar gasped.

Siebrecht spluttered. 'Aye.'

'Then dig!'

The distinctive form of Gausser staggered over, supported by Bohdan. The big Nordlander had taken a nasty blow and was leaning heavily on the Ostermarker.

'By my heart,' Siebrecht gasped when he looked about him. Where Jungingen's banner had been scant moments before was now just another slope upon the mountainside. Siebrecht counted three dozen knights or so who were struggling back to their feet. The rest were trapped beneath the rocks.

Beside him, Delmar uncovered Alptraum. The Averlander squirmed and pushed as Delmar pulled him clear. Alptraum struggled to his feet, breath rasping, chest heaving. He grabbed at the straps of his helmet; he had to get it off. He had to breathe.

'No, Alptraum, keep it on!'

Alptraum tore the imprisoning armour off and took a great freeing breath.

'Get down, brother!' Delmar cried, then ducked on instinct as he heard the flurry of arrows fly over. He felt a couple bounce off his plate, but all thoughts of his own safety were as naught when he heard Alptraum's scream.

'Gods! Gods! Gods!' was all Alptraum could gasp with the agony of the black-shafted arrow embedded in his cheek.

'Get your head down, I say!' Delmar ordered, and tackled the shocked knight to the ground, covering the wounded man with his own body.

'Sergeants! Sergeants!' Delmar called, but there were no sergeants to come. Those who had been digging the knights out had run into cover from the goblins' shots. Delmar dragged Alptraum into the lee of one of the hovels still standing and sat him there. Siebrecht, aiding Gausser and Bohdan, followed.

'Get it out, brother!' Alptraum shouted, but then he yanked at it himself, breaking the flimsy shaft and leaving the arrowhead embedded still. Alptraum gritted his teeth against the pain.

'Ah, Shallya's mercy,' Siebrecht said as he saw the metal barb in Alptraum's cheek.

'Cannot push it through,' Bohdan spoke dourly. 'He shall need a surgeon to dig that out.'

'You take him then,' Delmar declared, 'I shall put an end to those that did this.'

Delmar was already rising, sword ready, when Siebrecht caught him. Sigmar's breath, Siebrecht thought, he was going to charge up that slope against those goblins single-handed. He really did wish to die.

'Wait. Wait! Delmar!' Siebrecht shouted. 'Wait 'til we are all ready. Wait 'til we can go together.'

Through his visor, Siebrecht saw that his words had impact: the wild look in Delmar's eyes dimmed and he gave a curt nod of agreement.

Siebrecht relaxed a fraction. 'Finally, some sense' he muttered. 'And it only took a half a mountain to knock it back into you.'

If Delmar heard him he did not acknowledge it. Instead, he peered over the fungoid roof of the hovel. 'We go together,' Delmar repeated Siebrecht's words. 'The others are still dragging themselves out. We must clear those goblins from over our heads or we will never get the rest of our brothers free. There's a path up the rockfall to the goblins' position. It is narrow and steep, but it will serve.

'Two men in front, shields high. No swords, for we shall need the spare hand for climbing.' Delmar pulled his shield from his back; there was no doubt he would be one of the two. As to the second: 'Gausser?' Siebrecht asked the injured Nordlander. 'Are you recovered? Can you do it?'

'That is certain!' Gausser declared, swaying only slightly.

'No, Gausser, not you,' Delmar countermanded. 'Bohdan, you are with me.' The Ostermarker looked up, thick eyebrow raised. 'Gausser is too big. They will focus their fire upon us and the shield will cover you better. Siebrecht, Gausser, you follow with your swords. We shall need you right behind us or when we reach the top we shall be slaughtered. Ready?'

His brothers nodded their assent.

'Then, brothers, advance!'

* * *

DELMAR SMASHED HIS shield into the goblin's face, the arrow barbs embedded within it merely adding to its potency. The goblin, its bow broken, was knocked bodily off the cliff and the black-robed creature slipped down into the waiting arms of the knights climbing below.

They had begun their charge with four knights; they had finished it with forty. Each one of Jungingen's banner who could still walk had seen them run, had heard their calls to battle and had followed.

'Your sword, Delmar! Don't forget your sword,' Siebrecht reminded him, his own blade flashing out, cutting one goblin down and sending another scrambling away. Delmar hurled his shield at a knot of the greenskins huddled together in defiance, then drew his sword and set about them with Bohdan.

'Reiksguard!' Gausser bellowed beside them, flying the squadron's banner. Ignoring his weapon, Gausser simply plunged the pole forwards with such force as to impale the evil creatures.

'Falcons!' Falkenhayn called as he, Proktor and Hardenburg struck together.

The goblins were breaking in front of them, Delmar saw, and they were not retreating up the mountain back to another defensive line. They were running left and right, fleeing to the Karlkopf's other faces in hopes of escape. Throntoad's lair had to be close.

The goblins fled, but the knights did not pursue. They had thrown back the immediate threat, and now their concern returned to their squadron-brothers still struggling from the avalanche. First, the walking wounded turned, then a few of their brothers to aid them. Then a few more to aid the sergeants desperately clearing the rubble. In the face of such disaster, the battle could wait a few moments. Their brothers needed them and their brotherhood called them back.

Thanks to their actions, sixteen more brothers were saved from the rockfall than would otherwise have been found in time. Five knights who had survived the fall had died, trapped and waiting for rescue. Twenty-nine knights were already dead, crushed in the first few seconds. Amongst their number, the banner's gonfanonier, his blood seeping from his armour and staining the banner's standard, and Preceptor Jungingen himself, his fast-rising career within the order cut short along with his life, buried under a ton of rock. Of all his knights, only one squadron obeyed his final order, to climb and keep on climbing.

It had been because of Bohdan.

'Not this way.' Bohdan said when his vigil-brothers turned to go back. 'Up. We must go up.'

'What? Why?' Delmar asked.

The Ostermarker's eyes flared. 'Evil is there.'

'Look!' Siebrecht shouted, pointing above them. Nearly hidden within the mouth of a cave above them, a robed goblin stood alone. Its head bobbed as it chanted, its voice raising to a familiar screech. It was that same noise the knights had heard before the rockfall, and now it was once again channelling its power.

'Shaman!' Bohdan blurted, and ran towards it. Monstrous green shapes were forming around its body as it readied to strike again.

Bohdan shifted his grip upon his sword and then hurled it like a javelin at the shaman. One of the green shapes became an arm, and shot from the goblin knocking the flying sword to one side. Then it formed a fist and struck Bohdan hard, lifting him from the ground, knocking him twenty feet down the slope and leaving the indentation of four bony knuckles on his helmet.

Bohdan fell, but his attack had broken the shaman's concentration. The green shapes faded, and it ran back into the darkness of the cavern. The knights followed it, Bohdan stunned but waving them on, and they stepped into the gloom.

'Look at this place,' Falkenhayn whispered, his eyes adjusting quickly. 'It's a throne room.'

Hardenburg was the first who chanced to look up. 'In Sigmar's name,' he gasped.

'What are those things?' Proktor asked.

The ceiling of the cavern went high and was criss-crossed with taut cables and rope; the sloping roof was embedded with steel rings right to the top.

'It's a web,' Delmar said.

'If that is a web, then where is the spider?' Gausser intoned, ominously.

'You just had to ask...' Siebrecht muttered, but his eyes did not stop searching for the threat. The knights slowly backed towards each other, each of them feeling the darkness bear down upon them.

'Enough! We are not here to fear the monsters. We are here for the monsters to fear us!' Delmar declared, and the oppressive moment passed. 'The shaman came in, it must be here. Search about and find it before it brings the mountain down again upon us.'

The squadron divided, but there were at least half a dozen passages leading away from the central chamber. These goblins evidently did not like to be backed into a corner. Delmar even saw light at the end of some of them and heard the echoing sounds of the assaults on the other faces of the mountain. The shaman could be hiding down any of them.

'Here, brothers! Look at this,' Hardenburg called from behind them. He motioned to Falkenhayn and Proktor to join him and peeled away the surface of lichen from the wall to reveal a pink, fleshy nose.

'It's a dwarf,' Hardenburg said. It was strung up against the wall, covered with fungi feeding off the body.

'Is it dead?' Falkenhayn asked.

Hardenburg raised his visor and held his face close to the dwarf's. He felt the wisp of breath against his cheek.

'He's alive,' he exclaimed.

Falkenhayn and Proktor used their blades to cut through the binding ropes, and Hardenburg took hold of the dwarf and eased him gently from the parasitic arbour.

As they lowered him, Siebrecht saw the shaman. It had climbed into the web, and was crouching across two of the ropes, gorging itself on the toadstools growing on that section.

'There,' he whispered to Delmar.

'Where?' Delmar replied, looking around.

'There!' Siebrecht shouted as the shaman began to glow with power once more. Siebrecht threw his sword as Bohdan had done, but the weapon went wide. The shaman turned and hissed down at them, except the hiss turned into a roar, a roar that shook the cavern, that shook the very base of the mountain.

'It's going to come down right on top of us!' Falkenhayn yelled. 'Anyone? A bow? A pistol?'

Siebrecht drew his pistol, took a moment to aim and fired. The shot flew true, heading straight between the shaman's eyes, then struck a shield of energy about the goblin and ricocheted away. Both Falkenhayn and Siebrecht swore. Delmar looked around, searching through the web of ropes illuminated by the shaman's light. One of them that the shaman stood upon was buried in the wall just above Delmar's head. He took up his sword and swept it up. The blade bit into the rope, but it cut only halfway. The rope shook and the shaman shifted off it and onto another. Delmar looked to see where the rope ran.

'Gausser!' he shouted, and pointed to the other rope's anchor. The Nordlander drew his blade in a mighty arc and cut it with a single blow. The rope whipped back at the shaman, but it leaped up and caught hold of another. This one though, its anchor loosened by the tremors rippling through the mountain, came loose in its hand. Desperately, the shaman clawed out and grasped another, dangling from it by its nails, all the while burning brighter and brighter with the power building up inside.

Delmar traced the rope back, but it was too high.

'Gausser?' he shouted in desperation. The Nordlander swiped as high as he could, but it was just out of his reach.

'Siebrecht?' Delmar called, but Siebrecht shook his head. His spare powder and shot were in his saddle.

Frustrated, Falkenhayn whipped his sword up at the rope, but it struck without effect. Then Delmar saw it.

'Gausser! Falkenhayn!' The two knights looked back as Delmar rushed over. 'Proktor,' he said, motioning up.

Proktor looked at Delmar and understood. The three knights seized him by his legs and lifted him from the ground. Gausser took the strain, while Delmar and Falkenhayn pushed the legs of the smallest of their number as high as they could. The rocks fell down around their feet, but they ignored them. Proktor swung, and cut, but not hard. He swung again and the shaman began to twist to try and swing to another rope. Proktor swung a third time, and the blade skimmed away.

'Come on, Laurentz,' Falkenhayn shouted. 'For your brothers!'

Proktor swung up and hit the spot of his first cut, shearing the rope through. It spiralled away. Proktor overbalanced and the tower of knights tumbled. The shaman dropped down and bounced upon the floor, the power dissipating through the stone.

'I have him!' Hardenburg shouted and plunged his blade twelve inches through the shaman's black heart.

The shaman burst and a cloud of red spores ripped from its body. The other knights could only watch as the red spores hung in the air for a moment, glistening with unholy magic; then they were suddenly sucked up into Hardenburg. They flew into him, slipping through every hole and chink in his finely crafted armour.

Hardenburg's eyes bulged wide. Then he clenched and twisted, and he gave a great wail of pain as the spores went to their vicious work. He collapsed, tearing at his helmet and his collar; his armour trapped the spores against the skin, their protection rather than his own.

The knights clustered around their fallen brother. Hardenburg gave another agonised cry and slipped from consciousness.

'We must get him down to the sergeants at once,' Proktor said, and this time no one disagreed. The virulent red spores gave the fair-faced Reiklander the look of having been butchered. Delmar reached to lift him.

'Proktor and I shall carry him, Reinhardt.' Falkenhayn's tone brooked no disagreement. 'You may carry the dwarf.'

But none had a chance to lift either of them, for beyond the throne they heard the commotion of more men coming down a passage. The leading knight bore the markings of one of Helborg's personal guard. It must be Griesmeyer! Delmar's hand grasped his sword. But the knight raised his visor and Delmar realised his mistake. It was not Griesmeyer, but another of the guard.

The knight looked at them and then turned to his brothers who were following behind him. 'Pass the word back, the Karlkopf has already been taken!'

HELBORG FELT THE trembling stop and then saw the Reiksguard flag fly from the top of the Karlkopf. He felt a surge of his old excitement at a battle won. The militiamen struggling in the valley against the goblin tribes saw it too and raised a rousing cheer, just as the goblins gave a creaking moan and turned to retreat.

The ogres had never appeared.

WHILE GAUSSER AND Bohdan took the dwarf down the mountainside, Siebrecht followed Delmar as he passed through the tunnel and out onto the eastern face. There he found Griesmeyer amongst the rest of Helborg's personal guard.

'We should talk, you and I,' Griesmeyer said. Delmar nodded, and Griesmeyer led him by a rough path onto a plateau near the peak itself. Siebrecht reluctantly let the two knights go.

To the west Delmar saw the Stadelhorn Heights and beyond those the Achhorn ridge. To the north was the wooded Predigtstuhl stretching down to the Dragon's Jaw below. To the east were only the frosted peaks that hid Karak Angazhar from sight, and the deep blue mountain lake that fed the Reik. Although there were thousands of men all about them, on the mountain slopes and on the flats below, here they were alone. They would have privacy enough to fight.

'It is fitting enough,' Delmar decided, as he looked about.

'Fitting enough for what?' Griesmeyer asked.

'For what other reason are we here?' he said, raising his sword and taking his guard.

'Reiksguard do not fight Reiksguard,' Griesmeyer declared.

'You wish to hide behind that, do you?' Delmar had been calm, but the older knight's stubborn impenitence reignited his rage. 'Very well. Here.'

Delmar reached inside the collar of his armour. He pulled off his Reiksguard insignia and threw it to the ground. 'I hereby quit the order. There, now, let us go to it; for since Wolfsenberger told me his tale I cannot endure both our existences. One must end. And it must end now.'

'To quit the order? And seek to kill me?' Griesmeyer was angering as well. 'You've placed great belief in that knight's words.'

'Why should he lie?' Delmar challenged the older knight.

'Why should I?' Griesmeyer shot back.

The sharp exclamation hung fixed in the frozen air between them. Delmar weighed his sword in his hand, as he weighed Griesmeyer's words in his mind.

'Whether you have lied or not… you have not told me the truth,' Delmar said.

'I have told you all the truth it is safe for you to know.'

'And who are you to judge that for me?'

At last, Griesmeyer's restraint shattered completely and he thundered: 'I am a knight of the Reiksguard, ordained of the inner circle; I have faced daemons and beasts beyond your imagination, and I carry the Emperor's life as my greatest honour and my constant burden.' He sucked in a breath of the cold air. 'That is who I am. Who are you? Answer me that, Delmar, who are you?'

Delmar had never felt such anger from Griesmeyer before. The calm, tempered knight he knew was gone, replaced by a savage warrior filled with heat. His sudden rage struck Delmar like a blow.

'I am his son.' It was all Delmar could answer and

Griesmeyer found he had no reply to that.

'Then listen, Heinrich's son, to what I say,' Griesmeyer began. 'For I now, here, break the oath that I once swore, never to reveal what I am to tell.'

'Take the boy!' Reinhardt ordered. The young knight, Wolfsenberger, held Nordland's son tight and spurred his horse away through the reeling Skaeling horde.

Griesmeyer cut down another too-eager northern warrior and then looked back to his brother.

'Give me your hand!' he cried. 'Brother, your hand.' Griesmeyer reached out to pull his friend up onto his horse.

'No, brother,' Reinhardt replied, calmly, hefting his sword still by its blade. 'Here I will stand. Here I will fall.'

Griesmeyer swore. 'Do not be a fool, Heinrich. Just take my hand. Think of your wife! Think of your son!'

'They have never left my thoughts.'

Griesmeyer yanked his horse around. 'I shall not tell them, Heinrich. I shall not be the one they despise, the one they shall blame for taking you from them.'

'Yes you will, brother. For you could not bear for them to hear it from another,' Reinhardt said. 'And I shall beg one more favour.'

Reinhardt raised his sword high, handle first, to his brother, and Griesmeyer instinctively caught its grip.

'Give it to Delmar. Give it to my son.'

'Gods damn you! Gods damn you!' Griesmeyer's sight began to blur with frustration.

'They have already, my brother.'

'No!' Delmar cried. 'It was not so! My father would

never…'

Delmar screamed his denial, raised his sword and charged. Griesmeyer drew his own and held it straight. Delmar's cut crashed down and the old knight's guard gave way. But Griesmeyer had already stepped aside and Delmar's swing went wide. Griesmeyer's blade spun and whirled across his brow; the knight uncoiled and struck Delmar square in the back of the head.

Delmar staggered. His fingers went numb. His sword slipped from his grasp. The blow was with the flat; it had not penetrated his helmet, but it had been delivered with such force as to knock him senseless. Delmar's legs buckled and he collapsed upon the rock.

With the tip of his blade, Griesmeyer raised the young man's visor. Delmar blinked up into the cloudless sky.

'Just lie still, Delmar. Just lie still,' the old knight soothed. 'And listen to your elders.'

'It was the year before Emperor Karl Franz's election,' he continued. 'The Patriarch's expedition started badly. Heinrich had come with us, though I knew it pained him to leave you and your mother behind while you were still so young. In our first action, a champion of theirs, a sorcerer of some kind, cast a bolt of dark energy that fair tore our squadron to shreds. I was lucky. Heinrich was not, but he held tightly to his life and defied Morr at his very gates. Battered, we came home, and while I prepared to march forth once more, he returned to you and stayed there whilst he recovered.

'The year progressed. The campaign was done. And then, that winter, he called me to your home. I arrived, joyous to see him so recovered, and he had a surprise for me: your mother's belly was swelling again. She was due on any day, and he wished me there for we were family.

'The birthing came upon her suddenly, and it was most terrible. A day and a night she suffered in bed, whilst your father tormented himself with the thought of her loss. You were so small a child, but you were already brave. And it was you and I, together, who kept him sane.

'The gods, however, had already marked him down. The babe, when it came, was a hideous thing. I cannot describe its horror in mere words; it was no mortal creature, it was a darkling child of Chaos.

'Your mother, mercifully, was already collapsed in exhaustion. Your father though, was left to gaze upon it: its horns and claws and mottled skin, its limbs twisted, confused and too great in number. He took it away, into the chill night, and returned next morning with it gone.

'I had hoped, I had prayed that that would be the end of it all. A grievous shock to any family, yes, but not unknown. Your father had taken the right action, harsh, but quick. And now it was simply time to heal. Your mother improved, you made yourself her constant companion and though she hurt she never forgot what a blessing she had in you already. Heinrich, though, he slipped away, and naught that I could do would prevent it. The foe he fought was not one to be defeated with sword or lance. It was one inside him. He prayed, morning to night, to rid himself of the taint he carried; the corrupting strain with which that dark sorcerer had left him infected.

'I tried to talk to him, but he would not listen. The sermons of Sigmar's priests hold a man very strong. When he said that prayer had failed him, he journeyed back to Altdorf and I went after him. I caught him steps before he declared himself to the witch hunters. I told him that if he did, then it would not only be his life that would be forfeit but yours and your mother's as well, and he at last relented. I brought him back to the chapter house, thinking to bring him to his brothers' care. But there we argued for days on end, until all the words had been said, and we spoke to each other no more.

'And then Karl Franz was elected and he led us north to fight against the Norse harrying Nordland's coast. When I heard we were marching I feared that in my absence your father would destroy himself. Imagine my joy then, when I learned he was to come with us. Imagine my joy, then imagine what I felt when I realised that he had come north to end himself.

'I brought the news to you myself. Your mother, at first, accepted my words. To marry a Reiksguarder is to accept that such loss might befall you at a moment. But as the next years passed, and your father's face appeared in your own, I saw her feelings harden towards me each time I returned. When I did visit, it was a reminder of all she had lost. And when I told you stories of my life, and duelled with sticks as swords, she only saw the true father you had been denied, the father I should have brought her home.

'She told me then I was no longer welcome. And thus I have not been, until my oath to your father brought me back to present his sword to you.'

The old knight finished his tale. Delmar slowly picked himself up from the ground and walked to the edge of the plateau. There to the east was the mountain lake from which the Reik poured. Somewhere there was the well-spring that fed that lake, the source of the Reik, the greatest of the rivers from which the Empire drew its power. This was no place for endings, Delmar decided. It was where journeys commenced and the past was washed clean.

CHAPTER FOURTEEN

HARDENBURG

BURAKK THE CRAW looked out over the green and fertile plains of southern Averland. The army of men had been left well behind, distracted by the goblin fortress, assuming that the ogres were fleeing deeper into the mountains. Not a chance. Not when the Empire's army had left this soft province undefended, with its beasts and men fattened from their harvest. No. This was Burakk's reward from the Great Maw. Never again would he play humble before a greenskin creature. Now it was he who was their chief; the trickle of goblins who had come to give their service had become a flood once it was clear that their great stone goblin was lost. As he and his bulls had raced across the slopes that night, the goblins had sprinted after. They knew Thorntoad was lost, and their praises of him turned to curses; his plans to become goblin-king of the dwarfen hold were scattered as the dust. Instead, his goblins joined the ogres and became their willing servants.

'Tyrant!' One of his bulls approached him up the slope. He was dragging something through the dirt behind him. It looked like some hairy animal, drowned in the river.

'Found this. Washed up on the bank.' The bull held it out for Burakk to examine.

Thorntoad unravelled and came up screeching. He whipped one arm around and his spines made a dozen tiny slices in Burakk's outstretched hand. Thorntoad spun about and dug his teeth into the wrist of the bull holding one of his crippled legs. The bull shouted in pain and let go his grip as the goblin freak took a chunk from his flesh. Thorntoad, though, did not fall, he held on tight and scrambled up the bull's shoulder. He flipped himself over and sat upon the ogre's shoulders, clamping his arms around the ogre's face and letting his thorns dig in. The bull's shout turned into a strangled bellow and he blindly grabbed at the goblin on his shoulders, only to grasp handfuls of razor spines. Thorntoad was screeching again, this time in triumph, as he dug his heels into the ogre's back as though to ride him to safety.

Burakk swung his hefty club and smacked them both hard. The ogre, brained, fell to the side and Thorntoad tumbled from his shoulders. Burakk raised his club again to finish the goblin off, but the freak sprang up and raced up the cliffside out of the ogre's reach.

Thorntoad was not done. No sooner was he safe than he turned back. The struggle had been heard by the ogres and goblins alike, and now both came to see. Thorntoad looked over his goblins newly sworn to the tribe of the Craw. There were still enough, he could win them back!

'My fiends!' he called, hanging onto the rockface with one hand and reaching out to them with the other. 'My magnificent fiends! Your black hearts are in *my* chest. Your broken teeth within *my* mouth. Do not submit your fates to these betrayers who will have you serve them in the day and then will gorge themselves upon you at night. Let yours be the first blow! Seize your blades and set upon these hulks. Rend their bodies and drain their spleens. Our own great victory is still within–'

The heavy stone struck the goblin's temple. Burakk's aim had been good. Thorntoad crumpled and fell from his perch, landing in a spindly mass at the feet of his goblins below.

'Take his thorns,' Burakk ordered. The goblins' blades came out and they cut Thorntoad's spines from him. As they were cleared, the mighty Thorntoad was revealed beneath for what he truly was, a pitiful, slight freak.

Burakk lifted him by his leg above his head, and his breath roused the denuded freak to consciousness. It was too late. The mouth of the Craw opened and engulfed its victim. Burakk felt it wriggle as it slid down his gullet. He swallowed and then it went still. His bulls cheered and his goblins cackled, and he acknowledged their ovation as he strode back to the edge. Out there, upon the plains, Burakk could see a farm: both cattle and humans, plump and juicy. The Feast of Averland would begin with them. His tribe's course was set, and it would prove satisfying indeed.

THE COLD METAL prongs of the grey instrument forced the flesh of Alptraum's cheek apart even wider and the

Averlander howled in pain. His attempt at quiet stoicism had long since been abandoned.

Alptraum crouched before the sergeant who was slowly opening up the side of his face to extract the arrow's tip. He clenched his jaw against the agony for a moment, then gave up and continued in his systematic defamation of the Empire's lower pantheon.

Delmar, Siebrecht, Gausser and Bohdan watched from a few paces distant. As Alptraum's oaths progressed onto the lesser goddesses and took on a more lurid tone, Siebrecht turned to Gausser.

'Can we not get him a horse's bit to bite down on?'

'The swearing helps him, he says,' Gausser replied.

'I do not doubt it,' Siebrecht said. 'I am just not certain it's helping anyone else.'

The sergeant twisted and pulled, and Alptraum's shouts rose to new heights. With his own cry of triumph, the sergeant extracted the arrow with his pincers. Alptraum, exhausted and hoarse, collapsed onto his back as his brothers congratulated him.

As they set about bandaging the wound, the sergeant held the arrow point up to the light of the torch. 'Would you like to keep it, my lord?' he asked. 'Many of our brother-knights do. A memento of battle?'

Alptraum looked at him as though he had recommended they should fling themselves onto hot irons for fun. 'Throw the cursed thing away! I never want to see it again.'

'As you wish, my lord,' the sergeant said, slipping the arrowhead away, and passing Alptraum a draft. 'Here, drink this. It will help fight the infection.'

That it did, and it also swiftly put the young Averland knight to sleep. Delmar watched as his knotted face finally relaxed.

'I'm going to see Hardenburg,' Delmar told Siebrecht.

Siebrecht nodded and then, after Delmar had left, he stepped over to the sergeant who was putting away his surgeon's tools.

'I'll give you half a crown for the arrowhead,' Siebrecht whispered.

The sergeant almost asked why he wanted it, but then he saw the twinkle in Siebrecht's eyes and decided that the less he knew the better.

'Two crowns,' the sergeant countered.

'One.'

'One and a half.'

'One,' Siebrecht said, more firmly this time.

'Done.'

Siebrecht smiled and turned back to Gausser. 'Brother? Our wager? Delmar lives. Pay the man.'

Growling something beneath his breath, Gausser reluctantly reached for a coin.

DELMAR STEPPED PAST the other convalescing knights. Most of them here would survive, cared for by the order's sergeants, who carried their knights to battle and carried them home again. The dying were kept separate; the sergeants did not want to tempt Morr when he came for the dead to take the living as well. Their last hours would be spent with the prayers of a priest, until they passed and their bodies could be moved. At least, Delmar thought sombrely, his father had been spared that slow dissolution of life.

The Reiksmarshal had confirmed all of Griesmeyer's words. At last, Delmar knew the truth of what had happened to his father. And yet, in gaining knowledge, he had lost his certainty. The order had concealed the taint of a man to allow him to keep his honour. It had deceived and sinned, broken the faith of knights like Wolfsenberger, but in pursuit of a noble goal. Griesmeyer had lied to his brother's wife and his son, but all for the purpose of protecting them from those who would consider them tainted as well.

By all the priests' teachings Delmar had ever heard, Griesmeyer was wrong, the order was wrong, dangerous, complicit even. Where there was mortal taint, there could be no exceptions made. And yet Delmar held in his heart the fervent belief that they had been right in what they had done. He could not resolve it.

But then Delmar thought back to the crippled masters of the chapter house: Verrakker, Lehrer, Talhoffer and Ott. The order cared for its own, no matter what befell them in its service. No matter if their wounds were self-evident, or hidden inside. Brotherhood – that was the order's true strength.

Hardenburg lay amongst the living. His entire body was swathed in anointed bandages that were fighting the spores that covered him. His flesh had become a tiny battlefield of its own as the infection and the medicine waged war.

'Tomas?' Delmar announced his presence.

Hardenburg's eyes looked over; his head was too bandaged to move.

'Delmar?' he croaked. 'I am glad you have come.'

'I have something for you.' Delmar was holding a piece of plate, a shoulder pauldron. 'It is from your harness.'

Hardenburg focused upon it. 'What are those markings?'

'The dwarf we freed from the goblins' lair. The one you saved.'

Hardenburg nodded a fraction.

'That dwarf,' Delmar continued, 'was King Gramrik's son.'

Hardenburg gave a hollow chuckle beneath his bandages. 'Is there a reward? Is there gold?' he joked, his voice weak.

'No, brother,' Delmar laughed. 'But in his thanks, he ordered this rune carved upon our armour. Of all our squadron.'

Delmar held the pauldron forwards so Hardenburg could see, and the injured knight peered at the markings.

'Do you know what it means?' he asked.

'No,' Delmar admitted, 'but I think it must be a mark of strength, and of courage. I thought it should travel back to Altdorf with you, not in some caravan.'

Hardenburg shakily reached out with his hand and traced the pattern lightly.

'Yes,' he decided, 'yes, you are right. Strength and courage.'

Hardenburg continued to touch the rune, but Delmar saw his eyes glass over with worry once more.

'Do you not like it?'

'No, it is not that. I am just afraid, that is all.'

'Of what, Tomas?'

'Of what people will think of me back home in Eilhart. I do not think many of my friends back there will wish to see me like this.'

'Your real friends will.'

'Maybe, then, it is *I* who does not want them to see me like this. Even if I heal, they shall never look at me the same again.'

Hardenburg brushed one of his bandages aside slightly and Delmar saw the virulent work of the goblin's toxic spores upon the young man's body. Hardenburg would survive, Delmar knew, but he would bear those ugly scars upon his skin forever.

But the order cared for its own. No matter what.

'Then do not go back to Eilhart just yet. The chapter house is no bad place to heal,' he said. 'You will get the finest treatment from the sisters of Shallya.' Delmar got to his feet. 'Consider it, Tomas. For when you are amongst your brothers, you have nothing to fear.'

'I know,' Hardenburg replied, replacing the bandage. 'I think I will,' he decided.

Delmar placed the pauldron down on the bed by his brother's hand.

'I will tell you, Delmar,' Hardenburg said. 'I knew this was to happen to me.'

Delmar looked back up at him. 'How so?'

'I had a dream, back in Altdorf. It was the night before our vigil. It was so vivid, so real.'

'You dreamt this?'

'Aye, I think I did. It's hard to picture it now.' His eyes closed. 'But I know it was a nightmare. I was marked, scarred, like this, and there was some bargain, I could make myself whole again.'

Hardenburg opened his eyes. 'I remember thinking when I woke up that to be so disfigured was the worst that could happen to me. Worse even than death. I wanted to talk to you about it but...'

Someone coughed behind them. It was Falkenhayn.

'If you are finished, Reinhardt,' he said, stiffly. 'Then I would appreciate some time to sit with my brother.'

Hardenburg acknowledged Falkenhayn, but then beckoned Delmar to lean down close to him.

'But now the worst has happened to me, and I have survived,' he whispered, 'and so I have nothing left to fear.'

Delmar leaned up. 'I'm glad to hear it, Tomas.'

He stood and took his leave, but as he passed Falkenhayn the other knight stopped him.

'Do not think,' Falkenhayn said quietly, 'that the order has mistaken your desperate race up that mountainside for anything more than it was. They can discern the difference between a proper leader and an ill-balanced mind, yearning for its own destruction. You and your Provincials will not take this squadron from me.'

Delmar looked closely into Falkenhayn's eyes, searching for some kind of comprehension on his part of what was truly happening.

'There are no Provincials, Franz, not any more. Nor Falcons, nor Reiklanders.' Delmar motioned to the rune both he and Falkenhayn wore on their shoulders. 'We are united. For we are brothers.'

'Oh,' Falkenhayn replied, 'do not think you can catch me that way, Reinhardt. I am no fool. You may be the more able warrior, but you shall never best me in this.'

Falkenhayn raised his voice a degree, just so it would be heard by the others nearby. 'Stay with me, Reinhardt. Sit with me over our fallen brother and let us comfort him together.'

Delmar could not believe it had taken him so long to see how small a man Falkenhayn truly was. But then they were interrupted; more pressing news had arrived at camp.

'UNCLE! UNCLE!' SIEBRECHT hurried down the slope. At the bottom, Herr von Matz watched a line of men and dwarfs loading a riverboat. 'Have you heard?'

'What is it, Siebrecht?'

Siebrecht caught his breath to answer, and then noticed that one of the men loading the riverboat was Twoswords. Then he realised that all the rest were his uncle's keepers as well. 'Wait. What is this? Where are you going?'

'Back to Nuln,' Herr von Matz replied. 'Now the goblins are broken the river is open again, and I can get my shipment safely there. I had begun to think that it might have been trapped in Karak Angazhar for good.'

'What? You already had a shipment here?'

'I admit,' Herr von Matz smiled, 'I was perhaps overly modest about my relations with the dwarfs of Karak Angazhar. We have been trading partners for some years now. But you seemed so heartened to hear that I had a trace of altruism that I did not want to disappoint you, especially going to war.'

Siebrecht stopped the next pair of men carrying a crate.

'Open it,' he ordered. They looked at Herr von Matz.

'Go ahead,' Herr von Matz said wearily.

Using a pick, they levered the crate's lid open. Siebrecht looked inside.

'It's pistol shot?' he said in disbelief. 'You came all this way for a few crates of pistol shot?'

'There is a war on, Siebrecht.' Herr von Matz waved at his men to close the crate up. 'There has never been greater demand for fine dwarfen shot. For nobility only. And perhaps I might interest the Reiksguard in some as well. They're worth a small fortune, I can tell you.'

Siebrecht had no interest in his uncle's commercial enterprises; there were events of far greater importance unfolding. 'You can't leave now, uncle. You haven't heard about the ogres.'

'What about them?'

'They didn't disperse into the mountains. They've gone down the Reik valley, and they've taken the goblins with them.'

'They are not blocking the river, I hope.'

'No, they're into Averland. They're heading for the villages.' Herr von Matz ignored his nephew and carried on supervising the loading. Siebrecht took hold of his shoulder to gain his attention. 'You don't understand. The militias are here, the villages are defenceless.'

As Siebrecht gripped his uncle, Twoswords suddenly appeared behind him. Herr von Matz gestured for his guardian to hold back and gently removed Siebrecht's hand. 'So, what would you have me do about it?'

'We can ride ahead of the army; as soon as we catch up with the ogres you can talk to Burakk again. I know it was you who convinced him to break with Thorntoad; you can convince him to return to the mountains.'

'Why would I do that?'

'Why?' Siebrecht blinked at his uncle's impenetrability. 'Burakk is going to lay waste to Averland! The army is in the north, the militia is here, there's nothing to stop him.'

'No, Siebrecht, I understand what Burakk will do. I mean, why would I go and renege on our agreement?'

Siebrecht was about to repeat himself when he realised what his uncle had said. Herr von Matz motioned to his men to hurry loading the last few crates.

'You… agreed this?'

Herr von Matz regarded him coolly. 'Of course. How do you think I convinced him to give up Thorntoad's lair? How do you think I convinced him to stand aside as the Reiksguard rooted the goblins out?'

Siebrecht was staggered, 'I thought… I thought you had given him money. Or offered him mercy, so he could escape into the mountains.'

'Money or mercy? If you had listened for a single moment when I told you about them,' Herr von Matz said, the scorn and disappointment clear in his voice, 'then you would know perfectly well that ogres have no use for either. They want food. And at this moment Averland is full of villagers, fat from the harvest. It was ideal.'

'Gods, you are a traitor.' Siebrecht's hand went to the hilt of his weapon. In a flash, Twoswords whirled and Siebrecht felt the man's two blades crossed under his chin like scissors at his throat.

'You are developing a habit, Siebrecht,' Herr von Matz said, 'of reaching for your sword at the most inopportune moments.'

Siebrecht swallowed carefully. The rest of his uncle's men were watching from the boat with interest; the dwarfs from Karak Angazhar were nowhere to be seen. He dared not turn his head to see if there was anyone behind him who might come to his aid. He released his grip on his sword and it slid back into its scabbard.

'There's a good boy.' Herr von Matz said it as though he were speaking to a child. Twoswords did not lower his blades though.

'So it was all for coin?' Siebrecht began. 'You gave up Averland for trade? For this one pathetic shipment?'

'Listen to me, Siebrecht. Truly listen for once. Burakk and his ogres will gorge themselves on cattle and villagers, they will burn a few towns, then they will get bored and move on. It is nothing that Averland has not endured before, and nothing they will not have to endure again.'

'They are going to kill hundreds of our people.'

'Yes,' Herr von Matz agreed, 'they will only kill hundreds of our people. What price is that? Karak Angazhar is safe. Black Fire Pass is safe. The Empire is safe.'

The last crate was placed aboard the boat and his men gathered up Herr von Matz's personal belongings.

'I am a patriot in my own way,' he continued. 'No one will acclaim me as they will your friend Reinhardt, no one will sing sagas about me as they will for Gausser. But everything I do is done for the good of the Empire.'

'So you are the good man, with the righteous cause.' Siebrecht spat.

Herr von Matz paused as the memory of their conversations in Altdorf clicked into place.

'Now that, my nephew, is simply impolite. That quick tongue of yours will get you into trouble wherever you go. Let us just hope that your sword stays quicker.'

'It will. It will be quicker than today.' Siebrecht scowled at Twoswords and, able to do little else to him with his blades around his neck, stuck his tongue out at him. Twoswords smiled back, and then opened his mouth and displayed where his tongue had been cut out.

'I know,' Herr von Matz said, climbing over the side of the boat, 'that's why I shall watch your future career with keen interest.'

At that, Twoswords sheathed his blades and stepped into the boat just as it pushed off from the bank. Siebrecht rubbed his neck where the sharp steel had pressed against his skin, and watched the boat row away.

'So,' Siebrecht called after his departing uncle. 'Reinhardt will have the acclaim and Gausser will have the sagas?'

'Yes?' Herr von Matz called back.

'Then what will I have?'

'You get the best of it, my lad. You will have the choice!'

Still smarting, Siebrecht traversed the base of the Karlkopf. The mountain was surrounded now with pillars of smoke: from pyres cremating the corpses of the goblins and from the fires lit by the dwarfs and the Reiksguard to flush the tunnels clean of any goblin survivors. It was a forlorn task, they all knew; the grobi, as the dwarfs called them, could never be finally defeated, they were a disease that infested these mountains. Their power in this area had been broken for a time, but it would not be long before their kind migrated once more from the west and south and took up residence again.

Snow was beginning to fall, blowing over the peaks and down the valleys with bursts of chill wind. Down on the plains, Siebrecht knew, Rhya still held sway, but up in the mountains Ulric, the god of winter, had taken residence. Two riders approached him along the bank of the river. They were Delmar and Gausser. Siebrecht raised his hand in salute.

'Brothers!' he cried, against a flurry of snow.

They reined their horses in, Delmar in the lead. 'Siebrecht, we heard that you might have left with your uncle.'

'Not a chance, brother. Not a chance.' Siebrecht looked past Delmar and nodded at Gausser. 'Where are you headed?'

'Sternberg has taken command of Osterna's and Jungingen's knights. They are to remain behind to guard the wounded and the bodies of our fallen brothers. The rest of the order is to chase after the ogres. Zöllner's banner will lead the way and we have permission to join them...'

'I am coming too,' Siebrecht stated suddenly.

'I am glad to hear it,' Delmar replied, 'for we have brought your horse for that very purpose.' Delmar looked behind him and Gausser, a look of deep satisfaction upon his face, led forwards the spare steed.

'You are good brothers indeed,' Siebrecht declared as he mounted up. 'To victory or death!'

'No, Siebrecht,' Delmar amended, his gaze fixed down the Reik valley and into the green lands beyond. 'Just to victory.'

COUNT VON WALFEN, the Chancellor of Reikland, strode briskly through the halls of the Imperial Treasury. His haste was not caused by urgency, but by eagerness. This was to be a great day for him indeed.

He arrived at his destination: a vault, unlocked and empty aside from the neat stacks of crates and a single figure. Walfen bowed deeply.

'My Imperial Majesty.'

'Let us proceed,' replied the Emperor Karl Franz.

'As you say, majesty.' Walfen stepped forwards and unbolted the nearest crate. Normally, he would not have performed such manual work himself, but he had done far worse in order to keep this secret. The bolts loosened and he opened the lid.

'Pistol shot,' the Emperor stated.

Walfen nodded. 'Who would take special interest in cases of pistol shot? But beneath the tarnish they are purest silver, majesty. The first instalment of the war loan from High King Thorgrim.'

'Ingenious.'

'This is nothing, majesty. The true ingenuity was your persuasion of the High King, that he might put his silver to work rather than add it to his hoard.'

The Emperor ignored the flattery. After two decades of rule, he did not hear it any more. 'Will it be enough?' he asked. 'Will it be enough to rebuild the walls, to replant the crops, to bandage the wounds of my broken realm and set its lifeblood flowing again?'

'It will, majesty.'

The ghost of a smile tugged at Karl Franz's lips, and a fraction of the heavy burden he always bore lifted from his shoulders.

'And who else knows?'

'A few on the High King's Council of Elders, also King Gramrik. Recent events aside, Karak Angazhar is a far better route for future payments than Black Fire Pass. It is far quicker down the Reik, and those dwarfs' preference for isolation greatly reduces the chance of discovery.'

'I believe we can rely upon the dwarfs' discretion,' the Emperor said.

'And then just you and I,' Walfen replied.

The Emperor, though, appeared thoughtful, and so Walfen continued. 'We agreed, majesty, the common citizenry is not ready to know how indebted we are to the dwarfs. As we rebuild all that has been destroyed, your citizens must believe that it is a result of the strength of our great nation, and that we are not subordinated to any others, even to our oldest allies. Should the mob prove fickle, it would imperil the safety of every dwarfen citizen of your Empire.'

'We did so agree,' the Emperor concurred. 'And none of your couriers knew what it was they were transporting? None of those sent to retrieve it after Karak Angazhar was besieged?'

Walfen's instinctive response was to agree, but then he caught the stern look in the Emperor's eye. The same look that had faced down kings and elector counts, and held the fractious Empire together throughout twenty years of strife and war.

'There is one, majesty.'

'And you trust him?'

'I have done for many years.'

'Keep a watch on him, nevertheless.'

'I will, majesty.'

'You shall have to tell Chancellor Hochsvoll, of course.'

'Of course.'

The Emperor raised an eyebrow at Walfen's quick response.

'It will be her responsibility to keep this money safe, to spend it where we need it most and, ultimately, when we are strong again, to make our repayments to the High King. She must be told. You cannot keep your secrets from all your fellow council-members. Though I know you would prefer it that way. And you might consider some reconciliation with the Reiksmarshal. This came at some cost to him.'

Walfen stood firm. 'My only desire is to serve you as best I can.'

'Yes, my councillor, yes,' Karl Franz relented. 'And you have done that today.'

'My thanks, majesty.'

'No, count. My thanks to you.'

Count von Walfen bowed again. Karl Franz took his leave, his mind already turning to other matters.

EPILOGUE

THE FEAST OF AVERLAND

The foothills of the Vaults
Early 2523 IC

THE OGRE ONCE known as Burakk the Craw stumbled and fell upon the stony ground. Each time he did so he found it that much harder to rise again. The ever-present hunger within his gut maddened him. He could not think, he could not reason, all he could do was drag his emaciated body towards the mountains rising in the distance. His clothes hung off him, slack; his prized gut-plate had long since slipped off his shrinking belly. He lay face down upon the ground, mouth slowly trying to grind the dirt in his teeth. He did not have long left; starved this way, the ogre body turned to consume itself. Its last act of worship of the Great Maw.

It should not be like this. He had been a tyrant, he had had a tribe of bull-ogres of his own, and a thousand goblin servants to wait upon them. The land of men was defenceless, an open larder filled with the plumpest stock. His first days had been glorious, his ogres had run wild through the villages they reached, plucking beasts and men from within their flimsy homes with ease and gorging upon them. The Feast of Averland, they had called it, a banquet with a table the size of a province, and as many courses as there were men and beasts remaining.

Even then, though, Burakk had sensed that something was amiss. His bulls ate their fill time and again; the scraps were plentiful, though the goblins still squabbled over them as was their way; but he, no matter how much he consumed, could not quench his unnatural hunger. He ate all he could, until his jaw ached with chewing, taking what food he wished even from the mouths of his bulls. It was all for naught, for his hunger still burned.

Then those men in armour, with banners of red and white, had come after him. Mounted on their heavy horses, they charged his greenskin servants down and ran his bulls through with their lances. Some of them were killed, of course; his bulls tackled their steeds, and then crushed the fallen knights with their mauls. But the rest came on, unfearing, unwavering, relentless in their pursuit. While their number seemed without limit, each bull Burakk lost could not be replaced.

Food was no longer so plentiful. The easy meat had fled beyond their reach, and now these knights herded them even further distant. As each skirmish bought fresh losses, Burakk's hunger grew even more intense. His body began to waste away. As his proud gut diminished, his bulls began to drift away, no longer in awe of their leader. As they went, so their goblin servants went with them. These splinter tribes struck out on their own, and more than most were quickly fodder for the avenging knights.

Then Burakk had been left with only one bull-ogre to follow him. The first morning this last survivor saw Burakk was alone, he drew his carving knives and set about to make Burakk his meal. Burakk was weak, but was no birthling, and it was he who broke his challenger's bones and drank the marrow from them.

Yet even as he consumed the body, his hunger ate at him from within. He was done. He had nothing left. He set his sights upon the nearest mountains, those mountains that reminded him of his distant home, knowing he would not reach them.

And here he lay, alone on some nameless slope, no victor's sword at his throat, no cannon shot through his chest. His final foe, the betrayer he could not best, was his own body which had turned on him and judged that he must die. Why it had, Burakk did not know. The Great Maw was calling, and he would go.

As the sun dipped low, the ogre's corpse began to cool. Its blood no longer flowed, its muscles would not move. But there was motion still. A pulse, a beat, within that barrel chest. A shape that grew larger, pushing up with violent struggle.

'Ah! Freeeeee!' Thorntoad screamed, as he pulled his broken form up through the ogre's slack throat and out its lolling mouth.

'Freeee!' Thorntoad cried again, his regrown thorns still glistening with the ogre flesh to which they had clung to keep him from the ogre's stomach.

'Free…' Thorntoad said once more, before collapsing as his exhaustion took hold. He had survived, though survival was too grand a word for the baseness of his existence these last few weeks, living an inch from destruction, feeding on the masticated bola that came down the ogre's throat. It had been plentiful at least for a time, and then it had ceased. But Thorntoad's starving time was over now; his head dipped down across the ogre corpse and his razor teeth took a bite. Burakk the Craw would attend one last meal, not as the diner, but as the feast.

'Is this the place?' Delmar asked.

'No. It was a little further down,' Griesmeyer replied.

The two knights guided their steeds carefully down the snow-covered slope.

'Was it as cold as this then?' Delmar wondered.

'Worse,' Griesmeyer stated, with great bravado.

Delmar chuckled. Griesmeyer pulled his horse up and looked in each direction to check his bearings.

'This is it?'

Griesmeyer paused a moment. 'Yes, it is.'

Delmar swung himself out of his saddle, patted his horse and took the last few steps to the edge of the bank on foot. He looked down its length. It was smaller than he thought it would be. Such a small gap, and yet twenty years before, in this very place, two hundred men of Nordland had lost their lives. Two hundred men of Nordland, and one Reiksguard knight.

'Is there anything left?' Perhaps it had been a foolish wish, but he had thought, had hoped, that there might be something left; something to mark the event that once happened here.

'Perhaps, beneath the snow.' Griesmeyer knew Delmar's wishes. 'But there is nothing left of him here, Delmar. All that remains of my brother is in you.'

Delmar nodded and looked out across the endless grey of the Sea of Claws. He had wanted to see this place, wanted to gaze upon that same horizon as his father had done at his end. But Griesmeyer was correct. There was nothing of his father on this ugly coast.

'Come on, Delmar.'

THE TWO KNIGHTS crested the last hill. Arrayed before them stood the army of Nordland. The grizzled regiments of halberdiers and spearmen had covered their blue and yellow uniforms with thick coats to keep out the cold, and, in the centre of the line this time, the Reiksguard knights had swapped their scarlet cloaks for furs. Delmar broke company with Griesmeyer and returned to his brothers. He touched his gauntlet to his visor in salute as he passed his squadron's standard-bearer.

'Your errand is done?' The hulking knight handled the standard with ease.

'It is.'

'Then rejoin our squadron, Brother Reinhardt.'

'At once, Brother Gausser,' Delmar smiled.

Delmar directed his steed towards the far end of the line of knights. He nodded on his way to Bohdan and Alptraum, the Averlander's grin crinkling the scar running down his cheek. Delmar turned his horse about and stepped into formation. The knight beside him raised his visor.

'I have had a letter from home,' Siebrecht said.

'It reached you all the way here?'

'Aye, Delmar, they have civilisation beyond the borders of Reikland, you know,' his friend admonished. Siebrecht pulled off one of his gauntlets and produced a parchment. 'It is in the hand of my father, though I believe we both may guess who the true correspondent is…'

Delmar readily agreed. Herr von Matz had not reappeared since they broke the siege of Karak Angazhar, but the sight of each devastated Averlander village in their pursuit of the ogres had been reminder enough.

'My father writes,' Siebrecht continued, adopting a haughty tone, 'to posit to me that once this campaigning season is done, I might consider interrupting my time with the order for a while. Apparently, an opportunity may arise to raise the family's fortunes, should I join the service of my uncle.'

'And how have you replied?' Delmar inquired.

Siebrecht looked pointedly at Delmar, and then slowly began to tear the letter to pieces.

'I would not be so hasty if I were you,' Delmar said. 'We may need the parchment for kindling.'

The two of them laughed at that and, as if in agreement, their horses snorted underneath them. Their merriment was interrupted by another rider who drew level beside them, a rider who gripped his reins in one hand and with the other drummed upon his saddle, even though that hand had no fingers.

'Still the disrespectful tongue, Matz,' Master Verrakker said pointedly.

The two young knights turned to their master. 'How goes the training of the Nordland troops?' Siebrecht asked.

'We will see today,' Verrakker judged, 'how they will fare against a real enemy.'

'It is strangely fortuitous timing, Brother Reinhardt, is it not,' Siebrecht said archly, 'that Elector Count Theoderic should have had such a sudden change of heart on the Reiksguard to invite them to come and train his new army, just before this new threat is spotted off his shores.'

'Stranger still,' Delmar replied, 'that the Reiksguard should have agreed so readily and dispatched a whole banner commanded by Lord Griesmeyer, a banner that includes the elector count's grandson, no less, to escort the three fightmasters.'

Verrakker harrumphed without further comment.

'A suspicious man,' Siebrecht concluded, 'might be led to believe that all was not as it appeared to be in the grand province of Nordland. Would you not agree, Master Verrakker?'

Verrakker gave Siebrecht a baleful look. 'Griesmeyer was right about you, Matz. You perceive secrets and shadows, when the truth could not be more clear. Both of you!'

'Brother!' Fightmaster Talhoffer called. He and Ott were mounted, both upon the same steed. Ott sat behind his brother; his eyes were bandaged against the light, but he had a great smile upon his face as he drew deep breaths of the sea air.

Talhoffer continued, 'We are needed, brother...' Talhoffer looked to say more, but then saw the other knights listening, 'about that certain matter.'

Verrakker shook his head at Talhoffer's clumsy attempt at subterfuge, then turned his horse, and the three masters trotted off together.

A stir went through the army: some news had been received. Sails had been spied on the horizon, the foe had been spotted. Delmar and Siebrecht could see the gonfanonier preparing to raise the banner's standard. Griesmeyer rode to the head of the knight squadrons. He drew his sword and pointed it straight in the direction they would take.

'Reiksguard!' he called. 'To battle!'

ABOUT THE AUTHOR

Richard Williams was born in Nottingham, UK and was first published in 2000. He has written fiction for publications ranging from *Inferno!* to the Oxford & Cambridge May Anthologies, on topics as diverse as gang initiation, medieval highwaymen and arcane religions.
In his spare time he is a theatre director and actor. His first full length novel was *Relentless*.

Visit his official website at
www.richard-williams.com

NEXT IN THE SERIES!

AN EMPIRE ARMY NOVEL

IRON COMPANY

COMING SOON!

CHRIS WRAIGHT

WARHAMMER

UK ISBN 978-1-84416-7784-4 US ISBN 978-1-84416-779-1

TIME OF LEGENDS

HELDENHAMMER
The Legend of Sigmar
GRAHAM McNEILL

NAGASH THE SORCERER
The undead will rise...
MIKE LEE

MALEKITH
A Tale of the Sundering
GAV THORPE

This all-new series
explores the tales of
the legendary heroes
and monumental
events that shaped
the very fabric of the
Warhammer World.

WARHAMMER

MATHIAS THULMANN
WITCH HUNTER

WITCH HUNTER · WITCH FINDER · WITCH KILLER

Buy this
omnibus or read
a free extract at
www.blacklibrary.com

C·L·WERNER

UK ISBN 978-1-84416-669-5 US ISBN 978-1-84416-554-4